# THE
# OLIGARCH

by

# Joseph Clyde

GIBSON SQUARE

This is a work of fiction, in which the events are entirely imaginary.
Any coincidence between living persons and named characters
in the novel is purely fortuitous.

This edition published by Gibson Square for the first time

UK   Tel:  +44 (0)20 7096 1100
US   Tel:  +1 646 216 9813

    info@gibsonsquare.com
    www.gibsonsquare.com

*Eire* Tel:   +353 (0)1 657 1057

        info@gibsonsquare.com
        www.gibsonsquare.com

        ISBN      978-1908096715
        eISBN     978-1783340620

# 1

What does an ex-MI5 man in need of a boost to his pension do with the rest of his life? For Tony Underwood the question arose when a note on his desk invited him to a meeting with the head of personnel. A bad moment. Judith Thornberry was new in the job. Her predecessor, a chum from Tony's Cold War days, had told him not to trouble himself about his official retirement date, he'd be all right for a few years yet. Thornberry, on the other hand, was said to have a brisk way with old-timers, and there was talk of premature retirements.

Four-thirty that afternoon, the note specified, for Tony a less-than-ideal time: the first he saw of it was when he got back from lunch exuding a warm glow and a whiff of cigar a little after 3.30. On the way to the lift he put his head round the door of Dick Welby, the friend whose birthday they'd been celebrating, and who'd worked with Thornberry on the IRA in her early years in the service.

'I've been summoned by la Thornberry. Our paths never crossed, what's she like?'

'Judith?'

Dick's sharp nose and oblong glasses seemed designed for contemplation. Before answering, for a long moment he examined the wall above his desk.

'Did a great job in Belfast. No jitters, cool as they come.'

'A one-word description is all I need.'

Dick thought some more.

'Metallic, it has to be. Gutsy as hell but a bit of a dum-dum bullet, and now she's up there in personnel it'll be your guts she's after. Good luck.'

Tony took the lift to her floor.

'Sorry to call you in at short notice,' Thornberry's secretary told him. 'The four-thirty slot was meant for someone else but he called in sick at the last minute.'

He took a seat, and waited. Was this the end of the line? He thought back to the day they'd taken him on, in the old HQ in Curzon Street, Mayfair, before MI5 moved to Thames House on the Embankment. *A4, Intelligence Resources and Operations* was the branch he'd been assigned to, and to a twenty-three year-old the words had sounded imposing. What they meant was that he was to be trained as a humble watcher before taking his place in a team specializing in the routine surveillance of diplomatic personnel.

After nearly forty years service on communist countries, Northern Ireland, then in the anti-terrorism branch he'd risen above that level, though not too far. Now he was back in the diplomatic surveillance business, a middle-ranking post where his job was to oversee people younger than himself and watch them rise past him.

Not that he resented his lack of advancement. It was the way of the world. In the security game the importance of a good background and education were the same as anywhere, only more so, and having neither one nor the other – his father had been a tobacconist and he'd never made it to university – for Tony the ceiling on promotion wasn't glass, it was concrete.

He wasn't a complainer. He'd done all right for himself, though a top job, a comfortable income and a rewarding family life – none of them had come his way and it was too late now. What kept him going all those years had been a plain man's patriotism, that and the club-like feeling, the belonging. He'd had his place in the intelligence family, he got on with people and in his undemonstrative way he'd enjoyed it mightily. Now he felt differently. The idea that there might no longer be a place for him, that they might throw him out early, filled him with a numb fury.

Four-thirty came and went. Another poor superannuated sod must be in there, on his knees pleading for a stay of execution. He wouldn't do that – though he'd given no thought to a post-retirement job. Where would he get one, and what would it pay? The way things were going in his family God knows he would need the money.

Had Dick been joking about Thornberry? Maybe she wasn't so bad, and if it came to the worst he could appeal to her better nature. *I know I've had my day, but could we look at the human angle? It isn't just the vacant days I'm afraid of. The truth is I need the money. It's to do with my daughter, you see, Penny. It's taken her till the age of thirty-six to get off drugs, and we still have to support her.*

*Then there's Heather, her ten-year-old. Fatherless, naturally. A delicate girl, but so gifted. I can't tell you the pain of seeing her grow up in a rubbishy school in a down-market part of London. We need to get her into a good area and properly taught, but my wife Jean had to give up her job prematurely – muscular dystrophy – and spend her savings on private treatment. So if there's any flexibility, if you could see your way to keeping me on for another couple of years...*

\*

'Good lunch?'

Thornberry put the question without looking up, her eyes on her papers. Tony had sat down opposite, his breath vaporized alcohol and the smell of his half-smoked cigar seeping from his breast pocket, polluting the sanitized air.

'Very good, thank you.' He pried open a smile. 'HMG didn't pay, I assure you. A private celebration...'

Her eyes flicked to the top of the page.

'It's not your birthday.'

She read on. He stared at her clean-cut, close-trimmed auburn hair. He didn't like that hair, any more than the functional desk, the new bookcase with its prissily-ranged volumes, or the blown-up copies of MI5 recruitment ads pinned to the wall. It wasn't the personnel office he remembered, with its armchairs, ashtrays, drinks cabinet and comradely chats.

The fact that he faced being dismissed by a woman did nothing to put him at ease. There'd been women in the service he'd joined all those years back, though in junior positions mostly. Now they had degrees, spoke hard languages and could be technologically savvy. Accomplishments he had never mastered.

'Tony.'

Thornberry looked up from her papers. His name came out in admonitory fashion, like a teacher addressing a child. Then, her hands joined before her, she began.

'My predecessor indicated that it might be possible for you to stay on beyond your retirement date.'

'Three years was the number mentioned, as I recall.'

'A verbal assurance, was it? I'm sorry Tony, that may have been the way things were done in the past but it's not how I intend to run matters now. I know the years you have given to the service. I'm conversant with your background and no one is questioning the breadth of your experience. The Soviet bloc, the IRA, Muslim fundamentalism, I see here. A meritorious record over several decades…'

Oh Christ, he thought, it sounded like a farewell speech.

'…It's just that the timing is unfortunate. New blood is always needed and there's been a rush of well-qualified recruits as a result of the recession. We have to press on with restructuring the service.'

She pointed to one of the framed recruitment ads.

*Around 3,800 people work for the Security Service. 41% are women, 56% under the age of 40. 8% are from black and ethnic minority backgrounds, and 3% have a disability.*

'Then there's the question of qualifications. It's graduates and technicians we're after now. Especially Farsi and Urdu speakers.'

Wrong age, wrong sex, wrong ethnicity, no degrees and lamentably able-bodied. Dick had it right, Thornberry was a dum-dum bullet. Gets under your skin then mushrooms, to maximize the pain.

'But what about this?'

He pointed to another recruitment ad:

'*Opportunities throughout your career,*' it says. I'm not arguing against diversification, but don't you need to keep some of the old lags around to help bring the young ones on? Experience it used to be called, stuff you build up over time. Now it's like something you clear out like lumber from a shed.'

'No-one is underestimating your contribution, Tony, but we have our career structure to think about. So I'm going to have to include you in our premature retirement programme. There'll be the usual compensations.'

Tony stared at his lap with a blank expression. It was one that came naturally. His was an expressionless face, one that had settled over the years into a default mode of non-expectation. Not that it had aged him: good health and a placid nature had kept him youthful-looking for his fifty-nine years. A smudge of grey at the temples, a line or two on his cheeks when he smiled, which from time to time he did, quietly, and that was all.

For a moment he sat on, staring down. He wasn't interested in the usual compensations. He wanted a regular income, a job of work to do, the comradeship that had become a substitute over the years for his dysfunctional family life. He felt crushed, wounded – and afraid. Was this the time to say his piece about his daughter, her child, his wife, his financial problems?

Out of the question. When he looked back up at her he couldn't bring himself to do it.

'So that's it?' he said.

'I fear so.'

As he got up she held out a sheet of paper.

'What's that? A P45, is it? I've been here so long I've forgotten about them.'

'No – my secretary will be giving you that. It's your terms of service. Confidentiality and all that. A copy of what you signed when you joined, a reminder of what you can and can't do after you leave the service. If you're interested in another job you may like to refresh your memory.'

Tony took the paper and turned to go.

'Anyway, all the best for the future, Tony. And I'm sorry.'

The words felt like pennies thrown at his back. *No you're not, if you were you wouldn't have fucked up the rest of my life and my family's future.* Anger in a placid man can be volcanic, and it took an effort not to say it.

'Don't worry,' he muttered over his shoulder. 'I'll get something, no problem. As for what I'll do I'll make my own judgments, if you don't mind. I don't think I've got too many obligations left to HMG in that regard.'

Looking back later, after the drama and the mayhem, it occurred to him that his parting words to Judith Thornberry could have been construed as a threat. But then he wasn't to know that within months of leaving the service he would find himself embroiled in a conspiracy to assassinate a President.

# 2

*Don't worry, I'll get something, no problem.* It was bullshit of course, bravado. Three weeks spent replying to advertisements on the Internet had resulted in a single response. The job was security manager for a chain of half a dozen high street jewellery stores, the interview in an office above a shop in Shepherds Bush.

The owner, Mr Forbes, wore a black leather jerkin, sideburns and a sceptical smile.

'So what kind of money you looking for?'

'Well, maybe fifty.'

It was no random figure. His early retirement money would go to help pay down his mortgage. The amount he would need on top of his pension, he'd worked out, was £30,000 post-tax at least: £10,000 for a bigger loan on a better flat for his daughter, £15,000 to get Heather into a private day school, the remainder for medical expenses for Jean.

'Fifty *grand?*'

Mr Forbes' intonation was not encouraging.

'*Salary depending on qualifications and experience,* the ad said, and I've had almost forty years in the Security Service.'

'That MI5?'

'It is.'

Digging his hands deeper into the pockets of his jerkin, the manager lay back in his chair.

'I looked at you and I thought, maybe a soldier? That'd be fine, but MI5? Jesus! We don't want someone to bump people off, just stop the bastards smashing in windows. And if we was to take you on who'd you be working for, us or the government?' He gave a nervous laugh. 'Any rate, we don't pay that kind of money. Still, thanks for coming. Now I can tell my son I've met a real live spook.'

There were other interviews, other failures. With a detective agency specializing in marital breakdowns, £32,000 plus performance-related bonus. As a sales representative for home alarms, £30,000. And so on, down. The best-paid job (£55,000) was the least enticing: deputy chairman, officer training board, Tanzanian security authority, Dar Es Salaam.

*

Then the breakthrough, courtesy of Dick Welby. A few years older than himself and a former specialist in the recruitment of Soviet agents, Dick had been a colleague in his Russian days. By now he was senior to Tony – most people were – but somehow the two of them had stayed close.

A tiny man with a confidence-inviting manner, Dick's personal style helped explain why he'd been so good at getting the opposition to work for him. Knowing of his friend's family problems, he'd been mortified at his news and listened sympathetically when Tony had vented his feelings. What troubled him was when, after a few drinks, he'd begun sounding off about Thornberry and her kind.

'When she told me I had this urge to explain why I needed the job. Her being a woman, I thought, maybe she'd understand? Just as well I didn't. Afterwards I looked her up. Well-to-do background, private school – the usual. Imagine me explaining to little Miss Prim with her preachy fucking recruitment ads all over the wall what it's like to have to downsize from a nice house to a two-bedroom cottage so as to put a deposit on some ghastly flat south of the river for your druggy daughter. Or that you need to get your granddaughter out of a lousy inner-city school into something decent.

'She'd think I was a screaming racist. And if I'd said the NHS performance with Jean was a scandal I'd have got a talking to about that too. Oh yes, Ms Thornberry will have insurance, won't she, plus she looks as healthy as a horse.'

'Come on, Tony, you can't hold people's backgrounds against

them. That's a travesty. I worked with her, and she's no daddy's girl I can tell you. OK she's got to be a bit officious, but she's smart and she's tough and she's professional. We were on a job once in South Armagh, in an unmarked car, when this guy just steps out into the road with an AK 47 and she – '

' – I don't care what she did to the opposition, it's what she's doing to the service. And to me.'

Dick let it go, though he'd worried about his friend. What Tony needed was a new job, fast. Without telling him, so as not to raise his hopes, he'd been on the lookout for a position in the private security business, and six weeks later something had come up.

'Fella who used to work for me is in the market for someone from the service.'

'You don't say. And who's that?'

Tony looked back, sceptical.

'Russian émigré, name of Golosov, Mikhail Golosov. Not his real name, what we ended up calling him. Businessman and occasional informant of · mine in the old days. Now he works for Arshile Grekov, the billionaire.'

'And ex-GRU colonel in military intelligence, I seem to recall,' Tony laughed. 'I'm mad as hell with the service but I wasn't thinking of defecting.'

'Grekov's been out of all that for a long time now. He's not some cosmopolitan fly-by-night, lives here full-time and taken to England in a big way. Thinks we're a model for his country, that what the Russians need is a constitutional monarchy.'

'He has political ambitions?'

'Too old for that. His first ambition is for himself and his son to stay alive. Which is why he wants someone from the service to head up his security. A man with his background and money needs to watch his step.'

'How did he make the money?'

'First it was the swords-to-ploughshares stuff – converting arms factories to car plants after communism collapsed. Then agribusiness.'

'So our ex-GRU man is a sort of ethical investor?'

'He's a man with ideals, the cleanest oligarch around. Another thing the Kremlin don't like about him. Gives them no hold over him. They can't imagine that someone who doesn't kowtow isn't up to something, so they're always trying to get alongside him.'

'Plants?'

'Man called Dombrovsky got himself appointed as his head of his security. Turned out he was in our bad books – something to do with criminal contacts – and we tipped him off. Since then he's conceived this immoderate admiration for British security. Ultimate guarantor of our lives and liberties and all that. He'd buy MI5 if he could. I told Mikhail he should do the next best thing – take on a retired officer. He sounded out his boss and the boss said yes.'

'So what would be the job exactly?'

'The slip-up over Dombrovsky shook him. The first thing would be to check out his security team. Then you'd be monitoring any threats from hit men, mafia types or political intriguers – not to mention the FSB.'

'You say there's a son. He need protecting too?'

'Sounds like that'd be a big part of the job. Sasha is what you'd expect – Eton and Oxford – but maybe not as smart as he thinks. Mikhail says he's got himself involved in Russian émigré politics and his father's finding it hard to keep tabs on what he's up to.'

Tony considered.

'Want me to mention your name?' Dick persisted. 'Or are you worried what the service might think?'

'Absolutely not!' Tony flared. 'They can't throw me out then dictate where I can and can't work. It's just that I never expected to end my career working for the other side. Anything to do with Russian intelligence, post-communist included, and you're in trouble. Shit doesn't just stink, it sticks. And whatever you say your friend Grekov is a GRU man.'

'*Ex*, Tony, *ex*! The Russians have a saying: 'That was a long time ago and it was never true anyway.' Grekov is basically a businessman, a philanthropist and a thinker. Kind of Russian George Soros. And

the salary would be competitive I imagine. Shall I tell Mikhail you'd
be prepared to be interviewed? Nothing against an interview, is
there?'

Nothing at all, Tony finally decided. And if Judith Thornberry
had the nerve to object there'd be trouble. There was no shortage of
ex-diplomats and politicians pulling in easy money on the boards of
Russian companies, dodgy or otherwise, whose owners had been in
the intelligence game. And a competitive salary from a billionaire
sounded good.

*

One of the humiliations of serving out his notice were the restric-
tions on what he could and couldn't see, though with a little help
from Dick he got hold of Grekov's security file. The Russian had
served in France and Britain under diplomatic cover. One of those
nailed by a KGB defector in the Seventies, he'd been thrown out
during the expulsions of intelligence men from Britain that had followed. Thirty years later he was back in London, an oligarch with a
two-billion fortune.

His business interests were international, though that wasn't the
only reason he'd left Russia. Someone in the FSB seemed to think
he'd been recruited by MI6 in his intelligence days: that before the
British had thrown him out they'd turned him, and that he'd worked
for them till the Berlin Wall came down. Not true, as it happened,
the file confirmed, but something the Russians continued to suspect.
No wonder Grekov kept a seven-man security team.

His wife had died some years earlier and in émigré circles he had
the reputation of a recluse and an eccentric, who lived alone with his
son. Sasha, his only child by his second wife, was 27. His father was
76, and unwell.

His poor health and unusual working habits, Dick had warned,
meant that his office might not be able to give him a precise time for
their meeting. And so it turned out. The date was fixed for April 10
and notice of the hour, his personal assistant told him, would come

in the course of the day.

Tony got into his interview clothes and waited. The morning passed, then the afternoon. At seven o'clock he stood himself down, poured a whisky and told Jean that he'd be in for dinner. At twenty minutes past the personal assistant rang to say the interview would be at eleven.

'In the morning?'

'No, Mr Underwood. Tonight.'

'Ah.'

The woman, whose sensual foreign accent made 'wood' in Underwood come out like *wooed*, sounded sympathetic.

'I'm sorry you've been waiting all day. Sometimes Mr Grekov likes to work late in the evening.'

The white stucco house in Belgravia was one of a terrace, with colonnaded porches and glass canopies shading first floor balconies. For a billionaire it didn't seem extravagantly large – till you entered. The single house was in fact composed of three, a lateral conversion taking in its neighbours on either side.

For all Grekov's anglophilia there was no feeling of an English mansion. A vast entrance hall, with corridors disappearing into the distance, made it feel more like an embassy than a home, and every-thing in the place seemed foreign: the servant who relieved him of his coat ('I take for you, Sir?'), the heavy, central-European décor, the portraits of dignitaries lining the hall.

The largest was of a luxuriantly moustachioed figure in black uniform with a blue sash, a chest full of medals and a ceremonial sword. He glanced at the label: *Alexander II of Russia, 1855-1881.* Beneath a second label had been appended: *The Czar-Reformer.*

He waited on in the hall. Three burly fellows (chauffeurs, body-guards?) sat in a corner talking Russian, fingering cigarette packets longingly and taking turns to go outside for a smoke. A pretty maid in a white headband and Russian pinafore walked past, followed by their mournful eyes.

'Mr Underwooed?'

He looked up. A woman was descending the curved mahogany

staircase. Forty or so and dressed in a high-necked blouse and old-fashioned pleated skirt, she would have looked prim were it not for the smile she threw him over the banister. The penumbra of the hall lightened a shade.

'I'm Lisa, Mr Grekov's personal assistant. We spoke on the phone. I apologize for keeping you waiting. Thank you for coming so late.'

She took him up the stairs to the first floor and along a corridor cut into the adjoining building. Now the house began to feel like a hotel, except that the rooms on either side looked like offices. One of the doors was ajar, a light slicing across the hall. As they passed a young man's voice roared:

'Oh fuck off, Eddie, you bastard. I was only kidding!'

No foreign accent there: the voice was public-school, loud, slightly tipsy.

Lisa turned to smile.

'That is the office of Sasha, Mr Grekov's son.'

'He works late, like his father.'

'Only when he has to.'

Lisa ushered him into her office.

'I will tell Mr Grekov you have arrived.'

She pressed an intercom, waited, shrugged.

'I may have to ask you to wait some more. Sometimes he takes a nap before work.' In a smaller voice she added: 'His health.'

'Of course.'

'Can I get you anything? A coffee?'

I don't drink late-night coffee, it keeps me awake, he was about to reply, but didn't. It would make him sound old and, for all her sober clothes, something in Lisa made him feel younger.

'I'm fine. He must have a busy social schedule.'

'Before, yes, but now not so busy. He is not like, I don't know, Abramovitch or the others.'

Tony nodded understandingly, as if a confidant of them all.

'Please take a seat.'

The moment he did the intercom buzzed. A low voice, like a

grunt, reached him.

'Sooner would be better. He is waiting.'

Another grunt.

She got up, opened the door, and indicated that he should follow.

Grekov's office was at the end of the corridor. The demands of Tony's career had taken him to some fancy places (embassy premises at night time, unattended private houses, luxury hotel suites before the occupants were due to arrive), though never to an oligarch's office. When Lisa opened the door he hesitated before stepping in.

It was as if the room was in darkness. The walls, wood-panelled, were lined with unlit portraits peering from the shadows. Except for a small TV on the modest-sized antique desk every taint of modernity had gone.

The only light in the room was a green-shaded standard lamp by the desk, scarcely enough to illuminate the figure behind it. As they stood in the entrance Grekov said nothing, his head bowed low. For a moment Tony thought he'd fallen asleep.

'Mr Underwooed,' Lisa announced.

'Where?'

The figure looked up, its eyes searching the semi-darkness.

'Here, beside me.'

'I can't see him. There's no light.'

'That's because you turned it off.'

Lisa reached for a panel by the door. A slow glow lit the room: first the pictures – Old Masters, more portraits of worthies with sashes and medals, more imposing beards – then gradually the depths of the cavernous office, the size of a small ballroom.

'Not too much!'

Lisa adjusted the panel. The pictures receded, the rest of the room became shadowy.

'Come in then.'

Tony walked towards him. It seemed a long way to the desk. Behind it he made out a chaise longue, with a pillow that was still indented. Grekov must have just got up.

'That's better. Sit down, Mr – '

' – Underwood.'

'Underwood, yes, very good, I like that name. For a security man it is perfect. It has something confidential about it.'

Still half in shadow, the man smiled. Taking his seat Tony saw a long, thin face that finished in a smallish beard.

'Lisa is a fine woman,' the voice said when she'd closed the door behind her. 'I told her not to wait, my son would let you in, but she is loyal.'

'She seems very efficient.'

'You like women?'

'I'm married…'

' – no no, I mean as people.'

'I have no problem with women.' For something to say he added: '40% of my former colleagues were women.'

'Good, because I am a feminist, a historical feminist, a feminist before it came into fashion. Queen Elizabeth, Queen Victoria, Catherine the Great of Russia…The best sovereign Russia ever had. And she was a reformer.'

'Like Alexander II,' Tony got in quickly.

A silence. After a minute he felt the need to break it.

'You must travel a lot.'

'Not so much now,' Grekov replied in a regretful tone. 'And before you ask, no, I do not own a football team and I do not have a yacht. For not having a yacht I am famous. But we must talk. Do you know what I want you for?'

'I gather it was to oversee your security arrangements.'

'You put it diplomatically. In London there are two kinds of Russians: those who come here for the security and those who come to kill them. So the job is to keep me alive, together with my son.'

'Are there threats?'

'That is for you to discover. There have been problems…'

'Because of your attitude to the regime?'

'About the regime I say nothing. But they know my view of them.'

As he spoke, with an effort Grekov got to his feet. At first Tony thought he was wearing a dressing gown, but it seemed to be some sort of antique cape.

'But if you don't say anything, I don't see why they're afraid of you.'

'That is *why* they are afraid. Afraid of my silence. They think there is something happening they know nothing about.'

'You said there'd been problems.'

'They told you about Dombrovsky, I imagine? To think I appointed such a man to head my security! It was my fault, my guard was down, I am getting old... So your first task will be to clean up after him. Get rid of anyone unreliable.'

His eyes glinted. Paranoid? For a Russian oligarch in London that would be natural, a default state...

'I know about these things,' Grekov went on. 'I worked for the GRU, in London and Paris. MI5 was better than French security at tracking us, I remember.'

'You were in London in the Seventies, I gather, when I was working on Soviet diplomatic personnel. Maybe I tracked you myself?'

'You must have done it well. I was never aware – except once. Somebody kept breaking into my car, though nothing was taken, and eventually we saw why it was. In those days it was no use bugging the car radio. You could wire it up, but the transcribers had a problem disentangling the engine noise from the conversation. So your people built a microphone into the chassis. The trouble was they had to renew the battery from inside.

'Every time it was the same person who did it. I knew because there was always a faint smell of cigar – a cheap cigarillo. When we discovered the microphone I left a box of cigarillos on the dashboard, with a note saying please smoke these before breaking into my car next time, they smell better. And you know what? When they came in to replace the battery and found the mic had gone, they took them...'

They'd been top quality, Tony remembered. Delicious, miniature

Havanas.

'I hate smoking. You smoke, Mr Underwood?'

'I, er – '

' – so it wasn't you. A pity. We could have reminisced about the games we used to play in those days. And then you threw us all out, myself included.'

'I remember. We had a big celebration.'

'Later I celebrated too. It was the best thing that happened to me. My name was blown, I couldn't be sent anywhere interesting abroad, so I resigned. Got out before the collapse of the whole rotten system. You know what Brodsky said about stealing secrets?'

'I'm afraid – '

' – the Russian poet, Joseph Brodsky. He said that when you steal secrets the theft possesses you. And it was true. We were good at stealing people's secrets, but not at thinking about the future of the country.

'Now I have made money I have to take care of my security, so again I am in the intelligence business. As a Russian you never escape it. I am glad I came to London. In my years here I came to admire your country. Its Parliament, its monarchy, its traditions...' His eyes lightened. 'You admire your monarchy, Mr Underwood?'

Well, yes and no, was Tony's position.

'It helps give us stability,' he said.

'More than that – dignity. It was stupid to kill your king, no?'

'Charles I? Of course, very stupid,' Tony said, decisively now, his royalism growing by the minute.

Another silence. Where was this going? Grekov was shuffling up and down behind his desk, the conversation erratic. It wasn't that his mind was wandering, it just didn't stay in the same place for long.

The intercom buzzed. Lisa's voice:

'You have a visitor.'

'One minute.'

He turned to Tony.

'Good, it is agreed. In one week you will start. You will see Mikhail about money. Also about the people you will oversee. I await the result of your purge.'

Grekov bent over his desk and began fiddling with some papers. He seemed in a hurry to be on his own. Tony got up.

'Can I say how – '

' – me too, I am glad you will work for me. Well good night, Mr Underwood.'

*

He walked back to Lisa's office. There was no-one there and the lights were out. So no visitor. The message must have been pre-arranged to get him out.

He made his way towards the stairs. The light was still on in Sasha's room, the door open. After he'd passed a voice called out after him:

'Hey, Mr Underwood.'

He turned. A tall, heavy, flaxen-haired figure had lurched from the office and was lumbering towards him.

'Hello, I'm Sasha. Lisa said to look out for you. I'm just leaving. Let me give you a lift.'

'I'll get a taxi.'

'No no, it's late. Come on, I have to go out, I'll drive you.'

As they passed through the hall, one of the bodyguards made to get up from his chair. Sasha waved him down. His car was a small convertible, a Maserati GranCabrio, less than ideal for his six-foot-three frame. From twenty metres away Sasha zapped the doors and canopy open.

Following him as they walked towards it, Tony was struck by his shambling gait, a combination of Russian torpor and old Etonian languor, it seemed to him. The sight of him cramming himself behind the wheel of the Maserati was a study in dislocation.

In the car he turned towards him, so close he caught the smell of his vodka-laden breath.

'So where is it you live?'

'Chiswick. If it's out of your way –'

' – no problem. And we can have a chat as we go.'

The engine revved, and they roared off.

'So how did you find my dad?'

'He's very…distinguished.'

'He's that all right, but he's not well. Has these problems no one can explain. Sometimes I think someone's doing something to him.'

'You think that's possible?'

'Well they did the polonium thing, didn't they? And no one knew about it till the guy was dead. If they think dad was a traitor they're capable of anything.'

'But he wasn't, was he?'

'Absolutely not! But it's not just that. The Kremlin hates anyone they can't control.'

As he spoke, Sasha's flushed, meaty face was turned towards him. At the speed they were taking Hammersmith Broadway Tony would have preferred him to keep his eyes on the road. To him they looked a little crazed as he went on:

'All they need is to feed him something, slowly. A few grammes a day, right?'

'I can check out the cooks.'

'Yeah, do that. None of them are Russian but the way those bastards spray money around all it takes is, you know –'

' – I know,' Tony said, gravely.

'People laugh at my dad for going on about the Russian royal family, but it's not so weird. Technically we're still a monarchy, you know that? A line of descent interrupted by the assassination of the Romanovs. Even that the communists botched. Murdering bastards shot them, then stabbed them to death with bayonets. But the succession was only suspended, and there's still Romanovs alive…'

Tony nodded dutifully, his eyes on the red lights Sasha was about to run. A few more minutes on the return of the Romanovs and he was back on the President:

'Only things my dad and him have in common is that they were both spies and neither of them drink. The difference is my dad's smarter. Him, you seen how he ponces around the Kremlin?'

'Like a monarch himself,' Tony threw in.

'That's right! Think of it – a KGB dynasty! A dynasty of thieves and assassins…'

It was well after midnight on the dead streets, and in a little more than a quarter of an hour they were at Tony's house in Chiswick. They drew up.

'That was kind.'

'Good to have you aboard, Tony. Any problems, let me know. We work as a team, me and dad. Close as lips and teeth.'

Inside the house he watched from the darkened window while the car made its three-point turn. Immature, none-too-bright and obsessive were the kinder descriptions of Sasha that occurred to him. There'd be problems with that boy, he could sense it coming.

# 3

The Maserati lurched to a halt on a double yellow line at an indolent angle to the kerb. Before Sasha cut it the engine gave an alerting rasp. In a normal street the sound would have enraged a hundred sleepers, though not here. One of those Chelsea squares bought up by foreign investors and where except for security guards you rarely saw anyone day or night, the homes were mostly empty.

The slam of the car door was another signal of his arrival, and it was answered: as he crossed the street a light came on in a third-floor window. A few seconds' wait and a click released the tall wrought-iron gate before he walked down the path and up to the front door, the indolent legs quickening now, taking the steps three at a time.

A second click, the front door opened to his touch and he was through the hallway and into the lift. A third and he was in the flat. Minutes later his clothes were off and he was climbing into a fragrant bed.

'You're late,' the occupant murmured over her shoulder. 'I have to be up early.'

'Poor darling. What for?'

'Interpreting for the Ambassador. A social breakfast. Something to do with the arts.'

'Just be late! Tell the bastard you had a prior commitment – with me.' A hand fled over her thigh in a preparatory caress. 'You'll sleep soundly, I promise.'

'Depends what you've been drinking.'

'A love potion, my princess.' The hand gripped a shoulder, drawing her to him. 'Litres of it.'

'*Bolshoi durak,*' she sighed and turned towards him. 'My big, clumsy fool. I can smell your potion. Vodka. And it's measured in grammes, not litres.'

In the midst of moving onto her he paused and rolled away. With a grunt he heaved himself from the bed, groped for his shirt and, as always before they made love, threw it over the Russian icon that hung above them, obscuring the sacred image.

*

In calling her his princess he wasn't being mawkish: technically that was her title. In pre-revolutionary Russia princesses had been two a penny, more than a few of them self-invented, but Svetlana was from genuine, if minor noble stock. The family, ruined under the Bolsheviks, had survived when her father, a scientist, contrived to keep his head down till a chance came in the Gorbachev era to emigrate to London with his wife and daughter.

A startlingly pretty woman, with not much money but a high sense of her worth, at Oxford she had worked hard and played ferociously. Not that she was immoral exactly: Her autocratic instincts had left her with little idea of what morality was. The only thing she didn't do at university was experiment with drugs – it would have threatened her sense of control – though it was she who drove Sasha to them.

With her looks and his money to their friends the couple seemed a natural pair, and the weekend house Sasha had bought in a Cotswold village was the natural scene for wild behaviour. What did it matter if the parties she organized for him went on till daybreak, or if she selected someone other than Sasha with whom to spend the early morning hours? He might not have liked it – he didn't – but her insistence on sexual autonomy meant he had no choice.

The truth was that the perfect pair had never slept together. Finding him unappealing she saw no reason to fall into his bed. One day perhaps, if circumstances required, but what was the hurry? She was not in the habit of responding to the desires of others and, rich as he was, Sasha was no exception.

Her indifference to what anyone thought of her extended to her clothes, or lack of them. At the Cotswold house she could be seen swimming in the heated outdoor pool naked, sunning herself in nothing more than a pair of high heels she was breaking in with a book on her lap, or returning bare-chested from a boyfriend's bedroom to her own in the early hours.

'I don't sleep with men,' she would pronounce, 'I value my privacy too much. I fuck them, that is all.' (The 'u' in fuck would be drawn out – it was her habit to retain her Russian accent when it suited.)

Sasha watched her passing parade of lovers, uncomplaining; it would have made no difference. Public humiliation was avoided by a rumour that they were cousins, several stages removed. It wasn't true but Svetlana saw no reason to deny it, and Sasha couldn't, because it saved his face and because it was she who'd put it about.

To make things worse she had a penchant for practical jokes. Once she'd hidden in a bedroom cupboard and watched him at work on a girl. At the time he hadn't discovered her, she'd told him the day after the girl had gone.

'Can I give you some advice?'

'Go on.'

'You really have to do something about your sexual technique.'

Sasha's brow lowered.

'What do you mean?'

'I mean you can't just go at it like a bulldozer. You flatten them.'

'How do you know?'

'Because I watched you the other night with Alice.'

'You watched us! How could you do that? It's disgusting!'

'*Byedni kuzenok*! My poor little cousin! Don't be so puritanical! I'm only trying to help. It's like you're an adolescent and I'm an older woman. One day – who knows? – we may hit it off together, like in *The Graduate*. You'll be Benjamin to my Mrs Robinson – except I get to lick you into shape before we get started.'

The truth was that Svetlana was less than a year older, but no matter. For Sasha what mattered was the prospect she dangled from time to time of getting started.

She didn't leave it there.

'Now Carlos, my Spanish Carlos, there's a role model for you! You want to watch him? Take a lesson from a pro?'

Carlos, a minor royal, was her latest, who was staying that weekend at the Cotswold house.

'*Watch* him?'

'Why not?'

'With *you*!'

'What's the big deal? People are always coming across each other when they're at it, especially in the same family. And if it's true what they say and we're related, little cousin...'

Where Svetlana was concerned Sasha could be a patient fellow, but this was too much, and for the first time he lost it.

'You don't let me sleep with you and now you want me to watch you with someone else! Don't you have *any* idea how other people feel? The way you treat them, it's, it's − ' his arms threshed about as he grasped for the word − 'fucking autistic!'

'*What did you say?*'

It was a warm weekend and she'd been sprawled with a book in a wicker chair next to the pool, topless. Now she sat up, coiled like a spring ready to fly up at him.

'You heard.'

In an instant she was on her feet, as close to his face as she could reach, as she spelled out her words slowly and with a chilled intensity.

'You ever say that to me again − ever − and it's the last you'll see of me. Understood?'

'I'm sorry, I didn't mean it... It was just that...'

That it was a modish term of abuse, and that in a fury of frustration he'd thrown it out without thinking.

Hapless as ever, he stood watching her walk away from the pool towards the house. Next to the door to the changing room hung a large mirror, and as she passed before it he saw that her eyes were streaming. It was the one time he had seen Svetlana in tears, and it would be the last.

\*

It was only after they'd graduated that they finally slept together. For Svetlana the first time was an accident, a moment of inattention (she was drunk). The second, some weeks later, she'd been sober. The occasion was to celebrate her moving into the flat he'd bought her, a grand affair in whose spacious bedroom they were sleeping tonight. Sasha was promised more, on condition that news of their affair did not get around and they held to the story that they were related.

In London she needed his money more than ever. Everyone had expected her to land a top job in the media, and fancying herself as an interviewer she'd got a trial recording on ITV, but it didn't work out. The problem was her style. Self-confident women were in fashion, but in the words of an executive who took part in the trial, 'it was like being interviewed by Catherine the Great.'

Tests for other channels produced more rejections. 'Pushy pussy is fine,' a Channel Four man sighed after subjecting himself to the same experience, 'but when she trains those eyes and those tits on you, you don't want to answer questions, you want to stick up your hands, surrender and get the hell out. Attack is the only kind of relationship she understands. Bloody autistic, the way she behaves.'

It was one of those accidental still-on-air moments: the Channel Four man had been relieving his feelings with his mic still in his buttonhole, live, so on her way back to her changing room Svetlana heard every word, as did the cameramen and studio hands clearing the set.

*Autistic.* The first time she'd heard the word was when she'd overheard her parents discussing her behaviour late at night. Having no idea what it meant, she forgot it. Her scientist father, however, was concerned. Disturbed by her stubborn conduct and tendency to monomania, when she was twelve years old he asked a psychiatrist colleague to observe her over a period, and report back.

No, not autism, had been his friend's conclusion, though maybe a personality disorder. 'She's a willful young lady all right, and she's not in the habit of taking other people's feelings into account. Might just be a question of character. Either way it could ease off over time as the child grows up.'

It didn't. When she was preparing to go to university, choosing his words carefully her father did his best to convey to her that there was a problem. And by now she knew the term.

'You're telling me I'm autistic?'

'Not at all, darling, not exactly. Whatever it is it's a sign of intelligence. Just something to bear in mind when you're under stress, or when you come to choose a career.'

But Svetlana had already made her choice. She enjoyed being admired for her looks and her sassy spirit and had determined that her career would be on television. And now, after three failed trials and three refusals her broadcasting future was over before it had begun.

It was the first setback in her life and she didn't like it. It couldn't be lack of talent, so it had to be because she was Russian, at a time when a new Cold War seemed to be brewing. From now on her adopted country would be against her, she privately decided, and became even pricklier than before.

To disguise her failure she put it about that she was in no hurry to commit to a career, amusing herself meanwhile with this and that: a little modelling of the up-market kind, a job in a well-known gallery of contemporary art and, more recently, occasional interpreting. Not for anyone – and most certainly not for business – but for the Russian Ambassador at prestigious artistic events.

How she got into it was accidental. Her gallery had hosted a festival of Russian art, where the sleek princess caught the Ambassador's eye when she'd interpreted for him to open the show. A Kremlin trusty, when Oleg Mikhailovitch Ivanovsky had been dispatched to London during the Ukrainian conflict with orders to polish up his country's image he had wisely decided to begin by improving his own. Employing a startlingly pretty woman with aristocratic status as his personal interpreter on cultural outings had seemed to him a clever stroke.

When the Ambassador's social secretary telephoned her with the proposal, at first Svetlana had laughed it off.

'Me, work for the Russian Embassy? You're not serious! Think of the security and bureaucracy for a start.'

There would be none of that, the woman rang back to assure her, after consulting her boss. As nothing confidential would be involved, the Ambassador would be happy for the arrangement to be informal.

To a young woman who still harboured the dream of a TV career, the idea of circulating amongst the *beau monde* of the arts world had its appeal. Though not for Sasha. The first time she'd told him about it he too had laughed it off. When she said she was thinking of accepting, he was horrified.

'You can't, it's crazy! It's like consorting with the opposition. What would my dad say?'

'Firstly, he doesn't know about us. Nobody does. Secondly, he stands to benefit. It's a job where you run into people, and you pick things up. And it's only occasional, for God's sake.'

So Sasha's misgivings had been soothed. And sure enough, charmed by his glamorous companion, Ivanovsky was more loose-tongued than he ought to have been in her company. *Moya lichnaya shpionka* – my personal spy – Sasha would call her when she was able to satisfy his craving for Russian political gossip and intrigue.

Tonight was to be one of them.

\*

For a while they lay watching the play of shadows on the curtains produced by the languidly swaying chestnut outside the bedroom window.

'*Dushka...*' Sasha began, and reached out a hand. It was as far as he got. Turning her back, she said irritably:

'English, if you don't mind. I can't bear you speaking Russian.

Your grammar is terrible.' She yawned. 'Now I'll never get back to sleep. What kept you? Your father on night shift again?'

'He was interviewing someone to replace Dombrovsky. I took the fellow home. Gave me a chance to check him out. Lives in some backstreet in Chiswick. Low-level guy, I would think.'

'I thought you were taking over security yourself?'

'I did for a bit, then Dad got it into his head we needed a professional to clean things up.'

'So who was he interviewing?'

'Guy called Underwood. Ex-MI5.'

'*Bozhe*! He must want to buy into the security service. How is he, by the way?'

'Still not well. I go on telling him to change his doctor but he won't hear of it. He's got this doddering old professor, been with him for years, only man he trusts. Won't let anyone else touch him.'

'Another paranoid Russian. The story of our motherland. Everyone's paranoid and nothing gets done. Speaking of which, if your dad's going to give you an MI5 nanny, you'll be able to do even less than now.'

Sasha lay silent. He didn't like her way of dismissing his one-man campaign against the Kremlin as pinpricks. It wasn't the first time.

'You'll end up like your father,' she went on. 'He used to be a man of action but he went soft, turned into a Russian dreamer. A constitutional monarchy, in Russia? We've got one already. He's the King *and* the constitution. With him in charge, your father's dreams are a waste of time.'

Sasha lay frowning.

'So you think this MI5 guy will keep an eye on me?'

'Of course he will. And report to the authorities so they can keep tabs on you too. Not that there's a lot to keep tabs on. Except us.'

He thought for a moment.

'Maybe you should live somewhere else?'

Svetlana turned to him, startled. It was she who had selected the flat.

'You're joking! I've only just moved in, and I love it.'

'I mean find somewhere more discreet. It's a bit poncy round here.'

'Where do you want me to live? In some godforsaken suburb, full of blacks and Islamics and God knows what?'

Laughing, he edged closer.

'Ah, my little racist! I adore my little *rasistka*!'

Svetlana backed away.

'No, let's talk. I've got a secret for you.

'Tell me.'

'He's coming to Europe.'

'Who?'

'The President, for Christ's sake.'

'Where? What for?'

'France, on a state visit. The first time he's done a big trip since the Ukrainian business. With his election coming up I suppose he thinks he's got to show he's a big noise in the world and not everyone hates him.'

'France! Brilliant! I've got contacts over there, we could do something.'

'Such as?'

'I dunno… Fuck things up for him a bit.'

'Like how?'

'Get some articles going, maybe a demonstration.'

'A couple of placards and an article no one reads?' She gave a derisive laugh. 'You think that'll make a difference? Is that the height of your ambition?'

'I need to think about it. How long's he going to be there?'

'The Ambassador didn't say.'

'I have to see his itinerary, and the dates. They'll keep the London Embassy informed, won't they?'

'I imagine. And they're asking for French speakers to go over there to help out, the secretary told me.'

'You speak French, my pigeon.' He kissed her hair. 'Perfectly. Why not volunteer?'

'Why should I?'

'So you can keep me informed.'

'For your piddling demonstrations?'

Again he relapsed into thought, then said:

'Maybe I'll think up something bigger. Something that may surprise you.'

'From you, darling, something big would certainly surprise me. Now how about letting me sleep?'

'You'll let me know about the itinerary, won't you?'

'If I can. It won't just be Paris. The secretary said he was going to take a break somewhere while he's at it, in the South probably. So he'll be on form for the elections.'

'Where exactly? If we're going to get something going I'll need to know where. Come on, *dushenka,* make an effort. There'll be a little present...'

'Little, only?'

'Maybe not so little. In fact I brought something tonight.'

'A present! Where is it?'

'Next to you.'

Groping the bedside table her fingers encountered an envelope. Without opening it, she felt the thickness of the notes.

'You're right,' she turned, 'it's not so little.'

As her outline curled towards him, and Sasha's straightened, the forms under the sheet came together.

# 4

'Good morning Mr Underwooed! I am so glad we are to work together. You are the only Englishman here, it will be good for my English. The first thing is to meet Mikhail.'

'And what does Mikhail do exactly?'

'Everything, he will tell you everything.'

'So he's the factotum.'

'What is factotum?'

'The man who does everything.'

'You see?' She shot him a shy smile. 'Already I am learning.'

She led the way to the office two doors along from Grekov's, knocked and opened the door.

'Mikhail, this is Mr Underwooed.'

Closing the door, she left the men alone.

Mikhail was lounging on a sofa, his feet on a glass table, drinking coffee and reading *Novaya Gazeta*, an opposition Russian paper.

'Mr Underwood, our English spy! Welcome!'

With a struggle he got up and shook his hand. A block of a man, smallish but broad-shouldered and barrel-chested, Mikhail stood close, in the Russian fashion, so close that Tony could see that his eyes were reddish, as if permanently bloodshot, and his features leathery, yet somehow kind.

'First, I tell you about house. Sub-basement is cinema, Mr Grekov love cinema. Anything with kings and queens. *The King's Speech*, you have seen? He see it twenty times. Sub-sub basement is swimming pool, and *banya*. Like me he hate exercise but he swim. At night mostly, if he can't sleep he swim a little.

'Ground floor reception. First floor Mr Grekov's office, my office, his son's office, and Lisa. She is Czech. Very nice woman, very cultured. Second and third floor accountant people. Fourth floor bedrooms, top floor for guests. Mews houses are garages at back. You have questions?'

'I hope you can tell me about the security arrangements? Or do I ask Mr Grekov's son?'

'No, is me you ask. Yes security we discuss. But for that we need drink, to celebrate.'

'It's a little early.'

'Early?'

'The time, I mean.'

It was ten forty-five.

'For me no early! Russia has eleven time zone, this house like Russian territory, so here Mr Grekov make own time. This morning he want start at six o'clock, so for me is almost lunch.'

A full-sized fridge stood in a corner. Opening the door he displayed the contents proudly.

'So what you like?'

'A beer perhaps.'

'Beer no good for celebration! Vodka better!'

He poured two shots, and raised his glass.

'A toast to English security man who will find Moscow spies!'

They drank, and sat down. Mikhail held out a cigarette packet.

'No thanks, I don't smoke often. Only cigarillos.'

Mikhail lit up and drew in, deeply.

'In Russia, two type of people only: no-smokers, like Mr Grekov, and chain smokers like me.'

'So, who supervises the security people now?'

'You know about Dombrovsky, yes? After that Mr Grekov think maybe Mr Sasha, but he change his mind.'

An hour and three vodkas later, Tony had what he needed: the names, addresses, photographs, functions, car numbers, curricula vitae and personal descriptions of Grekov's security detail: six men and one woman. Closing his notebook, he asked:

'One thing puzzles me. If Mr Grekov doesn't do business in Russia, and if he isn't politically active, what has he to fear from Moscow?'

'They know he is thinker. In Russian history is thinkers who make trouble. But he is oligarch, with money, so when he finish thinking what he do? They know he admire English Queen so maybe he active with émigré royalty? Put Romanovs back on throne!'

'Isn't that a bit far-fetched? I mean a bit fantastic?'

'In Russia everything fantastic! You no read Gogol?'

No, Tony had not.

'Something else I need to know: his security people, do any of them carry weapons?'

Mikhail reached over and patted his knee.

'Tony, my friend, why you ask question when you know answer?'

'Which is?'

Mikhail looked scandalized.

'In Britain is illegal carry weapon! Only hit men carry weapon!'

'So they don't?'

A sigh.

'Remember how Russian people used to say how one day Moscow will be third Rome? Rome, Constantinople, and then Moscow.'

'I can't say – '

' – never mind. Today Moscow not third Rome, it is second Chicago! If they send more hit men here London will be third Chicago!'

'So you're saying Mr Grekov has to defend himself.'

'Tony, you have MI5 pension, no? Weapon against law, so why you speak about them? Why you ask questions you don't want to know answer?'

Tony smiled, faintly.

'Maybe better we talk about salary?' Mikhail grinned.

'Mr Grekov didn't say anything – '

' – I know. He hate talk money, money he leave to me. He is reasonable man, he pay well.' His face creased in a parody of laughter. 'He like being alive so if nobody kill, you get bonus.'

'And in terms of salary...'

'First year, one hundred fifty thousand. You will be personal employee, not on books, so pay will be cash. You want to tell to taxman – ' his hands went up, defensively, like a footballer's after a foul – 'is up to you. Just no names, OK?'

'I shouldn't tell anyone I work for Mr Grekov?'

'You tell everyone you work for MI5?'

'No.'

'So why for Mr Grekov?'

'Including the people I supervise?'

'Especially people you supervise. They no need know you are here. Beside Mr Grekov three people know: Lisa, Sasha, and me. For anyone one else you are banker. OK?'

Going behind his desk, he opened a safe.

'Banker need money, so here.' He held up an envelope. 'Ten thousand.'

'Well, thanks.'

'Mr Grekov like everyone dress nice. Like old days, in jacket and tie. Even me I must dress nice!' He stroked the lapel of his suit. 'From Harrods! Like uniform we have to wear, so Mr Grekov pay. Maybe you get, I don't know, more shirt, more suit!'

Tony took the envelope.

'You like advance on salary, you tell me, OK?'

Tony didn't decline.

'Oh and please you sign this.'

He handed him a piece of paper.'

'A receipt?'

'No, receipt not necessary. Is confidentiality agreement. Mr Grekov hate things in press.'

Tony read it and signed.

'One more thing.' Mikhail was looking grave. 'Is about Sasha. Mr Grekov love his son like he was prince. He not want him get in trouble, but Sasha young man, who is not thinker. He do things without thinking – do too many things! Of course he drink, of course he has girls, that not worry Mr Grekov. What worry him is politics. Sasha is nice young man but a little hot in head.'

'Hot-headed.'

'Correct. So Mr Grekov want you cool him down. He try do too much against Kremlin, so we cool him.'

'Mr Grekov didn't say anything about that.'

'He not want say, he want me say. Is sensitive person, not want ask English spy to watch his son. And his son's friends. Strange friends sometimes.'

'Dissidents you mean?'

'Dissident only talk, Sasha's friends more than talk. While he run security he take on new man. He is personal protection officer, he tell me, but I never see him. All we do is pay him.'

'What's his name?'

'Daudov, Thoma Daudov. He is on list of security people but no photo or detail. All I know is he is Georgian. I not tell Mr Grekov yet because anyone from Caucasus – Georgian, Chechen, Dagestani – he worry. First I want you see what Daudov does. If it worry Mr Grekov we find way get rid of him. But without tell Sasha, OK?'

He was on his way to the door when Mikhail said:

'One more thing. Is delicate. Somebody tell me Sasha has Russian girlfriend. Something else I not tell Mr Grekov because he not like. For him anything Russian mean problem. We need find out who she is. See if she is problem. Maybe you check out, no?'

# 5

His room in the Belgravia house was a cut above the open-plan office where he'd squatted during his last months in the service. Now he had an antique desk, a three-piece suite in black leather and equipment so high-tech he wasn't sure how to use it. The drinks cupboard, munificently stocked, looked easier to handle.

A quick shopping trip – a suit from Harrods, some shirts and a £300 pair of shoes – and he got down to business. The files on the security staff Mikhail had supplied lay before him, and if it proved hard to focus, it wasn't only his alcoholic morning. All his life he'd worked in a structure: bosses telling him what to do, a team to work and grumble with, tech guys to keep him abreast of the latest methods.

Now he was on his own, an organization man without an organization, a one-man surveillance operation reporting to two bosses and overseeing staff who didn't know he was there. After a while he got up, worked out how to operate the coffee machine, poured himself a cup, sat back down, stared into space. Where did he go from here?

The answer he knew before he asked the question. He'd sworn he wouldn't do it, told himself that he'd keep in touch with his old friends in Thames House socially but nothing more.

And the alternative? Finishing his coffee, he reached for the phone.

*

The pub where he drank with Dick Welby, a thirst-giving stroll from Thames House, was the sort of place new recruits were specifically warned against frequenting. Which was strange. With its youthful clientele and explosions of falsetto laughter when the white wine circulated too quickly amongst the groups of young women the place seemed to attract, the noise levels were so ear-rending it was hard to imagine anywhere more secure. The problem at the Cumberland Arms wasn't being overheard, it was to make yourself heard at all.

Dick arrived first. When Tony turned up in a sharp new suit he leant across to caress the pinhead worsted.

'Wow! Looks like you've sold out to the oligarchs after all. You seemed to have doubts.'

Tony gave a guilty laugh.

'Wait till it's your turn. And Grekov was a pleasant surprise, I have to admit. Bit weird, but a genuine anglophile. Not one of those smarmy bastards who've come over because their money's safer here than there and are still in touch with their Kremlin friends.'

They were a few drinks in before he broached the purpose of the meeting.

'As you said, the first thing Grekov wants me to do is look over his security team.'

'So you want me to check them out.'

'Since you offer.'

'I didn't and it's unethical.'

Dick was half-smiling, but Tony was down his throat in an instant.

'What's unethical is to give you to understand you've got another few years in a job then tell you to fuck off. The least they can do is help a man earn his living.'

'Woah, cool it Tony! Of course I'll help. No one has to know. Providing it's just background – '

' – that's all I need, background. Seven of them need checking.'

'Much as my job's worth, but then the rate they're chopping out the old wood it's not worth much as it is.'

Two days later they were strolling in the streets behind the Embankment.

'I ran a check on the magnificent seven. Six of them seem clean

– at least there's nothing definitive on them. There's just this one.' He pulled out a photo. 'Fellow called Daudov.'

'Good.'

'Why good?'

'Because he's the one I'm interested in.' Tony studied the photo. A youngish man, late twenties, light brown skin, jet black hair. 'Protection officer, so-called. Anything on him?'

'Mixed background, half-Georgian, half-Chechen. Incendiary combination. Used to live in France. Came here via Marseille a year ago – there's a Chechen colony there. The French think he was involved in a bit of drug-running and anti-Russian agitation. Done a bit of it here, which is why he's on our books, in that large category of people we haven't troubled looking into.'

'Why not?'

'Too low-level. Plus he's not in the jihadi business.'

'Anything else on him?'

'His girlfriend's an illegal immigrant. Ukrainian, a dancer. Klara Stepenko's her professional name.' He held up a snapshot. 'Here she is. Dancing.'

She was, at the Club *Elle et Lui*. Nude, on a table, with Daudov applauding in the background.

Tony returned the photo.

'Not bad-looking for the trade,' he mused. 'She'll be expensive. Where does he live?'

'Maida Vale.'

'Fancy address for a protection officer. And the girlfriend?'

'Lives with him.'

'Any suggestion she's a Russian nark?'

'We don't think so. Doesn't seem Moscow-friendly. Got out of Eastern Ukraine during the troubles in 2014.'

'And what about Daudov? Could he be in with the Embassy?'

'The opposite. I told you, he's involved in anti-regime stuff.'

'So he's the kind of man who could get Sasha into trouble.'

'Could, I suppose,' Dick agreed. 'Though he sounds to me a piddling sort. You're absorbing your boss's paranoia.'

'That's what I'm paid to do. How do I get him thrown out?'

'You can't. He's got a visa he's just renewed and he's done nothing wrong. Whipping up anti-Russian sentiment is his human right. Maybe you should just get Grekov to fire him?'

'If he's doing stuff for him, Sasha won't like that.'

'Well there you go. You'll have to think up some other way of persuading him to leave the country. Just one thing.'

'And what's that?'

'I'd rather not know how you do it.'

*

His first stop was Lisa. Calling by that afternoon, he found her at work in her office. The sight of her demure, uncrossed legs under the desk, her high-necked blouse and a skirt that was longer than the fashion was somehow affecting.

'Daudov? I don't know the name. He's a bodyguard?'

'Well, yes and no. Apparently he works for Sasha. Here's his photo.'

She looked at it briefly.

'He must be new, I've never seen him. But now you mention it, Ruth told me Sasha had taken on a Georgian who's lived in France.'

Ruth was Sasha's personal assistant. A severe-looking lady of sixty, she'd been imposed on the boy by his father, Lisa had told him, and had watched over his affairs since his late teens.

'Whatever this Daudov does he's not based here,' Lisa went on. 'The only time Ruth hears from him, apparently, is when he sends in a chit for expenses to pass on to Mikhail. She says they're outrageous, but he has to pay up because he gets Sasha to sign them personally.'

'Anything else I should know?'

'Well, Ruth thinks he's Sasha's ...No, I'd better not say.'

'His dealer?'

Lisa avoided his eyes.

'Maybe you should ask Ruth.'

'Do I need to? I think you've given me the answer.' He smiled. 'I know it's awkward for you, me asking you about Sasha. I'll try not to make a habit of it, I promise.'

'Oh don't worry, I understand,' said Lisa, with a look that conveyed that her boss's son was not her favourite.

*

If its window display was to be believed the café on a main road in Maida Vale was famous for its sarnies and full English breakfasts. At the start of one of his periodic health regimes – there were new clothes to fit into – Tony confined himself to a croissant and black coffee. Selecting a high stool at the window that affording him a diagonal view into the street where Daudov lived, he waited.

The two-storey mews house was fronted by a curtained bay window and pots of withered plants. At 9.10 the door opened, and Daudov emerged. Closing it gently – he must want to avoid waking his girlfriend – he glanced up and down the empty mews warily, the way someone would before crossing a busy road.

A tallish, athletic figure, he looked younger than in the photo, somewhere in his late twenties. In his denim jacket, chinos and trainers there seemed something at once nervy and cocky about him. Slugging back the remains of his coffee, Tony waited for him to unlock his garage. Instead he turned into the main road and, with a jaunty, spring-heeled step, strode towards the café.

The *Daily Telegraph*, selected for its broadsheet cover (Tony was a *Mail* reader) screened him while Daudov crossed the road. When he opened the door a swivel of his seat kept him safely obscured.

'Takeaway coffee and zani.'

'You mean sarnie.'

'Same I always have.'

'I remember.'

The woman's smile was half-amused, half-flirtatious. With his rich dark hair and southern looks, the Georgian must do well with the girls.

Aware of him waiting for his bacon sandwich behind him, Tony decided to be on his way. But a lone surveillance man needs luck, and that morning he had it. The moment he'd folded his paper and was about to depart he heard the Georgian talking into a mobile.

'Is me, Mr Sasha. You say I telephone after nine clock... Of course Mr Sasha. Today you want? Yes I come, where you like go?... Yes I know Queensway. *Cafe Anglais*?... At Whiteley? How you write Whiteley? Like white...? So café in big shop, yes?... OK, one o'clock Mr Sasha.'

*

'And where would Sir like to sit?'

Tom Sandiman, a tall man with a stoop in his late sixties, surveyed the large, half-empty room at the Café Anglais with approval. For his purposes, the place was perfect. Not too smart for his worn tweed jacket, so he wouldn't stand out, and the tables not too close, with clear, open lines between them

It was just past one. He checked out the customers. In the far corner a lone male in a denim jacket sat waiting at a table for two next to the window. While his eye was measuring the distance from the dark-haired fellow to an empty table opposite a tall, fleshy-faced young man in a sort of up-market anorak mooched through the entrance and, ignoring the waiter, shambled towards the denim-jacketed figure.

'Over there,' Sandiman indicated the empty table, 'facing the window. I'd like to sit there if it's free.'

'Certainly, Sir.'

The waiter pulled back his chair. Sandiman sat down, his briefcase at his feet.

'Anything to drink?'

'Glass of light ale, if you wouldn't mind.'

'We have lager, or – '

' – all right, a lager will do.'

After scanning the menu he opened the briefcase and took out a

hardback copy of Tom Clancy's *Clear and Present Danger*. Opening it
at a bookmarked page, he placed it to the left of his napkin.
Glancing across at the two men opposite and adjusting his book in
the manner of a fussy old gent, he began reading.

His lager arrived.

'And to eat, Sir?'

'Mushroom soup and baked cod.'

He could have ordered something fancier – the meal would be
on expenses, Tony had assured him – but Sandiman, from a modest
background, had simple tastes. Thin-faced, glasses, intelligent-
looking, he resembled one of those telephone engineers you see in
the street disentangling cables of unimaginable complexity, who
except for their brown overalls you could imagine as an academic.

Which was exactly what Tom had been – a Polytechnic lecturer
in telecommunications – before his recruitment by the security services in his late thirties. From then on his career had gone downwards, ethically speaking, while his job satisfaction had gone sharply
up. With his inventive mind, his powers of persuasion and preference for fitting his eavesdropping contrivances into position personally, soon he was insinuating himself into the homes of foreign
intelligence men, terrorists and drug bosses of all nationalities and
persuasions.

After bugging his way through a long and meritorious career he
was supplementing his pension with occasional work for a detective
agency, occasionally of a kind that might have landed him in trouble
with his previous employers. But then as Tony had discovered when
they'd worked together tapping into mosques, Muslim bookshops
and the homes of militant imams in the North of England, Tom
was inclined to charge ahead with or without official sanction. As to
the morality of his work, he was happy for others to judge. A man
devoted to his craft, his priority in life was not so much a clear con-
science as clear reception.

Today's job seemed straightforward enough. Lucky he'd been
available at short notice when Tony had called that morning.

The waiter approached on his left and stood with his tray next to the book, his eyes inviting him to shift it. Leaving it where it was Sandiman pointed, imperiously, to his right. While the man served him his soup he glanced across at his quarry.

Ignoring their first course, Daudov and Sasha were putting back vodka while engaged in low but animated conversation. When his waiter had gone Sandiman took a spoonful of his soup before inclining his head back over his book. As he did so his thumb grazed the control of the directional microphone concealed in its spine, increasing the volume a notch.

The soup wasn't up to much – not enough salt – though the baked cod was delicious. He ate it with relish, remembering to glance at his book between mouthfuls but forgetting to turn the pages. The trouble was he'd read *Clear and Present Danger* before, many a time, so if Tony had more of this line of work for him he'd better get himself a new Tom Clancy.

*

Sandiman lived in Hammersmith, half a mile from Tony's place in Chiswick, and delivered the recording of the Café Anglais conversation to his house at nine next morning. Luckily they'd talked in English.

'Can't say I took to your Russian friend,' he said, handing over the memory stick. 'Treats the other fellow like shit. Mind you, I'm not much of a fan of the guy in the Kremlin either, so anything they can pull off has my vote.'

'Against the President?'

'You don't know what they're up to? Never mind, you'll find out when you listen. Anything else I can help you with?'

'May well be. Be in touch Tom, right?'

In his upstairs office he listened to the recording. Tom was right, Sasha was domineering with the Georgian, Daudov pathetically ingratiating towards his Russian boss. After suffering an ear-bashing for taking his money and failing to come up with new projects, the Georgian finally got a chance to speak.

'Mr Sasha, is good we talk. I have idea for you. Very good one.'

'And what's that?'

'Soon there will be visitor, in France.'

'I know.'

'Big visitor.'

'I know.'

'Is not in papers. How you know?'

'Never you fucking mind. How do *you* know?'

'Émigré people in France tell me.'

'He's going to Paris in October, for a state visit. That's why I wanted to talk to you. I want you to go over there, sound things out, get onto people, see what they can come up with.'

'I have many friends not like him, can make visit difficult.'

'That would be good. But I don't want something piffling.'

'I no understand. What is piffling?'

'Small, I don't want anything small.'

'You mean not just write things?'

'Yeah, not just bloody articles and posters and stuff. I want new ideas. Big ones, right? It's what I pay you for. So get in touch with your friends over there and let's have something serious.'

'If I need people help me it cost money. How much Mr Sasha like to spend?'

'Whatever it takes.'

'And what kind of thing you want?'

'That's what I'm asking you to come up with, for Christ's sake! Think it through. Why is he going to Paris? Because he's got elections coming up and wants to play the statesman, put on a show to take their minds off the poverty he's got them into. And tell them he's got away with annexing the Crimea and beating up on the Ukraine and the West has to deal with him, like it or not.'

'And what's he going to do there? Parade down the Champs Elysées, probably. The uniforms, the guards of honour – Russians love that stuff. Reminds them of 1812, Alexander I riding through Paris. But if something happened on the way, in front of the world's cameras...'

'So what you like happen?'

'Whatever. Something that buggers up the whole visit. Something that'll make the front pages over the entire bloody globe.'

A silence while the waiter served them, then Daudov:

'Maybe we stop the parade? With leaflets. Maybe we organize naked girls, with leaflets.'

'Oh Christ no, too jokey. Anyway it's been done. Those feminists, when he went to Germany, remember? Stripped off to show their tits and wrote *Fuck Off Russian President* on their backs. And it didn't work, did it? Bastard didn't move a muscle. Just did that macho thing of his – gave the girls the thumbs up so the Russians thought he was a great guy.'

As the vodka took hold (Sasha kept calling for more) there were endless tirades against the President. Daudov was eager to add his bit.

'You are right, Mr Sasha. I know what you say. I am Georgian and Chechen, he attack both my country, kill people I know. When he invade Georgia in 2008 I in army. Shoot many Russians, but they take me prisoner.'

'Well, now's your chance to have a shot at *him*.'

A silence, then.

'Shoot him?' Another silence. 'Is joke, Mr Sasha, no?'

'What do you fucking think?'

Nervous laughter from Daudov.

When they were leaving the Georgian said in a low voice:

'You want something nice, Mr Sasha, for have fun? I have new stuff. Maybe for you and girlfriend?'

'What girlfriend?' Sasha's voice was harsh suddenly. 'Who's talking about girlfriends? My girlfriends are no business of yours.'

'I am sorry Mr Sasha, you are right, is not my business. I only say because is not too strong. Maybe you like take some with you now, so you try?'

'Not here for Christ's sake. Next time, I'm OK for now. And it better be good. The first stuff you gave me I couldn't sleep, the next time it gave me nightmares.'

'No nightmare, I promise. Is really clean. So how much you like?'

'Whatever, five grand. And here, I brought something for you. It'll take you across to France and get your imagination going.'

The rustle of an envelope.

'Thank you Mr Sasha. With this I have good idea!'

And that was it. Tom, as always, had come up with the goods. Tempted to give the recording to Mikhail, so as to prove he was on Daudov's trail, he decided against. The Russian would think he couldn't have done it without inside help, and conclude that the security services were at his beck and call. Not the image he wanted to project. Best preserve a bit of mystery about his methods.

So much for Sasha's personal protection officer. With his drug supplies, his crazy political schemes and foreign contacts, Daudov was everything Grekov must be afraid of. It was his job to keep his boy out of trouble, Daudov was trouble all right, so the Georgian would have to go.

*

8.50 next morning and he was back in Maida Vale, parked on a meter up the road from the mews. At nine thirty Daudov crossed the road to the café, returned four minutes later with his coffee and his bacon sandwich, took his car from his garage and drove off. Interesting to have known where, but Tony had another task in hand.

His dancer girlfriend would be a late riser; *Elle et Lui*, he'd established, had a license till 3 am, so he'd give her till 10 o'clock to get up and dressed.

It wasn't enough: when he rang the bell of the house there was no response. He pressed it again. Finally a voice came over the intercom.

'Who is it?'

'Immigration.'

'I no understand.'

'The immigration service.'

'I not up. Can you come back?'

'I'm afraid not. It's an official call. I have important information for you.'

Silence.

'You must wait I dress.'

Dress for Ms Stepenko turned out to be a relative affair. Minutes later she answered the door wearing a shift over her bra and pants. A comb had been passed through her straw-blond hair, to little avail.

'May I come in?'

The light blue eyes were mistrustful, and a little frightened.

'You have identity?'

He had: his immigration official's card, one of several mementoes he'd taken the liberty of appropriating from Thames House, this one from his Islamist days. In the name of a Mr Patrick Firbank, its validity was a little out of date though the photograph was kosher. Just as well: the woman checked it against his face before letting him in.

The front room of the mews was tiny and a mess: a sofa, a table bearing the remains of last night's dinner – pizza crusts, an empty bottle of Rioja – and a guitar slung up on the wall.

Ms Stepenko clutched a hand to her chest.

'Why you come? I no problem with immigration. I am dancing artist. Look.' She pointed to the wall, where a poster from her club (*Klara Gets It Off*) was hanging. She was slimmer in the picture, by a wide margin.

'Is nice, eh?'

'It isn't about you. I've come about your friend, Mr Daudov.'

'His visa OK. He tell me he just renewed.'

'I am aware of that, but there's a problem. The visa doesn't automatically mean he has a right to stay. It's conditional on good behaviour.'

'What he do? He not make trouble.'

'We've been told he's consorting with undesirable people.'

'What is consort?'

'Mixing.'

'Who tell you?'

'The appropriate authorities.'

'Security people you mean?'

'I am not at liberty to say.'

'So what I do?'

'I want you to give him a message.'

'I tell him to stop consort, so no problem, right?'

'Unfortunately it's not so simple. My personal advice – my strong advice – is that he should leave the country. Quickly. Otherwise – ' he shook his head – 'there could be complications.'

'What kind complication?'

'Investigations about drug use and supply. Arrest, the immigration courts – it could be a long business.'

'This terrible. How can happen?'

Her mouth went down, her face wrinkling, like a savvy child preparing tears. Then a smile.

'Maybe we fix unofficial? We just sit and think what we do.' Taking a step towards him she pointed at the sofa.

'Maybe you like drink?'

A hand lingered against the collar of her shift, as if to suggest that it was adjustable.

'Thank you, I've just had breakfast.'

Her face reverted to tearful mode.

'And me? If he go where I live? Who look after me?'

In a second she was next to him, a hand on his arm, her face close to his. She smelt of old scent, of sleep, maybe something more. When he moved away she said quietly:

'I tell you secret I not tell boyfriend. Soon I have baby. It is he rent house. He leave I have no home, with baby.'

If she was acting it was a creditable show, her hands cupping her cheeks, her eyes glistening. Tony looked back at her, sceptical.

'You no believe? Wait!'

Hurrying from the room she came back clutching a letter and thrust it silently in his face. *The Royal Free Hospital, Department of Antenatal Care*, the title read.

'I'm sorry, there's nothing I can do. I suggest you give your partner my message.'

Driving back to his office he marvelled at his performance. The NHS letter looked genuine. Throwing pregnant women out of the country... Hard to believe he'd done that. But then he had a family of his own to take care of, and his hundred and fifty grand to earn...

*

Three days later the telephone rang at home in the early evening.

'It's me. I'm on my way home, in a phone box. You've got me behaving like a bloody nark. Just to say your man was on an Air France flight to Marseille first thing this morning. With his naked lady.'

'Excellent.'

'Nothing we did, I assure you. So you'd better dream up some way to collect the credit.'

'Dick, I can't thank you enough.'

'You'll find a way, give it time. Just don't tell me what you're up to, right? Anything less than legal I don't want to know. I mean that, understood?'

'Understood. From now on you'll be in the dark.'

'That's where I'm happiest.'

Mikhail was ecstatic:

'This good, very good! This need celebrate.' He strode towards his fridge. 'Tell me,' he said, pouring, 'how you do so quick?'

'Hacked his phone. Found out he was in with a bunch of agitators. Informed the relevant authorities, and he's out.'

None of it was true, but there was no need for details. Nor did he say anything about the Presidential visit, or what Sasha was up to with Daudov in France. It was too early to worry him – or Sasha's father – and the boy's schemes sounded more than a little halfbaked. Best wait till he knew what Daudov came up with, see how things developed.

'I tell Mr Grekov you throw out Chechen. He will be pleased. Chechen people very wild, crazy wild!'

'He's only half Chechen.'

'Half is enough.

'And Sasha. Don't we have to explain?'

'No, we say nothing. People like Daudov they come then they go. If Sasha use him for things he know his father not like, he say nothing.'

Mikhail was right. A week went by and the boy didn't mention that his personal protection man had disappeared. And he was right about Grekov's contentment: the reward for Tony's expeditious operation, a £5,000 cash bonus, came a day later.

# 6

Daudov sat in his vest and pants on the balcony of his one-roomed flat overlooking a dilapidated *quartier* of Marseille. He was out here because the flat was a dump, and because Klara said she couldn't breathe any more of his cigarette fumes now that she was pregnant. She wasn't there at that moment – off for another check-up – but after giving up smoking herself she was at the stage of renunciation where she could sniff out a fag a mile away.

All part of the new life he was facing. A shot of something to help him through the day was what he needed, but in her new phase of clean living she'd banned that too. He preferred the old Klara, the Klara who liked some fun and pulled in cash. If she'd told him about the baby before they'd come he wouldn't have brought her.

Too late. She was here and he couldn't send her back. Here with her morning sickness, her doctor's bills and her endless gripes about money. Why not do a bit of dancing, he'd told her, you're not far gone, people would hardly notice. And lose the baby, she'd said, though what would you care if I did? Not too much, would have been the honest answer.

The flat was on the eighth floor. He stared at the scabby buildings opposite. Washing lines, balconies stacked with rubbish, wailing Arab kids, wailing music. A long way from their mews in Maida Vale. In London he'd had it good, now he'd have to begin at the beginning, pick up where he'd left off before.

The main thing would be to keep in with Sasha. The Russian wanted him to come up with something on the President's visit, and he'd had an idea all right, though not one he could talk to Sasha about. One that had come to him like a revelation during a sleepless night in their airless, mosquito-ridden room. The scheme he'd dreamt up was risky, he knew it, but there could be big money in it, and for him these were desperate times.

The sound of Klara coming back. Stubbing his cigarette he opened the balcony door, went in, closed it – she'd complain of smoke drifting in – and asked:

'So how'd it go?'

Busy double-locking the door top and bottom – you had to here – she was displaying a rounding rump encased in over-tight jeans.

'A hundred twenty euros! In London it would be free! But she asked me for papers, I don't know, some forms or something, so they made me pay. I didn't have enough for a taxi back, and the heat, and those stairs… Aiya, I'm exhausted.'

On the edge of the bed she kicked off her shoes.

'So what did they say?'

'They said to be careful, it would be fine if I rest.'

'Well that's what you'd better do.'

It was June. What would it be like when it warmed up, a suffocating Marseille heat, and her up here on the eighth floor, swelling and swelling? Though if his idea worked they'd be out of this place soon enough.

He began putting on his jeans.

'Where are you going?'

'To see some friends about a couple of things.'

'To drink I suppose.'

'Well I may have a drink, yes. That's how you do business.'

'What business? And who are these people?'

'Klara, I told you, I lived here, for six years I lived here, so I know my way around.'

'The kind of people who got us thrown out of London?'

'The kind of people who'll help pay your doctors' bills.'

'And get us somewhere decent to live I hope. Maida Vale, it was so nice, so civilized… And here, all these Arabs. And the stairs…'

On his way to the door, he kissed her. She smelt of something medicinal, and of sweat.

\*

The two men sat alone outside the café, a hole-in-the-wall place with half a dozen rusting tables. Behind the bar ragged posters advertised meetings, speeches, rooms to rent and concerts by *Lean Young Wolf,* a Chechen rapper.

'You know about the visit?' Daudov asked his companion, Kasym, the moment their beers came.

'Whose?'

'The President's! The Russian President's! Haven't you heard? He's coming to France, for a state visit.'

Kasym looked back at him, silent, disbelieving. Early thirties, thin face, wiry, close-cropped hair, he was poised on the edge of his chair, smoking. With his urgent puffs and nervy demeanour Kasym always seemed to be on the edge of something.

'Not just that, he's coming down here.'

'To Marseille?' Kasym snorted into his glass. 'You're joking. He hasn't got the balls.'

'Not Marseille, he's not stupid. It's the Camargue he's coming to, for the riding and hunting. At the end of the state visit. Taking a break, to get himself on form for the election.'

Kasym was unconvinced.

'How do you know? Has it been in the papers?'

'Not yet – but he's coming. The Embassy's booking up all the hotels for four days in October, the duck-hunting season. Someone I know has a sister who works in one. A chambermaid, in Saintes-Maries-de-la-Mer. Whole blocs of rooms they're booking, she says, for his minders.'

'Well he'd better have plenty of them,' Kasym shot back, 'otherwise he'll be a sitting duck himself.'

He didn't smile as he said it, his deep brown eyes as intense as ever. Intensity was his default state, intensity and implacable loathing for the Russian President.

For a full minute he sat brooding.

'We have to do something,' Daudov said. 'You'd be up for

it, right?'

The Chechen's eyes flamed.

'Of course we'll do something!' He drew on his cigarette, nervily.
'The question is what? You got any plans?'

'Not so far, but I'm thinking.'

It was too soon to sound out his friend about his own idea:
Kasym was a jumpy fellow, he mustn't alarm him. The first thing was
to get him interested, and for more than an hour they sat hunched
over their table, Kasym talking earnestly while Daudov listened.
Most of what the Chechen had to say about the President wasn't
new, though this time it came out stronger, his lips twitching, as if
he'd developed a tic. When he got excited, with Kasym it happened.

Someone sat down at a nearby table. At a signal from Daudov he
lowered his voice, and they leant closer. When they parted the
Georgian's final words were:

'Whatever we do we'll need money. I'm not saying I can promise
anything, but I'll talk to a few people I know. And you – go on thinking.'

Out on his balcony next morning, the door shut against Klara,
Daudov made two calls on his mobile. The first was to Sasha, and
before dialling he took a deep breath.

He hated these conversations. The way the Russian dealt with
him, like he was some Georgian orange-seller, put him in a silent
rage. Today more than ever he must control himself. As always he
spoke in English – it wasn't too good, but then neither was Sasha's
Russian.

'Hello?'

'Is Mr Sasha?'

'Who's that?'

'Monsieur Henri here.'

'Where are you calling from?'

'From pay-you-go, new one. Is OK.'

'I mean what country.'

'France.'

'Good.'

'No, not good Mr Sasha. After I see you I had to go from London, quickly. Immigration people make problem, so I come back to Marseille.'

'Shit. How can you do anything down there?'

'I have friends here, already I find out something. He not just go to Paris, he come here for holiday. You know that?'

'To Marseille?'

'Not Marseille, in Camargue he come, to hunt. You know Camargue? 30 kilometres from Marseille.'

'Course I bloody know. How do *you* know, about him going there? Can you be sure?'

'Is certain. In Marseille people tell me.'

'Well talk to them some more.'

'Yes I talk. Already I have ideas.'

'Like what?'

'Maybe not say on phone. Later I tell you. But Mr Sasha, there is problem.'

'What problem?'

'I have no money. You help me, no?'

'Bullshit. I gave you some, to go to France.'

'Yes but before they throw me out. I still must pay rent for London house even if I no live there. So I no money left. And my girlfriend, she come here too, she tell me she going to have baby. In Marseille we have no free doctor, nowhere to live. You send money, yes? So I can help with big visitor. Go and look at Camargue, see where he going to hunt. But it cost money. So please Mr Sasha, you help. It urgent.'

'Send me an address and I'll see what I can do.'

Daudov's second message was a text addressed to *Santa*, to fix an urgent rendezvous. Within an hour a reply came back, agreeing to a meeting the following day.

*

Kasym's conversation with Daudov left him in a state of turmoil.

Anything about the Russian President always did, and the reason was his father. A doctor suspected of treating Chechen guerrillas during the second war with Russia, including a notorious warlord, he'd been forced to flee the family home. Was it true? Kasym had never known, and refused to think about it. All he knew was that there'd been a price on his father's head, and that in the end they'd got him.

The day they'd run him to ground soldiers had surrounded the block of flats where the family lived on the fifth floor. For safety his father, on the run and home for a clandestine visit, had been sleeping in the basement, and it was there they'd found him.

As they'd marched him off he'd made a break for it. Hearing a shot and a cry, disobeying his mother her son opened the window, looked down, and watched as the soldiers took his father's body away. By a leg they'd dragged him, like a dead bleeding stag. The image of his head bouncing lifeless along the stony ground never left him.

With no future in Chechnya, at 17 he'd stowed away on a merchant ship from Odessa that brought him to exile in Marseille. His elder brother Batir came with him but they'd lived apart, under different names. Their temperaments too were different. Batir was a pious, bearded fellow, Kasym clean-shaven and with little time for his country's religion. All he knew was that the war had wrecked his family and his country. The Russians were to blame for his father's murder, and the jihadis for involving him in their infernal violence.

As a *sans papiers* for some years he'd worked at this and that – a waiter, a docker, now a car mechanic. Holding down jobs hadn't been easy. It wasn't bad health exactly – he was fit and strong – just a propensity to suffer prolonged and violent headaches, as if someone had inserted a needle beneath his skull, stealthily, and was probing his brain.

The attacks had begun not long after his father's death, and his mother had assured him they would ease with time. They hadn't, they'd got worse. In Marseille a doctor near the port who treated *les sans papiers* for thirty euros a time shrugged them off, recommending the powerful painkillers he'd already begun taking. Which to

Kasym suggested that this was something he would have to live with.

He'd married a Chechen girl, fathered a son and found a squat to live in, though settling down had never been his ambition. And all the while the attacks continued. When they began it was impossible to think of anything else, but then Kasym was a worrier, obsessive by nature, and more and more two things haunted his dreams: revenge for his father and escape from the Marseille ghetto, with its rotting tenements and stinking alleys. Thieves and degenerates everywhere, it seemed to him, human flotsam from the world over, people with no hope and no education, who if he stayed would drag him down to their level, and his son with him.

Though how was he to get away? It was here that his dreams collided. It wasn't only lack of papers and money that kept him where he was. Leaving Marseille would mean cutting links with his émigré circle, whose anti-Russian schemes and agitation had become a focus of his life. So for years he had stayed, trapped between his urge to get away and vengeance for his father.

Daudov he'd known before he'd gone to London – known him but never been close: something about his Georgian swagger, his drug dealing and boasts of gangster connections. As a half-Chechen he'd hung around Kasym and his group, helping out with money for their pamphlets and posters and concerts and demonstrations. The two of them were friendly enough, though at the same time Kasym kept a distance. How much was Daudov in it for the cause, he sometimes wondered, and how much for the underworld contacts?

He'd had it out with him once – and got nowhere.

'I'm in it for both,' Daudov had said, 'and so what? In Marseille it's the same game. Don't talk to me about Russians, I fought them in Georgia, 2008, and I've seen the inside of their stinking fucking prisons. And don't preach at me about drugs. You and your friends, you're in it too, because when you take my money I don't hear you asking questions.'

Next thing Daudov disappeared. It was the summer of 2012, the year when there'd been forty murders in shoot-outs between gangs on the Marseille streets. Paris had had enough and troops were drafted in to sort things out. To hear him talk you'd have thought that Daudov was up there with the big guys, a *chef de bande,* but that was just his style: in fact he was a small-time dealer, nothing more. Yet his suppliers were bigger fish, and rather than risk being caught up in police sweeps he'd fled to London.

And done well for himself there, so Kasym had heard, for a while at least. Now he was back with his woman, his new alias (Monsieur Henri), his earring and long hair – but no money. Which didn't prevent him throwing promises around, some of them in Kasym's direction, about how he'd be in a position to resume his help for the cause just as soon as he'd re-established himself in the city. Which was why Kasym had kept in touch.

*

In the days that followed their meeting rumours about the President's visit grew, along with Kasym's agitation. After a week of reflection he rang Daudov's mobile. No reply. Next day he rang again, and the next. Still nothing. It was several days before the Georgian rang back, and they met again in the café.

'I've been ringing every day. Where the hell have you been?'

'I told you, sounding out a couple of people.'

'Like who?'

'Serious people don't flash their names or nationality, but there's interest all right. And you, you said you'd do some thinking. What have you come up with?'

Kasym hunched forward.

'Whatever it is it has to be spectacular.'

'Right. So?'

'I was thinking, maybe the Consulate?'

'The Russian Consulate?'

'We could force an entrance. Ransack the place, get some documents, then burn it down.'

'You mean *fry* people?'

'No. At night, when it's empty.'

'A burnt-down Consulate.' Daudov rocked his head, as if considering. 'Well that'll scare the shit out of him, won't it? Ruin his vacation.'

'Well maybe a demonstration as well. I could – '

' – my friend, let me ask you something. How many times have you told me that the Russians shot your father? What if he knew his killer was holidaying a couple of hours from where his son lives, and the best revenge he can think up is to torch an empty building?'

Kasym looked away, frowning. The needle in his head had begun its probings, his tic the outward symbol of his pain.

'I'm a Chechen as well as a Georgian,' Daudov went on. 'The bastard killed a lot of my friends – but not my dad. And you, you saw it happen, with your own eyes. How they dragged him away like an animal, you told me. And now you talk about the Consulate. God, if it was me – '

'Shut the fuck up!'

Kasym half-rose in his seat, spilling his beer.

'Easy!' Glancing round the café – it was still empty – Daudov waved him down, then signalled the barman for another beer. After it came he said:

'I told you, the people I spoke to, they're serious. And for a serious job they'll pay serious money.'

'So what are we supposed to do?' Kasym made a despairing gesture. 'Shoot the bastard?'

There was a pause, before Daudov said softly:

'Not necessarily shooting.'

The Chechen stared back at him. Daudov wasn't smiling.

A pair of bearded old-timers shuffled in past their table. Waiting till they'd gone, Kasym lowered his voice to an incredulous whisper.

'You want to have him *killed?*'

'You don't think he deserves it?'

'Course he bloody deserves it!' Kasym rasped, 'but the security, the protection... Who we going to get to do it? Fucking jihadis?'

Daudov shook his head, swiftly.

'Those maniacs? Absolutely not.' Another pause. 'Trouble is, who else is there?'

Kasym blinked, and stayed silent. To stop his fingers trembling he grasped his beer. Daudov must have noticed.

'Don't worry,' he said with something between a smile and a leer. 'I'm not suggesting you get involved personally. Your hands would be clean. We'd just have to come up with the plan and the money. So don't be afraid.'

'Afraid?' Kasym's voice was indignant, though his eyes were troubled. 'Why would I be afraid?'

'Because however we do it we might get caught. Mind you, whatever we do… I mean if we trash the Consulate we'll get five years in jail, and at the end of it no one's going to pay…' He leant to within inches of Kasym's face. 'But if we take him out, then get ourselves abroad – Canada, South America, wherever – we can get big money, and we're safe.'

'I don't see how –' feeling his tic going uncontrollably, Kasym winced and stopped.

' – well I do. The people I know, they can do anything. Get you papers, passports, tickets out of the country, money to live…You and the family. We'd be all set up, and your dad,' he pointed upward, 'would be a proud man.'

In a hesitant voice, Kasym asked:

'So these people, you're going to go back to them?'

'I would, but – ' Daudov threw up his hands – 'what's the point? I mean if we've got no idea of what we're going to do, or who the fuck's going to do it.' He shrugged. 'I can't do it alone. And you're out, I take it?'

His eyes invited confirmation. Calmer now, Kasym looked back at him steadily and said nothing. His silence was his answer to the question, and with a tremor of excitement Daudov understood.

\*

When they'd parted Kasym had said he'd come back to him, that he needed time to think. For a week he agonized, and day by day what Daudov had said turned from an impossible fiction to a plausible reality. He had no truck with the terrorists threatening his country. But the Russian President, that was different. With him it would be family business, family honour.

The question was, how? In Paris the protection would be total, yet out there in the Camargue, on horseback, in the open... There he'd be vulnerable, couldn't ride around in a posse of security men. Would it have to be a suicide attack? No, not that, his father would never have asked it of him. He was no Islamist crazy.

On Daudov he had few illusions. Whatever he said about being half-Chechen and the rest he'd be in it for the money. God knows who he was lining up as backers, but that was his affair. For himself it could be the turning point in his life. The risks would be huge, but so was the prize. His father avenged, the slums of Marseille behind him, a new life for them all.

He was not in the habit of seeking his brother's advice, though now he did. Apart from Daudov there was no one else he could talk to. Batir had heard about the President's visit. Should they do something, Kasym asked him? Before replying, Batir reflected.

'It's not by accident that he's coming here,' he finally intoned in his quiet, priestly way. 'It is providential. Allah has guided his steps into the path of his enemies.'

'And so?'

'So it is our duty to do as He wishes.'

'Which is?'

His brother's plump round face creased for a moment in thought before he smiled his guileless smile.

'Make sure he never goes home.'

Kasym was startled. Did he mean it, or was it his brother's child-like simplicity? When they talked some more it was clear that he was serious. For Batir it was as if the answer were obvious, as if they had no choice. Their mortal enemy coming to a place just two hours away? How could they mistake such a sign? It was God's will that the President be punished, the fact that He had sent him to the

Camargue meant he and his brother were His chosen instruments, and to allow him to escape their vengeance would be a crime itself.

Normally his brother's pietism annoyed him. This time it set him thinking. Retribution for his father's death was the only course. If he succeeded it would be his escape not just from hopelessness and penury but from the duty of revenge that weighed on him. And if he failed to make the attempt he would curse himself for the rest of his life.

# 7

Working for a Russian tycoon was a boon for Tony's health as well as for his bank balance. Mikhail encouraged him to make use of the basement gym, a flamboyant affair constructed to Sasha's personal design. Other billionaires had subterranean pools surrounded by statues, Greek pillars or murals of desert landscapes. Sasha's extravaganza had palm trees, a jazzy bar, tables with sunshades emblazoned with *Campari* or *Dubonnet*, a vast golden sphere emitting adjustable heat, even a raked stretch of sand. Lucky no one could see him doing his lengths next to a perennially sunny Mediterranean beach thirty feet beneath the Belgravia streets.

An incident in his first few days, when he decided to take a dip after work instead of in the morning, made him careful about when he swam. With Grekov away for a hospital check-up there was no risk of running into his boss. Instead he'd run into Sasha.

He was halfway down the spiral stairway leading to the pool when he saw him. The boy wasn't alone, and he wasn't swimming: he was lolling on a waterbed attended by a pair of blondes as naked as himself. One rocked it mischievously while the other, head down where his trunks should have been, ministered to his needs as best she could between mouthfuls of water and bursts of gurgling laughter.

A glance was enough; Tony retreated.

The next night he was working late. The architect of the castle Grekov was restoring in Suffolk wanted urgent comments on the security implications of his designs and he was stuck at the office till eight. On his way out Sasha hurried past him. Instead of his usual slobby clothes, for once he was smartly dressed.

'Have a nice evening,' he called after him as the boy thundered down the stairs. At his appearance in the hall one of the bodyguards leapt from his chair and began following him to the door. Sasha turned on the man brusquely, barking something in Russian.

'OK, OK.'

The minder retreated to his chair, hands raised as if in surrender, as Sasha left the house. Tony threw him a smile.

'What was that?'

The bodyguard, the Latvian, shrugged and grinned, displaying tragic teeth.

'He no want. Maybe he meet girlfriend?'

And maybe she was Russian, Tony thought.

He emerged from the front door in time to see Sasha clambering into the car a chauffeur had driven round from the mews garage. Waiting till it had thundered off, he hailed a cab.

'I'm with that Maserati,' he shouted to the driver. 'No room in those bloody things, and we're picking someone up. Just don't tailgate him. He's allergic to being crowded, right?'

'No problem.'

There was little trouble keeping Sasha in sight in the slow-moving traffic. After turning right into Sloane Avenue the car made its way through Knightsbridge along Kensington Gore. Opposite Kensington Palace Gardens, it turned into a narrow street.

'Pull in on the far corner,' Tony yelled at his driver.

The taxi stopped. Tony looked down the street. Towards the end Sasha had pulled into a parking bay and was sitting in the car, waiting.

'Move along and give me a few minutes, OK?'

Leaving his cab he took up position on the corner, eyes alert for young ladies who might answer the description of consort to the son of a billionaire. Minutes later she came, a girl so obviously a rich man's date you couldn't miss her. Obvious because of the Frenchified scarf, the handbag with its burnished gold hardware, the chiffon skirt glued to slim thighs and the vermilion boots that rose to meet them.

Also because she emerged from Kensington Palace Gardens

before crossing the road in his direction. Which fitted. A tallish woman, she seemed high-toned, haughty, embassy-looking. Sure enough, she went into the side street and, with a glance behind, climbed into Sasha's car.

He got back into his taxi.

'OK. On we go.'

The driver followed the Maserati at a distance, Tony slumped low in the back. It led them to a cobbled cul de sac not far away, in Knightsbridge.

'OK, this will do.'

From the top of the street he watched Sasha stop outside a discreet-looking restaurant, *Bellagio's*. Handing the keys to a doorman he went in with his date.

The cabbie unlocked the cab, and looked round.

'You're not getting out?'

'No – sorry. Something I forgot. Back to Kensington, if you wouldn't mind.'

Past caring by now, the fellow shrugged:

'Whatever you say.'

At Kensington Palace Gardens he paid off the taxi. The gated road, he knew from long experience, was home to the embassies and residences of a dozen countries: India, Romania, France, Israel, Russia… A dark blue gatehouse bristling with antennae and security cameras guarded the entrance. Ambling past, he glanced in the window.

Inside, two guards were sipping coffee, one of them Larry Merchant. He waited till a diplomatic car drew up at the barrier. Larry dragged his portly, peaked-cap figure from his hut, bent to the car window, grunted at the chauffeur, signalled to his mate to raise the barrier and waved him through.

He was on his way back to his coffee when Tony approached.

'Larry, how's it going?'

Larry's dour face brightened.

'Tony!'

For 28 years Larry had worked the gate of the embassy enclave, and for twenty-two of those he'd been an MI5 informant on the Russians' diplomatic personnel. The joke about Larry was that he was a bit of a Bolshie himself, a one-man trade union forever griping about his pay and conditions, and it was when he'd threatened to withdraw his labour that Tony, his contact man at the time, had been sent to soothe him. He liked the old curmudgeon, with his eagle eye and train-spotter's memory, and after listening to his grievances negotiated a 20% increase.

A chat about Tony's retirement led naturally to the point of the encounter.

'I'm in private security now, but it's the same game, and I could use your help.'

With his confidential look, Larry nodded.

'Who's it you're after?'

'The girl who walked out twenty minutes ago. Classy-looking one in vermilion boots. Who was she?'

Larry's long face grew longer. The names and photographs of embassy personnel were provided and he prided himself on his powers of instant recall. The woman in vermilion boots, however, he couldn't place.

'Must be new. Hold on a tick.'

He went inside, checked a camera, came back out.

'She is. Svetlana Morensky, Russian Residence. Ambassador's social interpreter. Does all the art stuff with 'im. Comes in coupla times a week on average. Been there coupla months.'

'Great man, Larry.'

Tony shook his hand, heartily. A folded £50 banknote materialized in Larry's palm.

'No come on Tony, you don't have to – '

' – I do. Take it or I won't be able to call on your services again. Don't worry, I've been privatized, the boss can afford it. More if you could see your way to letting me have some stills of the lady. Preferably with other people, with names and functions attached.'

Slipping the cash into his pocket, Larry said no problem.

Back at *Bellagio's* there was more luck. After a Dover sole and a half-bottle of Meursault in a classy little place en route (why stint himself?) Tony arrived in a cab at ten, and they came out fifteen minutes later.

The house Sasha drove to was in a Chelsea square. With their iron gates, steel-grilled windows and winking alarms the houses stood like a row of elegant fortresses, daring assault. The kind of place where the Middle Eastern/Russian/Chinese owners would live a month or two a year, for the same reason they were rarely to be seen in their alternative mansions in Paris, New York, Los Angeles, St Tropez.

It was Svetlana, he noted from his taxi, who produced a key. Smart place for an interpreter, Tony thought.

*

Dick's reward for checking her out was a lunch at an up-market restaurant in Piccadilly, a difficult place to book on short notice though Lisa had managed a reservation using her boss's name. Since it was the boss who would be paying, this seemed sensible. Thank God for his providential oligarch, Tony reflected as he paused to check out the cut of his second new suit (bespoke, this one) in the glass door of the restaurant.

He waited till the brandy and cigars arrived on the terrace to put the question. When it came the sound Dick emitted was somewhere between a laugh and a sigh.

'I had a hunch there'd be someone. Who's it this time?'

'Embassy girl. Name of Morensky, Svetlana. Nice-looking, fine-featured, cheeky little nose. Sort of girl you can imagine on the front of Russian Vogue in nothing but a sable.'

'Sounds one-up on the sacks of potatoes the Embassy used to employ in the old days. How come you're interested?'

'Last time we spoke you said you didn't want to know what I'm up to. In any case I'd rather not say. Sorry Dick, but I owe it to my boss.'

His friend pulled a mock-aggrieved face.

'And *my* boss? Her Majesty? Don't I owe loyalty to her?'

'Her Majesty isn't paying for our lunch. And neither are we.'

The bill came out at £274, so it was just as well.

Dick came back by phone two days later.

'The girl you were interested in, she's locally engaged. Impoverished aristocrat by the sound of it. Would never have got through the class sieve in Soviet days. Now they think aristocrats are sexy, but there you go, that's the Russians for you. Either executing them in cellars or loving them up.'

'So she's not – '

' – no sign of it.'

'Anything else on her?'

'Nothing on file.'

'Great. I enjoyed our lunch. We'll do it again.'

'Love to. Just don't expect – '

The line went dead. Dick must have run out of change.

He checked out the place in the Chelsea square. Luxury flat, two bedrooms, two receptions, basement swimming pool, large, communal garden, it said on the Internet. Sold just under a year ago for £3,500,000. The impoverished princess was living in style.

Larry's stills arrived at his house two days later, and there were plenty. Busy woman, Ms Morensky. He went through the photos. Svetlana on foot, in sunglasses, swanky as a model. Svetlana in her car, a sports number, courtesy of Sasha no doubt. Then in the back of a Mercedes with the Ambassador en route to some arts function. In the front, alongside the driver, was a stocky man with a beard. *Victor Bulagin, First Secretary for Cultural Affairs,* Larry had noted on the back of the photo in his meticulous way.

The picture was coming together, and it didn't make sense. Sasha was using Daudov for his one-man campaign against the Kremlin, now it turned out that his girlfriend worked at the Russian Embassy, with Sasha's knowledge. The embassy that was doubtless keeping tabs on his father.

'Who-whom?' was the question, Lenin used to say, and it always was. In Svetlana's case someone must be fooling somebody else, and there was only one way to discover how and why.

# 8

Tom Sandiman stood before the iron gates of the house in the Chelsea square. He knew that the owner of the third floor flat was not at home that morning, because he'd seen the woman from Tony's photo leave at 8.15. Also that her boyfriend was not in residence, having spent the night at his father's house.

In addition, he knew that the landline in the flat wasn't working, for the excellent reason that an engineer of Tom's acquaintance at the local exchange had been kind enough to break the circuit. And finally he knew how he could be admitted to the flat: the cleaner, a minuscule Filipino in a green beret, Tony had informed him, would be there at nine sharp.

At ten o'clock he rang the bell.

'Who's there?'

'Telephone engineer. The exchange says there's a problem. I tried to dial in a minute ago. Didn't ring, did it?'

'No call.'

'Well I'd better fix it.'

At the entrance to the flat she stared up at the man sporting BT overalls, a wide smile and his engineer's working bag. For her Tom was a giant, though a friendly one. While he frowned over the phone she chatted away about her daughter in Manila, a clever girl, she assured him, who was hoping to go to university.

'Tell you what, love. I could use a spot of coffee. Would you mind?'

'What kind you like?'

'You have espresso?'

Tom preferred the instant stuff, sweet and milky, but then in smart houses the coffee was fresh, and grinding it took time.

'Of course we have.'

In keeping with the décor of the flat it was an arty phone, with a tortoiseshell handle. In the minutes the Filipino was in the kitchen, off came the fancy cover and in went the mic.

She returned with his coffee to find Tom on his mobile. Smiling his thanks, he dialled a number, waited then said:

'Hello, mate. Check on a line, if you wouldn't mind.' He read out the number, and hung up.

They stood watching the phone. Nothing happened, which was no surprise, the number he'd dialled on his mobile being non-existent. Opening the cover he fiddled with a wire, replaced the receiver, asked for another test, waited. The phone rang.

'Great. Thanks, mate.'

No surprise there either: the second number was his friend at the exchange, who'd restored the service.

'There you go,' he beamed at the Filipino. 'It's working.'

'So good you mended. I wait my daughter phone. She give me result of examination.'

The espresso she'd brought him was the strongest he had tasted. He stood sipping it, thoughtfully. A bedroom, he'd noticed, led off the far end of the drawing room. The door was open and above the bed hung a chandelier, a large, psychedelic affair composed of clusters of gaudily coloured flowers. Instinctively his eyes measured the distance from bed to lights.

Boudoir filming wasn't on Tony's specification. On the other hand he was here, with his bag of tricks, and the florid chandelier would be perfect for a camera.

'Very nice,' he said to the Filipino, finishing his coffee. 'Short and sharp.'

'You like more? Maybe long one? Maybe biscuit?'

'Wouldn't say no to a long one.'

And away she went.

'Better check the bedroom extension,' he called after her.

Hearing the coffee grinder start up again he fished in his bag, stepped onto the bed, reached for the candelabra, did his stuff, and got down just as the Filipino returned with her tray.

'The extension's fine,' he called through as he smoothed the bed-spread and came back to the drawing room.

'You like chocolate?'

With motherly satisfaction she watched him put away a luscious-looking brownie.

'Delicious.'

'Miss's boyfriend, he like. I get from Harrods.'

'By the way.' Swallowing the last mouthful he looked straight at her. 'I don't think it would be a good idea to tell your boss there was something wrong with the phone. She might think you broke it, or you know, been using it for calls. Anyway I've fixed it now, haven't I?'

He said it through a smile but with a warning look that registered. No, she nodded, nervously, she wouldn't be telling anyone that someone had had to come to fix the phone.

'Well then better be on my way. Good luck to your daughter.'

And he meant it. Lovely little lady. Girl who lived here probably didn't deserve her. Good-looking woman though, to judge from her photo, you had to admit. And from now on he'd be seeing a lot more of her.

\*

The first take from the flat he delivered to Tony three days later.

'Maybe there's a little more than you wanted,' Tom explained, handing over the memory sticks. 'I slipped a camera into the bedroom while I was at it, so you've got intercepts plus illustrations.'

'How did you manage that?'

'Mattress.'

'Sorry?'

'In classy places they tend to be nice and hard, so you can stand on them, and there's a chandelier over the bed, horrible modern thing. Couldn't resist. The camera's one I'm trying out. Magnetic, so it takes seconds to fix. Battery's built into the base of a lamp so it charges whenever the light comes on. Download from the street, and away you go. I've had a look at the first take and on the lady in question I can guarantee the quality of the goods.' He grinned. 'Enjoy.'

Tony sat in his bedroom office, the memory sticks running, listening and watching and taking notes. First, the drawing room mic. Svetlana railing against the Filipino for failing to clean the bathroom to her liking. Then ordering stuff from Peter Jones, quoting an account in Sasha's name. Then dialling a mobile number and leaving him a recorded message:

'OK, you can come over around nine. Just don't turn up high. If you do I won't let you in. Understood? *Poniatno?'*

Before going out she orders the Filipino to prepare a lobster salad for the evening.

'Make sure you crack open all the claws. And don't leave bits of shell like you did last time.'

'Sorry, Miss.'

The door slams.

Eight thirty p.m. The bedroom camera shows her coming in, drawing the curtains, hanging up her coat, entering the bathroom. The sound of a shower running. Ten minutes and she emerges, naked. She opens one of a row of wardrobe doors, then the next. Inside are two facing mirrors, automatically lit. She stands between them, examines herself front and back.

Tony examines her too. All in the line of duty. She is not disappointing. Smallish breasts, rather pointy, still a young girl's thighs. Svetlana is clean-shaven – for a princess who could imagine otherwise? She flicks away a lock of hair the better to see over a shoulder, and passes a hand over a hip, as though smoothing away a redundant millimetre of flesh.

He gazes on at the woman gazing at herself. The spectacle ought to be sexy, but with Svetlana, somehow it isn't. Something to do with the hardness of her look, her frozen self-regard, a kind of chilled erotic autarchy.

A second later she is slipping into her underwear, then the first thing that comes to hand – a short blue dress. The moment she's finished the mic picks up a motor's roar from the street. The Maserati. After checking at the window she walks to the bedside table, smoothing her dress as she goes, presses a button, waits, then another, then a third.

The sound of the flat door opening.

'Hi sweetie!'

Sasha comes into the bedroom, dressed in his usual junky clothes. They kiss, briefly.

'You smell,' Svetlana complains, 'like a *muzhik.*'

'Warm evening.' Sasha loosens his collar. 'Been running around.'

They go into the drawing room.

'Anything to eat?'

'I have a salad.'

'That all, *golubchik?*'

'For your weight. You eat late, it piles it on.'

'I didn't know you cared.'

A scuffling sound.

'Leave me alone, for Christ sake! I'll get the salad, you get the champagne.'

Footsteps, then:

'Here.'

The sound of pouring. Silence. Then a blare of TV voices: the remains of the nine o'clock news.

'Turn it off,' Svetlana instructs. The TV cuts out. 'Come on, sit down and eat. I want to talk.'

Svetlana speaks sharply. Over the clink of cutlery she says:

'Remember they wanted people to help out in Paris, for the state visit? Well I didn't have to volunteer. The Ambassador here knows I speak French so he's offered to lend me to the Embassy there. For his *cher collègue.*'

'And you'll go?'

'I could do some shopping. And how could I turn down a chance to work for our great leader? They want me to help out in the information department. Then maybe with interpreting.'

'Jesus! You're going to interpret? For *him*?'

'That's what they tell me. Not the official talks in Paris – he's got his normal interpreter for that – just for the private part of the visit. Apparently he's taking a few days' break.'

'I heard.'

'How?'

'Daudov told me.'

'Oh him, your druggie political fixer. A genius you keep telling me. How come *he* knows?'

'Immigration threw him out so he went back to Marseille. He's got contacts there – the Chechen mafia. I asked him to nose around about the visit and he heard he was going to do some horse-riding and hunting in the Camargue.'

'That's right, that's what they told me. It hasn't been announced yet.'

'So you'll be with him down there, all the time,' Sasha mused. 'With him wherever he goes.'

'It's easier to interpret that way.'

A silence, then:

'Fuck it.'

'Here, give it to me, you're so clumsy. Stupid bitch of a woman, she forgot to break it.'

The crack of a lobster claw.

'There.'

'Thanks. Think of it – you and him together! Amazing! I bet it was him who asked for you.'

'I told you, it was the Ambassador who suggested it.'

'And he grabbed at the chance. He'll want a pretty woman, for the media, and it'll give him a kick having a princess work for him. He's on the loose now he's got rid of his wife, so don't let him make a grab for you!'

'Your vulgarity is distressing. Anyway he's got that gymnast woman, hasn't he?'

The sound of eating, then Svetlana.

'So what are you going to do about it?'

'The visit?'

'Yes, the visit. You said you could get something going.'

'I've been thinking. Paris will be crawling with cops, so I was working on something in the Camargue. Daudov's talking to his friends and looking over the terrain. It's wild down there, you know? The Rhone delta, lots of swamps, a nature reserve. Riding, bird-watching, duck-shooting, all that stuff.'

'So what will you do? Wave a couple of placards in the middle of nowhere, and that's it?'

'I told you, I've talked to Daudov. We're going to do something serious. Daudov says... '

A droning sound drowns his words. A low-flying plane. The Chelsea square is on the Heathrow flight path, Tony remembers. Three and a half million for a flat where you can't hear yourself talk.

'...so he's thinking about it.' It is Svetlana speaking. 'Good to know that *someone's* thinking! Don't *you* have any ideas? You said you'd amaze me, and you have – with the poverty of your imagination.'

'I'll find something, give me time... That's a promise.' The sound of him getting up. 'Any more champagne?'

'In the fridge.'

Footsteps in the corridor, there and back. A cork popping.

'Want some?'

'I'm tired. We'll drink it in there, maybe watch TV.'

They come into the bedroom, where the camera takes over. Sasha fills their glasses, empties his own, puts his hands on her hips. She leaves him to it, takes a swig of her glass. Now he moves on her greedily, his left hand round her neck, his right fumbling at her dress. Her champagne spills. She tears herself away.

'Leave me alone for Christ's sake, *durak*! What do you think I am – your peasant girl? It's you that's the fucking peasant!'

Sasha backs off, sits on the bed. She stands over him, glass in hand.

'Now, ask forgiveness.'

She points to the floor, imperiously. Is she drunk? Only half,

Tony decides.

Sasha kneels, cumbrously, and takes her hand. Is she amused, or gratified? Neither. Her expression is curiously detached, as if she is absent from the proceedings. And him, was he enjoying his humiliation? Not by the pained set of his face. A strange look, as if the pain were as much for her as for himself. *Why do you have to do this?* the look seems to say.

Maybe there is something wrong with this woman, Tony wonders? Who would behave like this otherwise, drunk or not?

'Princess, I am sorry.'

'In Russian!'

'*Princessa...*'

'Old Russian!'

'Darling, I've forgotten.'

'*Knyazhna* for God's sake! And to think you went to Oxford... What did I get there?'

'A first in history.'

'And you?'

'A third in modern languages.'

'Which qualifies you to be my servant. So you can get up and give me some more bloody champagne.'

She holds out her glass. Sasha gets the bottle and fills it.

'Now undress me.'

Tony watches, awed. This must be a joke, and yet Sasha looks serious and Svetlana has that same detached expression. She stands before him, nonchalantly, while he takes off her dress, her brassiere, her pants. He leans to kiss a breast.

'No touching! Now get into bed.'

He undresses and lays down, the sheet up to his chin, as if to spare her the sight of himself. Not that she is interested. She is parading round the room, the bottle in hand, beneath his adoring eyes, with the blank, uninvolved look of a model. The display isn't for him, it is for nobody but herself. She even stops for a moment before a mirror.

The bottle empty, she gets into bed. He moves towards her.

'No! I told you, you smell!'

'I'll take a shower.'

'Don't bother. I don't make love with cowards!'

Now she *is* drunk, slurring a little.

'Why am I a coward?'

'Because you know where the great man will be but you haven't the guts to go after him. You keep telling me he's poisoning your father and you do nothing about it. Jesus, in your place – '

'I will – I am. I'm giving Daudov some cash.'

'Cash for what?'

'Something to help him bugger up the visit.'

'Giving him money! I'll tell you what he'll do with it. He'll have a pamphlet printed and piss away the rest on drugs. You'll never have a better chance. I'll be with him down there for Christ's sake! I'll know his programme, his movements, from one minute to the next.'

Svetlana switches off the lights, but the room is not entirely dark. Filtered through the leaves of the giant chestnut a streetlamp casts a ghostly glow through the curtains, so Tony can see their outlines. Svetlana is curled up, her back to Sasha. He lies there rigidly, four feet away on the colossal bed. After a minute he edges in her direction.

'*Niet!*'

Sasha moves back, and lays still.

# 9

Monsieur et Madame Thody were southern gentry in the French fashion, which is to say folk of an age and class where paying the wealth tax was getting to be a problem. Jewellery in bank vaults, securities in off-shore accounts – there were ways to conceal most things from *le fisc*, but a large, princely house on the northern edge of the Camargue was impossible to hide.

The solution had been to rent it out. The disruption was minimal: they just moved up the hill to the old farmhouse, a charming place in itself and for the two of them a more sensible size. With horse-riding in summer and duck-shooting in the autumn and winter months a steady flow of tenants was guaranteed, and the 6,000 euros weekly rent took care of the wealth tax bill.

There was another benefit from renting: for a homebound couple (her hip, his gout) their tenants could provide an inexhaustible source of interest, and the latest were a curious trio. Most of their clients were Americans, Russians or Japanese and with the exception of some of the Russians, well-bred folk. Whereas these three were…What exactly? Some sort of minority?

They spoke accented French to each other and yet they looked like…well, it was hard to say. Monsieur Henri's name was English-sounding, but that was all. With his light brown skin, long black hair and earring, he seemed like some kind of cosmopolitan hippy. As for Monsieur Kasym, his complexion was whitish and yet the sharp features and close-cropped hair suggested a light-skinned Turk or – *Dieu nous préserve!* – an Arab. The third, Monsieur Batir, looked like nothing so much as a monk, though of a non-Christian persuasion.

Not the sort of clients you would select if you had the choice, though there'd be no trouble about payment: Monsieur Henri had settled the rent for the week in advance in fresh €500 notes, with no request for a receipt. On the other hand it couldn't be said that the three of them offered much in the way of entertainment. Watching the house in the evenings through his opera glasses M. Thody made none of the salacious discoveries that had warmed his old heart in previous lets.

This time there were no carloads of henna-haired North African harlots driven in from Marseille you could see stripping off through the windows, no nude bathing in the late evenings in the arc lights over the pool accompanied by screeches of drunken laughter, scenes he could sit at the window in the darkness of his room and look down on like a naked opera.

With Messieurs Henri, Kasym and Batir – so far nothing. They couldn't be hunters – it was too early in the season and he saw no guns – though they were excellent horsemen, he'd heard from the owner of the stable where they rented. In fact riding about the Camargue was all they seemed to do from dawn to dusk.

*

Tony's plane touched down at Marseille Provence airport at three thirty. It had been a pleasant flight: he'd taken the liberty of booking himself business class, a luxury unknown in his security service days; in his new job nobody took any interest in his travel costs, and he was on *bona fide* business.

The reason he'd come was a chance remark by Lisa, whose closeness to Sasha's secretary Ruth was proving a handy source of gossip. They'd been talking about the boy's madcap way of life and strange friends when Ruth had mentioned a phone call she'd taken from a Monsieur Henri.

He was ringing her, he'd said, because Sasha's number wasn't working (he'd forgotten to charge his pay-as-you-go mobile, Ruth supposed). The message he'd left had been to say that he'd found a place to stay in the Camargue but coverage was bad, so if Sasha needed to get through urgently he could try reaching him on the landline of a M. Thody, whose number he had left.

Ruth had been tickled because Monsieur Henri spoke with a comically thick accent, and Thody reminded her of Todi, the Italian town in the Peter Ustinov comedy *Romanoff and Juliet.* Though when she'd passed on the message Sasha was not amused, he'd been livid. She was never to take messages from Monsieur Henri again, he'd shouted, never. Fine by her, Ruth told Lisa. He was probably another of Sasha's suppliers, or a pimp for his high-class whores.

Operating as ever on a need-to-know basis – it was in his blood – Tony forbore to tell Lisa that M. Henri was Daudov. He'd been wondering whether to keep track of what the man was up to in the Camargue, though till then he'd had no leads, no addresses. Now he knew where the Georgian was staying while he reconnoitred the terrain.

Investigating what would probably turn out to be no more than some hare-brained publicity stunt to make the Russian President look stupid was hardly a compelling reason for a trip to France. On the other hand, Svetlana seemed to be encouraging Sasha to go for something bigger. Tony had finished some more security work on the castle, there was nothing urgent in his in-tray, Marseille was a town he'd never visited, and the prospect of exchanging a damp and chilly London summer for a day or two in the Provençal sun clinched the argument for the trip.

*

He put up at a five star place overlooking the Old Port. The Thody residence, *Domaine des Hirondelles,* he discovered from the telephone directory, was a kilometre or two from St Gilles, a town just north of the Camargue. Hiring an inconspicuous Renault, he set off next morning.

A small place of 6,000 souls, the town turned out to have a big ego:

*Did you know that St Gilles is the gateway to the Camargue? Did you know the town was at the forefront of medieval architecture? Did you know that you can see more than 200 birds in the St Gilles museum without getting stung by mosquitoes?*

He arrived just before one and a vine-covered restaurant in the main square beckoned. Over coffee and a cheroot he chatted to the proprietor in the creaky but serviceable French he had learned on a schoolboy exchange, his sole linguistic achievement. After extravagant compliments on his cuisine and praise for the Languedoc wine – a heavy-ish brew Tony had never cared for – he enquired about the *Domaine des Hirondelles.*

'Ah yes, a fine house, eighteenth century, ten minutes from here.'

'Can I visit?'

'It's not open to the public. *Les Thody* are an old couple, it's a big place, too many rooms, and the last few years they've been hiring it out. If you want to rent it for the hunting season, you'd better be quick.'

'And why's that?' Tony deadpanned.

'Everything's booked up for the Russian *services de sécurité.*'

'The Russians?'

'You don't know? Well you'll soon find out – it's the talk of the town! Any day now it will be in the press but here everyone knows already. The Russian President's coming early in October after his visit to Paris. Spending a few days in the Camargue hunting and riding. You know he likes horses? I've seen pictures. *A cheval il est formidable,* like a cowboy President!'

'Will the French President come down riding as well?'

'Our little fellow, on horseback?' The proprietor guffawed. '*Ah monsieur, toujours l'humour anglais!*'

*

That evening two pairs of eyes were trained on the lighted windows on the top floor of the *Domaine des Hirondelles.* Tony had an excellent view: the night was clear, and by an oversight his government-issue binoculars had found their way into retirement with him.

Not the most expensive in the range, but the Zeiss Compact

model were an advance on M. Thody's antique opera glasses, even if
the Frenchman had the advantage of surveying his guests from the
comfort of his bedroom rather than from roadside bushes, where
the warm evening air pullulated with insect life.

A bedroom window was open and the light was on; an anti-mosquito grill, however, clouded his view of the interior. As he watched
a youngish, bare-chested male with long dark hair appeared at the
casement, and lingered. The Georgian? He focused closer: yes,
Daudov it was, in hippyish mode, complete with new earring.

The shutters of the next window along were open too. A bathroom. A figure in the shower, its back towards him, was soaping and
rinsing. Brownish neck, shortish hair, slim-bodied. Man or woman?
The figure stepped out of the shower, turned towards him, dried
itself and began dressing.

A woman, mini-skirted and whorish-looking. Minutes later she
joined Daudov at the window. The sight of him and his tart sent the
Georgian's plausibility as a serious conspirator, already low, down
several notches.

When Monsieur Thody made the same discovery it was with a
twinge of anticipation. The woman was the one he had seen arrive
by taxi an hour before. Action at last.

*

Next day he was doing a series of passes in front of the house when
a white Citroen emerged from the gate behind him. Allowing it to
overtake he saw Daudov at the wheel, with two others in the back.
Keeping well behind, for three quarters of an hour he followed it
south to the Camargue, where they wriggled along narrow roads
through the marshes and ponds of the Rhone delta.

A sign in two languages pointed left: *Mas de Solange, equitation.
Horses to Rent.* The Citroen took it. Tony motored on, U-turned at
the next junction, came back and drove to the *Mas de Solange.*

Drawing up in the car park, he watched Daudov saunter towards
the stables with his companions: one slim, one plump-looking, both

of them dark-haired, all three of them in riding gear, new by the look of it. Daudov and the slim one had cameras and binoculars slung from their necks, while the fat man hefted a good-sized saddle bag: food and drink, presumably, for a long day's ride.

As they approached the office a middle-aged woman in jodhpurs emerged to greet them. Minutes later stable girls appeared with three horses, ready saddled. A brief conversation, the men mounted and headed for the gate before disappearing along the road.

Tony got out of his car and followed the woman into the office. When he entered she was at her counter, head down over what looked like a rental agreement, ticking off days and the names of her customers' rides. Waiting for her to finish, he read the form upside down: it was their second day's riding and the names were Henri, Kasym, and Batir. Why had Daudov not bothered to invent another alias, he wondered? Amateurism again…

Finished with the form, the woman looked up.

'Can I help?'

She addressed him in English. It must have been his straw hat and sweat-drenched face.

'I was thinking of renting horses with my wife and daughter, later in the season.'

The woman handed him a list of dates and prices.

'You're English?' he asked.

'I am, but I moved down here twelve years ago.'

'On your own?'

'I have experience of running stables.'

A clumsy start.

'Seems to be going well.'

'I get by. Would you like a drink? You look warm.'

'I'd love one.'

She spoke, in French, to a lad behind her. Orange juice, iced, was produced. He indicated the road where Daudov and his friends had ridden off.

'Your clients ride by themselves? You don't do guides?'

'We do, but these ones seem to know their way around, and

they're at home on horseback. North Africans I suppose, they tend to be good riders, or some kind of minority. Marseille is full of them.' She looked wary, then went on. 'Can't say they're our customers of choice.'

'Why's that?'

'Some of them go in for horse smuggling, so if they hire our mounts for days at a time we get worried. They could be on the lookout for wild ponies. When they get them they break them in then rent them out.' She grimaced. 'Not good for business.'

A sympathetic nod from Tony.

'You've got the Russian President coming soon I heard. Should pep up demand.'

The woman pursed her lips.

'Yes I heard, but I doubt it. The security could put a lot of the regulars off.'

A family of Americans came in, all harassed parents and insistent children. Tony got up.

'Well thanks for the drink, and the brochure. I'll be in touch. I'm going to drive around a bit, get a sense of the terrain. Is there a trail people follow?'

'Left along the road, then straight on, south, is where most people start out.'

\*

A mile or two from the stables he saw them. They had reined in their horses and were talking amongst themselves. Pulling into a passing point on the narrow road, for a few minutes he watched through binoculars, and took some shots. Daudov seemed to be asking questions, the slim one providing answers. As he spoke he was pointing out features of the landscape, an arm sweeping the horizon like a general mapping a campaign. The third, the fat one, said nothing.

Knowing he'd be in rural terrain, the surveillance kit he'd brought included a long-distance parabolic microphone, on loan from Tom Sandiman. Tony wasn't that handy with the latest gear –

too many years in middle-management – but Tom had provided instruction. He'd tested it on the house from the bushes the night before, with no luck: with the windows closed and music playing in the room, he'd been denied the pleasure of eavesdropping on Daudov's conversation with his whore.

Time for another go. Best thing on the market, Tom had boasted, voice interception at a range of up to 500 feet. The horsemen ahead of him must be all of that, but what the hell. He fetched the mic with its foot-long boom and appendages from the boot of the car, together with a wheel brace. Kneeling between a hedge and the nearside front wheel, straw hat well over his eyes, he began unscrewing the nuts. Under cover of the brace he angled the mic in the direction of the horses and switched it on. A long shot, in every sense, but worth a go.

While Tony made a meal of pretending to change his tyre, Daudov and friends went on talking. A nasty moment came when the fat one, left out of the conversation, began casting around idly with his binoculars. Feeling them trained in his direction, in a semblance of exasperation he tugged despairingly at his wheel, obscuring the mic in the process. The binoculars wandered elsewhere. Moments later, after taking some photos, the three of them spurred their horses, rode round a bend in the road and were out of sight.

Re-tightening his wheel nuts and stowing his brace and mic, Tony got back into the car. What now? Spending the remainder of the day attempting to track three horsemen from his Renault seemed a waste of time. He'd done what he could and the open air recording – assuming it came off – was a trick you could only pull once.

He checked his guidebook. A tour of the Camargue in the brilliant sunshine, with a leisurely lunch in Saintes-Maries-de-la-Mer on the coast, seemed a more attractive proposition, and it proved a picturesque drive. Wild white horses grazing in meadows, the long grass shivering in the softly stroking breeze, flamingos stalking importantly through a shallow lagoon, and from time to time the glimpse of a mounted *gardian* – the local rangers – ambling along sandy paths with his broad black hat and trident, it was a magical place.

The President had made a good choice for his break. And by the look of the DIY plotters – there was something comical about the three of them trotting along in their neat new riding gear – Daudov and his friends seemed unlikely to inconvenience the Russian's protection team too much.

By seven he was in Marseille. In his hotel room he played back the recording. To think that any terrorist, two-bit criminal or private dick could pick up eavesdropping equipment as good or better than government issue. A scandal, he used to think in his MI5 days, but he didn't think that now. Tom was right, the thing was a marvel. Even in the countryside at the limit of its range the parabolic mic had done its job.

Amidst a murmur of wind, occasional bird calls and distant planes, the recording was a thing of threads and patches, though the conversation was mostly audible.

Daudov: 'Look at it, goes on for fucking miles. And we don't even know where the bastard's going to ride.'

The fat one: 'They say he's this great horseman, but I bet – '

Daudov: ' – shut it, Batir. I was asking your brother.'

So Batir and Kasym were brothers.

Kasym: 'Yes, it's all marsh and lagoons. But the lagoons are mostly shallow, and the horses don't mind, they like it.'

Daudov: 'So he won't even stick to the paths? He could ride on the water, like Jesus Christ.'

Kasym: 'That's right, he could stick to the lagoons, like the tourists. And he'll probably do some duck-hunting.'

Batir: 'Shooting down birds, like he shot Chechens.'

Kasym: 'He'll need a base for that. A blind, they call it. Normally they hire them out, but for him they'll build one specially I'd imagine, like for the richest clients. Make sure he gets a good bag. And for security.'

Daudov: 'OK, but where?'

Kasym: 'No idea.'

'Well you'd better find out. He'll go riding in the same area he does his duck-shooting, won't he?'

Kasym: 'Probably, but it's early in the season. He's not due for another couple of months and they run these blinds up in a matter of days.'

Daudov: 'Well you'd better come out again closer to the season. Keep looking till you find where it is. You and Batir. There's a limit to how much time I can spend wandering around this godforsaken wilderness. Make out you're hunters, come out with some guns, do some shooting. And keep your eyes open.'

Kasym: 'We don't have shotguns.'

Daudov: 'Don't worry, I'll hire a couple. And you'd better…'

They must be moving away. The sound began fading, then stopped. Only the wind and the bird calls. He switched off the recording.

*

A long way to have come for a few minutes' inconclusive chatter, but the evening helped make up for his trouble.

At seven o'clock the representative of the car hire firm, a runty, wheedling fellow in a flowery shirt, turned up at the hotel to collect his Renault. After declaring himself ready to overlook some scratches he claimed to have detected on the bonnet he engaged him in conversation, dilating on the late-night attractions of his town and enquiring what plans his client had to entertain himself that evening.

'*Monsieur* is alone?'

'Yes, on business.'

The runt smirked.

'*Alors une compagne, peut-etre?*'

Was Tony in the market for a lady that evening? If so, he was ready to be of assistance, the Frenchman implied, at reasonable cost. In fact for *monsieur* himself there would be none at all, since the lady would be thrown in with the price of the Renault, so as to enable *monsieur* to claim his *compagne* on expenses. And it wouldn't be just anyone – *ah non!* – but a shapely young woman of his acquaintance.

*Non merci,* said Tony, with a crisp shake of his head, though his

decisiveness did not extend to declining the personal business card
the man pressed upon him.

'Maybe you change your mind later, *non*?'

And following a sumptuous supper in the Michelin-starred
restaurant at the top of the hotel, accompanied by a bottle of
*Pernand Vergelesses* and two brandies, change it he did. On one point
the runt was as good as his word: the woman who tapped at his door
an hour later, a *petite brune*, turned out to be a class or two above his
Renault.

It was not something he would have succumbed to in his MI5
days, but then that was beginning to seem another life. This was no
Travelodge in Middleborough or Corby, it was a five star hotel
abroad, the cost was immaterial and the risk of detection non-existent.

And so it proved. Unlike Thames House, with its demands for
receipts and signatures in triplicate after every trip, Mikhail had a
cavalier way of handling his expenses claims: he would toss his
receipts into his waste paper basket without a glance, check the total,
amble to the safe behind his desk and reimburse him in cash to the
nearest round number.

So it was that the Russian failed to notice that the airfare was for
France, the fee for one day's hire of his two-door Renault came out
at £480, or that the hiring had taken place in sunny Marseille rather
than rain-sodden London.

*

Next morning his flight home was delayed. Waiting at the
airport, he noted the impressive numbers of soldiers and police
toting sub-machine guns patrolling the departure lounge. And
this well before the President was due. Part of the beefing up
of security since the drug feuds had exploded onto the streets
of the city, he assumed. If they put on this kind of display for
the drug guys what would it be like with the Russian leader in
the region? It didn't look promising for Daudov and his boys,

who would never get within a mile of the President.

Though maybe he should play it safe? Have a heart-to-heart with Sasha about getting mixed up with Georgians and Chechens, and warn him off. Protecting the boy from spivs and chancers was what he was paid to do – and yet how was he to do it without revealing what he'd learned about Daudov, and how?

Warning him off could only confirm what the boy must already suspect – that one reason Tony was there was to oversee his political activities. So that was out. Ought he to keep Mikhail informed, at least? No, not that either. Better to keep the fact that he was onto Svetlana and had bugged her flat to himself. The need-to-know principle…

Was it time to bring in MI5? It went against the grain, he'd sworn he wouldn't go out of his way to help them, and yet a state visit by the President of Russia… A word with Dick Welby would do it, so they could tip off the French that something may be afoot in the Camargue. Though there too there were risks. If MI5 were to enquire about how he'd got onto the Daudov group in the first place, it could land his friend in trouble. Anything less than legal, Dick kept telling him, and he didn't want to know.

And if the DCRI – French security – got involved, and traced Daudov back to Sasha… No, his obligations to the service had ceased the moment they'd shown him the door three years early. Judith Thornberry had taken care of that. If you gave the piper premature retirement, you couldn't expect to go on calling the tune.

Finally there was his own position, in the sense that every course of action could end up putting his hundred and fifty grand on the line. His daughter's rehabilitation, Heather's education, Jean's new peace of mind over the costs of private treatment… Always it came back to that.

The alternative – to say nothing to anyone and let Sasha and Daudov have their fun with the presidential visit – seemed increasingly attractive. From him all that was needed was a watching brief. Which meant checking out Kasym's background (Batir didn't seem to count for much) without telling the French what he and Daudov were up to. Another chore for Dick…

This time the feedback took longer. Then the call from a phone booth to his mobile.

'Me again, your anonymous informant. Regarding your Marseille friends. The frogs think Kasym's a *sans papiers*, one of the illegals who came in after the Chechen War. Involved in agitation, leafleting, couple of anti-Russian demos. Then he disappeared from the radar. Last heard of in the North African area of the city working as a car mechanic.

'Said they'd let us have his address if they find one. Meanwhile they're not unduly concerned. With the President coming in October they've got bigger fish to fry. It's the jihadis they're looking out for, and there's no suggestion your friends have any links with Islamists. They haven't even seen Kasym at a mosque.'

'Thanks Dick. Very helpful.'

'At your service – for the moment. Saw my old friend Thornberry yesterday.'

'Oh Christ, how did that go?'

'As expected. She explained that she'd found someone better-qualified, better-looking, half my age and happy to work for half the salary, if I understood her correctly. Underneath the management-of-human-resources-speak that seemed to be the message. So would I mind clearing my desk and getting the hell out in three months' time?'

'So that's it then? I'm so sorry. Bloody woman.'

'Oh come on, Tony, it's not her fault, it had to come. She just doesn't do smooth talk – not even to old colleagues. I prefer it in a way, to be frank. I've had my fun, I can't complain, and complaining didn't help you much, did it? Meanwhile anything else you need, you'd better get on with it before I'm out.'

For the moment there wasn't. He would see how things went. His main worry had been the Chechen connection, though if the French were relaxed about Kasym then so was he.

# 10

Kasym crouched in the marsh, his shotgun patrolling a great arc of sky. For almost an hour he waited, before a bird arose from the rushes fifty metres away. A rustling of air, a flapping, a crack from his gun and down it came.

He waded towards it, his rubber boots swilling with water and his feet dragging in the tangled reeds. Just as well there was no-one around. Masquerading as a hunter with his brand new camouflaged waterproofs and rented gun, he felt stupid. Rabbits he had shot with an airgun, but birds only once before.

It was when he was a child. His father had taken him on a hunting trip to lake Sari-Su in Azerbaijan. It was the top place for ducks. The best shots could get up to 50 a day and his father, a fine hunter, had scored 34. With a little help lifting and aiming the Baikal shotgun he'd had a go himself, and brought down two. Not bad for a twelve-year-old.

Rowing about in boats, spending the nights in blinds, he'd loved his first duck shoot, every moment, and begged to be taken back the year after. It was promised as a birthday present but never happened. The next year was 2000, the year Moscow had launched its onslaught on Chechnya, the year his father had gone from hunter to hunted. Their duck shoot together was his last, treasured memory.

The bird he'd shot today had come down in the reeds. He picked it up, swore, and threw it back.

'Fucking egret!' he shouted at his brother as he waded in his direction. Bulkier than ever in his hunter's outfit, his shotgun over his shoulder, unused, Batir plodded on through the brown-green water towards him. Even more of a hunting novice than his brother, he looked an unhappy man. For one thing he'd taken against

Daudov. Before they'd come back to the Camargue the Georgian had insisted that Batir get himself shaved. No point in drawing attention to yourself by skulking about with a gun and a beard, he'd said, like some bloody jihadi.

Kasym was feeling gloomy too.

'Brother,' he said as they met, 'it's no use, I see no point in what we're doing.'

'Why?'

'Because it isn't going to work. We can dress up as much as we like, but we'll never pass as duck-shooters or horse trekkers. Look at us – we're Chechens! In any case they'll seal off the whole area with gendarmes and soldiers and God-knows-what special forces. We'll never get within range, not remotely. Even if we pulled it off I don't think we'd get away.'

'Daudov said there could be a boat waiting, at Saintes-Maries-de-la-Mer. A speedboat that – '

' – fantasy. We'd never get that far. They'll block every road. What could we do? Slog across country, through marshes? It would take us hours. They'd pick us off as easy as them.'

He pointed to a group of flamingos in the shallows of a lagoon, their beaks twitching from side to side. Watchful, alert, and ineffectual-looking.

Batir said nothing. His expression, permanently glazed, made it hard to know what he was thinking.

'Maybe we are not meant to escape,' he said finally. 'Perhaps we are destined for sacrifice. Our glory will be in – '

' – in punishing our father's killer and getting away. That's the only glory I'm after. This talk of martyrdom, I've told you, it's selfish. Don't think of yourself in the hereafter, think about those you leave behind.'

'Surely it is fear of martyrdom that is selfish?'

'I don't want to hear about it. You sound like those jihadi scum. I don't want to blow myself up and kill women and children so maniacs can call me a hero. What God could justify that?'

'Maybe Allah wants us to be martyrs so we can do it, is what I meant. Otherwise, how can we?'

'Brother, leave it there. We've been through it before and nothing will change my mind. If they hunt us down that's one thing, but I don't *aim* to be dead. Paradise will have to wait, I have things to do on earth for my wife and son. We only need one martyr and that'll be the President, *Inshallah*.'

Rejoining their horses for hours they went on riding around, sticking to the edge of ponds and lagoons as they searched for a blind. They were rounding a bend in the track when Batir stopped and pointed.

'Look!'

The path they were on skirted a lagoon. A hundred metres from the shore, working from a flat-bottomed boat close to an outcrop of reeds, a dozen figures were constructing something on a floating platform. At this point the lagoon was deeper, the platform anchored to the bottom by chains. The structure they were erecting looked like a camouflaged hut, the men like boys setting up a secret camp covered in nets and branches. Except they were soldiers in army fatigues.

'That's it!' Kasym reined back his horse, his frown lifting. 'That's what we're looking for! And see who's doing it. It's for our distinguished visitors, their duck-shooting base.'

'So they'll be in there, waiting.'

'Waiting the whole night,' Kasym echoed, 'so as to be there for the dawn flight. That's what they do, that's the ritual. That's what I did with dad. It's a whole business. They'll have decoy ducks to draw them in, then the retriever dogs, when you've downed them in the lake, to swim in and fish them out...'

They stared on. A soldier on the platform, resting on his spade, began taking an interest in the two horsemen with shotguns on the deserted road. He signalled to a mate, who began staring at them too.

'Ride on,' Kasym instructed. 'We can't take a photo but try to remember everything about it.'

\*

'*Papa! C'est fantastique!*'

Kasym raised the shotgun above his son's reaching hands, and stood it in the corner of the room.

'Where did you get it?'

'From a *monsieur.*'

'What monsieur?'

'Never you mind. He lent it me, and I have to give it back, so don't touch it. It isn't a toy.'

Ten years old, his large brown eyes set in a narrow face, Alik was a clever child, doing well at the school he had no right to attend, technically speaking. His father had ambitions for his son. The way the boy was shaping up – he seemed to have inherited his grandfather's scientific interests – he would study technology or medicine, get a good job, do better than his father. And keep well away from Chechnya.

While he struggled with his boots, Alik stared on at the gun.

'Where've you been hunting? Did you get anything? Not as many as granddad, I bet!'

The story of the 34 ducks had been often told.

'One or two, but they weren't edible.'

'Was it in the Camargue? I've got a friend with a dad who shoots there, and he takes him. Will you take me?'

'One day.'

'And can I shoot?'

'We'll see.'

The boots off, for a moment he stood casting around for somewhere to stow them. In the cramped, two-room flat there wasn't an inch to spare. Eventually he went to the bedroom and stuck them under the bed, the shotgun with them. Now there was something in the flat to steal – the new television and laptop Daudov had come up with – it could be useful to have a gun around for a while.

'I'm hungry.' He checked his watch. 'When's your mother back?'

'She didn't say. Maybe she'll bring something nice for dinner.'

Layla, his wife, worked shifts in a *supermarché*. A timid, self-sacrificing woman, she didn't come off well when the workers fought over the out-of-date food destined for the skip at the end of the day. Mostly she ended up with mushy fruit and vegetables, rarely meat or fish.

Kasym got himself a beer and sat staring from the single window, smoking. Later that night he would meet Daudov at his new flat in a better part of town. God knows who was paying the rent. It must be whoever had given him the money for their stay in the Camargue, the horses, the hunting gear, the rented shotguns.

What would he tell him about their latest trip? He'd be pleased about the duck-blind, though not the location. The area round it was meadows, mile after mile of them, totally flat, with no cover, hardly so much as a few trees or bushes. When the President came the whole place would be surrounded, they'd never get anywhere close, not even at night. Yet nothing seemed to put Daudov off. If anything he was getting more determined, and freer with his cash. Somebody must have promised him big money.

'Papa, can I watch the TV?'

'No, you can't. You get on with your homework.'

Seeing his father in one of the preoccupied moods that had assailed him lately, Alik went back to his textbook, did his best to focus. It was no good: the older kids in the flat next door had got home and put on their music, loud. Always it was the same, Chechen rapping, always the same singer, *Lean Young Wolf*, and often the same songs.

Alik knew them by heart and he didn't like them. The lyrics, invariably about death and killing, were scary. Tonight the riffs from *Islamics Are Not in it for War* pounded like hammers through the thin partition walls:

*Fuck off Russki bastards, you're on top for now*
*But whoa, watch you don't get too clever 'cos one*
*Day Inshallah it'll be you lying down there in*
*The shit while we pour on the pepper, rat-tat-tat-tat,*
*Rat-tat-ta-ta.*

He'd thought of asking his dad to complain, tell the boys' parents his son couldn't work with all that racket, but he never had. He didn't want the bigger kids to get back at him, and anyway his father was becoming a *Lean Young Wolf* fan himself, chanting along absently under his breath. He was doing it now, while he read the paper.

His fingers straying to the new laptop – he was allowed to use it for homework – he typed in *duck shooting in the Camargue*. Half an hour later he was a master of the subject: the guns, the blinds, the decoys, the tricks they used to get the ducks to fly over. Which led him on to model birds.

Ten minutes later he looked up at his father.

'*Papa*, I've had an idea. When you're hunting ducks you don't need blinds or decoys to fool them into flying over. Birds follow their leader, don't they? So you could use an ornithopter to lead them into the path of the hunters. You steer it where you want them to go, the ducks all come over together then – bang, bang, bang! Twenty, forty at a go! More than granddad!'

His father glanced up from his paper.

'*Ne dis pas de conneries.* Don't be silly. I thought you were on your homework.' His eyes went back to the paper, then looked up.

'What's an ornithopter?'

'A robot bird. Like a model plane, radio-controlled, so you can fly it anywhere. I know a boy's dad who made one for him. It's fantastic, they look just like birds. Eagles, falcons – whatever you want.'

A silence, then his father said:

'I don't suppose they can fly very far, these ornithopters of yours? They're just toys, aren't they? For kids.'

'They didn't go far to begin with, but they do now. My friend's plane only went for a few hundred metres, but now they make ones that can go for – I don't know, a whole kilometre or more. They use them at airports – pretend eagles to scare away birds so they don't get sucked into engines. You can bring down a plane like that, did you know?'

Kasym got himself another beer, drank a draught:

'Flap their wings, can they? Dive and swoop and things?'

'Everything, like a real bird. Here, I'll show you.' Alik's fingers played over the laptop keys. 'There's a video of one flying. Come and look.'

His father got up and stood over his shoulder. A man was in the countryside, releasing his robot eagle. It looked simple: he just ran a few steps then threw it into the air, his arm well back, like launching a spear. Then he worked on his wireless control box, with its long aerial, pulled a few levers and up the bird sailed, way up, soaring and swooping then flying with its wings flapping – a little stiffly but flapping all right. Then he let it glide and cruise, with exactly that rapacious look eagles have, before making it dart downwards, in a steep descent, pulling it back up just as it was about to hit the ground.

'Play it again.'

Alik wound it back. His father watched, intently.

'Do they have a robot duck?'

'It doesn't say. I suppose they could, I told you, you can make anything. But who would want to fly a fat-arsed duck around when they could fly a falcon or an eagle? Unless you used it for hunting.'

'That's true. Plus a duck would be heavier...' He went back to his chair and sat down. 'How much load can they carry, these things?'

'Let me see...This eagle's 4 kilos, it says.'

His father thought some more.

'But you'd need a bigger motor for that. I suppose that makes them noisy?'

'They used to be, when they had little petrol engines. My friend's plane makes a racket, but apparently they've got them with batteries now. And when they use them for model planes you can fit all sorts of extras, like bomb doors that open. All by radio. Sort of like a drone.'

'That's it,' his father said. 'Birds like miniature drones. A duck drone!'

'Except ducks don't fire anything but shit! Imagine! You could use an ornithopter to bomb people you didn't like! You just steer it till it's over them then – pow! – make it poop on their head! *Super!*'

'Ha!'

Hearing his laugh the boy glanced over his shoulder. A laugh from his dad had been a rarity these last weeks. Before he'd been more cheerful, as much as he ever was, except when anyone mentioned Russians. Then he'd learned to leave him to himself: sneak into the bedroom to read, go for a walk, anything to get out of the way. He understood why he was like this – his grandfather's murder – but Alik had never known him, it was so long ago.

He could hear his mother's steps on the stone stairway. They sounded heavy. Maybe she'd got a good haul from the skip for once? That would put his dad in an even better mood.

# 11

Tony sat waiting in Lisa's office. Grekov had come back the previous day from a stay in Morocco, his latest attempt to shake off his illness, and for the first time since he'd begun working in the house his boss had asked to see him.

The wait was a long one but he didn't mind. He liked watching Lisa at work. Her fingers were long and fine, and something in her movements as she rearranged papers or wrote a note was soothing to him.

Grekov's doctor had been checking him over, she told him. It was the doctor who had advised him to escape the vagaries of the London summer and get away somewhere warm and dry for a few weeks, but his patient had come home feeling worse than before.

Newspapers in English, Russian and French lay on a table, and the front page of *Le Figaro* caught his eye. On it were two pictures of the Russian President: one with his usual 'don't-mess-with-me' expression, the second of the same man bare-breasted on horseback in some wild-looking Russian backwater, a hand to his eyes, gazing into the infinity of his homeland. Beneath was another picture of horses: a group of grey-white ponies splashing through a lagoon.

It was the announcement of the state visit to France. He picked up the paper.

*Visite du Président russe en France,* the headline blared, and lower down, something about his love of horses and his private trip to the Camargue: *Le Président, un grand amateur des chevaux, a l'intention de visiter la Camargue à titre privé.*

He checked the British press. Only *The Daily Telegraph* had commented on the story. Inside a column was headed: *Welcome to Paris, Monsieur le Président – Just Don't Come Here!*

'If he came,' the columnist argued, 'it would be a signal that everything would be forgiven and forgotten: the London murders, Syria, the Crimea, his thugs marauding in the Ukraine. The only reason for welcoming Russia's head honcho to London would be that we might get a few days' reprieve from his hit men roaming our streets.'

The door opened and an elderly man with a beard and a brief-case entered. A ramshackle figure – a leather patch on an arm of his jacket had come loose and the flap of his briefcase was open – he seemed more academic than doctor.

'Lisa, we are finished. Here are the prescriptions.'

Fishing them from a pocket he handed them to her. For several minutes they talked about diets, injections, sleeping pills. The doctor's tone seemed sombre. When they'd finished she said:

'I'll get you a car.'

'No problem, I prefer walking. I'll be off.' Halfway out of the room, he turned back. 'And don't forget the bedroom temperature at night. Most important.'

When he'd gone Lisa turned to Tony:

'You can go in now.'

'You're sure he's well enough to see people?'

Lisa gave a sigh.

'Such an active man, all his life. He'll never admit to being unwell. That's part of the problem.'

He went along the corridor to his office and knocked. No reply. He waited, knocked again, opened the door a foot or two.

As before Grekov was at the end of the room, at his desk. His head was bowed, as if over papers, but as Tony approached it was clear that his eyes were shut. A step closer and he saw that he was sitting in a wheelchair, a shawl covering his shoulders. Beneath it his body seemed shrunken. Extraordinary, he thought, that a man could have aged so quickly. It was a little over three months since they had last met.

As he stood wondering whether to stay or go, Grekov's head jerked upwards.

'Mr Underwood, forgive me. So many pills, I must have nodded off.'

His eyes shone weakly from his wasting body. Tony sat down. Grekov leaned back and, speaking with an effort, began:

'I have heard good reports of your work, here and in the Suffolk castle. But it is Sasha I want to talk about. I didn't say anything when we first spoke because I am his father. Now you have met him I think you will know the problem.'

'His political interests, you mean?'

'Not his interests – I am in favour of that – his activities. His schemes, his agitation, his wild thinking. Put enough money in the right places, he seems to believe, and you can bring the whole regime down. We talk about it, of course, but I am afraid he doesn't tell me everything. I don't want him to get in too deeply. There are dangerous people in that game.'

'I know what you're saying. I've been keeping an eye.'

'I will be frank with you. I love my son but I am not blind to his faults. Sasha is impetuous, he has strange ideas. He's got it into his head that they are poisoning me, because they believe I was another intelligence traitor. I have told him it's nonsense, but he won't listen. He does not believe his father can have a normal illness, die a normal death. He has these extravagant notions.' He sighed and shook his head. 'Very Russian.

'Now I must trouble you with my health. My doctor has just seen me. He is not happy with my progress.' As if in illustration, he gave a sepulchral cough. 'If I die I intend to ensure that Sasha keeps you on. I want you to go on watching over him. I don't want him taking on the FSB. If it looks like he's going too far, you must restrain him. A line out to MI5 will keep him safer.

'My son has money already – too much of it, an old man's weakness – but when I am gone he will have millions more. Enough to do things not just here but over there. He had this idea of running agents, of getting onto FSB people and using money to turn them, in a sort of one-man intelligence war. He asked me to finance it, and I said no. In that kind of game only one can win, and it wouldn't be him.

'Plots, cabals, assassinations, intelligence work – it is my country's disease, a Russian sickness. But you see how the marches and demonstrations are building up as the election approaches? People are getting bolder, more civic-minded. The West thinks we are a hopeless case, but one day Russia will become a country of culture, of elegance, of moderation.'

Russians? Moderation? Tony thought of Sasha's rants, of the girls in his pool, his drink and his drugs, and of Svetlana: her absolute domination over him, his infatuation with her.

'So when I go, you will stay and watch over him Tony, won't you?'

'So long as Sasha wants me.'

'It's not what my son wants. I have *instructed* him to keep you. I have made it a provision of my will, so he will have no choice. A link to British security is a condition of his inheritance.'

Tony looked back at him gravely.

'I understand what you're saying and I'm grateful for your confidence. One thing troubles me. The way you describe it I'll be like a mentor to him, and I'm not sure he'd take kindly to that.'

'I hope that isn't a no? To encourage you to stay in your post, we will sign a contract. First I will increase your salary. Then I will leave you a sum, conditional on you staying. The lawyers will insist on specifying a period, and seven is a good number. So seven years, shall we say, with a fund of three million for your pension?

'After which you will be contracted to find a reliable successor. The FSB will never relax its interest in our family, so our agreement will be like an insurance policy.' His smile was lugubrious. 'Except that it will be *post mortem* – and cheaper.'

All at once he stopped, and his gaze fell. Because he was tired? Or because he realized that he was fooling himself, knew in his heart that whatever arrangements he made Sasha would do what he wanted and would never abide by his will?

He raised his head.

'I apologize, I have had a bad morning. With tax advisers, accountants, lawyers, signing papers I no longer understand. And then doctors… It is heartening to know you will be here, whatever happens. You and Mikhail. You get along with Mikhail?'

'I do. He's very…down to earth.'

'A rough diamond, is your English phrase I believe. But him too you must keep an eye on. I don't want him playing things too rough with my son after I've gone… So tell me Tony, apart from Daudov, what have you to report? Nothing more about Sasha?'

What could he say? That he was back in touch with Daudov, and involved in intrigues against the Kremlin? That he had a Russian girl-friend ensconced in a Chelsea flat, who was goading him on? How much could he tell a sick father about a reckless son?

'It's difficult. I don't want to interfere, do things that will make him think I'm on a surveillance mission.'

'About technical matters I do not want to hear,' Grekov said sharply. 'That is for you. I just want your impressions.'

'He's getting up something in France, for the state visit. I'm keeping an eye…'

'Ah yes, he does things over there from time to time, about the Romanovs. France is their second home they say. Provided it's just publicity and he keeps his hands clean, it will do no harm.'

He paused, then looked at him keenly. 'So you will do it? Take in charge the security of my heir?'

'A big responsibility.'

'If I didn't think you were up to it I wouldn't give it to you.'

As Tony walked to the door, Grekov called after him in a melancholy voice:

'I'm not gone yet, mind you. I hope to see the castle finished. Is it going well? It's so long since I've been there.'

'It's looking splendid. We're making sure the security's world-class.'

'Good. If my doctors agree, I plan to come next weekend. Maybe you'll be there?'

'As you wish, Mr Grekov,' Tony said, and left.

# 12

Kasym came back from his garage before his wife or son were home and went to work on the laptop.

*Ornithopters*

*Recent progress in wing-flapping birds has been remarkable. Robotic birds are now capable of bearing considerable payloads, and are easier to manipulate than in the past. Flight control has also improved enormously. In a series of tests a bird with a 30 cm wingspan was brought down within a radius of 0.4 metres of the target...*

*Gliding means they use less power, which is then available for ascending or landing. Then there was the problem of battery power, but advances have been made.*

He searched for models for sale. Flying ornithopters was a flourishing sport, it appeared, with a growing range of birds. A dizzying profusion showed up on the screen, from toy-like creatures with popping eyes and brightly coloured beaks that flew no more than a few metres to advanced experimental models.

Amongst them were startlingly realistic falcons or eagles with full plumage capable of flying several kilometres. One – a falcon made by a specialist Dutch firm – showed it cruising over a flat remote landscape, not unlike the Camargue. *In flat terrain,* the advertisement said, *the motor consumes less energy, so birds can fly further.*

As he stared on at the screen, *Lean Young Wolf* struck up *Fuck off Russki Bastards* in the neighbouring flat. The falcon was flying in a mountainous area now, and as he followed the soaring and plunging bird with fevered eyes he sang along with the rapper.

\*

The cliff in the Calanques – rocky inlets southeast of Marseille – fell precipitately to the calm waters below. Wild olives and tufts of sea lavender were all that relieved the surface of the hard bare rock. Along it a boy was running towards the sea holding what looked like a stuffed bird, shoulder-high. A few metres from the cliff edge he stopped, drew back his arm and launched it into the void.

A childish fantasy, an onlooker might think: a few seconds in the air and the bird would end up shattered on the narrow, rock-strewn beach below. Yet after dipping from view for a brief moment, it soared suddenly upwards into the clear Provençal sky.

The boy stood staring up while his father, a few steps behind, fiddled with a control box sprouting a metre-long aerial.

'*Super!*' Alik cried. 'And look over there! There's a real one – a falcon! Make it chase it! No, not like that, here, give it to me.'

Running back to his father, he grabbed the control box and, his fingers manipulating the buttons and switches expertly, put the falcon into cruise mode. At the sight of it the real bird – native to this part of the Calanques – turned and swooped towards it, then veered skywards, startled.

'You see, it thinks it's real!'

For a minute or two Alik played on with his bird, then his father took over. In his control the falcon cruised back and forth high over the water, then suddenly dived.

Alik stared, horrified.

'*Papa, t'es fou?*'

Kasym wasn't crazy, he was intent on what he was doing. Advancing closer to the edge of the cliff, he stood with the joystick on his control box in a downwards position, his eyes alternating between the plunging bird and a spot in the sand a few metres from the shoreline.

'*Papa,* don't, it's too low! Pull it up!'

Rushing towards him, Alik made a grab for the box. For a few moments they tussled, their backs to the sea. Behind them a soft thwack was audible above the wind.

They went to the cliff edge and looked over. The bird had come

down vertically, like a rocket, a hundred feet below, its beak implant-
ed deep in sand, its tail protruding absurdly. As they stared down, the
real falcon appeared from nowhere to swoop low over the shore, as
if in triumph.

They climbed over rocks down to the beach, Alik scrambling
ahead to prevent his father seeing the tears in his eyes. When he
tugged the bird tail-first from the sand it was impossible to hide
them.

'You've ruined it,' he said. 'Our falcon, you've ruined it!'

He held up the bird in a hand, the other one smoothing its feathers. It must have struck rock beneath the sand. It's head, seat of
most of the electronics, was smashed in.

'It's like its brain,' Alik sobbed over the tangle of tiny circuit
boards, 'you can't mend it. And you did it on purpose!'

'I'm sorry.' Kasym put an arm around his son. 'I had a sort of
compulsion to bring it down in the water. You know, like you see
birds doing when they dive for fish. I aimed for the shallows but I
missed. Stupid.'

Except for his contrition over Alik's tears none of it was true.
His voice was sad but his eyes were contented. The plunge into the
sand was no mistake. He'd meant the bird to land exactly where it
had, equidistant between two rocks that he'd used as markers in
guiding its descent. The only thing that had gone wrong was its
encounter with the rock beneath the sand: he'd hoped for a softer
landing. It was their third outing with the bird, he'd tested it to its
limits and the precision of the guidance system was extraordinary.
The trial bombing had worked.

They climbed back up the cliff, the damaged bird dangling forlornly from Alik's belt.

'Never mind,' Kasym said soothingly, 'we'll get another, I
promise.'

In a fit of dejection, Alik tore the bird from his waist and threw
it to the ground.

'Well that one's no use, anyway.'

His father picked it up.

'No, we'll keep it for spare parts.'

'Suppose we'd better,' Alik said grumpily. 'If you go on smashing them up like that, we'll need them.'

They started out on the long trek from the Calanques that would take them to the main road and the bus back to town.

*

His father was true to his word. The same afternoon he telephoned the Dutch firm that produced the birds from his pay-as-you-go mobile. Delivery, as before, was to his garage, and like the first time the firm was paid by a cash transfer in advance: 580 euros, in the name of a Monsieur Henri. And as before, when the DHL van drew up at the garage he was careful to take delivery personally, on the pretext that the wooden crate was spare parts he had ordered for a friend.

This time the crate was bigger.

'One each, OK?' he said to Alik after he'd lugged it up the stairs and into the flat that evening. 'You take responsibility for yours and I'll do what I want with mine. And if I make a mistake, no whining, right?'

'Right.'

Alik's eyes were part joyous, part puzzled. Was his dad going to go on dive-bombing his bird into the sand? When he began bringing it down at an ever-sharper angle towards an inflatable plastic boat he'd positioned in the water close to the beach, then jerking it back up at the last moment, his puzzlement increased, but he said nothing. It was good to be spending time with his dad, good that their games with the birds seemed to have cheered him up. Best of all, for over two weeks now he hadn't hit him, or his mother.

They could tell when it might happen. It wasn't that he drank too much, it was his moods. When his brow darkened and creased as if in pain and his lip began quivering, it was time to watch out. Anything could set him off. The last time had been when the TV was showing a news feature about Russian forces hunting down rebels in Dagestan, finishing with a gory shot of soldiers standing over dead jihadis shot up in a car.

'Murdering bastards, both of them!' his father had shouted, 'they deserve each other!'

Then he threw his beer can at the screen. His mother went to examine the new television, appalled.

'Why do you do that? Just because they're Russians? You can't spend your life in a rage, you have to forget.'

It was the wrong thing to say, even Alik could see it. His father got up from his chair, lurched across at his mother and slapped her face, so hard her nose began bleeding.

For Alik it was the familiar dilemma: should he get out of the way before he turned on him, or stay to comfort his mother? He stayed and began crying.

'Don't stand there blubbering! Get some toilet paper!'

Afterwards his dad had seemed sorry, mumbling an apology as she wiped her bloodied face in silence. Then it all passed. Alik had become used to these sudden rages: his father flaring up at him and thumping the side of his head so that his ear ached for days, or lashing out at his mother, hard sometimes, the way he might strike a man. Sometimes he would flail at them both, for no clear reason, leaving them sobbing in each other's arms. Then he would hurry to the bathroom and take a pill, while his mother soothed her son, pointing to her forehead and whispering 'it's not him, it's his head.'

Nobody ever talked about it, but Alik had grown up knowing that his father wasn't well. The nerviness, the quivering lip, the constant pills... Once, when he'd been sent to buy them, the *pharmacien* had asked whether they were for him. If so, he couldn't sell them, they were far too strong. *Ça, c'est pas pour enfants, c'est pour les grands malades!* The pills weren't for kids, they were for seriously sick people.

At first he'd thought that it was his bad mood that had made his dad smash up his bird, but it couldn't have been, because he hadn't blamed him, he'd said it was his own fault. And it didn't happen again. His dad was getting really good at bringing it down low now. Again and again he watched as he came close to another crash-landing, but never quite.

To soften the impact if he didn't manage to pull it out of its dive in time, he'd taken the precaution of covering the bird's beak with a kind of putty, but it wasn't needed. Soon he was expert enough to bring the bird down to within a foot of the plastic boat, every time, then making it soar up.

There was something else he'd done to it, something his son would never know, because his father had taken to fiddling with his falcon incessantly behind the closed door of the bedroom or whenever Alik was out. Under the pretext of fixing a tear in its feathers he'd fitted strips of lead into the bird's body, stuffing in more and more to see how much it would take before the payload became unmanageable.

The answer was three strips. At that point he became over-ambitious: when he went for four the piloting became erratic, and when he took it up to five – that was it. As he tried to steer it down as if to bomb the plastic boat the whole thing veered out of control and spiralled into the sea a hundred metres from the shore.

Busy with his own bird, at first Alik didn't notice. Only when he turned to see him standing at a distance along the cliff, his control box on the ground in front of him while he puffed thoughtfully on a cigarette, did he ask what had happened. Afraid that he might be in a mood, he kept his distance, but his tic wasn't going and his dad appeared calm.

'It went down,' his replied, shrugging. 'Had to some day.' He grinned, morosely. 'It's like a test pilot in an experimental plane. Sometimes they push it too far, and they have to bale out. At least it's not me in the water.'

'Maybe it'll be washed up.' Alik looked up at his father, doubtfully. 'It'll float, won't it?'

Not with all that lead in its belly it won't, Kasym thought.

'Maybe.'

For some time they went on staring out to sea, but the bird had disappeared, and there was nothing.

Days later his father brought home a third crate with a fourth bird. The cost was another 290 euros (Alik had caught sight of the bill), so maybe he would finally learn his lesson about pushing his bird too far.

Alik never found out. With the new one, he stopped taking his son to play with their birds together, and began going to the Callanques to fly his own with a friend. They wouldn't take Alik.

# 13

Tony and Lisa were staying in a hotel in a village a mile from the Suffolk castle, waiting for Grekov's visit. He'd bought it because of its royal associations (Henry II had stayed there once, it was said) and had poured millions into its restoration.

Built in the 12th century, for the last two or three hundred years the place had been a ruin: crumbling towers, its roof fallen in, the moat a pit of nettles. Now the work was mostly complete: the moat was brimming, the walls newly crenellated and the living quarters between the towers in the last phase of decoration.

The task of overseeing the security arrangements had been complicated by constant interference from Sasha, whose assumption seemed to be that the castle would be under perpetual siege. It was he who had insisted on a super-sensitive type of biometric access control, one that not only checked your fingerprints before letting you in but retained a sample of your DNA for future use. On top of that, specialist firms had installed state-of-the-art technology with a coded connection, so as to monitor and adjust surveillance cameras from anywhere in the world.

Finally a panic room had been installed, its walls and door reinforced with sheets of steel, Kevlar and bullet-resistant fibreglass, with external ventilation systems and a protected telephone connection. From it an escape shaft had been dug under the moat – another of Sasha's personal touches. 'By the time he's finished it'll be like *The Great Escape*,' the architect told Tony, sighing, 'except that Sasha will be his own prisoner. And unlike Steve McQueen's his tunnel will be air-conditioned.'

It wasn't the first time Tony had been down here with Lisa. Knowledgeable about old furniture – she'd once worked in the antiques trade – as the residential parts of the castle began taking shape she was charged with scouring the area for antique furnishings: iron bedsteads, wood-panelling, cavernous wardrobes, vast gilt mirrors.

They had arrived late on Friday; Grekov was due on Sunday morning. On Saturday night they had dinner in the hotel restaurant, and inevitably the conversation turned to Sasha. Protective about Grekov himself, she needed little encouragement to speak her mind about his son.

'He's a parasite. He speculates on his father's feelings for him as an only child.'

'Strange there's just the one. I would have thought he would have had a big family.'

'I think he would have liked that, but he couldn't.'

'Why?'

'An accident. He was a big skier, every year at Meribel. He had his own chalet – more of a small palace really – where he would entertain, in the days when he saw people. Then the accident. He was a daredevil on the slopes, it was a bad fall, and there were complications.'

'What sort?'

'He was impotent.'

'Ah.'

It was his second marriage, she explained, the first had been when he was still in the GRU. It hadn't lasted; his wife had been a Party woman and he was moving away from that. After he'd given up intelligence work and made his fortune he married again. Another mistake, this time a Russian model he'd met in London. The gossip was that after they had Sasha she refused to have more children, said it would ruin her looks.

She'd lost them anyway: when her career was in trouble she'd started drinking. Then it was drugs, and he divorced her, in the days you could do it without giving away half your fortune. After that, she'd gone back to Russia.

'And where was Sasha?'

'Here – his father got custody, because of the heroin. Not that she'd seen a lot of him before. God knows what effect it had on him – he was seven at the time. What must really have damaged him was when she started writing things against his father in Moscow, for the Russian press. Hints that he'd been a traitor, that his money was stolen, that kind of thing. Before that he'd been to Moscow a couple of times to see her, but when they began using her to attack him he never went back. Too dangerous. She died a few years ago, in a sanatorium.

'So there he was, a man in middle age desperate for a new wife and family. He found a girlfriend – a marvellous woman, Ruth said, a young British historian. She was staying with him in Meribel when he had the accident. No-one ever knew whether she dropped him or it was by mutual agreement.

'That's when everything changed. No more sport or skiing, no more women, no more socializing. Apart from his business and his interest in Russian history, Sasha was all he had left, and when he finished Oxford he insisted on him moving back home. His son is his world. Not sentimentally – literally.'

'The boy's grown up. Maybe he needs to get away.'

'Grown-up?' Lisa laughed softly. 'Not Sasha. He's one of those people who never will. It's his father's fault, of course. He's too indulgent, but at the same time he's old-fashioned. It's almost Victorian. When they're by themselves Sasha calls him papa! Can you imagine?'

'And what about women?'

'He'd like him to marry but there's no sign of that. Whores he goes with, no one regular.'

Tempted to disabuse her, Tony held his peace.

She shrugged.

'And he does drugs, of course.'

'In the house?'

'Never, but Ruth knows everything – especially how much he's spending. The sums he carries in cash – you can't imagine. Mikhail gets it for him. Sometimes he tells him it's too much to have around, but Sasha won't listen. At university it was tens of thousands. Last week – I shouldn't say, but – '

' – come on,' Tony smiled, 'if it's a security risk it's my job to know.'

'Well, Ruth says she heard him asking Mikhail for a million dollars. He tried to talk him out of it, find out what it was for, asked why he couldn't use a bank transfer. Sasha told him to mind his business, and he backed off. I love Mikhail, such a character, but with Sasha he's softer than you'd think.'

'Why's that?'

'He's afraid he'll complain to his father. Anyway, he got his million. Two fat parcels of $100 notes, Ruth said. She saw him toss them into a drawer, just like that. I wonder what it was for.'

Expenses for Daudov and his friends? And maybe he was replenishing the boy's cocaine supplies while he was down in Marseille. But a million? The Georgian must have bigger reception plans for the President than he'd thought. Unless, of course, he was just conning Sasha. Probably the latter…

He switched the conversation to Lisa herself. Till that evening she'd been reticent about her background, now she volunteered that she was divorced from a Russian lawyer. A decent man, she explained, but he'd got himself mixed up with a pair of financial sharks from Moscow. Hard to be a Russian lawyer in London without that happening. As a result he'd spent four years in jail, his career in London was ruined, so he'd gone back home. She couldn't face Russia, so they'd split up. There'd been no children.

How could he have let her go, Tony wondered, listening to her story? This quietly alluring woman, with her quick intelligence and air of restrained sensuality?

It was at the end of a fine September day they had spent hunting for antiques together. The hotel was friendly and intimate, the restaurant superb and the Camargue a long way from his thoughts. Away from the forbidding London house Lisa seemed more relaxed, and Tony at his smartest and most agreeable.

With money in his pocket and his family affairs on the mend –

his granddaughter had got a place in a private school in Wimbledon and his daughter was looking for a place nearby – he felt lighter-hearted, and it showed in his appearance. For the first time in thirty years he paid attention to his clothes. Now there were tailored suits and stylish casuals rather than his usual clumping brogues, an end to the feeling that he was undressed unless he was wearing a tie.

The invisibility that had been part of his career had been over-taken by a more man-about-town image, and his swimming was still keeping him trim. All in all, he looked and felt younger: a man who a year ago had been in danger of looking more than his age now seemed to have lost a year or two.

That night Lisa too looked less than her age, her hair cut in a less severe fashion, her heels higher, a modest décolleté. Unconsciously for them both, their friendship had played a part in this mutual reju-venation. Tonight had been their first real talk together and Tony had been charmed. In fact rather more.

*

At two thirty in the morning there was a soft knock at his door. He opened. It was Lisa, in a dressing gown, holding her mobile.

'Him,' she said, 'for you.'

Taking the phone, he beckoned her in and closed the door.

'Mr Grekov, how can I help?'

Oblivious as ever to the time of day, it turned out that he'd been looking over pictures of the castle and something about the gate-house had caught his eye. Too modern, he sighed, far too modern, security was becoming obtrusive, interfering with the antiquity of the castle's façade.

The short answer was 'speak to Sasha,' but Tony refrained.

'Well, we'll talk about it on Sunday.'

'Unfortunately I won't be coming,' Grekov replied, his voice fainter by the minute. 'My doctor won't allow it.'

'Maybe Monday, if you're better? Lisa and I could stay on here.'

'I doubt it,' Grekov said, and rang off.

'He can't make it,' he said to Lisa. 'His health…'

'I never expected he would. I'd better go back tomorrow.'

'That would be a pity. Couldn't we stay another night? I really enjoyed today.' The words were stiff but his eyes conveyed something more. 'Anyway now we're up, let's have a drink.'

He opened his fridge and poured the half bottle of champagne. As they drank Lisa agreed to stay on a second night, and they planned the day together.

Till now the simmering warmth between them had stayed under control. It was a genteel, old-fashioned business: a hand on her arm, a touch to her waist, a goodnight peck. Now, when the champagne was drunk and she got up to go, the peck turned to a kiss and the kiss into a night together.

# 14

Alik sat on the landing outside his flat, doing his best to read in the semi-darkness. He didn't like squatting out here alone – the boys next door might come home any moment – but his father had visitors. To get him out of the flat before they'd arrived he'd given him money to buy *Les Naufragés du Temps,* his favourite science fiction comic. He'd started reading it in a park then come back in when it began raining. If he'd known he'd be stuck out here he'd have brought a torch, though better here than on the hallway stairs, with the scary passers-by and the stink.

The story was that the planet is under attack from plague, and two people – *The Castaways of Time* – are placed in hibernation capsules and sent into space. He liked it because he thought of himself as one of the heroes. He wouldn't mind being whooshed into space, or just to another country. Anything to get away from his rotting tenement. Somewhere with a proper house where he could invite his friends and where no one would know he was a Chechen.

And it was no longer fantasy. Not long ago his father had talked about them going abroad. It was the time when he'd suddenly begun buying things, like the laptop, the plasma television and the birds, and he'd asked him how they could afford them? Because he'd had a stroke of luck, his dad told him, a collective bet he'd placed with some friends at the garage that had come good. Enough money for them to go on a long trip.

'*Super!* Where to?'

'Maybe Canada. And who knows, maybe we'll stay? You can speak French there, you know. But you have to be a good boy. Don't tell anyone we've got some money or that we might take a trip abroad, or about the laptop or the new television. And especially not about the birds.'

'I know about Canada, a friend at school told me, a Chechen like us. It sounds great but you can't just go there, they have to allow you in. He says his father's tried to go to Canada for years but they won't let him.'

'We're lucky, we know someone. Someone who can help with visas and things.'

'My friend's dad says you can buy a visa if you've got enough money.'

'Never mind your friend. I'm telling you we're going to have visas for Canada, all three of us. You and mummy will go first then I'll come too, when I've finished at the garage. Over there we'll have a proper place to live. A nice kitchen and bathroom and your own bedroom where you can do your homework, and no one will piss in the hall. But remember, you're not to tell anyone we're going. Mummy knows, but no one else.'

Alik went on peering at his comic. It wasn't the first time he'd been banished from the flat. There'd been several of these meetings with the nameless visitor, always in the early evenings when his mother was still at work. Whoever the man was, from the little he'd seen and heard he didn't like him. Partly it was the way he looked – he'd caught a glimpse of him once, out in the street, with his long dark hair and leering face, sort of cocky – though mainly it was because he was the one his dad had taken to the Callanques to fly his falcon. The man with the car who'd refused to take him.

He'd worried about what the two of them would do with the bird, rightly as it turned out: the second time they'd gone out there together his father had come back saying his friend had crashed it. There wasn't another one ready at the factory where they made them, so his dad had taken his. He'd bought him a radio-controlled helicopter in consolation, but it wasn't the same.

Giving up on his comic – it was getting darker by the minute – he put his head to the door and listened. All he could hear was a low murmur, interrupted from time to time by his father's rising voice. At that moment he burst out in Russian:

*Daudov, Daudov – ty durak, chto-li?*

Alik didn't speak Russian, though that bit he understood. *You an idiot, Daudov, or what?* Sometimes his dad asked him the same question. The next voice he heard was that of his uncle Batir. He'd come to one of the earlier meetings but he didn't say much, he wasn't allowed: whenever he spoke his father or his visitor cut him off.

Alik wasn't too fond of his uncle, a dull fellow who never brought him anything nice, not even sweets. All he did was ask how his Koran-reading was coming along. He'd given him a copy in French for his birthday and followed up with a lecture on his next visit, when he saw that the pages were unopened.

His dad got lectures too sometimes, about his smoking and beer drinking, till he lost patience and shouted at his brother to keep his sermonizing to himself and shut the hell up. On top of that Batir had a funny kind of face, sort of round and soft and silly. It seemed even sillier now he'd shaved his beard off.

So the nameless man was Daudov. As far as he was concerned Daudov *was* an idiot, not just because he'd crashed his dad's bird but because he'd been messing around with his. One day he'd come back from school to find it on the table, after Daudov had gone. Seeing him pick it up his dad stormed in from the bedroom, grabbed it from his hands and put it back in the locked cupboard.

'Can't I just hold it?'

'No you can't.'

'Can't I even *look* at it?'

'I said no!'

'It was *mine* before.'

'Well it's not now!'

He'd had time to sneak a glance. The feathers seemed OK, though when he'd felt underneath there was something hard and long jammed in its gut.

'What's that man being doing to its belly?'

'Never you mind.'

'Is it his now? Is that why you lock it away? Have you sold it to him?'

The answer was a smack on the ear that had made him cry. His dad wasn't in one of his moods and the blow was unexpected.

'I've told you, forget about the falcon! Just leave it alone. If I find you touching it again…'

He didn't say what he'd do, didn't have to. He'd get a bigger bash than the one he'd just received. He'd gone for a walk till the tears had dried and when he'd come back up, his father was drinking beer and watching the news as always. He hoped it wouldn't be about Russia. It was.

He was going to the bedroom to get away when his father switched if off and called out:

'*Viens ici.*'

Come here. For a second he'd hesitated. Was this some new offence?

'*Viens, je te dis.*'

He took the three steps back to the cushion-covered wooden boxes that served as the family sofa. His father drew him down.

'The falcons,' he said. 'Just so you understand. The thing is they were never ours. Just someone who asked me to keep them here, do some work on them, because I'm a mechanic. Like a garage for falcons, right?'

Alik had done his best to smile. He didn't like it when his father spoke like this. It sounded as if he was making things up. He'd never said the birds were someone else's before, he'd said he'd bought them.

He sat on by the door. When would the meeting be over? He pressed his ear closer to the panel. The talk from the flat was fainter, then somebody said in French in a sarcastic voice '*Monsieur le Président*', and there was a boom of laughter.

It must be about what his dad had seen on the news the night before. He'd laughed then too, loudly, and when Alik had asked what was funny he told him that there'd been a row over a cartoon in *Le Figaro* that had made the Russian leader look ridiculous.

'Good,' Alik had said, keen to please, 'because he is.'

Inside the flat the talk stopped suddenly. A sound of chairs moving. Steps towards the door. Springing to his feet Alik rushed down the blackness of the stairs and out into the rain. If his father discovered him listening his chances of seeing his falcon again were zero. And he might never get to Canada.

# 15

The Church of The Dormition of the Most Holy Mother of God and Royal Martyrs was on the outskirts of town, visible from the M4. On his way to and from Heathrow Tony had often admired the blue onion dome exploding above the suburban townscape, wondering why it was there and what a newly-constructed Greek Orthodox Church would be like. Now, at the funeral of Arshile Nikiforovitch Grekov, he would discover.

The sadness he felt was made worse when Grekov's death became the occasion for his first confrontation with Sasha.

'The funeral has to be delayed,' the boy told him two days before it was due to be held.

'You're withdrawing the invitations?'

'I am.'

'Why?'

'I need to find out how he died.'

'I really don't think that would be wise. The press will get hold of it, there'll be a scandal, lurid speculation. Is that what you want?'

'What I want is the truth. There has to be an autopsy.'

'Sasha, be reasonable. We've been into that. I checked out the cooks, spoke to his doctor. We knew he suffered from abnormal heart rhythms and the doctor says he died from cardiac arrest.'

'In the Kremlin they have a personal taster, you know that? And it isn't just the cooks, anyone could have put things in. Slowly, over time, so the doctors wouldn't notice. I've seen stuff on the Russian Internet saying the CIA had dad on their books, that it was how he'd got started in business. It used to be MI6, but now it's the CIA. The same people who say that all these years he's been secretly backing a coup. Don't you see? They had every motive.'

It was like reasoning with an obsessive, and yet Tony, a patient mentor, kept his cool. It had taken him over an hour but eventually Sasha calmed down. When Lisa told him that the funeral was to go ahead it looked as if Tony'd won the argument. This was not quite the case.

According to Orthodox rites the body should be buried three days after death. The same ritual stipulates that the deceased should be on display in his coffin in his home in white clothes, his head on a pillow, his legs pointing towards the door through which he would finally depart the house. It was there that Grekov's colleagues and acquaintances came to mourn him, and take their farewells.

What Tony didn't know, until Mikhail told him, was that after the last mourner had gone on the last night and the room was closed the body was taken away. By nine next morning it had reappeared, in all its funeral regalia, and the leave-taking and lamentation came to a close. It was during those night hours, by arrangement with a specialist whose services Sasha had procured in exchange for a £25,000 fee he'd got Mikhail to come up with in cash, that toxicology tests were performed, and samples taken. Nothing, of course, had been proven.

The funeral arrangements had brought Tony another run-in with the boy. When the list of invitations went for his approval and he'd seen the name of the Russian Ambassador he stormed into Tony's office.

'Who put that bastard on?'

'Lisa, I imagine.'

'Anyway he's coming off.'

'Hold on, there's a reason. Your father's tactic was to preserve a façade of normality with the regime.'

'Oh, come on, Tony, that's typical diplomat's hokum. A façade of normality while they had the FSB onto him? Anyway that was then. Now that he's gone why do I have to keep up the façade?'

'For the same reason as your father. And because you're your father's son. Now they'll be watching you closer than ever.'

'If you think I'm going to shake hands with the man in charge of the goons who – '

' – you must do what you want,' Tony cut in, tired of this over-grown adolescent lumbering about his room, shouting. 'I'm here to offer advice. It's for you to decide whether to take it.'

'Tony.'

Sasha came up and put a hand on his shoulder, his voice suddenly maudlin. Tony gave an inward sigh. It had happened before, and he knew the mood: it was one of his abrupt transitions from outbursts of half-crazed irrationalism to Etonian smarm.

'Don't think I don't appreciate all that you did for Dad. He wanted you to stay on and I'm grateful you agreed. But this time I can't accept your advice.'

'If the Ambassador's not there there'll be even more press speculation. How much attention do you want to draw to yourself? You don't have to hobnob with him. Just invite him.'

In the end, Sasha gave in. It had been a wearing business, not a great start to their new relationship. And to think there would be seven more years of this… Could he take it? With the new salary of £200,000 stipulated in Grekov's will and a payoff of three million at the end of it, he decided that perhaps he could.

*

Icons, candles, incense, chanting, and a swarm of white-robed priests. Tony watched from the back of the church while the mourners filed in. Amongst the first to arrive was the Ambassador, a portly fellow with an imperious manner: a 'puff-ball with a power complex,' as he'd heard Svetlana describe him. And there she was herself, alongside the puff-ball, sombrely enchanting in her fine mesh veil and black fur coat. Instantly he looked at Sasha: prepared no doubt for Svetlana's appearance he took no notice.

Alongside her stood a shortish fellow with a jutting beard. From the clips of the ambassadorial car Larry Merchant had sent him Tony recognised Victor Bulagin, the cultural attaché who sat silently in the front on their artistic outings. With his grey unhealthy features and bleary, drinker's eyes, from time to time he exchanged remarks with the Ambassador though never a word with Svetlana. Perhaps he resented her presence? In any event, there appeared to be a frost between them.

The coffin was carried in feet first for the burial service. Set in the centre of the nave facing the altar it was opened, an icon of Christ positioned in the dead man's hands and a wreath placed on his forehead. Next, the priest distributed candles to the worshipers.

After the Dismissal, people came one by one to the coffin to say a last good-by. Like most of the others Lisa, pallid behind her veil, bent to kiss the icon in his hands. When it came to the Ambassador a stiffening could be felt in the congregation: would he do it too? He didn't. Sasha, his face puffy with tears, stood next to his father for several minutes.

When it was over the coffin was closed and carried from the church. The choir sang and the bells pealed slowly. The mourners stopped at the grave. Till that moment Sasha had contrived to avoid contact with the Ambassador. Now the fellow approached with Svetlana and spoke to him in Russian: his commiserations, Tony assumed. Sasha nodded woodenly, didn't reply. Nor did he glance at Svetlana. It was over in seconds but for Tony, knowing what the three-way encounter represented, it was an eerie tableau.

He drove Lisa back to the house. Neither spoke. He had never been a believer and his experiences of Northern Ireland and of Islamism had done nothing to raise the status of religion in his eyes. Mysticism of any kind was not for him, and yet the incense, the chanting and the spectacle of the open coffin of someone he had known and respected had worked their effect. Many things had happened in his life that he would never have predicted, but feeling his eyes dampen at the burial rites for a one-time GRU operative…

Grekov had been born into an atheist, anti-monarchist, anti-capitalist regime, one that he had served faithfully half his life. Yet he'd died a rich man, a royalist and a believer, the Orthodox Church part of his vision of his country's future.

Tony had come into the world as a Christian in a free country and spent a fair part of his career in the anti-communist struggle. At the end of it he'd found himself an atheist in the service of a Christian oligarch who had been his enemy, felt moved by his death, and had sworn to spend the rest of his working days protecting the life of his son.

A strange world, that was about to become stranger.

# 16

An urgent summons from Sasha. It was a Sunday and apart from the endlessly hovering security men (all of them smoking now) the vast house seemed empty. Sasha had taken over his father's office, the huge TV and drinks fridge he had moved from his own room incongruous amidst the antique opulence.

When he entered Sasha was at the desk, his chair tipped backwards, a trainer-clad foot resting on its mahogany surface. At his appearance the foot shot down as he sprang to his feet and began pacing the long room.

'Drink?'

'Not just at the moment.'

It was four o'clock. Not that it mattered to Sasha. An empty whisky glass stood on the desk and his fleshy cheeks were white and strained.

'Tony, thanks for coming. I need your help. There's a girlfriend of mine I sometimes visit. Thing is, I've just found out that someone's bugged her flat.'

'You're sure?'

Tony's frown of concern was unfeigned.

'Course I am. Fucking camera, in the bedroom.'

'Ah.'

'It's bloody worrying. You think it was the Russians?'

'Well they'd certainly be candidates.'

'Jesus, the things they could do with stuff like that. Threats of publicity, blackmail...'

'Has anyone tried?'

'Not yet, but I'm not going to wait and see. Anyone you know who can take a look? Tell me how long it's been there, see if there's any others? Somebody in your old line of business, someone discreet?'

Tony considered.

'I think there is.'

'Good.'

Sasha went on worrying away while Tony sat nodding, confining himself to sagacious remarks. After that came another tirade against the Russian President and ramblings about the reinstatement of the Romanov dynasty, so by the time Tony got away an hour later he wished he'd accepted the drink.

*

For a backroom boy Tom Sandiman's representational skills could be impressive. Standing in the bedroom of Svetlana's flat in his neat grey suit and sober tie, a briefcase at his feet and an eyeglass in position, deep in study of an object the size of a cigarette lighter, he looked for all the world like a jeweller or an auctioneer.

Sasha stood waiting for his verdict. In his jeans and shapeless sweater he resembled some hulking street scruff who'd lifted the object from a lady's handbag and was keen to sell it on.

Sandiman walked to the window and, his back to Sasha, held the bug up to the light.

'It's a neat job. Very professional. How did you come across it?'

'Something was wrong with the wiring in the bedroom. The lights went out in the chandelier. An electrician came and found it. I look after the flat for her so the guy gave it to me.'

'And who has access to the flat? Apart from Miss Blackman?'

It was the name Sasha had given Tony.

'Nobody. Only a cleaner, a Filipino. You think she could have done it? I'm going to have a word with her.'

'That would be a mistake,' Sandiman opined, 'on several counts. When did your friend buy the flat?'

'She rented it. 'Bout a year ago,' Sasha lied, badly.

'It's been up there some time I would guess' Tom mused, 'so it could have been there when your friend moved in. Also,' he held up the bug, smiling, 'it's not working. In fact, I doubt it ever has.'

'You sure? Jesus, that would be… But how can you tell?'

'Here, have a look with this.' Tom handed him his eyeglass. Sasha put it in and peered at the tiny camera. 'See that pin?' He indicated a minuscule spur of metal, fine as a tendril. 'End's snapped off, hasn't it?'

'Yeah. I can see. When did it happen d'you think?'

'Probably when they put it in.' A minute and a half earlier was the truth, the pin nipped off between Sandiman's agile fingers as he'd stood at the window. 'Maybe it was installed in a hurry. Or the person who did it was an amateur.'

'Thought you said it was professional?'

'The camera itself I meant,' Tom backtracked smoothly.

'But if it *wasn't* here when she rented the place who the fuck put it in?'

Sandiman affected a solemn look.

'Mr Grekov, do you mind if I ask a question? I'm afraid it may sound indiscreet.'

'Go ahead.'

'On the basis of my experience, I can only say it's rarely the one you suspect. In bedrooms especially. I assume you, er, shared the room from time to time?'

'Naturally.'

'So the person with the best access would be Miss Blackman.'

Sasha frowned, angrily.

'You know, that's such shit.'

'I'm sure it is. I have to mention it because…' he sighed, 'as I say, experience. Have you told your friend about it?'

'Thought I'd better not. No point in worrying her.'

'Very wise, if I may say so. Especially if the thing's never worked. Why upset her, pointlessly?'

'Is it Russian?'

'Things like this don't have a maker's stamp. Could be, mind you – they're well up in the field.'

His lips pursed, he gazed round the bedroom ceiling.

'Of course this is only one. There could be others. Then there's the rest of the flat.'

'Bloody hell. Maybe you should sweep the whole place?'

'I haven't got the equipment, but I could come back and do it if you like.' He nodded his head, soberly. 'Be safest.'

*

Over a drink with Tony that evening Tom was in expansive mood.

'I have a look at the take from time to time, check the quality. Doesn't half put herself about, your young lady. Got to be a bit of a connoisseur of Slavic women over the years, and they're not what they used to be, thank Christ. Seen 'em come down from this' – he spread his arms a metre – 'to this.' He indicated a wasp waist. 'Some of the fat cows we used to get, you wouldn't believe it... Didn't stop 'em wearing those nifty nighties mind you. There's one I remember, KGB man's wife, built like a T72 tank. Had this boyfriend, one of the Embassy heavies, and the pair of 'em...' He closed his eyes, shuddering. 'Thirty odd years ago it was, but you don't forget...'

'I'll take your word. And how was Sasha?'

'Worried stiff. Asked if I could sweep the place, pronto. So what do you want me to do? Put it back in the ceiling, or leave it in the chandelier? Last place anyone would suspect it. Bit more time, do a better job hiding it. Put another one in the drawing room if you wanted. Just say the word.'

Tony reflected. If Sasha had the place swept by someone else and the new bugs were discovered it would be the end of his job. Though if he thought the flat was clean, he'd be even more indiscreet...

'Put it back the way it was.'

'As you like. Anything else I can do for you?'

'I'll need you to come down and do the castle before the decorating's finished.'

'Sweep it?' Sandiman grinned, 'or fit it up?'

'Both, I suppose, now it'll be just Sasha living there.'

'That's what I like to hear. It's all work, isn't it?' He raised his glass. 'Bless you for easing the pain of a poor old boy's retirement.'

Tony's finger pointed upwards.

'It's Grekov we should both be blessing.'

Looking at the ceiling they raised their whiskies and drank.

*

A few hours to himself when the Filipino wasn't around and Sandiman had the camera reinstalled in the chandelier, plus another in the drawing room ceiling. Two days later he passed by the house in a green Loden coat (last time it had been a plastic parka) carrying a holdall, one of a large array of containers (satchels, briefcases, backpacks) he used to vary his appearance and for his downloading gear.

'Seems OK,' he said when Tony came to his door to collect the delivery later that night. 'Thought I'd stick in another one in the drawing room while I was at it.'

'I didn't say – '

' – I know you didn't, but you hesitated. Plus it's got this ornate cornice, so I thought, too good a chance to miss...'

It was the evening before another of Tony's trips to the Suffolk castle. Tossing the recordings into his suitcase he told himself that he'd check them in a spare moment. Viewing them was getting to be a chore. Apart from Sasha, Svetlana never seemed to have visitors, and there was limited mileage in listening to her barking commands at her Filipino or watching her prepare for bed; a small treat at the beginning, the novelty had worn off quickly. And when Sasha came round they'd developed an irritating habit of leaving the TV on when they talked, even when they were eating.

Nothing much was coming in about her from Larry Merchant either. Keen to justify the cash Tony dropped off for him, from time to time his man at the barrier to Kensington Palace Gardens was inundating him with clips from his security cameras, each of them much like the last: the Ambassador leaning towards Svetlana in the back of his limousine with his ingratiating, podgy man's smile, and Victor Bulagin, the Cultural First Secretary in the front, invariably silent and frosty-looking.

The spare moment came in his hotel two nights later. The architect working on the castle he was seeing for dinner, a gossipy fellow full of stories about his dealings with Sasha (it was he who had designed his underground pool), fell victim to a bad Suffolk oyster. Alone in his room with a brandy after his solitary meal, he remembered the memory sticks and, a finger poised on the fast-forward button, plugged one in.

Daytime. Svetlana goes out at nine a.m. and gets home about eight-thirty. After dinner (a skimpy affair, the woman watches her weight – though not her drinking) at ten Sasha turns up.

She gives him a kiss, pleased to see him it appears, and as always, the champagne comes out. They talk excitedly but the sound of the television overlays their voices. Svetlana goes to the bedroom. Sasha pours himself a large whisky, checks his watch, and sits before the TV.

The bedroom. Svetlana has a bath, comes back and views herself pink and fresh from the tub in the wardrobe mirror, before slipping on a nightie. Sitting up against the pillow she zaps on the TV at the foot of the bed. A news programme. There are now two TVs going in unison, the same channel. Are they waiting for a particular item? Something about the President? And why isn't Sasha in the bedroom, eager to join her?

The drawing room. Sasha is still drinking and watching the TV, distractedly it seems. A mobile rings. He draws it from his pocket, hurriedly, lowers the volume of the TV, jumps to his feet and answers. He speaks English but the bedroom TV makes his voice unclear. After a minute or two Svetlana lowers the volume for a moment to shout:

'Sasha! I'm waiting!'

*Her* calling *him* to bed?

'Hold on.'

He talks on for several minutes, pacing the drawing room, then switches off and hurries to the bedroom.

'That was him.'

Sasha, triumphant-looking, is tearing off his shirt and pants.

'Good. So what's he up to?'

'He's got this idea.'

'What exactly?'

'Well he's not going to spell out the details over the phone, is he?'

'So it could be anything. Or nothing.'

'It'll be something all right. Here, I'll show you.'

Down to his underpants, his gut wobbling, Sasha goes impetuously to the drawing room and comes back with a laptop. He opens it on a table alongside the TV, goes online and brings up a map.

'Here, look.'

Eagerly, Svetlana jumps from her bed. They pore over the map together. Sasha zooms in and marks an X with the cursor. Their heads are close to the TV, still chattering softly, so their voices are indistinct:

'So where will he be?'

'Here.'

'And so the idea is – '

' – exactly!'

'So it'll…' The next phrase is lost.

'With any luck.'

'Brilliant!'

Svetlana, on tiptoes, gives him a kiss. Sasha is radiant.

Next something peculiar happens. Her arms extended, she circles the room like a demented ballet dancer before diving head-first onto the bed. Then lies there yelling above the TV:

'You're right – he's a bloody genius!'

Sasha watches her, grinning, before diving alongside, landing heavily. They cuddle. At this point she is in the habit of reminding him to take a bath, though tonight she doesn't. Encouraged perhaps by his whisky and her welcoming mood, Sasha is in a hurry. Forgetting to cover the icon over the bed he stretches a hand to turn off the light.

The TV is still going. In its glow Tony sees Svetlana peppering him with kisses. Whatever he's told her about Daudov's plans she is grateful – to the point of offering an instant reward, of a kind that has Sasha stretching blissfully on his back and Tony reaching for the rewind button.

He went back to the scene where they were standing over the laptop staring at the map. Freezing the frame and zooming in till the title was clear, he read: *Institut Géographique National: Arles et Camargue*.

He peered closer. The map was detailed, the scale 1:25,000, the equivalent of ordinance survey. The mark Sasha had left on the screen was on the shore of a large lagoon with a small island in the middle. Find the blind where he's going to do his duck shooting, he remembered Daudov instructing Kasym and his brother when he'd recorded their conversation. This must be it.

Before switching off the laptop he checked back to make sure Sasha and his girl hadn't conversed after their amorous interlude. They hadn't: Sasha was fast asleep, though Svetlana was still awake – and crying to herself quietly. At least that's how it looked. She was lying as far away as she could, her back towards him, her face to the window, from which the faint light from the streetlamp picked out the glow in her wet, wide-open eyes.

Strange. Before servicing Sasha she'd seemed unusually perky, and he'd never seen her cry before. So Svetlana had feelings – who would have thought it? – though feelings of what? Revulsion for her lover, perhaps. The tears must be of anger for him and of pity for herself. If so, Tony was unmoved. Well, darling, he thought, if you're in there for the big money and nothing else, princess or no princess that's what you get.

He switched off his laptop and went back to his brandy. The boy was still busy with his anti-Kremlin machinations, that was for sure, and with his father gone and no limits on his money there was little to restrain him. Daudov must be having fun spending his million dollars. On the Georgian's whereabouts he had nothing more, though on Kasym there was news: the previous day Dick Welby had rung to say that French security, bless their Gallic hearts, had come through with an address.

The idea of the boy getting mixed up in anything serious seemed as absurd as before, though how do you read the mind of the spoiled inheritor of a billionaire, a drug-user and political obsessive who's convinced that his father was murdered? And with Svetlana goading him on...

Another flit to Marseille? Somehow the prospect did not beckon. The airport hassle, the lush but impersonal hotel, killing time on his own by over-eating and drinking, the temptation to resort to another *compagne* for the evening...

A thought that led to Lisa.

He switched on the light and dialled her number.

'Sorry, it's late. Are you in bed?'

'Not yet. And you? You're in the country again?'

'Yes – and missing you. I'm done here, coming back in the morning. I had an idea. I have to go to Marseille for a day or two at short notice. I was thinking, maybe you could join me?'

A silence. He could see her conscientious face pondering, frowning a little.

'Wouldn't that look –'

' – no one has to know. Just a couple of days, I'm sure they could spare you. Sasha won't notice – and he won't know that I'm going. Just tell Ruth you're not feeling well.'

'I don't have to say that, I have a backlog of leave. Months of it.'

'So you'll come?'

'I won't get in the way of your work?'

'Oh it's nothing. Couple of things I need to check out, that's all.'

A flit to the Continent with a girlfriend. In more than thirty years of marriage it was the first time he'd done it, and a sense of delicious transgression was checked by guilt. Not that it stopped him, though ringing Jean to explain that he wouldn't be back next morning, as promised, and that he had to do another run to Marseille didn't feel good.

But then from now on this was the way of things, he told

himself, his new life, and it wasn't as if he was neglecting his wife and family; it was for them that he'd taken the job. And in a way, he persuaded himself as he fell asleep, it was because he'd never gone off abroad with a woman before that he deserved to now.

# 17

The July weather was perfect and with Lisa at his side the Provençal sun shone more radiantly and to greater purpose. Checking out the situation on Kasym and the Camargue during their stay would be no problem: she must have guessed that his trip had something to do with the Georgian Sasha had taken on who'd lived in France, but she never asked him about his work – part of her conscientiousness – and had said nothing on the flight down about why he was coming. All she knew was that Grekov had made provision for keeping him on for Sasha's protection.

As they planned their stolen days over an al fresco dinner in the Old Port, and he mentioned that they'd need to allow time for him to do his errands, it occurred to him that he might just as well tell her frankly why he was here. Then maybe they could take a spin to the Camargue together, and he could check out the spot on the lagoon Sasha had shown on the map?

He decided against it. He hadn't told Mikhail about the Marseille business either; in his drink, he'd discovered, the Russian could be alarmingly indiscreet, and in any event explaining to Lisa about the President's visit could put a damper over they stay, cloud their brief idyll.

Setting out for the address the French had given for Kasym at four o'clock next day was an awkward moment. Assuming it would be in a less-than-salubrious part of town, he'd brought a down-at-heel rig in his luggage. When he emerged from the bathroom wearing raggedy jeans, a light, scruffy jacket and trainers that appeared close to the point of disintegration, rather than his cream-coloured cotton suit, Lisa, reading on the bed at that moment, stared up at him before laughing.

'I won't ask,' she said, 'and I'd rather you didn't tell. So long as I don't have to walk around with you in that outfit.'

In the lobby the concierge looked askance as their formerly respectable English guest passed him on his way out.

'*Un taxi, monsieur?*'

'*Merci, non.*'

No point in the hotel knowing where he was going.

He strode out into the humid afternoon street, walked a few minutes in the direction of the centre of town to distance himself from the hotel, felt the trainers chafing and hailed a cab. When he gave him the address in the fifteenth arrondissement, the fellow swivelled in his seat, wide-eyed:

'*Le quinzième? Vous allez là? Vous êtes sûr que c'est la bonne adresse Monsieur?*'

No, he knew where he was going, hadn't got the wrong address. '*Absolument.*'

The driver, an Arab himself, knew his city. On his first visit, Tony had found time to wander around the old quarter behind the City Hall in the centre of town. *Le Panier* – the basket – the area was called, with its intricate streets, crumbling buildings sporting washing on high balconies, and occasional tourists' bars or artists' studios. Charming. The real basket case, however, was the area where the cabbie left him after a half-hour drive, at the end of a narrow street in the North African area of the city.

The address – number eight – turned out to be a derelict tenement. *EDIFICE DANGEREUX* a red notice at ground floor level warned. *UNSAFE BUILDING*. The same goes for the area, he reflected, walking watchfully along the ruined, malodorous street, empty except for a few mendicant-looking figures.

Windows at ground level were shuttered, the walls covered in graffiti in French and Arabic. *Fuck the Russians*, one of them read. *And all Christian sons of bitches!* someone had added. *Ici les Tchetchens gèrent tout* – round here the Chechens are in charge! proclaimed a third.

Maybe they were, but then this was Marseille, ethnicities changed from street to street and the Chechens had rivals on their patch. *Faites attention aux Roma!* was the last thing the cab driver had said before speeding off, and he'd been right: when Tony got to the end of the street, there they were.

Parked on the pavement was a ravaged pick-up, heaped with junk: broken furniture, car tyres, mattresses, a 1950s radio, a small refrigerator. Encamped on folding chairs beside it were two Roma, one with his paunch spilling from beneath a bright red jersey, the second in a tattered waistcoat, like a distressed bank clerk. Antique fellows smoking and drinking beer, they looked as though they'd been left in charge of the day's takings.

The first time he walked past the tenement the Roma ignored him. On his second pass they showed interest. With no shops or cafes from where he could keep watch on the building the only person under surveillance was himself.

Sauntering towards the pick-up he began poring over the junk. The fat one watched, expressionless. The waist-coated fellow stiffened.

*'Combien?'*

Tony pointed to the small, battered fridge. The big-gutted fellow raised a hand, fingers determinedly splayed. Five euros.

*'Nu, nu! Politia!'*

Fearing Tony was the police his companion reached to pull down the hand. Brushing his arm away the other persevered with the five fingers. Tony reached into his pocket and dug out a ten-euro note. The man made a show of fishing in his belt for change. Tony indicated not to bother.

*'Fait chaud. Vous avez quelque chose à boire?'* he asked, simulating a glass of beer.

*'Je vais voir.'*

Wheezing up from his seat the Roma went to the ruined fridge, opened it and returned with a can of something warm. Surreal… Tony took a swig, grimaced and glanced at the label. Lemonade, horribly sweet. He mopped his brow.

*'Je peux?'*

He indicated an empty chair on the pavement.

*'Bien sûr.'*

The fat one made a welcoming gesture. Tony took his seat, smiling weakly. This was going to be tricky. His spoken French was not good.

*'Vous habitez'*, he waved a hand round the spot where their pickup was parked, *'ici?'*

A shrug.

*'Ici n'y a pas de police.'*

No cops around here.

*'Pourquoi pas là?'*

Tony pointed to the deserted-looking tenement.

*'Y a des gens déjà. Regardez!'*

People already there. Look!

Tony turned in time to see a man accompanied by a young boy emerge from the tenement's shattered entrance and disappear along the street. From the back the man was slim, about thirty, steely-looking. He walked with the lithe gait of a jockey, turning out his elbows and swaying a little from side to side. The walk of the man he'd seen at the riding stables. Kasym, no question, Daudov's companion in the Camargue.

*'Là haut,'* the fat man stretched an arm towards the top floor. *'Ils habitent là-haut. Pas d'ascenseur! Pour moi, trop haut!'*

Too high for me, and no lift.

*'J'ai un ami là,'* Tony improvised, not too plausibly. *'Peut-etre lui donner le frigidaire? Je vais voir si'il est chez lui.'*

Finishing his drink and jabbing a finger towards his imaginary friend in the tenement, about to receive a clapped-out fridge, with a benevolent smile he got up, strolled towards the building, climbed through the broken door and into the hallway.

The smell on the stone stairs was of piss and worse. There were no lights or windows. Guided by a pencil-thin flashlight he'd brought he climbed the seven stories without stopping; his swimming regime was doing him good.

At the top were two doors, each with a metal grill, padlocked. On one of them a fearsome-looking poster, entitled *LEAN YOUNG WOLF*, was affixed. A singer, it seemed. *Just you try*! the hooded figure staring out at him from the gloom seemed to say. Tony went for the second door. A minute with his lock-pick and he was in.

Here there was light from a single window. He looked round. If this was Chechen poverty it wasn't so bad. The space was tiny and the furniture junk, yet there was a television, a new cooker gleamed in the kitchen alcove, and on the table there were schoolbooks and a handsome-looking laptop.

In a cramped back room stood an iron bedstead and a chair or two heaped with clothes. Opposite the bed was a wall cupboard, its doors secured, the padlock new. Picking it swiftly he peered inside. More clothes, books in Russian and Chechen script – and a bird. A falcon, stuffed it seemed.

He paused for a moment, smiling. The sight of it was unexpected and the way it stood facing him – head alert, glass eyes staring out fixedly, as if annoyed to be discovered in its cupboard – was somehow comic.

He shut the door, re-fixed the lock. Back in the main room he switched on the laptop and checked the website history. Homework programmes, model planes, toy birds… The laptop must be a child's, the boy he'd seen with Kasym. A quick check round with his Minox – papers in French and Chechen on the table, a family photo against what looked like a Chechen mountain background – and he was out.

Emerging from the building into the evening light, he looked around for the Roma but they'd gone, his five euro fridge with them.

In the main street he caught a taxi. The cabbie, a gnarled fellow with a stringy brown neck, was lively and a talker. It didn't need much to get him going.

'I gather you've got the Russian President coming to the Camargue,' Tony remarked, and that was it. The man launched into a soliloquy about the visit and for the rest of the journey scarcely stopped.

He was not enthusiastic:

'Coming for a private holiday, they say. Private? *Voyons, monsieur!*

The place will be crawling with cops. The gendarmes have closed some of the roads already, the Russkis have taken over a smart hotel and the rest of them are booked up with his guards and his officials. Too bad for the tourist trade… You a reporter, *monsieur?*

'That's right. I'm going out to the Camargue tomorrow, to get a feel for the terrain. See how he'll entertain himself.'

'He'll be shooting ducks, I imagine, and he'll get a good bag won't he, his goons will see to that, so he can pose for the cameras. Then he'll be off buying up property, like they all do. Scouting out a place for his retirement, way things seem to be going in Moscow. Seen the TV, have you *monsieur,* all those demonstrations? He's already got a place near St Tropez they say, but that won't be enough for him and his mafia friends. Not the kind of parties they give.

'There was one along the coast last summer, near Antibes. Pissheads got so drunk they started burning 500-euro notes, lighting 'em up and tossing 'em into the swimming pool for a laugh, telling the servants they could go in and get them if they wanted. Got a couple of 'em out, apparently, but they was all burned up. Two weeks salary gone up in smoke!

'That's what the French have come to. Scavengers, beggars, paupers – immigrants in their own country! But there you go, that's the way things down here are heading. First it's the Nazis wrecking the place in the war, then it's the *beurs* – it's what we call the Arabs, *monsieur.* Then the Chechens – *des gens féroces, monsieur, ah féroces!* – then the Roma, and now the Russians. Turning Marseilles into the arsehole of France between them, if you'll pardon the expression. Yes, a gangster city. Shoot-out between the lot of 'em would be the best solution…

'The Camargue's the right place for duck-shooting, mind you. Used to hunt myself, can't afford it now, the price of the ammunition alone… And now it's all regimented, not like it was. Pot one bird out of season and they're down on you like a ton of bricks.

'You hunt, *monsieur?* No? Well I'll tell you how we do it here. They have these hideouts – blinds they call them, camouflaged they are. Anchor them with these chains so they jut out into the lagoons.

Then they have these decoys, so as to fool the ducks. France is the only place in the world where they breed them live, you know that? It's for the quality of their voices, you see, *monsieur*?

'So there you are in the blind, waiting for the dawn flight of ducks. Nothing like it, *monsieur*, I can tell you! Take a bite to eat out there, bottle of cognac to keep you warm, it gets chilly in the mist… And when you've drunk your fill you can have a snooze in these cots they have while you wait, listen out for the call of the decoys…

'The flights come between dusk and dawn, dawn mostly, and when it's time to shoot they have these openings in the walls facing the water. Fold 'em down and boom, away you go! Then you've got plenty for your supper. *Ah oui, monsieur*, that's the life!'

'They'll have a special blind for the President I imagine?'

'Oh yes, you can be sure of that. Be like a camouflaged palace, I should think, full of caviar and vodka. Though they say he doesn't drink. What kind of a Russian is that?'

'You know this lagoon?' Tony passed him his map. 'Apparently that's where he's going to shoot.'

The driver glanced at it and passed it back.

'Yes, I know it. Used to drive for the guy who owns it, so he let me hunt on his estate. There's flamingos there too, artificial island they built for 'em in the middle of the lagoon. Russians will shoot them up too, I shouldn't wonder, they'll eat anything. If you want to go out there and have a look I can take you if you like. What time you want to go?'

Tony considered. He'd planned a trip next afternoon – though to do what, exactly? Watch them constructing the presidential blind – assuming he got that close? And what would be the point? In the tenement he'd found nothing, and on the Camargue the cabbie had told him all he needed to know. Another trip would take six hours there and back so he'd sacrifice most of the day, to no purpose. A good lunch and a siesta with Lisa would be more rewarding.

They had reached the hotel.

'Give me a card,' he said to the driver, 'and if I go I'll give you a call.'

*

'Successful trip?'

Lisa smiled up from her chair at her down-at-heel consort.

'Duty,' he sighed, stripping off his denim jacket. 'I did what I thought I had to, though why I bothered God alone knows.' He bent to kiss her. 'I'll get changed. Time for a walk and a drink before dinner.'

For the rest of the day Daudov, blinds and duck shoots were a long way from his mind. Lisa had caught the sun and looked vivacious in a bright new dress. It was another delicious evening. The only down moment came when they decided to stay another day and he rang Jean to warn her he'd be returning late.

'No problem,' his wife replied. 'You're lucky, it's miserable here, every day dank and chilly. So whatever it is you're up to don't let them overwork you. Make sure you get some sun and take a moment to relax.'

# 18

The President of the French Republic stood on the steps of the Elysée Palace, waiting. Against the ceremonial background – tricolours everywhere, the *garde republicaine* in full dress, sabres drawn – the President looked as he always did: small, grey, and anxious.

Only one thing was missing from the ceremony of arrival: the Russian President. Appearing too early on the steps of the Palace had been a protocol gaffe – the procedure was to stay out of sight till a split second before the cortège entered the courtyard from the Rue St Honoré – and the mistake was the host's. Eager to greet his prestigious guest – it was the Russian's first major visit to the West since the Ukrainian crisis – he'd disregarded the advice of the ceremonial officer to wait inside. Now he was stuck out there, in sight of the waiting press, and couldn't go back.

The minutes passed. An official appeared from inside the building and whispered into his ear. The French President nodded and began shifting from foot to foot, his eyes on the rooftops of the other side of the street, beyond the gaping gates. Anywhere but on the ranks of the press, where a murmur of surprise and impatience was spreading like a chill breeze.

'Always arrive late and be the first to speak. Know who used to say that? De Gaulle. Maybe our Russian visitor is taking his advice.'

The speaker was Raymond Baudoin, a freelance magazine correspondent and a rotund fellow. His remark was addressed to the young woman next to him, in a whisper that somehow carried. With a chuckle he added: 'Well our Russian de Gaulle's late all right, and he'll have plenty to say for himself, you can be sure of that! Once he's here our poor little fellow won't get a word in edgeways.'

A titter ran round the press corps, obliging the host to lift his eyes further, till he seemed to be imploring the skies for some *deus ex machina* to descend, preferably in the form of the President of all the Russias.

'It's intolerable, keeping him waiting,' the woman at M. Baudoin's side murmured. 'It makes Russians look like peasants. No sense of decorum.'

M. Baudoin glanced at her, an eyebrow raised. The young lady next to him with the deliciously haughty nose and a figure to haunt a man's dreams wasn't a journalist, and it wasn't the first time he'd seen her.

She was attached to the Russian Embassy, an interpreter doubling as an assistant press attaché, on loan from the London Ambassador because she spoke French as well as English and Russian. Also, he assumed, to give the ex-KGB colonel a bit of class, because apart from her more obvious qualifications she was a genuine princess. One reason M. Baudoin had taken a place next to her in the press throng.

He knew all this because the Embassy had approached the magazine where he wrote offering exclusive access for the trip south, the non-official part of the visit. While the President valued his privacy, the Embassy press attaché had explained, he knew how the French media worked and that an interview and photo opportunities would be essential.

The editor's choice had fallen on M. Baudoin because he was an experienced fellow, with the two qualities the story called for: a populist style, and no politics. Though in return for the exclusive the Russians had given him to understand the Embassy would expect sympathetic treatment.

He was still savouring his neighbour's remark about her leader's behaviour. The Russian President, a peasant? Even if he couldn't use it, the princess's comment intrigued him. He made a note to keep an eye out for Mlle Morensky when the talks were over and they travelled south to the Midi. A princess would speak her mind more freely than the bureaucrats you met on these occasions, give him less official bullshit.

At that moment the cortège swept in. While the principals did their handshakes and their waves and the cameras exploded, a colleague on the other side of M. Baudoin gabbled in his ear:

'We've been in the wrong place, *mon cher*. Missed a demonstration. Someone got through the barriers in the Champs-Élysées and made a dash for his car. That's why he's late.'

Finished with their waves and their smiles – the Frenchman's radiant with relief, his visitor's grim as ever – the Presidents turned to enter the building. In a gesture of false intimacy the host placed a hand on the Russian's waist.

As they retreated M. Baudoin whispered the news he'd heard in the ear of the princess, and asked:

'Sounds like somebody trying to disrupt the visit, *hein*? Who do you think is behind it would you say, *Mademoiselle?*'

'No idea,' Svetlana said stiffly, and walked away.

*

It was by accident that Tony saw the news of the Russian President's arrival on television that evening. Most of the bulletin was given over to a story about the Duchess of Cambridge's third baby (some routine infant illness) and if his wife hadn't been watching he'd have turned off the TV.

The incident in the Champs-Élysées came as the second item: an Asian man in denims vaulting a barrier, unfurling a banner and haring towards the motorcade so fast the goons in the car behind the President's scarcely had time to rugby tackle him before he reached it, scattering leaflets as he fell.

Instantly he thought of Daudov. Was this him? The first step in the campaign to foul up the visit? If so, it wasn't clever. The Russians would demand more protection, French security would tighten things up in Marseille and maybe round up Chechens for the duration, Kasym included. You could do that in France. On the other hand, why worry? If banner-waving and leaflet-scattering were all the million-dollar protests would amount to he could relax about whatever piece of foolery they were planning in the Camargue.

A later bulletin announced that the demonstrator was a Chinese immigrant, his leaflets demanding the return of territory in the Far East stolen by the Czars in the 19th century. So not Daudov. Still, Sasha would have enjoyed it. The close-up of the presidential face as a French plain-clothes man dived from a car, his revolver appearing for a second to point in his direction, was a gem: eyes like saucers, mouth agape, his teeth bared in a kind of skeletal smile.

*

While Tony watched the news Svetlana was walking in the streets behind the Boulevard Lannes, site of the ribbed concrete fortress that was the Russian Embassy in Paris, in search of a phone box. The call would be to Sasha's private mobile, and to avoid it being recorded on her credit card he'd told her to get herself a phone card – a *carnet téléphonique.*

Sauntering along the evening streets, glancing from time to time into dress shops or at her own reflection, she took her time. There was no hurry to get back to the embassy: the President was with his official interpreter at his welcoming banquet, no doubt bored as he always was on official visits, and as a non-drinker unable to take solace in the Élysée's most exquisite wines.

Though supposedly on call at the press centre till midnight, she was unlikely to be missed: until she did her interpreting in the Midi, her duties seemed to involve little more than hanging around looking glamorous. The rest of the time she was refreshing her hunting and riding vocabulary. Horse chat she could manage – she'd ridden as a child at the houses of French friends of her father – but duck talk? Blinds, decoys, mallards, pintail drakes, teal, widgeon – this was new.

A phone kiosk appeared and she stopped before it. Seeing her waiting the young man inside – black blouson, curly hair, a Parisian sharpie – lost interest in his call, intent on signalling through the glass that he wouldn't be long. *Oui, oui chérie, à bientôt,* she heard him say before slamming down the phone.

Holding the door open he came out and she took his place in the kiosk. After watching her fumble in her bag for her phone card he pushed open the door and said in English:

'You are English? I can help you?'

'*Absolument.*' Discovering her card, Svetlana rammed it into the slot without turning. '*Vous pouvez me foutre la paix.*'

('Certainly. You can sod off.')

The boy was searching for a comeback when the woman turned his way. The eyes that met his were full of such annihilating contempt that, lost for words, he stalked off.

Sasha replied at once.

'Er, Stephen here.'

She frowned: even his pretence of being someone else seemed cack-handed.

'It's me.'

'Darling, you OK?'

'Don't "darling" me. Just tell me what's going on.'

'Everything's fine, don't worry. All you have to do is keep me informed.'

'Anything you need me to tell you now?'

'I dunno. . Whatever's happening…' His voice seemed woozy. Had he been drinking? 'Like when you leave for the South, when you arrive, where you're staying, when you're going to be with him. And when he's going to do his, you know…When he'll be out there –'

' – OK OK, I get it. I don't know yet. They're still finalizing the programme. It changes all the time: who'll be with him, when he'll need an interpreter, when he won't. And you, make sure to keep me posted about what's going on at your end. I have to know when to be indisposed.'

'Yeah, right. So anyway, make sure to keep in touch when you're down there.'

'I'm calling from a phone box. I don't suppose they've got too many of those out there in the wild.'

'Well use your mobile. There'll be coverage where he's staying, won't there? Just statements of fact are all I need. Like where are you now?'

'They're putting me up at the Residence. I was supposed to be in some hotel but I complained, and the Ambassador – '

' – didn't dare refuse.'

'He's perfectly friendly.'

'Not too friendly, I hope.'

'I can handle myself, especially with some jowly old bastard who thinks he's God's gift. I'd better go. He says he wants to brief me personally.'

'Bet he does. Well, bye sweetie.'

'Bye.'

The briefing would be after the banquet, the Ambassador had said. She took a taxi to his Residence, the *Hotel d'Estrées* in the Rue de Grenelle.

'*Merde!*'

Fifty yards short of the street, the driver stopped and threw up his hands. A police cordon blocked his path. She paid, got out and marched towards it. Scanning her official pass briefly an officer gestured her through with a smile, then glanced over his shoulder at the imperiously stalking figure.

'Moves like she's on a catwalk,' he murmured to a colleague.

'Think she's his girlfriend? Supposed to be an interpreter, says on her card.'

'No idea.' His mate went on watching her, before shaking his head and sighing: 'Fucks like a dynamo I'd imagine, in any language.'

At the entrance to the residence, another security check. While she waited a commotion arose in the courtyard behind her. Sirens, motorbikes, pulsing engines – it was the presidential cortege returning from the banquet.

Inside the house, she lingered to watch. First in were the President and his guard. Leaping the steps two by two, the Ambassador panting behind him, he looked smaller than she'd imagined, scarcely as tall as herself. As they passed her in the hall the

Ambassador called ahead:

'*Gospodin Prezident!* Here is someone you must meet. Svetlana, your interpreter for your trip south.'

The President stopped, turned, snapped 'Later.', and strode on.

A private secretary, lean and anxious, approached at that moment to hand him a telegram. Stopping to read it the President shook his head, scowled and muttered:

'*Svinya.*'

*Bastards.*

Svetlana raised a brow.

'It's nothing,' the Ambassador murmured, smiling. 'Come along, the President is busy. I must brief you about our trip to the Camargue. Over a drink, perhaps?'

He led her through a colonnaded hall, along a passage and into the library, where they sat in Louis XV chairs, the Ambassador's bulk spilling over the sides. When a servant appeared with drinks he took a large cognac, Svetlana mineral water.

'The President seemed upset,' she said. 'Bad news from home?'

'The telegram?' The Ambassador made a swatting gesture. '*Nichevo!* I have seen it, it is nothing, nothing. Stupid, ignorant people causing trouble.'

'Trouble?'

'The demonstrations in Moscow, St Petersburg, they're still going. Before elections, always there are demonstrations. It is part of the democratic system. A few people will get their heads cracked is all that will happen – and they'll deserve it.'

Swilling back his cognac he called for more. After it came, he went on in a musing voice:

'Still, it is unfortunate. The problem it raises is this: would it look frivolous for the President to be amusing himself in the South of France when the Kremlin is besieged with riff-raff? Should he go back and oversee the situation personally?' He began to light a cigar. 'These are weighty questions. The President will be seeking my advice.'

His smoke alight, he leant forward.

'Come on, young lady, your ancestors must have had to deal with matters of state! So tell me, what would *your* advice to the President be?'

'My view,' she said coolly, 'is that a precipitous return risks over-dramatizing the situation. Also, the President needs a few days' rest, to conserve his energy for the electoral struggle ahead.'

'Bravo!' The Ambassador nodded, vigorously. 'My opinion exactly! You have a gift for concision! I shall put it to him in those very words!'

Tossing off half his second brandy he sat back and took a puff of his cigar.

'Have you ever thought of a diplomatic career? You clearly have the necessary judgment, not to speak of – '. His eyes swept over her figure, his moon face expanding in a smile. 'My London colleague is a lucky man! Interpreters are usually like schoolma'ams. The President will be delighted to be accompanied by a modern young woman. A statesman, a sportsman, a beautiful girl… You'll be photographed a lot down there. Together you will make an excellent image.'

With an expression of wistful appreciation, his eyes drifted from her face to her legs.

'The programme, Mr Ambassador. I wonder if we could discuss the programme? Where I need to be present to interpret, and where I don't. When they are duck-shooting, for example. That will be early morning, won't it? Will I need to be there?'

# 19

It was a Saturday and Alik woke in a torment of excitement. The previous night his father had told him that he and his mother would be flying to Canada the very next day.

'The immigration papers have come through,' he explained to his son. 'Now that we've got them we have to use them, quickly. So the flight's tomorrow.'

The truth was that the papers and passports Daudov had procured had been promised for a week earlier, so that they could get away well before the action. The documents would allow the family to settle in Quebec. They were keen on French speakers, Daudov had assured him, provided you arrived with enough to support yourself, and he'd promised to take care of that too.

'*Le Canada – demain? Fantastique!*' His eyes shining, Alik stared up at his father. A second later a shadow crossed his face. 'But tomorrow's a Sunday and I haven't told my teachers.'

Montreal was where they were going, his dad had said, and he'd looked it up on the Internet. *The City is located on an island…* A whole city on an island! If only he could tell his best friend Fabrice, who lived in a street close by.

'Can I go round and tell Fabrice? Then he can tell the teacher on Monday.'

'No you can't.'

'It's not too late. Why can't I just – '

' – I said no! I told you, I don't want you telling anyone. Anyone at all.'

It was nine in the morning. The flight, direct from Marseille to Montreal, was at seven that evening. His mother had been up since six, pulling their sparse belongings together in neat piles on the bed, all freshly washed and ready. Now she'd gone off to buy suitcases and provisions for the flight.

Alik had offered to go with her, help her carry the new cases, but his father had said no: he needed him to stay home and keep an eye on things at the flat. He had to go out himself in an hour or so, and wouldn't be back.

It was the last time he would see his wife before she left and before she went shopping they embraced. Alik stood watching. He'd never seen his father hug his mother so tightly. At the same time, there was a strange fierceness in his expression.

'We'll be together soon, I promise. The three of us. A new life...'

When his mother cried he hugged her harder.

'If only you would tell me why we can't go together. If only you would say...'

'There's nothing to tell you,' his father interrupted sharply, pulling his face from hers. 'How many times have I told you? I have things to tie up here, then I'll come.' Putting a hand on her neck, he pulled her back to him, his face softening. 'Just don't worry. It's all arranged. Someone will meet you, give you money, take you to a place to stay. You and Alik, you'll be fine.'

'I'll take care of you *maman*,' Alik echoed.

When his mother went off to buy her cases, his father retreated to the bedroom and shut the door. From the way he closed it and the sounds Alik could hear – a soft tapping, exasperated exclamations – he knew he was at work on the falcon. It had been like this for days.

He waited in the room. His father had been locked up by himself for more than three quarters of an hour and there was no sign of him coming out. The lavatory led off from the bedroom. Going in there when the door was shut was forbidden, and he needed to pee, badly. When he could hold out no longer, he went downstairs and began pissing in the entrance to the house. Only *les dégénérés* fouled up the hall like that, his dad told him, but what was he to do?

Halfway through he heard footsteps. Squeezing as hard as he could, he was buttoning his fly when his dad, treading cautiously, appeared on the stairs carrying an old suitcase and a box. He looked at his son, then at the puddle behind.

'I had to, I couldn't hold out.'

Setting his box and suitcase down with deliberation, his father took a step towards him. Alik half turned to the street.

'*Viens ici.*'

The boy hesitated.

'*Viens, je te dis.*'

The boy came towards him. He was still a foot away when his father reached out and grabbed him. Struggling feebly in his arms, he waited for the blow.

'*Ça fait rien, mon petit. Ne t'en fais pas.*'

*Never mind, don't worry, it's nothing.*

A hand seized his chin, raised his head. A kiss stamped his forehead and for a long moment an unshaven cheek pressed close to his.

'*Alors, au revoir, mon fils. Je t'aime, tu sais?* Do whatever your mother tells you, *hein,* till I get out there with you. Then we'll be together, all of us.'

Alik looked up at him. His father's eyes were wet and glistening. He'd never seen them like that.

'It's only a few day, right?' the boy said stoically, as if to soothe him.

'Maybe more. It's hard to say. There are things I have to finish before I can come. Grown-up things.'

Another kiss, then picking up his suitcase and his cardboard box he went towards the door, skirting the puddle of piss. Alik watched him go from the dark hallway into the morning sunlight of the street. With the back of his hand he wiped away the trace of his father's tear.

Upstairs he didn't go into the bedroom to check – he didn't need to. He knew what was in the suitcase and the box. No chance of his falcon coming to Canada.

*

Kasym walked from the tenement, his loads held steady at a prudent distance from his body. Passing the Roma camped at the end of the street, he hurried a little. The fat one gestured forlornly:

'Something for us, maybe? We give good prices!'

Ignoring him he walked to the next corner, glanced behind him – except for the Roma, the street was empty – and turned into the main road. Twenty metres along, an ancient Peugeot was parked. He leant in at the driver's window.

'The boot. Open the fucking boot.'

Daudov pressed a button. Taking them to the back of the car and padding them round with old blankets so they wouldn't shift he stowed his suitcase and his box and got into the back seat.

'Brother,' Batir's hand clasped his arm warmly. 'You have it? All is well?'

'Fine.'

He leant forwards towards Daudov.

'Remember what we've got in there. Watch out for potholes and don't throw the car about. Don't drive like a Russian!'

'Or a Chechen,' Batir added, which for him qualified as a joke. He seemed in a relaxed mood, his brother noted, happy to think of himself as a martyr in the making.

Touchy as ever, Daudov threw up his hands.

'You want to drive? Or you want me to?'

'I was only saying, take it easy.'

'I know, of course I know. We've got a lot of running about to do before we go out there. Stuff we need to pick up en route.'

'Plenty of time,' Kasym confirmed. 'We don't want to get there before nightfall.'

All afternoon they chased around the city picking things up: rubber boots, a groundsheet, some food, beer and water. Finally they drove out past a petro-chemical complex to what looked like a deserted warehouse beyond the city. When they stopped Kasym and Batir made to get out of the car. Daudov signalled that they should stay inside.

For thirty-five minutes they waited. What was Daudov up to?

The silence, Batir's patient, beatific face, uncertainty about why they'd come to this out-of-the way place – the wait began getting him down. Feeling the needle at work on his brain, his lip began twitching.

He got out of the car, swallowed a pill greedily and lit up a fag. It was when he threw it down half-smoked near the back of the car, without thinking, that the reality of where he was and what he was doing came to him. In the boot, a few feet from where the cigarette had fallen, a bomb was lying. Lurching towards the glowing butt, he stamped it out.

'You smoke too much, brother,' Batir called from the car window. 'It's really bad for you.'

*Smoking, bad for him?* He felt an urge to laugh. Instead he stared at the sun's reflection on the boot, imagined the heat building up around the falcon, wondered what might happen if they had an accident or hit a pothole. His brother was worried about smoking and they were driving about in a car that might go up any moment.

Though better to go that way than spending the rest of his life in jail. With the pain in his head came a moment of panic. What they were doing was crazy. How had Daudov talked him into it, and how could he and Batir go through with it, and stay calm? Should he leave them to it, walk across the empty parking lot to the busy road beyond, hitch a lift, get back to his family, change his ticket and fly out with them to Canada that evening? His father would understand...

At that instant, Daudov left the warehouse and came towards him, carrying a bulging plastic holdall.

'What's in there?' Kasym asked as Daudov stowed it in the boot.

'Change of clothes. Show you later. You'll love them.'

They got back in the car. After his pill he felt calmer, and as the afternoon went by and the night approached he did his best to stop the tension building, ignoring the tightness in his chest as he ticked off the hours till next morning. Fourteen more till dawn...

It was after six before they set out for the Camargue. As good as his word Daudov kept to a prudent speed, even when they'd crawled through the evening traffic and got onto the motorway.

'A little faster,' Kasym muttered when they reached it. 'The road's smooth enough and we're holding up the traffic. We don't want to draw attention.'

With a sigh Daudov took the Peugeot up to a hundred and ten.

# 20

The state visit to Paris was one of those international events where nothing seemed to have been accomplished yet everyone described as a great success. A reminder that *La France* remained a power in the world, a leader in *Le Figaro* exulted. For all the bad memories of the Ukrainian affair and the protests building up in his country, like it or not, the Russian leader was here to stay, and no amount of moralizing about human rights would change that.

In his press conference that morning in the gilded opulence of the ballroom of the Hôtel d'Estrées, the President said nothing to disrupt the conciliatory atmosphere. Cheered at the prospect of his stay in the Camargue, he was in upbeat mood. No question, he'd told the Ambassador over breakfast that morning, of giving a bunch of shitty-arsed demonstrators the satisfaction of seeing him scuttle back home in a panic.

After his statement, the questions came. Asked by a right-wing paper about the demonstrations and his prospects in the elections, the President shrugged and smiled:

'Last time I remembered to enquire, they told me they were pretty good.'

Had his stay in Paris been fruitful, a tame Russian reporter wanted to know?

'Certainly, I learned many things. Even the drive to the Élysée Palace was instructive. I read the leaflet a Chinese man seemed anxious for me to see. Very interesting, though you must excuse me if I feel unable to respond positively to the invitation to give away several million square kilometres of our Russian territory in the Far East to our Chinese friends.'

Amongst the correspondents present only the representative of the *People's Daily* declined to laugh.

Svetlana didn't laugh either, though no one saw her. Declining the Ambassador's invitation to 'embellish the front row of the audience with your presence,' she stood towards the back of the room, on her own, as if to distance herself from the proceedings.

A mistake. The moment she took up her position Raymond Baudoin edged in her direction. Seeing him approach she prepared to move away: as well as his other non-attractions Baudoin, she remembered, suffered from a bad case of halitosis.

Too late.

'*Alors Mademoiselle!* We met at the Élysée, remember? I gather you will act as interpreter on the trip south. You have interpreted for the President before?'

'No.'

'Maybe you are a hunting expert? A horsewoman – or a shooter of ducks?'

'I ride.'

'Wonderful! Together you will make a charming picture. You in your riding outfit and the President – who knows, maybe bare-chested?'

'It's October.'

'Ah but he is manly, very masculine!'

As he spoke the expression on the young lady's face hardened. She seemed bored, aloof, exasperated even. Because she saw her role as interpreter as beneath her? Assuming that was all she was... Baudoin, a specialist in lurid gossip, had his doubts. Maybe the remark that had escaped her when her boss turned up late at the Élysée, he'd begun thinking, told you something about the two of them? You didn't say your President was behaving like a peasant unless you knew him. The way she'd said it, as if she'd been alone with him, was like a lovers' quarrel...

The President and the princess. It wasn't so outlandish. At home he was bringing back imperial ceremonial – Czarist uniforms, Czarist balls – so why not a Russian princess to call his own? Fantasy perhaps, but it would make a good story, and when the moment came there could be a fine piece to be written.

Excusing herself with the look she'd worn when she'd made her remark about him – how seductive a princess's anger could be! – Svetlana began moving away.

'*Dans le Midi*,' he called after her, 'we shall meet again in the Camargue. Your press secretary has given me exclusive access, you know that? So remember – anything you wish to convey about *Monsieur le Président*, I shall be there. A great leader of men, *Mademoiselle*. I congratulate you for being chosen to work so closely with him.'

\*

The press conference over, it was clear that the President was impatient to start out on his travels, yet always there was something more. Before leaving, the Ambassador had prevailed on him to give a morale-boosting address to the Embassy staff. Again the ballroom was packed as the President went through the motions: your invaluable work, your inestimable contribution to the Motherland, our whole country is in your debt...

As he stepped down from the dais he turned to the Ambassador:

'That was like a mass demonstration. How many were there?'

'Everyone, Mr President. Absolutely everyone turned out to see you.'

'I know that. I'm asking how many?'

'Including wives?'

'Everyone. How many people have we got out here sucking on the state's teat?'

The Ambassador turned to an aide before answering.

'All in all about three hundred and fifty, I should say.'

'Absurd. I want that cut by a third. There is a limit to how much of our hard-earned foreign currency the government can spend on diplomats and their dependents living it up abroad.'

'A *third*?' The Ambassador swallowed. 'Including our *advisers*?'

The last word – a euphemism for intelligence personnel – he

spoke softly.

'How many do you have?'

'About 80, including technicians.'

'Not enough. I want more. We get better stuff from them than from all those smarmy diplomats with their four-hour lunches. So beef up the advisers and reduce the diplomats in proportion.'

'Certainly, Mr President.'

*

'It is as you said,' the Ambassador told Svetlana. 'The President needs a rest. Formal occasions are not his forte. He gets bored, so he's not in a good mood.'

They were sharing a car in the cortège that was racing to the military airport at Villacoublay a dozen kilometres southwest of the capital, from where the French President's personal Falcon 7X would fly them south.

'Do what you can to humour him,' he went on, 'assuming he speaks to you. I know him of old. You have to feel your way. Don't chatter at him, in some moods he prefers silence.'

'I can be silent too.'

'I'm sure you can, my dear girl, though if he wants to make conversation you must respond. Talk to him about your grandfather. He is interested in the old days, sometimes he sounds nostalgic for them. He loves the residence, it was built by the architect of Louis XIV, you know that? Perhaps I should have laid on a ball. Then you could have danced with him.' As if of itself, involuntarily, a pudgy hand brushed her knee. 'And with me, Svetlana, and with me.'

On the plane he sat opposite the President, who for a long time read in silence. Looking up suddenly he said:

'Petr Ivanovitch, tell me, what are you doing here? Why are you coming south?'

'I thought it would be a good opportunity for us to discuss the follow-up to your visit, *Gospodin Prezident*.'

'There's nothing to discuss. The follow-up will be in Paris, not the Côte d'Azur. Or maybe it's for the weather that you're coming? Is that what we pay you for, Mr Ambassador, to enjoy the weather?' He looked over his shoulder at the seats behind. 'And who are all these people? I gave clear instructions. I am having a brief holiday, I don't want to be crowded by officials. Only my security people, my secretaries and the interpreter. That is all. Understood?'

'Absolutely. I shall ensure they will not be in the way. The interpreter is traveling with us. Shall I introduce you? Just so you know.'

'Briefly.'

He went back to his telegrams.

The Ambassador raised a hand to summon Svetlana from her seat in a row near the back. Unbuckling her belt she walked, indolently, towards the front of the plane. One by one the heads of the security men behind her inclined, imperceptibly, into the gangway.

Reaching the President's seat she stood beside him. A twitch of his nostrils at her scent suggested he had registered her presence.

'*A kto vy?*'

*And who are you?*

With frowning eyes, he read on.

'Your interpreter.'

'Ah yes I'm told you're a princess. A genuine one I hope. Do I kiss your hand?'

He didn't, nor did he shake it, though he did look up.

'I gather we're going riding and shooting together. Maybe you're a hunter too? With young women today you never know.'

Her reply was a chilled smile.

A private secretary delivered more papers.

'It seems I have work to do. Well, I'm glad we met. We shall see each other down there.'

Svetlana returned to her place. The Ambassador sat frowning. There had seemed to be an instinctual chill between them. It wasn't him who'd suggested Svetlana for the job, the idea had come from London, and perhaps it was a mistake? Did the President think she was a haughty ex-aristocrat, who looked down on him? He could be sensitive about his origins. He leant towards him.

'She wasn't my idea, *Gospodin Prezident*,' he began. 'It was London. But it is good she is a young woman, because in France, the press…'

'I know about France, Mr Ambassador. And the press. And women.'

He went back to his work. The news was not good. A new poll recorded a steep drop in his popularity (*an apparent reverse*, in the telegram's words) on account of the failing economy. The oil price was wobbling again, and from Beijing came the news that *The People's Daily* had reprinted the Chinese demonstrator's demand for the return of the lost territories in the Far East, without comment, rather prominently.

Finishing the batch of papers he returned them to the folder, looked up and snapped.

'So where's that interpreter? Why isn't she here? I must give her instructions.'

The Ambassador summoned Svetlana back. Again, she stood over them.

'Your full name?'

'Svetlana Ivanovna Morensky.'

'She is the offspring of illustrious ancestors,' the Ambassador put in.

'*Former people…*' The President sat back in his seat, his lips tight, his eyes sardonic. 'You know the expression? That's what we used to call folk like you. Former people. People the Revolution deprived of their dominance in society and their luxurious lives. But none of that was the fault of your generation. Now you serve the nation.'

'From London,' the Ambassador came in. 'She helps my colleague in London, but her French is perfect too.'

'So you are an émigrée.'

'Not exactly.'

'You can't live in two countries at once forever. Even oligarchs have to choose.'

'I have chosen to serve my President. That is why I am here.'

'*Khorosho.*'

He stared from the window. For a few minutes nothing was said.

'Shall I tell you something about this plane?' the Ambassador volunteered.

'If you must.'

'It's a good story. When the first one was delivered to Nicholas Sarkozy, he got into trouble because they spent more than 100,000 dollars equipping it with state-of-the art ovens. A scandal! The press said he'd done it for his wife, so guess what they called the plane?

'Tell us.'

'They called it *Carla One.*'

The Ambassador grinned. There was no answering smile.

'After Carla Bruni. His wife, *Gospodin Prezident.*'

His boss turned from the window.

'You are wrong, that was not this plane. It was his long-haul plane, an Airbus A330, and its cost was 80 million dollars. You see, Mr Ambassador, you do not have to live in luxurious residences abroad to know things. We can buy a foreign newspaper, or cheaper still look it up on the Internet.

'As for Carla Bruni, I have met her, at conferences here and there. She's not bad, but we have our own beautiful women. Speaking of which, how can you leave a lady standing? Or do you think it demeaning to surrender your place to a princess?'

The Ambassador got to his feet, flushing. There being nowhere else to sit, he moved to a seat in the body of the plane. Coolly, Svetlana took his place.

They began talking about France, the Camargue, the riding she had done in her schooldays, London… Svetlana appeared respectful of his rank, though in a mechanical way, no more, while the President looked his normal self: by turns surly, offhand, and occasionally agreeable.

For two people who to outward appearances felt little interest in one another it was a long conversation. At the end of it, when they touched down an hour later at the Istres-le-Tube military airbase north-west of Marseille, Svetlana looked as she had at the beginning: as if she conversed with heads of state every day of her life.

# 21

'*The Russian leader arrived on schedule this afternoon at Marseille military airport aboard the French President's personal Falcon 7X.*' the car radio reported.

'Soon wish he hadn't,' Daudov said under his breath from the driver's seat.

'*He was met by the Mayor of Marseille and other officials,*' the announcer continued. *There were demonstrators outside the airport but no disturbances. Monsieur le Président is going straight to the Camargue for his holiday, where security is said to be tight.*'

'Tighter than a rat's arse,' Daudov sniggered.

As Kasym and Batir had discovered on their reconnaissance trips, it was true. In the weeks since they'd spotted it, access to the blind had been sealed off, checkpoints blocked the roads and gendarmes ringed the shore of the lagoon. A jetty had been built out in the direction of the blind. Behind it lay open meadows, now a prohibited area.

The closest they could get, Kasym had worked out over several visits, would be a field beyond the shore of the far side of the lagoon, a remote spot that could only be reached through rice paddies, waterlogged terrain and a wilderness of reedy marshes. For their purposes it was close enough.

The place where they'd planned to leave the car was an abandoned riding school. A doomed venture that had gone bust in the recession, it stood at the end of a weed-covered track several kilometres from the lagoon. The stables, for thirty horses, were occupied by nothing but a wrecked car and a pair of wild ponies foraging for scraps of hay. At the Peugeot's approach they galloped off, their long white manes flowing raggedly in the breeze before disappearing in the penumbra.

The reception building, half-demolished to salvage the tiles and timber, was no more than a shell. Kasym had wanted them to spend the night there, but Daudov had said no: better to leave the car here, walk through the paddies and marshes beyond and camp out in the wild till dawn. They'd argued about it, as about everything else, but eventually Kasym had agreed. He didn't feel strongly, he just didn't like being bossed about.

They stowed the car alongside the wrecked one in the stables so it would be invisible from the air. When they'd taken the stuff from the boot Batir fetched leaves and twigs to drape over the roof, artfully, so it appeared like a wreck as well.

'So here it is.' Daudov displayed the holdall he'd got from the warehouse. 'My little surprise.'

As he opened it the others stood watching.

'Brilliant!' Batir breathed when he pulled out three gendarmes' field uniforms, one by one. Everything was there: the kepis, the dark blue jackets and trousers, high boots, belts, the whole show. The belts held holsters complete with the SIG 9 mm pistols that gendarmes used, but unloaded; a discovery that prompted in Kasym a feeling of mild relief, he wasn't sure why.

Holding up the pants and jackets to gauge their width, and after selecting a size for himself, the Georgian tossed the others to his companions. Stripping off their clothes they clambered into them. For Kasym there was no problem: with his wiry build and close-cropped hair in uniform he looked neat and smart. Daudov's fitted, though he had trouble keeping his long hair under his kepi: bits kept straggling out, giving him a slovenly look. For Batir, securing the top buttons of his pants was a business.

'OK,' Daudov said when they'd finished, 'so how do we look?'

The three of them stood peering at one another in the near-darkness. In his stretched jacket and tightly belted trousers Batir seemed comic, a harlequin policeman, though no-one laughed. After surveying him carefully Kasym tucked in more of Daudov's hair, muttering:

'Maybe you should take out the earring. With the kepi it doesn't look right.'

Grunting, Daudov complied.

'And these leather boots, they'll be no good for the marshes. Better carry them with us till we get to the field.'

Tugging on rubber boots they set out, trudging and wading through rice paddies, damp meadows and waterlogged fields. It was weeks since Kasym had last reconnoitred the route – he hadn't wanted to be around too close to the visit – and now that the days were drawing in it was darker, a ground mist was forming and the trek to the place he'd selected for their camp seemed longer than he remembered. Noises you didn't hear or notice during the day – rustlings, croakings, the night song of birds, a plane high overhead – seemed louder.

After walking for forty minutes, Kasym in the lead with his suitcase (the box he had entrusted to Daudov), they stopped to let Batir catch up. Somehow he'd ended up with the heaviest gear. Finally he loomed alongside, panting.

'How far now?'

When Daudov turned to reply, Batir started: beneath his kepi was an alien's face. He was trying out his night-vision goggles.

When he'd first shown them to Kasym, the Georgian had been unimpressed.

'What's the point? If the dawn light is bright and the mist's not too thick, I don't see we'll need them.'

'Have you any idea how far you can see with these things? Of course we'll need them! Firstly to keep an eye on the blind at night, secondly for accuracy when I'm guiding it down.'

A frozen silence, then:

'*You're* guiding it down?' Kasym glared. 'Who said it would be you? I've spent weeks practising, you spent what – a couple of days? It's not some fucking game. We'll need pinpoint accuracy. Get it wrong by a few feet and the whole thing's buggered.'

'It won't go wrong,' Daudov had come back, breezily almost. 'I've got a good eye for these things.'

Boasting was part of the Georgian's style, though it was true. Daudov had practised for three days and learnt quickly, as adept at getting close to the plastic boat near the beach after a few dozen goes at the control box as the Chechen himself.

But their quarrel had been about more than just accuracy. For Kasym there was something else. For him guiding the bird to its target would be a personal business, like pulling the trigger on a gun. A squaring of accounts for his father. For that reason the row about who would do it had been a long one.

'And whose idea was it to use the falcon?' Kasym had asked, his mouth tight with defiance.

'And who came up with the cash? Not just for the bird, the whole operation. Fucking hundreds of thousands it cost – most of it for your Canada papers. And it's not finished. How are you going to live when you're there?'

There'd been no answer to that. Kasym swore and he raged, but it was hopeless: Daudov was adamant. It was he who would guide the bird down, not Kasym, and that was that.

'So how far is it?' Batir repeated, after dumping his gear to grab a rest.

'About three kilometres from the stable to our camp. We're halfway there, so about another three quarters of an hour. Bit more maybe. Depends how much dry ground there is.'

They went on in silence. After another twenty-five minutes sloshing and slipping about, they reached firmer ground.

'You saw the demonstration?' Kasym asked Daudov while they stood resting. 'The Chinaman in Paris? The TV had this close-up of his face through the car window, when the French security man pulled his gun. Terrified he was, must have thought the guy was going for him!' He pointed to the suitcase he had laid on the dry grass. 'When that thing's heading in his direction he'll have the same look. Pity there won't be cameras.'

'There'll be journalists around, don't you worry,' the Georgian assured him. 'He won't want the world to miss the macho President shooting his ducks. Oh yes, there'll be cameramen all right.' Daudov laughed. 'Trouble is, we'll blow the bastards up!'

Kasym went silent. Journalists, on the blind, at dawn? He hadn't thought of that. Would they be Russian or foreign? Either way he didn't want any dead journalists. Daudov must be wrong, the blind was too small, there'd be no room.

They walked on. To get out of earshot of Batir, Kasym drew Daudov along faster. He needed to double-check the arrangements for his wife and boy, be sure they'd be looked after if anything went wrong.

'The money…' he began.

' – when it's done.'

'I know, I know, I don't mean mine. I mean in Canada, for the family, when they arrive. Who is it who'll meet them at the airport? He'll give them enough to live on, won't he?'

Plodding on, Daudov gave something between a sigh and a groan.

'I told you, it's all fixed. It's a meet-and-greet service for immigrants. They'll meet them with a placard, with the new names on the visas. Then they'll take them to a place to stay and give them some cash.'

'And the papers? You're sure they're all right? They only came through yesterday – the last moment. They're flying out tonight.'

'So they're getting away. What's the problem?'

'And you're sure the visas will be valid? I read they're getting hot on Chechens over there, after the Boston marathon thing.'

'You won't *be* Chechens, you'll be Russians. And don't start telling me your boy doesn't speak the language. That's because he's been brought up in France. Just stick to the story – and that part's true.'

'And how long before I can join them?'

'How long is a rope? Till it's quiet, that's how long. Till then it's Nice. I don't know why you're worried. No one will bother you there and you'll be with your ethnic family. There's more Chechens in Nice than Marseille, you know that?'

'And Batir, you're sure – '

' – Batir we have discussed. You go, he stays. In Nice. Batir has no profile. He'll be fine, and whatever happens Allah will take care of him. That's what he keeps telling us anyway.'

Daudov marched on.

'And what about you and Klara? She must be getting close. Is she still here?'

Daudov's frown deepened. He hadn't wanted Kasym to know about Klara's pregnancy, or for them to meet, but she'd come across them one day in the café and had had to be introduced.

'No, I've sent her away.'

'To have the baby?'

'Yeah, the kid.'

It would be a boy, Daudov knew by now; a fact that had helped reconcile him to fatherhood.

'All these questions. You're making me nervous. The less we know about each another's problems the better for both. How about we concentrate on what we're doing?'

After fording a ditch they emerged into a large field. By now the darkness was closing in. Daudov stopped, rigged up his goggles and stared ahead.

'They're terrific! I can see every detail. For me it's like midday out there. Here, take a look.' Kasym fixed on the goggles and peered into the distance. Miraculous. Daudov was right to have got them. They were within sight of the lagoon now, and the trees on the far shore seemed as clear as the field before him. Where the ground was a little higher they'd be able to see as far as the blind itself.

The pain that had been threatening to start up again in his head receded as he felt a surge of hope. The plan was going to work.

# 22

It began with something Mikhail said after a couple of drinks one evening in his office.

'You see what happen in France? That Chinaman on television? I see him and I think – why he do that? No one do demonstration about Siberia before. Then I think – someone pay him. Maybe Daudov – one of his trick! Maybe Sasha still in touch? Sasha not around, I don't know where he is. In France, you think?'

'He's been traveling I gather, though as far as I know not in France. And he's been spending more time in the castle,' Tony explained, 'finishing things off.'

'Why he not tell me where he go?'

'No idea.'

Because since his father died he's been cutting you out of his affairs, was the true answer.

'I hope he not mixed up in nonsense over President. You not let him, no?'

'Don't worry,' Tony soothed. 'I've had my eye on it. Checked out a couple of things. He'll probably have a bit of a go, you know, with pamphlets and the press, too good a chance to miss. But no reason to panic.'

'Is good.'

Mikhail was on his sofa, one leg on a chair. After Grekov had departed his suits and ties had gone too: as always now he was dressed in baggy pants and an open-necked shirt. With little to do except to guard the cash in his safe after Sasha had appointed someone of his own as his manager-in-chief, he'd lost energy, let himself go. For the moment he was pretty much out of commission with a bad case of gout. Not that it affected his consumption. 'It not drink,' he'd told Tony, 'it hereditary, in genes.'

The gout wasn't all. There'd been a heart scare too. One way or another he seemed in a poor way. Russians like him tended to die in their late fifties, Tony had read: Mikhail was 59 and it looked like that's where he was heading. His state of health was another reason he hadn't bothered him with his suspicions about Daudov and his trips to Marseille. No point in worrying a sick man for nothing.

The Chechen connection, though troubling, seemed to be boiling down to very little. The papers he'd photographed in Kasym's flat he'd had translated, courtesy of Dick, and had turned out to be nothing more than a half-finished draft of an anti-Russian pamphlet and a letter from his mother in Grozny thanking him for some money he'd sent her. Nothing sinister.

Though it was some time since he'd been down there and tomorrow was Saturday, the day the presidential party was due to arrive. Ought he to check out Kasym's place again, if only to cover his back, and see if there was any sign of Daudov? Flying down there again would be a drag, and this time he couldn't take Lisa: she was off for a day or two staying with her mother.

On the other hand keeping Sasha out of trouble was what Grekov was paying him for, and now that Mikhail had focused on the state visit, if anything went wrong it wouldn't look good. So maybe one last trip, tomorrow, when the President arrived, to be sure…

*

The same hotel, the same pantomime with his jeans and trainers, the same reaction from the cabbie when he told him where he was going in the northern sector of the city (*'Vous avez du courage, Monsieur!'*)

He'd taken the earliest flight out so as to fit in a return trip in a day. Shortly before eleven he got out of his taxi in the main road and walked to the back-street tenement. As he approached the Roma's pick-up drove off, leaving a ravaged-looking armchair in the gutter, as if to reserve the space.

The entrance to the tenement was deserted. Skirting a fresh pool of piss he mounted the stone steps to the top floor. Ready with a variety of stories, depending on who opened, he knocked.

No reply. He knocked again, waited. Nothing – though the grill was open. Was it abandoned? He rapped one last time, harder.

'*C'est qui?*'

A young boy's voice.

'*Un ami de Monsieur Kasym.*'

The door, on a chain, opened an inch or two. Alik's face peered out, frowning.

Who was this? Another of his father's mystery friends? At least it wasn't one of the *dégénerés*, and he didn't sound Russian.

'*Je suis Americain,*' Tony said, in explanation of his overdone accent.

An American! Something to do with the trip to Canada?

'What's your name, *jeune homme?*'

'Alik.'

'Well Alik, is your father there?'

'No, he's gone out.'

'Ah. A pity. I owe him some money.'

He took out a fifty euro note and held it up. 'If I don't give it to him your father will be angry. *Tiens!*'

He thrust it inside the chink.

The boy eyed the note, stepped back and shook his head. Tony smiled, engagingly he hoped.

'And your mother, is she at home?'

'She's coming back later.'

'Well I'll give the money to her. Can I wait?'

'If you want.'

Alik let the American in, re-chained the door, hovered by the table. Tony stood in the centre of the room, looking round. The bedroom door was ajar and the wall cupboard was visible. It was open and empty, with no sign of the stuffed bird.

'Your dad out riding again is he? Hunts in the Camargue, doesn't he?'

'No, not any more.'

'Did he shoot that bird you had?' he persisted, for something to say.

'No, he didn't.'

'A falcon, wasn't it? Beautiful creature.' He looked round. 'I don't see it.'

'I think my father's selling it.'

'Ah, a pity.'

More minutes passed.

'When do you think he'll be back, your dad?'

'I don't know.'

'And your mother?'

'Maybe an hour. Maybe more.'

The boy stared at the floor. His brown eyes had darkened, he was troubled. He shouldn't have said that about the bird. His father had said not to tell anyone. In fact he shouldn't have let the American in at all.

Tony went to the window and peered through the grimy glass at the ravaged townscape. Another aborted journey. Dead ends didn't come any deader. Where did he go from here? Standing there waiting the fatuity of his position struck him. If he couldn't get onto Kasym, there'd be no hope of discovering what Daudov had planned. If the pair of them had gone off together they'd be out in the Camargue, preparing to sabotage the shoot, or whatever the hell they were up to. And there was sod-all he could do about it.

Behind him, Alik looked anxious. Now he was worried that the visitor might ask to go to the toilet, which would mean walking through the bedroom. Out of the American's eyesight, on the bed behind the door, their clothes were laid out waiting to be packed. And his father had said not to tell anyone they were going, anyone at all.

He wanted the man out.

'My mother, she could be two hours, more. She didn't say.'

Tony turned from the window.

'Maybe I'd better come back. What would be a good time?'

Alik shrugged:

'You can, *monsieur,* but I don't know when.'

'Well, I don't think I can wait. I'll just leave the money here.' He put it on the table. 'You'll give it your mother, OK?'

'*Oui monsieur.*'

Nice young kid. Intelligent-looking, and polite. His dad must be proud of him. With a son like that it was hard to believe Kasym would be up to anything serious.

'*Alors au revoir.*'

When he patted his head at the door, Alik flinched.

'*Au revoir, Monsieur.*'

He was halfway down the stairs when he heard the boy calling from the top landing.

'The money, *monsieur.* Who shall I say it's from?' Tony didn't reply.

'Was it for the bird, *monsieur?*'

Tony hurried on down.

At the hotel he got out of his slumming clothes and, resolved against spending another evening on his own, checked out and headed for the airport.

He should never have bothered coming. Did he care if Daudov and his pals succeeded in fouling up the presidential break? Not in the slightest. As to the extent of Sasha's involvement he preferred not to know – and whatever it turned out to be Grekov would never know either.

He was early for his four o'clock plane, which turned out to be delayed by another hour and forty minutes. As consolation for his wasted day he treated himself to a generous late lunch, and a good bottle. After that he strolled around the airport shops, where a pair of extravagantly priced loafers caught his fancy.

The plane was delayed a further hour, and it was seven before he boarded. Then they were stuck at the gate. It was while he was watching the French in-flight news over a complimentary glass of champagne that he saw Svetlana. It was a report on the state visit, the moment the President had arrived at the Marseille military airport that morning.

Emerging from the plane in dark glasses and casual wear, he made a brief statement to the press about the wonders of Provence and the Camargue, whose world-famous horses he was looking forward to riding. Responding to a question about his impressions of the French President, he said he'd found him in the best tradition of French leaders, adding with a rare smile that he was here for a short vacation and would spare its inhabitants any politics during his stay.

Svetlana interpreted for the President, including the smile. She was dressed in a light off-the-shoulder dress and the camera lingered on her longer than seemed necessary. As the two of them stood at the microphone Tony stared at the screen, scarcely able to believe what he was seeing. Somehow he had never taken the possibility that she would interpret for the President seriously – he'd assumed she'd been bragging – and for the first time the reality of what was happening struck him.

Sasha was a rich idiot in league with Chechens who were planning God knew what. And his girlfriend, in on the preparations, was about to spend four days at the President's side. And here he was flying home, leaving them to it and hoping for the best.

He ought to have stayed on in Marseille – though to do what, exactly? Sit around and fret? He was fretting already. When the attendant came to take away his champagne glass he asked for a double whisky, neat.

'After we've taken off, Sir.'

It seemed an age before they crawled to the runway and were airborne, and the whisky came.

# 23

The hotel the Russians had taken over for the presidential party was a sumptuous venue, in the style of a Provençal mas. All rose-tiled roofs, creamy arches and flowers, it stood at the end of a long private path well away from the tourist trail.

Svetlana stood on the balcony of her room in her riding hat and jodhpurs. After a spell of poor weather it was a fine day, fresh yet sunny, and the President was due to go for his first ride that afternoon.

She hadn't spoken to Sasha since she'd left Paris. With a car to herself she'd intended to ring him on her mobile during the ride to the hotel, but had left it too late; outside the airport area the coverage had been intermittent. Despite the presence of security men two or three rooms along the corridor, she rang him.

'Stephen? It's me.'

'How are you doing?'

'Fine. I've just arrived.'

'So you've met?'

'Yeah, we met.'

'And?'

She frowned into the phone.

'And what?'

'Nothing.' Sasha hesitated. 'I just wondered...'

'We're starting off with a ride. They've kept the tourists from the area so it's all ours, apart from the security.'

'It's tight I suppose?'

'Naturally it's tight.'

'And the ducks? When do you go hunting?'

'Tomorrow morning. I've been mugging up the vocab.'

'But you're not out there shooting with them, right?'

'Nobody's given me a gun or showed me how you do it, so I doubt it. You have to wear camouflaged clothes and I haven't got those either.'

'So it's certain. You won't be out there with them?'

'I suppose not. Just his security men I imagine. After all it's a private visit. And you?'

'Me?'

'Yes, you.' She waited a second. 'I'm asking you what you've been up to. You've been busy I imagine?'

'Yeah, busy getting on with things.'

'Good. So there's nothing new. Nothing that I should know.'

'No. Everything's fixed, pretty much.'

A knock at the hotel door.

'Sorry, I have to go.'

'Well, have a nice visit. And don't forget to keep in touch. Any changes – '

' – I know, I know.'

'Bye darling.'

'Bye Stephen.'

She opened the door.

'Bonjour, *Mademoiselle*.'

It was the French journalist. She must have looked startled.

'We have met. Raymond Baudoin! I came down in another plane.' He held up the photopass round his neck. 'You see, I'm offi-cial! I have a room in the hotel. Exclusive access!'

Her face morphed from exasperation into a welcoming smile.

'Of course. Well, come in. Have a seat.'

Charmed, M. Baudoin entered and sat down.

'You've come down with a photographer?' she enquired.

'Sadly not. It would have been good to have our own profes-sional pictures, but no...' He shrugged. 'Your press people said they'll provide them, it's part of our deal. Shots of him galloping around like a cowboy, I imagine. But the interview, it's guaranteed.'

'And where will that be?'

'They haven't told you?'

'Not yet.'

'It'll be out there on the blind, I gather, first thing in the morning.'

'After he's shot his ducks.'

'Well of course after.'

'So we won't be out there when he's shooting?'

'Not that I know.'

'So we'll meet for your interview, M. Baudoin. Meanwhile, how can I help?'

'*Mademoiselle,* I am a professional. You do not go into an interview with a man of his eminence without doing your preparation. Perhaps you can help to set the scene.'

'I'm an interpreter. I can't talk about politics.'

'Politics are not what I need. Only some background.'

'Background is fine. What would you like to know? I have a few minutes before the riding starts.'

'Allow me to say how splendid you look in your outfit.'

Svetlana looked back at him, stony-faced. M. Baudoin took out his notebook.

'I'm interested in how the President appears to young Russians. The New Russians, as they say.'

'Ah, that part is simple. Gorbachev, Yeltsin – Russia has had a tumultuous three decades, so people see him as the only man who can hold the country together and push it forward.'

'Forgive me, but everyone says that. A woman with your background, who lives in London and has seen the world, maybe you find him a little…'

'A little what?'

'I don't know. Unsophisticated.'

Svetlana's eyes widened.

'Not at all. Outspoken perhaps, but unsophisticated? No.'

'But at the Élysée, when he was late you said – '

' – oh, that was nonsense!'

It *was* nonsense, careless nonsense. She'd had her reasons for saying the President had made the Russians look like peasants, but she'd gone too far. It was why she'd let the journalist in, to correct any false impressions. Smiling half-sadly, half-playfully, she went on:

'Monsieur Baudoin! You're disappointing me! As a Frenchman I thought you would understand…'

'Understand what?'

'How with people you admire you become very critical if you feel they're letting themselves down… When he was late I was nervous for him. Afraid what the press might say, that my President would make a poor impression. But of course it was nothing to do with him. At the time I didn't know about the Chinaman…'

'*Mais bien sûr je comprends.*'

He made a hurried entry in his notebook.

'Another thing. People say that you are a princess.'

'Oh, that!' A modest, dismissive gesture. 'Technically I suppose it's true, but in the new Russia things like that no longer matter.'

'Ah, but not entirely, *Mademoiselle,* surely? How does it feel to be a princess serving a former KGB officer?'

She shrugged. 'Well he *was* in the KGB, and long ago my family were nobles. But Russian aristocrats were patriots and the President is a patriot too. He's not a narrow man, a vindictive man, he doesn't think in primitive social terms. His perception of history is broad, philosophical…'

She stopped. They were speaking in French and she felt herself getting carried away, a little flowery.

'And personally, *Mademoiselle,* personally how do you find him?' He gave a sly smile. 'We know he is susceptible to women. And women to him.'

'M. Baudoin!' Svetlana appeared shocked. 'What are you suggesting?'

'Nothing at all! It's just that, I mean, a beautiful young woman, a princess. He is a man – very masculine! He must be, you know, attracted.'

'His behaviour is very correct. He conducts himself like *un homme d'état.* A statesman.'

'If you say so, *Mademoiselle*.'

'I do.'

Svetlana tightened her lips, suddenly aloof. Russian princesses in the Czarist days, the Frenchman thought, sensing the chill, it must have been terrifying.

'Which leads me to another question. Does he mind you living abroad?'

'It's not something we've discussed, but why would he? Russia has come out into the world, London is full of Russians.'

Svetlana looked at her watch. She'd done enough to mollify the man, she decided. Why spend more time with this oily, malodorous slob?

She stood up.

'I'm going to have to go. The ride will be soon and the President will need me.'

M. Baudoin rose.

'It would be good to talk again, when you have a moment. And some pictures perhaps.' He patted his jacket pocket. 'I have no photographer but I brought my camera, just in case. Later in the visit, a few more words and some pictures? *Vous permettez?* It would make a good introduction to the interview. How Russia has come to terms with its past. How the old class preoccupations have gone, the hatreds have disappeared. *Une belle histoire*,' Baudoin concluded, his features folding into an unctuous smile. 'A fairy story almost, with a princess as heroine!'

'Let me think about it,' she said, sweetly. 'Now it's time for our ride.'

*

The stables the Russians had taken over for the President's outing were ringed by concentric circles of security. On the perimeter of the buildings a handful of military were skulking, their boots and fatigues incongruous in the bucolic gathering, their automatics a jarring presence.

Next came a posse of gendarmes on motorbikes, their peaked caps giving them a purposeful air, though apart from periodically revving their engines there was nothing for them to do. Russian goons with earpieces and stern, immobile faces formed an inner ring, leather jackets bulging and mobiles clamped to their mouths.

At the centre of it all was the President. Unlike the suits and uniforms surrounding him his outfit was informal. Dressed in helmet, riding boots, combat trousers and a sleeveless shirt rather too light for the crisp October weather, at that moment he was resisting the offer of a stable-hand to give him a leg up onto his horse.

Svetlana was at his side.

'*Le Président n'en a pas besoin,*' she snapped at the boy, motioning him away. 'He can manage. He's an experienced rider.'

As stable hands, photographers and officials pressed around the President's horse and a mêlée threatened, Svetlana took charge. Striding to a microphone set up nearby she announced:

'Gentlemen, move back a little, *je vous en prie,* give the President space!'

With a curt gesture she waved back the security men and summoned forward the small press party, so the cameramen could record the President mounting his steed all by himself.

Everyone obeyed. When he had swung up into the saddle and the photographers had had their fill, she turned towards a waiting figure.

'*Et maintenant, mesdames et messieurs, je vous présente* Monsieur Pascau Troupelen,' she announced into the microphone in French and Russian.

Some sixty years old, the Frenchman in question was in ceremonial garb: moleskin trousers, black velvet jacket and wide-brimmed hat, his hand gripping a long trident.

Monsieur Troupelen stepped up to the microphone. A fine, Provençal figure, a little stout now, his high colour owed as much or more to his drinking habits than to his outdoor life. Not that there was much of his face to be seen: a large moustache, almost achieving walrus status, obscured the lower half.

He was here because it was he who had been selected to make a welcoming speech. It was a natural choice. There was nothing about the wildlife of the Camargue – birds, horses, ducks or bulls – that M. Troupelen did not know or wasn't willing to explain at length. Smoothing his moustache and addressing himself to the President in his saddle, he took from a pocket the speech he had worked on long and hard, complete with humorous touches, and began:

'*Monsieur le Président de la Russie! Bienvenue dans notre pays!* Permit me to inform you that I too am a President: *Président de l'Association des Gardians de Camargue.* And please let nobody call me a French cowboy! Permit me also to inform you about the horse that you have done us the honour to select for your ride.

'The Camargue horse is not a horse like any other, but one of the oldest breeds in the world. For centuries they had lived wild in the harsh environment of the marshes and wetlands of the Rhone Delta. There they have developed the stamina, the hardiness and agility for which they are renowned today.

'How do I know this, you may ask? Because the Camargue horse is the traditional mount of the *gardians,* of whom I am honoured to be the President, as I have said. It is also the horse who for centuries has herded the black Camargue bulls used in bullfighting in southern France…'

Svetlana translated, briefly. The stable boy, trying not to snigger, held onto the horse's bridle. Irritated by the flashing cameras, the President leant down to his interpreter and said in a terse voice:

'How much more is there? I'm not a statue.'

'…Camargue horses are accustomed to living in salt water,' Troupelen went on. 'They are in fact often called horses of the sea…' He paused to turn the page.

'Excellent,' Svetlana cut in. 'The President wants you to know how interested he was in what you had to say and how much he looks forward to his ride with you.'

She indicated to the stable boy to let go the rein. The boy looked at M. Troupelen. After taking in Svetlana's steely smile, the Frenchman nodded and tucked away the remainder of his speech in a pocket.

'*Payehali!*' the Russian cried, and spurred his horse forward. 'Let's go!'

Nobody gave way. Scowling, the President rode straight for the rings of security surrounding him, forcing them to scatter. Stable boys brought up two more horses. Mounting swiftly, Svetlana and M. Troupelen followed.

The moment the three riders passed beneath the arch leading from the stables the motorcycles revved, the security men leapt into a car, the soldiers headed for their lorry and a clutch of cameramen scrambled for their beach buggy. Hearing the cacophony behind him the President reined in his horse and wheeled round.

'It's like an army,' he said to Svetlana, frowning. 'Tell them one photographer – our Russian – and one protection officer. They can share the buggy.'

Svetlana translated.

'*Merde alors*', a French photographer grumbled, exiting the buggy. 'I come all this way for nothing.'

The army reduced to five – the President, Svetlana and M Troupelen, followed at a respectful distance by the buggy – the party set off along the narrow road. Behind them officials, journalists, security personnel, gendarmes and soldiers, deprived of purpose, milled around aimlessly.

The track they followed led through rice fields and meadows. For a kilometre they rode at walking speed till they reached some shallow water on the shore of the lagoon. Led by M. Troupelen, they rode to the edge. On a signal from the President, they stopped.

'Wait for the cameraman,' he told Svetlana. 'We have to get it done.'

The beach buggy approached slowly, bumping over the rough terrain. Climbing out, the Russian cameraman set up his gear. This done, he turned to his President, grinning:

'*S obnazhennoy grud'yu, Gospodin Prezident,*' he called out. 'Topless. Like in the mountains!'

'You see who gives the orders,' his boss smiled at Svetlana before stripping off his shirt. From a silver chain an Orthodox cross dangled over the white, hairless skin. After glancing down at himself he turned towards the camera.

'And the helmet,' the cameraman called. 'No helmet!'

The President took it off, revealing sparse, slicked back hair. The cameraman studied the shot through his lens.

'The hair is too neat,' he called to Svetlana, lifting his eye from the aperture. 'It needs to be wild. Ruffle it.'

Svetlàna looked at the President, who smiled back, shrugging.

'I told you. He's the boss.'

Steadying her mount, she leant towards him. A smell of lemongrass came from his half-naked figure: advised that mosquitoes lethal enough to get through bull-hide swarmed the marshes, even in Autumn, and knowing he would be topless, he must have sprayed himself, liberally.

As she approached the President inclined his head as if for a benediction. Reaching out a hesitant arm – there seemed not too much hair for her to disarrange – with the tips of her gloved fingers she ruffled what there was.

'Now ride away a couple of hundred metres and gallop towards me. Not you – ' Svetlana and Troupelen had begun turning their horses around – 'just the President.'

He rode off. Steering his mount into the shallows of the lagoon, he turned towards them and with an exultant shout spurred it forward. Too hard. Rearing and stumbling, almost jolting him from the saddle it threshed around wildly before finally finding its footing. Then it shot forward, its hooves slapping the water. Thrown backwards by the sudden impetus, his face and chest soaked by flying spray, the President leant forward a little too far, as though clinging to his mount.

'*Opiat – medlenno nemnogo!*'

Again – but slower! the cameraman called out when the rider stopped, wiping the salt water from his eyes. The President obeyed, nodding and walking his mount to his starting position before turning and riding back at a canter.

The photographer, still unhappy, frowned and called out:

'Could we just – '

' – that's it, anything else you can edit.'

'*Khorosho, Gospodin Prezident.* That's fine, just fine.' Svetlana caught the hint of a sigh in his voice. 'Now we do a still. With the gardian, and the lady.'

The three of them shuffled their horses into line. Posing between Svetlana in her riding gear and the Frenchman in his splendour, the President, his wet hair splayed over his brow, looked like some delinquent brought to book. To perfect the incongruous image, he was grinning.

'And with the princess,' he said when it was done. 'A small piece of history. The princess and the President. Not for the press, for a souvenir.'

'*Niet, niet...*'

Modestly, Svetlana turned her horse away.

'I insist,' he said, with a sweep of his arm intended to be gallant.

Composing her features into a smile, one that contained something approaching a hint of condescension, the princess permitted the photograph to be taken. Next to her imperiously upright figure, this time the President resembled a villager encountered while out riding on her estate.

\*

Two hours of riding through meadows and marshes and they headed back to the stables, three abreast. The visitors talked in Russian as they rode. Left out of the conversation, Troupelen fell back, disconsolate; since they'd left the stables the President hadn't addressed a syllable to him.

'I think our French friend is unhappy,' Svetlana said quietly. 'Maybe a word, *Gospodin Prezident?*'

He turned to the Frenchman.

'Tell me, Monsieur – '

' – Troupelen,' Svetlana supplied, translating.

'Tell me, your horses, how is it they are always grey?'

Brightening, M. Troupelen drew abreast.

'*Monsieur le Président*, I shall explain. They are born with a hair coat that is black or dark brown in colour, but as they grow to adulthood it becomes ever more intermingled with light hairs until it is completely white. Yours, M. *le Président*, is a splendid example. Observe his short neck, deep chest, compact body, strong limbs and full mane and tail, and intelligent eyes…'

'I need to translate,' Svetlana interrupted.

'*Interesno*.' The Russian nodded absently when she'd finished.

'And our bulls, *monsieur le Président*,' the Frenchman hurried on, 'I must tell you about them too. The thing about *les taureaux de Camargue* –'

It was as far as he got. Spurring his horse forward, the President trotted ahead with Svetlana. Indicating the reeds and bamboo lining the road, tall enough to hide a human figure, he leant towards her and said:

'We must be careful, young lady. Hedges have eyes and ears.'

'Of course, *Gospodin Prezident*.'

A few metres further he said, idly it seemed.

'You have read Turgenev, *A Sportsman's Sketches*?'

'Of course I have, *Gospodin Prezident*. It got him arrested, but it helped liberate the peasants.'

'It is the book that made me into a lover of the countryside.'

For a while he went on about his Russian travels. Svetlana waited patiently. She had something to ask. When he stopped she said:

'So will you need me tonight?'

He shot her a look flecked with humour.

'Tonight?'

'For the duck shoot. Your secretary told me you may decide to go to the blind after dinner and stay out there all night.'

'Maybe I will, maybe not. I'll see. There may be work to be done. It depends on the news from Moscow. And you, young lady? Perhaps you aren't available? Maybe you have a rendezvous? With a Frenchman, perhaps. Please give him precedence.' After smirking at his joke he went on. 'The interview is when I shall need you, with the French journalist, when the shoot is over. Only for the interview. Otherwise there is no need.' He frowned. 'He didn't tell you that, the secretary?'

'It wasn't clear.'

'Well it is now. Till then you can get some sleep.' He smiled. 'If anything changes, they'll wake you.'

'Don't hesitate. Whatever you wish, *Gospodin Prezident*, I shall be ready.'

# 24

'There it is.'

Kasym took off the goggles and handed them back to Daudov. 'What?'

'Our camp.'

The place Kasym pointed to a few hundred metres away was a triangle of grass in the corner of a field beside a dry stream bed. On two sides a hedgerow of bramble and tall bamboo shielded it from view. Overhead rose a cluster of juniper branches.

When they reached the base of the tree he set down his suitcase, gently.

'Good spot, eh? Nice and flat.' He nodded towards the meadow. 'We'll need a smooth run for the launch. And the tree, see?' He pointed at the juniper. 'Aerial cover.'

Daudov looked around, nodded, and reverted to scratching his neck.

'Fucking mosquitoes.'

'They like your fine skin,' Kasym said.

'I'm a Georgian, Georgian and Chechen, not some fucking Russian.'

'Like some spray?'

Looking like a porter with his bags and his kepi Batir plodded up at that moment, put down his burdens wearily and reached into his trouser pocket. Daudov took it, with no thanks, and squirted his face and neck.

They changed from rubber waders back into their gendarmes' boots. Batir unpacked the ground-sheet and spread it out. The three of them sat down and stared round. It was past ten, the approach of night quickened by a light, rasping wind and a clouding sky.

'A drink,' Daudov announced, reaching for the bag of provisions.

'Not for me.'

Batir gave a virtuous shake of his head.

'We know, we know,' Kasym grunted at his brother.

'Here's to our success,' he said, clinking cans with Daudov. 'We come by darkness, and we go at dawn. In the mist.'

Daudov grinned.

'So you fixed that too, eh?'

'It's the pattern this time of year,' Kasym rejoined tersely.

Finishing his beer he reached for the night vision goggles, strapped them on and climbed the juniper. Some grew to six metres, this one was less than four, though high enough to command a wide view across the level landscape.

From his perch near the top he looked out over the patchwork of un-worked fields and marshes leading to the lagoon. Beyond its kilometre-wide surface, interrupted by the islet for flamingos, he focused on the reeds carpeting the approach to the far shore. Amongst them he picked out the blind he and Batir had spotted.

The soldiers who'd built it had done a good job of disguise. Its roof was a tangle of reeds and branches, the walls camouflaged with netting, the openings onto the lagoon closed and shuttered. From a distance it looked like an abandoned, overgrown hut.

After five minutes he came down from the tree. Daudov said:

'And so?'

Kasym grinned beneath his goggles.

'I saw it.'

'What?'

'The blind. Clear as day.'

'Don't tell me,' Daudov smirked. 'So clear you can see him pissing in the lagoon.'

'There were people visible, on the shore by the jetty. Security folk I suppose. They'll be watching out too. Which means we don't smoke.'

Peevishly, Daudov stubbed his cigarette.

'What else?'

'They have a flat-bottomed boat to liaise with the shore. I even saw the guy who rows it, snoozing in the back.' Unstrapping the goggles he handed them back. 'You're right, they're amazing. The darker it gets the better you see.'

'American,' Daudov grunted. 'Generation 3. Best you can get. So good they're embargoed.'

'So how did you get them? They must have cost a fortune.'

'Why do you need to know how much they cost?' Daudov had gone prickly again. 'You're not paying, are you? If money falls from the skies you don't ask who dropped it.'

'OK, OK.' Kasym frowned at his slip. From the moment Daudov told him that he had a backer, he'd been careful not to enquire what anything had cost or where the cash had come from, especially for his family's passports and visas, or the hundred and fifty thousand euros he'd been promised.

He made a note to watch his words. Daudov could be a moody fellow, light-minded and jokey one moment, snappy the next. What was lacking, it came to him suddenly, was the rage against their target he himself often felt. All Daudov would do was swear at him, followed by a shot of spit as though to cleanse his mouth of his name, and reminisce about volunteering for army service just in time for the 2008 invasion of his country.

Then it would be stories about the house-to-house battles he'd fought in South Ossetia and the Russians he'd killed – fifteen by his reckoning – while cursing the Georgian government for surrendering before he could shoot some more. He would vow to revenge his fallen comrades, yet Kasym had never heard from him the anger he himself felt for the Russian leader. Maybe your dead comrade had to have been your father, and you had to have seen him die.

Daudov was leaning back against the juniper, his kepi on the back of his head, his hands crushing his empty beer can. Batir, on his knees in the grass a dozen metres away, had worked out the correct direction, improvised a mat, removed his gendarmes' boots and was busy with his prayers.

Maybe he should offer up a prayer himself, Kasym thought, watching him: pray for Allah's help in destroying their enemy and for his deliverance from danger when it was done. He decided against. Religion was no part of the enterprise, and as for praying for success, Batir had done it for him.

*

It was getting on for eleven, time for supper. By mutual agreement they'd put off eating till late. The idea was to not feel famished in the morning, when there'd be no time for food.

Daudov unpacked dinner, consisting of a foot-long baguette sandwich apiece, squashed tomatoes, cheese, and bruised fruit for dessert. When he handed round the fare Batir peeled back his sandwich to peer inside.

'Ham!'

'Oh God, I forgot. Well just don't eat it,' Daudov growled. 'You can get your own fucking food next time.'

'I'll have it.' Kasym picked the strips of meat from their bed of butter, then turned to his brother. 'It's the gendarmes you want to be afraid of, brother, not a slice of ham.'

'Of the gendarmes I have no fear,' Batir said in his high, quiet voice, so at odds with his size.

Kasym gave him a troubled look. His fearlessness wasn't feigned – that's what worried him.

'So you're not afraid,' he snapped. 'Well we are, because we'd prefer not to get caught, so on the question of life or death you're outvoted two to one. And when we're getting away, don't you forget it. We don't want any heroics.'

'Easy now,' Daudov interjected.

Kasym bowed his head, contained his anger. It was easy to play the martyr if you had no wife and son. Ideally he would have preferred his brother not to have come, to have kept him out of the whole business, but he'd been in it from the start and Daudov had insisted. His idea was that Batir could act as porter and runner. He needed to stay in touch – he wouldn't say with whom – and out here in the wild they'd be incommunicado.

The stables where they'd left the car was in range of a transmitter covering a small town nearby, they'd established, and a mobile had been left in the car to receive messages. All it needed was someone to make the trek there and back during the night to pick them up. Another job for Batir.

They finished their food without talking, a silence punctuated with the calls of night herons, eagle owls and the low coarse croak of frogs. Kasym kept his head down, ate quickly, then sat pining for a cigarette. Batir chewed his bread slowly, his eyes staring round, entranced, it seemed, by the darkness. The moment he'd swallowed his last mouthful Daudov said:

'Time to check the mobile.'

'OK, I'll go and look.'

Pulling on his rubber boots laboriously, Batir hauled himself to his feet.

'Any messages,' Daudov said, 'just remember them. You don't try to reply, you just remember. Right?'

'Of course. And if there's no messages do I send anything?'

'I just want you to text *It's a fine night.*'

'And the address?' Batir asked.

'There's two. Whisky, and Santa. The same two addresses the last message was sent to. Whisky and Santa. Can you remember that?' He looked at him, doubting. '*It's a fine night.* Nothing else. To the same two addresses. Got it?'

'Of course.'

Batir stood over him, hesitating, a hulking figure in the dark. He was thinking: and if there turns out to be a message with a question and I'm not allowed to reply, even if I know the answer, does that mean I have to make the trip again? Another three hours walking?

He stood fingering his chin, something he did endlessly now that his beard had gone, as if perpetually shocked to find it naked. Daudov looked up at him impatiently.

'What's the problem?'

'Nothing.'

'Well, off you go then.'

When he'd gone Daudov grunted to Kasym:

'It's code. Just to confirm we're here, everything's fine, no problems.'

# 25

That evening Svetlana had dinner at the hotel with the presidential entourage: the cameraman, the goons, communications men, Kremlin aides, Embassy officials – though not the Ambassador, who'd been instructed to return to Paris.

Pumpkin soup with chestnuts, onion tart, wild boar – the local specialties the hotel served – found favour with the visitors, though not the Provençal rosé; too light for Russian tastes, it was scarcely touched. As the vodka they'd ordered in its place took its hold and decorum was relaxed, there was a joke or two about the President's hunt next morning.

Why wasn't he going out to the blind for the shoot, an Embassy man asked the cameraman.

'Misha said I'd be in the way,' the fellow shrugged. 'No photos till he's got his bag. Not that there'll be any problem. Misha will machine gun the little bastards if necessary!'

Misha, the protection officer, shot the cameraman a sour look. A burly, shaven-headed fellow, he was chewing through a second helping of wild boar, hurriedly. The President was intending to spend the night on the blind and Misha was due to go out later, to relieve a subordinate who was there now.

'The blind's a bit small, that's all,' Tobin, the presidential secretary in charge of the arrangements explained. A youngish man gaunt with worry, he seemed prematurely aged. 'He enjoys the feeling of freedom, of being alone in the wild. So it'll just be him and Misha out there, the President has confirmed, once he has completed his work.'

'So what's happening at home?' the cameraman asked.

'The demonstrations are continuing.'

'Pity the Cossacks can't ride into them with their sabres,' the cameraman sighed. 'That would show the stupid fuckers.'

'Watch your peasant language,' Tobin indicated Svetlana, 'we have a princess at table.'

Svetlana looked at him as if he didn't exist.

'And he's still doing the interview, right?' The press secretary looked anxious in his turn. 'After the shoot. With the Frenchman.'

'Yes, a dawn interview. In his fatigues, with his hunting gun, the sun rising behind him. A perfect setting.'

'It'll help take people's minds off the demonstrations,' the cameraman threw in.

'That's the point,' Tobin snapped. 'To put them in perspective. Focus on the country's international mission.'

'Your idea, was it?' someone teased.

'Actually,' Tobin replied, primly 'it was.'

A silence. The secretary wasn't known for having ideas, he was known for turning them down.

He focused on Svetlana.

'You'll have to be on hand for that. Promptly. You'll be there in time, won't you?'

Her reply was a withering look. He gazed at her a moment.

'Are you feeling all right? I must say, you don't look too well.'

Svetlana felt fine. Her pallor was because she'd spent ten minutes before dinner applying near-white *blanc de perle* powder to her healthy cheeks, and around her eyes a touch more kohl.

'Of course I'll be there for the interview. It's just that I can't stay up all night,' she said with a toss of her head. 'I need my sleep.'

'We all do, young woman,' the secretary chided.

'My name is Svetlana Ivanovna,' she rapped back smartly.

'As you wish.' The secretary flushed.

She had placed herself next to Misha, the lowest-ranking person in the room. With the others she was chilly, with Misha she was more friendly.

'So there'll just be the two of you out there, the whole night.'

'That's right.'

'It's quite a responsibility.'

'There's plenty of backup on shore. Our guys, the French…'

'But if someone comes at you from the water. I don't know, a speedboat or something.'

'Like in a film, you're saying?' Misha almost smiled.

'Exactly. Then it would just be you.'

'There are patrols, and they've sealed off the lagoon.'

'And overhead?'

'We've got that covered.'

'The sky, the water, having to watch over everything, you'll be awake all night. I don't envy you.'

'Can't leave him unguarded.'

'So he'll have a nap you think?'

'I should think so. Hasn't had a rest all day. All that travelling and riding.'

'I suppose you never drop off yourself.'

'We're trained not to.'

'Do they give you pills? Truck drivers take amphetamines, don't they?'

'We don't take drugs, we don't have to. As I say, we're trained.'

'I see you're not drinking.'

'Part of the job.'

'A tough part, isn't it?'

'The boss not drinking himself makes it easier.'

A few minutes silence then she said:

'You'll have to excuse me. I think I might have an early night. I have a bit of a headache. Maybe we'll meet in the morning. Meanwhile I'm sure everything will go well.'

'Me too.'

They exchanged smiles.

'And may I say how much I admire your professionalism and dedication.'

Misha didn't blush or say 'well thank you.' He simply nodded and went back to work on his wild boar, as if fielding compliments from pretty young princesses was all part of his training too.

Once in her room, she rang Sasha.

'Stephen here.'

'Hello.'

'So how's it going?'

'OK. We went out for a ride, and I've just had dinner.'

'You must be exhausted. Make sure you get some rest. You're not on night duty, I hope?'

'No. I told you, I won't be needed.'

A pause from Sasha.

'Hello?'

'Yeah, I'm here.'

Another pause. He's forgotten, she thought. Forgotten their code, forgotten what they'd arranged to say to one another when she rang for the last time before the shoot. She'd written it down for him phrase by phrase, but he'd forgotten. Drunk or drugged, probably.

'You don't sound too with it,' she said, sharply.

'I'm fine. I'm just a little…'

A third pause. She imagined him in his armchair in his father's office, a glass of whisky at his side, a cigarette on the go, groping for his crib. Finally he must have got it, and began:

'So how are things?'

'OK. It's a fine night.'

*(Everything's on track.)*

'The weather must be warm down there.'

'Warmer than I expected.'

*(Is the duck shoot still on for tomorrow? Yes it is.)*

'So you won't need all those clothes.'

'Well, it's chilly in the early morning.'

*(He'll be out there for the dawn flock of ducks.)*

To give him time she paused before adding:

'It can be even chillier on the lagoon.'

*(He'll be spending the night on the blind.)*

From Sasha's end, more silence. Then:

'Yeah, right.'

She was about to find words to convey that there'd be just one guard with him, then thought, why bother, what difference will it make? It would only confuse him.

'So that's all my news,' she said, curtly. 'I'm off to bed.'

'Take care, darling. I – you know – really mean it.'

'I will. Everything will be fine. Bye Stephen.'

# 26

It was almost three in the morning before Batir returned. A sad sight, he was limping, one leg soaked to the thigh and his gendarme's uniform torn and awry. He must have slipped into a ditch in the dark.

At the sound of his approach Kasym looked up swiftly.

'So brother, anything there?'

'A text message.'

'Saying?'

'*It can be even chillier on the lagoon.*' He looked down at them blankly. 'That's all it said. It hadn't come when I got there, it came after I sent your message saying *It's a fine night.* I waited to see if there'd be a reply, and that was it.'

He tipped back his kepi and made an effort of concentration.

'I remember which one replied. It wasn't Santa, it was Whisky. Definitely Whisky. From Santa there was no reply.'

He waited before adding forlornly. 'Doesn't make a lot of sense, does it?' He looked down at his soaked trousers. 'I won't have to go back with a reply to their reply, will I?'

'No you won't.'

Batir sat down to drag off his rubber boots and pants.

Daudov was looking contented. Whisky was Sasha. From Santa there would be no reply. Santa was for information only.

Kasym was curious to know who the recipients were but knew better than to ask. Outside contacts Daudov kept strictly to himself. Though he couldn't prevent himself saying:

'Anything I should know?'

'Nothing important. Just means he's staying the night on the blind.'

'Well, that's important, isn't it? I mean if it's certain he's staying the whole night out there we don't have to wait till morning.'

'What are you saying? That we should do it now?' Daudov spat, disgustedly. 'That is a shit idea. Forget it. We stick to what we agreed. We do it at dawn.'

'Why not now?'

Daudov cast up his hands in exasperation.

'For one thing the duck flight will give us cover. Otherwise they may spot it coming. OK, he's there now, but things can change. What if he's called away in the middle of the night to deal with something at the hotel, and we blow up an empty blind? No, best wait till we can be sure he's there. Till we can see the bastard with his head out of the window blasting away at his fucking ducks.'

'Maybe I'll take another look. See what's happening.'

Kasym got up and fixed on the goggles. Climbing the juniper he drew aside some branches. After ten minutes staring across the lagoon he scrabbled down the tree a little too fast, slipping as he neared the ground and tumbling on his back.

'It's true, he's there,' he panted, struggling to his feet. 'I saw him! Saw him! They have these openings for shooting and he put his head out. I could see him as if he was standing in front of me. He was wearing goggles.'

'Night vision, like yours,' Daudov drawled. 'Maybe he was looking back at you?'

'Then I saw someone coming out of the blind, a woman I think. A car was waiting, took her away. To the hotel I suppose.'

'A whore, probably.' Daudov grinned. 'High class tart laid on by his thoughtful hosts. Serviced the President and off she goes. She good-looking?'

'Couldn't see, she had a shawl on, against the cold. Could be anyone. A secretary bringing papers or a cook bringing food. They eat out there, don't they, hunters on blinds?'

'You are right, brother,' Batir threw in. 'It must have been a secretary or a cook. Certain.'

Daudov turned to him, puzzled; it was the first time he'd taken notice of anything Batir had said.

'How do you know?'

'Because if she'd been a whore Allah wouldn't have allowed her to escape before dawn.'

'Of course,' Daudov replied, with mock solemnity, 'of course.'

'The point is he's there,' Kasym mused. 'You said we should be sure, and now we are. So why are we waiting? Why don't we do it now?'

'And how am I supposed to guide the fucking bird in the dark?'

'I can do it,' Kasym said sharply, 'with the goggles.'

'But *I'm* bringing it down, that's been settled. And I'm doing it in the light! We're waiting for the ducks, end of story!'

'But that was the plan before we could be sure he'd be there at night,' Kasym persisted. 'If we do it in darkness it'll be easier to get away.'

Batir shook his head sadly.

'Brother, you are too anxious to cling to life. We should stick to the plan. At dawn we'll see everything. Allah will reward our courage with the spectacle of his death. The bird of vengeance plunging from the sky, the blind in flames, the ammunition exploding! Then we can enjoy our revenge for our father's martyrdom! But only if we are full of the spirit of selflessness and sacrifice...'

There was more. Daudov smirked but said nothing. Kasym's eyes were on his boots. The reason he wanted to do it now was one he could not have explained. It wasn't just to escape in the darkness – the police would have night vision too – it was something he felt deep in his gut: a gnawing impatience, mixed with fear. On top of that his head was beginning to ache.

He was still counting off the hours. It was nearly three. Four more to go, four whole hours in which anything could happen. Gendarmes could check out the derelict stables, discover the car. If they did they'd find the mobile, then follow their tracks through the wet grass to the camp. Or send up a helicopter with a searchlight: after the Chinaman had got so close the Russians would be paranoid, insist on a night-time sweep of the area around the blind...

As the night drew on he'd felt his fear mounting, and he was ashamed. The wind shivering the reeds, the warning calls of the birds – he never thought he'd be afraid of birdcalls. If only they could get on and do it, now, at once. Though Daudov was in charge…

The Georgian was sitting opposite, chewing on an unlit cigarette as he scrutinized his face in the dark, his eyes suddenly suspicious.

'Why are you always wanting to change the plan?' he said. 'First you want to stay with the car at the stables, then you want to push ahead before we're ready, next it'll be something else. You're not losing your balls, are you? If you are, remember what that bastard did to your dad. And he hadn't even been doctoring that fucking Chechen warlord, like the Russkis said.' He stopped, then went on in a leering voice. 'At least that's what you told me.'

'Leave it alone! I don't want to talk about it.'

Kasym looked away, his anguished expression deepening.

'Maybe you're just tired?' Daudov yawned. 'I am, I can tell you. Clapped out.' He reached into the breast pocket of his uniform, took out something silvery and got to his feet.

'A headache?' Kasym reached in his pocket and held out a pill. 'Here. It'll be stronger.'

'A headache!' Daudov smiled down at him, brandishing his tinfoil wrap. 'No my friend, this will do the job better than whatever you have there. Something guaranteed to keep you alert, and in good spirits.' Turning away, he threw over his shoulder: 'Like some? I brought a few wraps for the occasion. Maybe it'll help stop you worrying, wanting to change the plan every five minutes.'

Kasym looked up at him. Had Daudov taken stuff already? Was that why he'd seemed even cockier than usual, totally in control, with none of his own anxieties? Maybe he should have done the same.

He had a horror of drugs, yet for a second he was tempted. Instead he swallowed the pill he'd offered Daudov. The pain in his head was building by the minute, and what the Georgian had said about his father would make it worse. Only when he was revenged, he'd begun telling himself when he felt his brain about to explode under the pressure, would the pain go away and never return.

'Sure you wouldn't like a sniff?'

Daudov had come back and was holding up his silver wrap. Kasym shook his head.

'No thanks,' he said, 'I'm fine. As for changing the plan, let's forget it. It was just a thought. We'll do as you say: wait till dawn.'

# 27

M. Baudoin's alarm went off at five-thirty. Dawn was still almost two hours away but for him it was a big day and he was playing it safe. Everything was in order. The shoot would be at half-past-seven and arrangements had been made for him to go out to the blind at eight, when it was over. He'd be free to talk to the President about his life outside politics and his love of nature for half an hour, they'd promised, moving on to international affairs for another quarter. Just nothing about elections or demonstrations.

The Embassy pressman had vetted the list of questions he'd prepared. Not that M. Baudoin was an apologist for Moscow. In his youth he'd been a communist, but then in France who hadn't, and that was nearly forty years ago. What mattered to him today was not the fate of the international proletariat so much as the size of his pension, and an exclusive on the Russian visit, sold on around the world, could add a few thousand euros to his funds.

From his room in an outhouse of the hotel he made his way to the restaurant, where a handful of weary-looking officials were picking over the sumptuous breakfast buffet. Helping himself to a generous plateful – he'd be out there in the chill mist, he'd need warming – he saw Svetlana. Alone in a corner, she had her eyes on her plate as he approached.

'*Vous permettez?*'

She looked up. Her nod seemed reluctant but he was a journalist, used to that. She began finishing her coffee, quickly. He set down his plate, arranged his bulk on his chair and smiled across at her brightly.

'So you're breakfasting here? I thought you might be helping out on the blind.'

'No need. The President will be with his security. As soon as the hunt's over I'll be there for your interview.'

'Would you like to share my boat, so we can go out there together? I have one ordered.'

'No need, I have my own.'

'And would it help you to see my questions?' He reached for his folder. 'I have them here.'

'Don't worry, the embassy showed me.'

'Ah. Well, so much the better.'

She leant across to him, suddenly confiding.

'I'm so looking forward to seeing him out there, in his hunting clothes, with his gun.' Her eyes glowed as she spoke. She could make them do that. 'There's something' – she searched the air – 'so vital about him. But I must go. There are things to prepare. You must excuse me.'

A hand went to her brow, her vitality gone. To M. Baudoin's entranced gaze she looked suddenly pallid, her eyes clouded with a kind of fragile fatigue.

'You haven't slept? You're not well?'

'I have a headache, but I'll take a tablet. By eight I'll be fine.'

'And when we've done the interview don't forget the talk you promised. And the photographs, right?'

A slight frown morphed into a smile.

'Would after lunch suit you? I'll have had time for a nap by then.'

Collecting her coat from the back of her chair – she was dressed in jeans and a turtleneck sweater, equally taut – she got up. Tracked by the Frenchman's avid eyes, she made her way through the tables and out of the restaurant. What a woman! And a woman of moods. How swiftly she could go from vibrant to frail, and from forbidding to gracious! And that figure, even in jeans there was something aristocratic in its regally swaying motion…

'Tiens – M. Baudoin. Bonjour!'

The Russian press secretary, with his tray, interrupted his reverie.

'Bonjour!'

Taking his eyes off Svetlana, he smiled up at him, his ardour transferred from one to the other in an instant. 'You can take the place of our princess. She has a headache, poor woman. I hope she feels better by eight.'

The Russian, who'd had a taste of her haughtiness, set down his tray and shrugged.

'I think we can get along without her, *mon cher monsieur*. As you can hear she's not the only one around who can speak French. Now, a word about the interview…'

For another fifteen minutes the press secretary droned on about the questions he must be sure to pose to elicit the preferred replies. Getting twitchy, M. Baudoin checked his watch. Seven o'clock.

'Look outside.' He pointed to a window. 'You can see the light on the horizon. Maybe I should be going. A few minutes and the ducks will be on their way. No risk of them being late! It's like a fly-past, the locals say, timed to the last second. By the time I get out to the boat…'

Grabbing his briefcase and muffling himself in a scarf against the dawn freshness M. Baudoin hurried off. He was way too early, he knew it, though better to wait at the edge of the lagoon and watch the action than go out there in the company of the press secretary and suffer another lecture.

Outside the hotel his chauffeur was there. Ten minutes and he was at the jetty. When the driver stopped he stayed in his seat. Maybe he'd watch the shoot from the warmth of the car.

'You're not getting out?'

'Not for the moment, I'm a bit early. It's chilly out there, I'll wait here for a few minutes.'

'Unfortunately you can't, monsieur. I have to get back to the hotel. There are other passengers. Night workers going home, security people…'

'As you wish,' M. Baudoin sighed.

He got out and stood at the edge of the water, shivering. Behind him a row of gendarmes, interspersed with soldiers, lounged and chattered. They must have been out here all night, poor buggers.

The boat wasn't there but no matter, it was booked for later. As he looked out over the lagoon and his eyes accustomed themselves to the mist he saw that it was halfway to the blind, the boatman rowing gently so as not to disturb the water where the decoys had been placed.

He stared closer. The boatman wasn't alone. With him was a passenger, an indistinct figure sitting in the front holding what looked like a shotgun. He watched as the figure climbed onto the blind, the boat turned and came back to the jetty.

'Who was that?' he asked the boatman. 'I thought there were just the two of them out there. The President and his guard.'

'Gun trouble,' the boatman shrugged. 'The President's one is playing up, apparently. His own fault, insisted on using some clapped-out Russian model.'

'So who was it you were taking?'

'That was old Troupelen, gone out with a Remington and some ammo. Asked him when he wanted to come back and he says he'll probably stay there till it's over. Show him how to use it, make sure they get a good bag.' He checked his watch. 'You're the journalist, right?'

'I am, yes.'

'You're a bit early, *monsieur*. Thought you was booked for later. Never mind, hop aboard, since you're here, and I'll take you out now.'

'Maybe I should wait. There's the interpreter too, and the Russian press secretary. They'll be coming – '

' – I know when they're coming, I'll be back in time *monsieur, je vous assure*.' The boatman, a narky old salt, began looking impatient. 'Come on now, in you get. Take you out there before the ducks come. No point you hanging around here, shivering. Then I'll squeeze in a bite of breakfast while you're out there, and be back in time for the interpreter.'

M. Baudoin hesitated. Should he wait for Svetlana? On the other hand it would be good to get under cover, and maybe catch a bit of the action.

'I don't want to be in the way.'

'You won't be, there's a place where they can kip, you can wait
there.' The boatman frowned up at him. '*Eh bien, monsieur,* you
coming or not?'

M. Baudoin got in. The row out took a few minutes, bringing the
time to twenty past seven. He stepped from the boat to the blind
and opened the door.

The President, his guard and the Frenchman were crowded in
the tight space, preparing for the shoot. Troupelen was helping the
President with his new gun, the security man busy with his own.
Hearing him enter the guard shot him a dirty look. Tapping his
watch indignantly he sprang to his feet, grunted something in
Russian and strode towards him. Before he could explain what had
happened the Frenchman found himself backed into the bedroom,
and the door shut in his face.

He looked around the tight, Spartan room. The place was tiny,
no more than a few metres square. A single bed, its counterpane
ruffled. Next to it, on a small table, a bottle of champagne and two
glasses. He inspected the label – excellent stuff! – but what a waste.
The President didn't drink, so why the champagne – and two
glasses? And that scent in the air. Anti-mosquito spray, was it – there
were plenty around, he'd put some on himself – or perfume…

His imagination leaping, M. Baudoin considered the scene. Had
Svetlana been out here at night, secretly? Was that why she'd looked
tired at breakfast, why she'd invented a headache? Her boss had
divorced, a single man could do what he wanted, and it was the
perfect hideout. A tryst between President and princess amidst the
night calls of the birds, away from an inquisitive world… The article
wrote itself…

Fishing his camera from his briefcase in four quick shots he captured the main items in the room: the ruffled cover, the chair, the
cupboard, the bedside table with the champagne.

7.24. Dawn was eking through a gap in the bedroom curtains.
Agitated exchanges in Russian came from outside the room. The
ducks would be over in minutes, the President blasting away with his
Remington, he couldn't just stand here behind his door. The guard

seemed angry he'd come early but this he couldn't miss… He put an ear to the pane, turned the handle, eased the door open an inch.

The three of them had their backs towards him. The guard was opening the shooting apertures while Troupelen stood over the President, pointing to the breech of the Remington, and looking irritated. *Da da, OK, ponimayoo, I understan'*, the President was saying, looking irritated too.

Suddenly, with a gesture of impatience, he beckoned his security man across, took the Russian *Baikal* from his hands without a word and gave him the Remington in exchange. Turning their backs on the Frenchman the Russians stationed themselves at the apertures, held out their guns and waited.

Troupelen's lips tightened.

'*Eh bien… Dosvidaniye, Monsieur le Président,*' he called to his back. 'Au revoir. And the best of luck with that!' He pointed, disdainfully, to the *Baikal*.

No reply. Without turning, the guard jabbed a hand in the Frenchman's direction, signalling him to stand back from the shooting apertures, out of the way. Troupelen took out his mobile and dialled the boatman.

'His *breakfast?*' he spat into the phone. 'He's gone for breakfast! Well get him back! The President wants me out, and I'm not staying where I'm not wanted!'

A minute to go. Then right on time, in a faint light haze, the dawn began stealing in through the aperture where the President was crouching with his big old Russian *Baikal.*

# 28

U p in the juniper tree, Kasym raised his goggles to gaze into the pre-dawn light. Half an hour till sunrise. To him the view across the lagoon was heart-stopping. A stage where the curtain would soon be rising, where everything would happen...

Lit by a distant glow, slowly the wide Camargue sky began to infuse the vapour over the lagoon with a tinge of pink. Bird calls like a shrill, alerting summons rose around him as horses in damp pastures materialized from the mists, a ghostly white.

As he watched, with a sudden great rustle the island at the centre of the lagoon seemed to lift into the air, as the flamingos rose as a body and flew off low over the water. Startled – for a second he'd thought it was the ducks – he followed the streaming mass of gangling orange limbs till they disappeared.

The goggles down again, he stared over the water at the blind. A shutter on one of the openings had been drawn up, a head protruding. *Him,* he thought, his mind tensing. It's him, taking his last look at a sunrise... But no, it was a younger face, a security man by the look of his shaven head. He must be checking out the noise: along from the jetty a figure was releasing more live decoys into the lagoon to join the ones already paddling and calling around the blind.

As he gazed a second aperture opened and another face looked out. Now it *was* him, no question, his face craning upwards and his shotgun aimed skywards. Kasym's eyes focused on the gun. A *Baikal?* At that distance all he could see was an outline, but that's what it looked like: a Russian *Baikal.* With the choice of all the shotguns in the world he would go for that, of course he would, for patriotic reasons...

The sight of the gun stoked his rage. As he watched it the needles beneath his skull sharpened their probing yet he didn't reach for his pills, as the pain fed his anger.

The *Baikal* he recognized, the *Baikal* he knew well. It was an old model, like the one that used to stand in the corner of his father's office, his hunting gun. The gun he himself had fired at twelve years old. Though only once. The second trip his father had promised had never happened because the man he was watching across the lagoon had killed him.

Still at the aperture of the blind, the President began fiddling with the gun, frowned, then disappeared. Kasym stared on. For some time nothing happened. Then he saw someone being ferried from the shore, a tallish figure holding a shotgun. A second security man? Something wrong with the *Baikal*? The man stepped onto the blind, the boatman rowed back. Next thing the boat was taking out someone else, a short, fat fellow. Some sort of flunky, probably. Poor fools. Whoever they were, they'd chosen a bad moment…

The mist was still clearing, evaporating in the pre-dawn light. Further along the bank, a hundred metres from the jetty, a group of retrievers were waiting on leads. There'd soon be plenty for them to do, and this time there'd be more than ducks to be pulled from the water…

Minutes to go. The hours of waiting were over. His head was pounding, he was trembling. To steady himself a hand clung to a branch, tighter. He looked down, watched as Daudov opened the suitcase and gently, with both hands, as if cradling a baby, took out the falcon. Closing the lid he laid the bird on top. He took the control panel from its box and, extending the metre-long aerial, screwed it on.

If only he could have guided the bird himself, launched it with all the strength in his body then guided it to its target…

Batir stood watching Daudov.

'Out of my fucking way!' the Georgian muttered as he brushed past and began pacing out the field, calculating one last time the distance his running launch would take. Satisfied, he stood away from the tree, waiting, the falcon still on its case.

Everything ready, everything still. Then, from a distance, a whirring. The ducks? Kasym looked up, searched the horizon.

'A helicopter!' he called down in a low, tremulous voice. 'Heading this way! Get under cover!'

Telescoping his aerial with the flat of his hand Daudov scrambled back beneath the tree. When Batir lingered, a hand to his eyes, staring up, he jerked him towards the juniper so savagely he lost balance and tumbled to the ground. Then sat there, his kepi beside him, still gazing up.

'A Gazelle,' Kasym whispered down. 'Army reconnaissance.' He knew because Alik was a spotter. 'It's heading this way.'

'And so?' Batir murmured to himself, so softly no one heard. 'What does it matter? How can a helicopter stop a falcon?'

The whirring came closer. For a minute the three of them – Daudov crouching by his bird, Kasym in his tree, Batir on the ground – waited. Then the sky above the lagoon exploded in a discordant medley of sound. From the south the clatter of the Gazelle's rotors came ever louder, the first rays of sun picking out its green and brown camouflaged body. From the east the *aaaaaink...aaaaaink...aaaaink* of the ducks swelled and grew, and from the blind the boom-boom of a shotgun.

'Now!' Kasym shouted down. 'It's still coming! Now for fuck's sake, before it gets here!'

His mouth was dry, his words inaudible almost in the din – but Daudov heard. The falcon in his right hand, the control box in his left, its aerial re-extended, he lurched from beneath the tree into the meadow and ran twenty paces with an athlete's dash before casting the bird skywards, like a javelin, with a last desperate thrust.

Kasym stared from the juniper as the falcon flew up, dipped, wavered for a moment then levelled, shakily at first, then smoothly as Daudov worked the controls. Its wings flapping now, it soared upwards till it was cruising and looping high above the ducks, the low whine of its motor drowned in the surrounding hubbub.

The helicopter came on. Disturbed by the approaching rotors

the ducks began scattering, the flight in disarray, a gun from the blind firing a shot or two at the rapidly dispersing flock. It was then, as the flight was thinning as though to make way for it that the falcon swooped headlong, like a predator spotting a fish, down towards the lagoon.

From his tree Kasym heard and saw everything. The blast and the fountain of water, the Gazelle reaching the blind and hovering helplessly above it, the decoys scattering, squawking feebly, and the retrievers barking and plashing and breasting the lagoon.

# 29

M. Baudoin settled behind his laptop, poured coffee, lit a cigarette (forbidden in his room but what the hell) and began his article:

'I was there – there when it happened! A moment of history and a scene I shall not forget! Let me share with you the drama as it unfolded.

'It was a chilly October morning, the President of Russia was visiting the Camargue, and I had been invited to interview him. Our talk was to take place early that day immediately after a duck shoot. Why this unusual rendezvous? Because the President is an accomplished huntsman and it seemed a good idea to speak to him in his natural habitat.

'I was ferried out to the blind on the lagoon and instructed to wait, away from the shooting apertures, so as to keep clear of the action. I stood aside, and watched. It was half past seven, the day was breaking and the morning flight was on its way. The President and his guard, Misha, were at their windows, shotguns in hand.

'All night he had waited, and now it was to happen. Personally I am not a huntsman, yet I shared the exhilaration of the moment. The ducks came over, the President began shooting. Boom boom! – his Russian *Baikal*, a fine, trusty weapon, louder than his guard's Remington. And what a shot he was! A duck plunged into the lagoon, spinning, then another, then a third, in swift succession.

'Suddenly he stopped and frowned. The flock was dispersing. A distant noise had startled the ducks. For a second his eyes – those blue, fearlessly intelligent eyes – scoured the sky, and he saw it.

'A helicopter, bearing down on the blind! His guard had seen it too. Instinctively he reached for the President, seized his arm, attempted to drag him from the window, but he struggled free. He

swore, loudly. The word I could not understand but it seemed strong
– a manly curse! His emotion wasn't from fear of the approaching
helicopter – not at all – it was at the sight of the ducks scattering.
Determined to get his bag again he thrust himself at the window
and began shooting before the prey dispersed. Then he stopped.

'The whirr of rotors was almost overhead. What was it doing,
the President must have wondered, a helicopter in the middle of a
hunt organized in his honour? There were two possibilities: a pilot
who had lost his way – or an attack on his life!

'Realizing what might be happening he didn't hesitate. His first
thought was not for himself, but for us.

'*Vniz!*' he called out to me and Misha. 'Get down!'

'His voice was calm, his sangfroid amazing. We did as we were
bidden – threw ourselves to the floor. Stopping for a last glance
from the window – his courage knew no bounds – the President followed.

'We waited. The sound of the rotors passed. He was first on his
feet, at the window, with his weapon – and this time it wasn't for
ducks! He didn't want to cower there on the floor, he had a gun in
his hand and his instinct wasn't to wait for the helicopter to return
and – who knew? – drop a charge on the blind, it was to track it with
his weapon.

'*Niet, Gospodin Prezident!*'

'With a struggle his security man restrained him. The helicopter's
noise began fading. A false alarm, I was thinking, and began getting
to my feet, relieved. Then the explosion! A gush of water, nearby in
the lagoon, ten metres high – no it was twenty, fifty! A window shattered, the blind rocked violently on its moorings, tumbling us back
onto the floor. A bomb? A missile? There'd been a single explosion.
Would there be more? I lay there, rigid, waiting for another, for the
whole fragile structure to be blown to bits.

'Again the President was the first to rise. If he was to die it
wouldn't be like that, helpless… Flattening himself against the wall
he edged towards the window.

'*Niet!*' his guard shouted once more, imploring him to take cover, but it was useless. Again he was at the window with his gun. A leader! I thought, I am in the presence of a leader! Lucky Russians, to have such a man at their head!

'There were no photographers present – he guards his privacy fiercely – but by chance I had a camera, and pulling it from my pocket I snapped away. Here I will say something that journalists do not normally admit. When I came down south for the interview I wanted to write a different article about my subject. Colourful, playful, a little mischievous perhaps. About his private life, his tastes for food, sport, entertainment, and who knows, maybe women... About the man, rather than the President of all the Russias. But after what I had witnessed in those moments, I felt ashamed of my intention.

'There were no more explosions, thank God, and the helicopter had disappeared. Meanwhile the boat that had ferried us to the blind arrived. We took it to the shore. On board were more security men as well as the presidential doctor, on hand for such emergencies. He wanted to examine his charge on the spot but the President declined.

'From my place in the boat I watched him. He stood there, serene as ever, stood there erect, a man in full possession of his emotions, of himself, of the destiny of his country! As we approached the land he turned to inspect the scene of his near-assassination, his brush with death. Pointing to something in the water he shook his head, said something to his guard. My God, I thought! Somebody killed? I asked Misha.

'No, not a man,' his guard said in broken English. 'A duck. He has pity for animal.'

'I looked down. It was a wounded decoy, struggling in the water. A man who has narrowly escaped being blown to pieces spares a thought for a stricken bird...

'Out on the lagoon police in motorboats had appeared from nowhere, searching for any victims, scouring the surface for debris from the explosion. So far as I could see there was nothing. The boats were circling an area near a sanctuary for flamingos some distance from the blind. This was strange. Why there, I thought? To me the explosion had appeared closer.

'Later I understood. It turned out there *had* been a fatality: a conservation worker on his way in his boat from the flamingo island. Caught in the full force of the explosion his boat was shattered and he died.

'And the helicopter, had it played a part in the attack? Had it aimed something at the blind – a missile of some kind – and flown away? Not at all. A soldier I spoke to explained what had happened. It was an army Gazelle. Apparently they'd sent it up after detecting suspicious movements in a field some distance from the shore, on the opposite side of the lagoon. A gang of assassins, skulking in the corner of a field? No, a group of gendarmes in full uniform, it turned out, at an observation post! An embarrassing moment for the operators of the Gazelle, who will have some questions to answer. With security like that no wonder an attack was possible.

'Once ashore the President was engulfed in the waiting crowd. A first-aid team, the military, Russian officials with fevered eyes and white faces. '*Gospodin Prezident!*' some cried out. *Slava bogu* – God be praised – you are alive!

'All these he brushed aside. We drove back to the hotel. Avoiding the press was impossible. Although photographers were the last thing the President wanted at that moment, his composure was amazing. His shotgun still in his hand, a trickle of blood staining a temple, he stood there patiently while the cameramen did their work, with that expression of dignity and resolution his countrymen have come to know.

'We went into the hotel. Another throng of officials crowded round, at which point I thought, well that's it, that's the end of my interview, and turned to go.

'*Monsieur Baudoin!*'

'Detaching himself from his entourage the President summoned me back. One of his people translated.

'Was it you with us on the blind? So where are you going? We had an assignation, did we not? We must keep our appointment. It's not as if there's nothing to talk about!'

'*Gospodin Prezident!*'

His pressman came forward, tried to stop him, to persuade him to go with his doctor, but he waved him aside. With a firm hand on my shoulder he guided me along the corridor to his quarters.

We sat down and he gave orders to bring his interpreter, and for refreshments.

'Coffee, M. Baudoin?' he said when the maid arrived. 'Or something stronger? Maybe you are – how should I say – a little shaken?'

'It is you, *Monsieur le Président,* who must be shaken!' I said. 'For me, coffee and a cognac, if I may.' It was only eight in the morning but the President was right: I had been under fire, I needed steadying, I admit it. For himself he ordered coffee and a glass of water.

'Next came a touching moment. His interpreter, a beautiful young woman, a former Russian princess who works for the London Embassy, entered the room, took a seat behind him and said something in his ear. I don't know what it was but I could see the feeling in her eyes. They were dark, and her face was pale.

'So, M. Baudoin.' The President turned to me. 'I apologize for the delay. Now what is it you would like to ask?'

My first question you can guess.

'Who do you think it was?'

A magisterial frown, a slow smile, and finally a shrug:

'Who can say? My Chechen admirers, perhaps? It would not be the first time. They have tried before, so many times that I forget. Let me see… The first was in St Petersburg in 2,000, at a funeral. Then at a meeting in Yalta, I think it was. You see how desperate they were to see the back of me! Two in a year!

'Next it was a madman. "I've got to cut his head off!" he said when they caught him, and I understood his motive. Apparently I was a German spy… Then an explosive device on a highway shortly before my motorcade was due to pass. Then the British police foiled a conspiracy to assassinate me during a foreign trip. In addition there were some, shall we say, unexplained car crashes…

'So you see, it's part of the job, you get used to it. For myself I am not afraid. I have strong nerves and I have protection. It is for

the innocent victims of the extremists' atrocities that I am concerned. Also I worry about Russians who are taken in by their prop-
aganda. People who say we should get out and leave Chechnya and
the Caucasus to their mercy. I am not talking about foreigners but
our fellow citizens, who should know better. People who with their
actions are objectively aiding our enemy…'

'You're saying the people demonstrating against you in Russia are
traitors, the enemies of your country?'

Again, that slow, mischievous smile.

'It was you who said that, Monsieur Baudoin! Not me. All I will
add is that to my mind people who do things that encourage terrorists are no more than… No, I had better not say what they are. But
they belong in the water closet…'

'*De la merde?*' Baudoin supplied when Svetlana had finished translating.

'Ah, that word I understand, but again it is you saying it, not me.
Although I have heard it rumoured… With their lies and their dis-
tortions they are people who want to destabilize our country. While
I am alive I will not allow it. Which is why they want me dead. But
as you saw this morning, even at killing these people are incompe-
tent.'

He stifled a yawn.

'Perhaps I should leave you to rest?'

'Not at all, M. Baudoin. We still haven't covered international
affairs.'

'Maybe later today,' his pressman intervened. 'When the
President has freshened up.'

He stood up, smiling.

'I am sorry, they are dragging me away.' He held out a hand. I
took it. A firm, steady handshake. 'M. Baudoin, it has been a pleasure. Please tell your readers I have every confidence in the French
special services, and am convinced they will apprehend the criminals.
Meanwhile I apologize for disturbing your morning, and commend
you for your courage.'

'As she translated I heard the tremor in the interpreter's voice. It was then, as the President turned to go, that something extraordinary happened. Seeing a new spot of blood that had welled up on her leader's brow, without a word she took a handkerchief from her bag and wiped it, tenderly almost. A moment I could not allow to pass unrecorded.

'*Monsieur Le Président,*' I said. 'One last request, if you will permit. May I photograph that moment? If your interpreter could make that gesture again…'

He turned to his pressman.

'If there's enough blood left, why not?'

The pressman smiled. The interpreter retrieved her handkerchief, folded it, repeated the gesture. I took the picture you will see on this page. A staged shot, I admit it, but at the same time a genuine one, something that happened.

'To me it seemed a historic moment. For all their different backgrounds – she the descendent of an aristocrat, him from a humble family – in both there was a kind of shared nobility. The old, eternal Russia showing solidarity with the new.'

*

More coffees and half a dozen cigarettes later, and the article was done. He began reading it through, here and there raising a brow. It was destined for a popular readership, he could afford a little excess, yet there were phrases… *Magisterial frown* he replaced with *an expression of perplexity. Lucky Russians, to have such a man at their head!* came out altogether.

Finally satisfied he emailed it to his editor and lay on his bed. It was half past one but he had no appetite for lunch. Now that the tension he'd felt on the blind was gone – to think that he had come within metres of being blown sky high! – he was exhausted.

An hour later his editor roused him.

'*Félicitations!* Superb! A world exclusive!' M. Baudoin smiled silently, drinking in the praise. 'And the picture of the President and his interpreter – a sensation! What a woman – *une véritable beauté russe, et une princesse en plus!'*

As he dozed off again, he thought back to the room on the blind: the ruffled bedspread, the champagne... He prided himself on having a nose for these things, and now that he'd seen the pair of them together... But it was too early to write anything yet. He'd keep all that for his next sensation.

# 30

An attempted assassination, no question, but who was behind it and how could it have happened? The French press was as puzzled as French security. *Mystery of the Exploding Duck* was the best *Le Figaro* could do. The headline – a mystery in itself – turned out to be based on the report of an eyewitness, a gendarme on duty near the blind at the moment of impact.

No-one could see where it came from, he was quoted as saying, it was a moment of absolute confusion. 'The noise of the helicopter scattered the ducks in all directions, the sky was covered with startled birds. I was standing there looking up when one of them just seemed to dive from the flock into the lagoon, and explode.'

'*Outrage Without Malefactors,*' said *Le Monde*, more sedately, chastising the police for their failure to come up with clues, let alone suspects.

*Pravda*, on the other hand, was in no doubt who was to blame:

> Need we wait for proof about who was behind it? Why should it be anyone other than in the past? And now as then the Russian apologists for Chechen and Dagestani murderers must bear their share of the blame. They know who they are, and so do we. Yes, we refer to the kind of people we have seen soiling our capital's streets in recent weeks with their disorderly demonstrations, disgracing the election process and bringing shame on the country with their lack of patriotic feeling.

The rest of the Moscow press took a similar line, and here and there were insinuations that Western 'special services' may have been involved. 'After our triumph over the Crimea they are in a mood for revenge. If Russia's most stalwart defender of our national rights were to be eliminated,' a youth movement sympathetic to the leader declared, 'the question is: '*Cui bono?* Who stands to gain?' It went on to call for a closing of the ranks in the elections behind 'our hero-president.'

Which is what happened. Feeling themselves under fire, after a day or two of hesitation the organizers of the demonstrations issued a statement of their own:

From respect for the justified feelings of outrage of our compatriots, whatever their political views, at this monstrous act, future demonstrations have been cancelled.

\*

Alik didn't read newspapers any more that his mother, whose French was poor. For him the journey to Montreal – his first flight – had been an adventure. All the way his mother worried about their passports and papers but there'd been no trouble. The woman who'd met them at arrivals, a motherly-looking lady with a professional, cheerful manner, held a sign saying *Mme Simonov*, and from then on took charge. Her French was perfect, and she never tired of saying how welcome immigrants were in Canada.

Simonov, his mother had impressed on Alik on the plane, endlessly, was their new family name, and he must make sure never ever to use the old, Chechen one. To Alik this seemed logical – a new country, a new life, a new surname – though his father's choice of a Russian rather than a French one was puzzling.

The house the motherly woman had driven them to was on the edge of the island, in Dorval, a slightly forlorn suburb. She'd left them the keys, given his mother some Canadian dollars and told them that they should stay where they were till Monsieur Simonov joined them.

The house was small, a wooden structure, rather dilapidated-looking, but Alik was enthralled. For him it had everything he'd dreamed of: a bedroom to himself, a proper kitchen, even a small patch of garden.

Nervous that first day, by the evening of the second his mother was calmer. As for Alik, his only problem was to get to sleep. Midnight found him still awake, eating pancakes with maple syrup and deep in the latest number of *The Castaways in Time* that he'd found in a local shop.

*

With no more idea than anyone else about what lay behind the Camargue drama the British press had scrambled together what it could from the French media, and it was the *Daily Mail* that picked up the story of the exploding duck. The idea was so farcical-sounding that it took Tony a second or two to make connections. Then it hit him.

A duck – or a falcon? The falcon he'd seen in the tenement, the one that Kasym had gone off with. Absurd. The attack can have had nothing to do with Daudov, it must have been some serious jihadis, using a mortar that had missed...

And yet... An instinct to pass on what he knew to MI5 lasted no more than a minute. They would think him crazy. The duck theory was a newspaper headline, no more, though if they took it seriously, went after Kasym and ended up on Sasha's trail, it would be the end of his career in private security. Bad enough, though there was worse. If MI5 told the French, the French told the Russians, the FSB went after Sasha, discovered that Tony worked for him and got it into their heads that an ex-MI5 man was linked to an attack on their leader...

His mind played with these possibilities wildly, insistently, because he was drunk. Jean was away with their granddaughter and he'd spent the afternoon in his home office scouring every inch of the French and British press, a whisky bottle at his side. Good malt whisky that deserved better than to be used to numb his mind and fend off waves of guilt, mortification, and fears for the future.

Before falling into a doze he made a resolution. His instinct had been to lie low, and yet doing nothing was not an option. He would confront Sasha head-on about whether he'd been involved or not, and take it from there.

He woke in a sweat two hours later. In his doze he'd remembered how after Daudov's phone call to Sasha in the flat Svetlana had cruised the bedroom crazily, arms outstretched, before dive-bombing onto the bed. Now he made a second resolution, this one even firmer: to get onto Dick as soon as he could and come clean about the whole business.

\*

It was a sound decision, and Dick behaved as a best friend should. After listening to his story he didn't say 'shit...' or 'bloody hell', or roll his eyes in incredulity and despair. He didn't even ask why the fuck Tony hadn't told him before – remembering how many times he'd impressed on him that whatever he was up to he didn't want to know. Least of all did he say what he privately thought – that the depth of his friend's grievance against the service had warped his judgment, with disastrous results. All he said was:

'Tony, you're drinking too much.'

'In my position so would you.'

Tony took another gulp of his whisky soda:

'Right, let's look at it calmly. The Marseilles flat. Take me through that again. The business about the bird.'

'I told you, I had a good look round. There was no sign of anything, just the pamphlet. No weapons or explosives, just this bird.'

'You didn't check it out? Pick it up? Look underneath?'

'It never occurred – '

' – no reason why it should. Though in retrospect – '

' – in retrospect,' Tony scowled, 'we're all geniuses.'

'And the second time you went, it was gone.'

'I didn't think about it. Why would you? Stuffed bloody falcon sitting in a bedroom cupboard alongside some old books. When I saw it was gone I thought Kasym had sold it on. Bought it from the Roma near the flat, cleaned it up and sold it. His son seemed to think that's what he'd done.'

'Tony my friend, who are you trying to convince that you're in the clear? Me or yourself?'

'Both.'

'Well I wouldn't if I were you. You went down there again. You knew that Kasym had taken the bird away and that he'd gone off with Daudov.'

' I wasn't sure. I suspected. How was I to know – '

' – how much did you *want* to know?'

'Not too much, I suppose.'

'Afraid what it might mean for your job?'

Tony grimaced.

'Relax, I'm not blaming you. Just that birds are something the tech boys have been looking into. You have to think of them as miniature drones. Or in your case, a suicide falcon. The way the technology's going you could use a model bird for anything. Who's going to look up at some paunchy pigeon waggling about overhead and think it's on a surveillance mission? Or that the bloody thing's about to make a bigger mess of you than bird-shit, on account of how it's stuffed full of Semtex?

'And if we're talking falcons, birds that size you could use against anything: someone walking the street, the driver of a car, to hit someone in a building, fly it through the glass, and boom! The guidance systems are amazing. If you can put a cruise missile through a building's window, why not a remote-controlled falcon? And the way miniaturisation's going they'll soon be able blow your head to bits with a mechanized bloody sparrow.'

Tony looked back at him, troubled.

'So you buy the exploding duck theory?'

'In the absence of any other explanation, I can't exclude it.'

'Jesus…'

'The French, on the other hand, do.'

'How do you know?'

'Office chatter. Apparently the DCRI think it's more likely some-body lobbed a weapon from a distance, mortar or whatever. Plenty of room to hide one in that wilderness, and a mortar would explain why the shot went wild. Won't know for certain till they've finished dredging the lagoon.'

'If it's an exploding bird' – there was a note of hope in Tony's voice – 'there won't be much of it left, will there?'

'Enough,' Dick mused. 'Depends on the type of explosive. And on the water – salt or river. Affects the solubility. Then there's how much tidal movement there is. On polythene or aluminium you can detect traces of PETN – if that's what they used – providing they get in there quick.'

Polythene, aluminium? Tony did his best to focus. In addition to his other accomplishments his friend was something of a techno-freak, the kind of man who knew things. It could be annoying.

Dick was looking at him, hard.

'So what do you do intend to do now?'

'To say that I wouldn't start from here…'

Dick gave a sigh. When he was pondering something, his eyes and mouth fell in unison, making his face take on a tragic look. The way Tony felt.

'What should I tell Thames House?' he asked.

'Don't tell us anything. And we haven't spoken, right? Otherwise I'll have to come clean about our dealings, and we'll be duty bound to tell the FSB as well as the French. And if the whole thing turns out to be fantasy, as well as getting yourself in the shit you'll send us all on a wild goose chase, if you'll excuse the metaphor.'

'So what do I do?'

'Leave it a day or two, see if the French come up with anything. Then talk to Sasha. Put the screws on. Tell him that if he doesn't tell the authorities everything he knows, duty will oblige you to tell them as much as you've discovered.'

# 31

Sasha and Svetlana sat on a bench in the deserted square outside her flat. They were here because she'd refused to let him in. It was ten in the evening, a nervy wind was blowing and they were swathed in scarves.

'How much did you pay him?'

Svetlana's voice was terse.

'A bunch.'

'How much?'

'Million dollars.'

'*Bozhe moy!* My God! He says I've got this idea about assassinating the Russian President, so give me a million. And you do!'

'That's not what happened, you *know* it isn't. He came up with the idea about using birds, I told you. I thought it would be one of his publicity operations. Just, you know, bigger. Dropping pamphlets and stuff from the sky to scare off the flight, bugger up the hunt, make him look stupid, the tough-guy President in his hunting gear with his gun and no fucking ducks. Then get some journalist to film it, sell it to the world media. How was I to know he was thinking of bombing the bastard? He's not a hit man for Christ's sake, not in that game.'

'But you give him a million...'

'He was taking a risk, wasn't he? I mean if the French had caught him... And there were other people, he said he'd have to pay them off. It was you kept saying it should be big.'

'I don't remember saying you should bloody kill him. What about the money? Can they trace it?'

'It was cash.'

'From your bank?'

'I asked Mikhail to get it.'

'What did you say it was for?'

'I didn't have to. If it was over a million he used to have to check with dad, but now I just tell him and he gets it.' He paused, frowning. 'At least I think that's what happened.'

She glanced at him, sharply. He looked flustered, hesitant.

'You're drugged up.'

'No I'm not. Well a bit…'

'A million and he doesn't know, can't remember. Jesus…' She turned away, as if summoning the darkened trees to bear witness. 'Well you've done something big all right with your money. You've bought big publicity for him and big problems for me.'

'How could I know – '

' – that you were landing me in the shit?'

The Russian – *gavno* – came out loud and harsh.

'I don't see why it should affect you, darling.'

The hand round her shoulder was shrugged away.

'I was down there with him, for fuck's sake! I spoke to you.'

'We've dumped the mobiles, haven't we? They won't be able to trace the calls.'

'They can trace me to the flat.'

'They haven't so far.'

'They will when the French get onto Daudov and find out he worked for you.'

'He didn't, officially. That's why I never asked for too many details about what he was doing, and why I always paid him cash. So whatever he did was un-attributable.'

'Who's going to believe that? I'm surprised they're not onto you already.' She fell silent, shaking her head. 'Maybe it would be best to be out of the country.'

'We can't. It could raise suspicions.'

'What's this *we*? It's *me* I'm talking about. I'm not going to sit around and wait for the fucking balloon to go up, I'm going away and I'll need some money.'

'Where are you going?'

'Somewhere.'

'You can't just pack it in at the embassy and go abroad. How would that look?' He thought for a moment. 'You could go down to Suffolk for a while. No one knows you there. It's pretty much ready, and it's safe.'

'Safe from who?'

'Well, if the FSB think it was us...'

She looked around swiftly, as if suddenly afraid of the dark. As her face was averted from his a lamp outside the square captured a curious expression: her words were agitated, emotional, angry, yet her eyes were calm.

With Sasha it was the opposite. Till now the drink he'd downed and the spliff he'd smoked before seeing her had helped control his agitation. But now, when Svetlana muttered under her breathe 'imbecile!', instead of shrugging it off, as he would normally have done, he exploded.

'I keep telling you it was nothing to do with me, so why am I an imbecile? For fuck's sake listen to what I'm saying! I don't know what's the matter with you, you just don't know how to listen!'

'If you're not making sense,' she looked away, cold as ever, 'why should I?'

'You can't just go off on your own. Think of me.'

Her laugh was so strident he looked at her with a start.

'But I don't think about other people, do I? You told me yourself. That day in Oxford, remember? By the pool. Autistic, you said I was. If so you can't complain if I'm not all warm and feely, can you? It's just my autism coming out. So I'm not responsible.' She stood up. 'I'm going back inside.'

When he got up with her she held up a hand.

'No! I'm going alone. And don't forget the money. You owe me, putting me in this position.'

'How much will you need?'

'A lot. Ten big ones. Not dollars, if you don't mind, and quickly. Because if you don't...'

The glare of the lamp outside the square was full on her. In the second before she turned to go, he stared into her face. He was used to a certain remoteness in her expression, but nothing as distant as this.

'Don't worry, I'll fix it,' he said, and kissed the hard, chilled lips.

# 32

M. Baudoin sat at his desk in his flat in Paris, trawling the Internet for the latest reactions to his article. As always there was a flood, though not invariably complimentary. Today a Polish newspaper was accusing him of being a Russian stooge, describing the piece as 'slavish and celebrity-stricken.' The Frenchman was untroubled. Other papers had said much the same, probably because they couldn't afford the reprint fees his agent was demanding.

Never in his forty-year career had he been onto such a *bonne affaire*. 52,400 euros the article had netted him to date, and the pictures were fetching thousands more. The shot of the Russian leader clutching his *Baikal* while his security man, eyes ablaze, tried to drag him from the window had gone round the globe. Next in popularity (in the Russian press especially) was a close-up of him silhouetted against the lagoon with his watchful, intrepid expression. The quality of the shot wasn't perfect – the light on the blind hadn't been ideal – but the very greyness gave it an air of mystery and imminent threat.

He spread out the prints before him. On his agent's advice, not all of them had been released. A number were reserved for the piece he planned to write later, as a follow-up, about the President and his interpreter. And after that, the book. A near-assassination, a President and a princess – who could resist?

A contract was under discussion, with a starting figure 500,000 euros, a deal that would get him out of his fifth-floor bachelor flat not far from the Gare du Nord, where he'd lived for almost thirty years. Once the area had had its louche attractions, now riff-raff from the ends of the earth had taken to congregating there in the evenings, so you had to watch your step in your own street.

He gazed on at his prints. Lucky he'd taken those shots of the bedroom. The single bed, a cupboard, the bare boards, nothing could be simpler. And yet like those trick Japanese postcards, it could be read in two ways. The room seemed manly, austere, a hunter's lair, but seen through Baudoin's lubricious eyes the picture was transformed into a still life, full of atmosphere and suggestion.

Now you saw the hastily drawn curtain, leaving a shaft of light. Then the rumpled counterpane, the cloth rucked up as if by an amatory struggle. A man taking a pre-dawn nap on his own didn't flail about like that. And finally the champagne on the bedside table: *Louis Roederer Cristal Vintage 1999,* he had established, 500 euros a bottle. A princess's drink all right. And the contrast between that luxurious bottle and the rusticity of the room – perfect! Yes, the scene of a hunter's tryst with his mystery woman. The cover of his book could be nothing else.

Was there anything he'd missed? He took out a magnifying glass and slowly, forensically, his eyes inches from the print, scanned the photo. First, the floor next to the bed and the space beneath the chair. Might there be something there? Nothing but bare boards... Now the wardrobe. Its door was ajar, the shaft of light from the space between the curtains cutting through the gap and illuminating the interior like a torch.

Inside the light fell on two garments. One was a parka with a fur collar – a precaution against the October weather – while the other... He strained closer. Some kind of vest, sleeveless and in camouflage-type colours. It was hanging by itself, untouched and new-looking. Through the triangle formed by the coat-hanger he could make out a coloured label, though with the naked eye it was impossible to see what was written.

He went back to the pictures he'd downloaded onto his computer. Zooming in on the label he blew it up – too much: the picture disintegrated into pixels, like some abstract canvas. He shrank it, slowly, till a single word was visible:

*FLECKTARN*

It didn't sound Russian, and when he Googled it, it wasn't:

Latest issue fragmentation vest for the German military, comprising six kevlar panels and one cloth cover. Cover is in flecktarn poly-cotton. Has zip-open slits for easy removal and insertion of kevlar panels. Panels protect front, back, shoulders and neck. Weight is well distributed and the kevlar helps to spread the extra weight of webbing.

He brought up the illustration on the advertisement, and there it was: the one in the wardrobe, the latest version. A fragmentation vest.

Now why would the President want that on a duck shoot? He hadn't been wearing a security vest when the crazy Chinese had come within metres of his cortege, the media had claimed, in fact he never wore one at all. Part of his macho image. For all the attempts on his life the great man, who wiped the floor with his judo-teachers, was never afraid.

So why bring a fragmentation vest onto the blind, with his chief security man in tow and the shore a few yards away lined with gendarmes and military and plainclothes men? True, there were shotguns guns around, but flak-jackets, military-strength, for duck-hunting?

He went back to the other pictures. In the one where the security man was wrestling with his boss to get him away from the window he could see the top of the fellow's throat over his blouson. He zoomed that too, and there it was: the same Flecktarn vest. So they both had flak-vests on the blind, just in case. Though in case of what, exactly? And why wasn't the President wearing his?

He went back to the Internet, checked out the latest items on the explosion. 'The investigation is continuing' the official police site said. Of the twenty-six Chechens detained across the country in the days after the assassination attempt, twenty-five had been freed after questioning, the other one expected to be released soon.

And still no results from the dredging of the lagoon – a difficult operation, it turned out. Though relatively shallow, the sediment deposited over millennia in the brackish waters, it was explained, could have a high level of toxicity, making it hard to analyse precisely anything that might be found. And a sweep of the surrounding countryside had turned up no evidence, it had been reported, of a mortar or other projectile being fired.

In other words, an investigation going nowhere. He scrolled down further. As from the beginning the net was full of jokes at the President's expense, most of them infantile ('if the terrorists could-n't hit a blind on a lagoon it could only be the Donald Duck branch of Al Qaeda.') And inevitably there were the conspiracy theorists, plenty of those, which he read till he wearied of their fantastical inventions and accusations. Not one of them had the slightest evidence to offer, least of all anything about fragmentation vests.

*

But someone did know about the vests, and more besides. Pascau Troupelen was a man who had spent the weeks since the attack nursing bitter memories. It had been touch and go as to whether he would get the job of showing the Russian President around and he was beginning to wish he hadn't.

Conscious of the honour that had befallen him, when they were introduced at the riding stables, he in his full regalia, trident aloft, the President clutching his hand in a fine, huntsman's grip while the world's media snapped away, he was ready to be won over. But it hadn't happened, and he wasn't a man to hide his grievances. In the days after the botched attack *le vieux Troupelen* could be heard after a glass or two in the bars of Saintes-Maries-de-la-Mer spouting his views about this crap President (*ce putain de Président, ce Président de merde*) while reflecting in ironic terms on the amateurishness of his would-be assassins.

The reason wasn't politics; it was wounded pride. The voice of the Camargue had not enjoyed being cut off in mid flow by the President's interpreter in front of the nation's cameras. Arrogant bitch. Any more than he'd enjoyed it when during their ride the visitor, preferring the company of his pretty lady, had cut him dead. Stopped him from delivering the message he had prepared in advance about how bullfighting was in a Frenchman's blood as much as a Spaniard's, and how he for one would never allow those lily-livered abolitionist bastards to put a stop to a custom that had come down to them through the ages.

At that point the pair of them had exchanged glances – oh yes, he'd caught that look of derision – and ridden ahead, the two of them together, leaving him trotting along in their wake like some beggarly Sancho Panza.

Then there'd been the hunt itself. The arrangement had been that he'd be out there with them on the blind, yet it hadn't happened. After the man who knew more about duck hunting in the Camargue than anyone in the country had been informed at the last moment that his presence would not be necessary, he'd been hauled from his bed at dawn to take out his Remington when the President's antique-looking affair had jammed. Only to find that he'd decided to take his goon's gun instead. After which he'd been obliged to stay on for the shoot and bloody near got himself blown to bits in the process.

Then the media storm. Had anyone troubled to ask him for his impressions? No they had not. Baudoin's article had scooped the pool and he'd been edited out of the whole affair. He'd said nothing about his grievances to the press, though now that the world and his dog had given their version of events – and what shit they talked, all of them – a man must tell his story.

So bit by bit in one bar then another out it came – or some of it – to whoever would buy him a drink and listen. And always the response was the same: *come on Pascau, say what you like about him, the guy's a hero. You must have read the Baudoin thing.* Which really got him going.

Never mind that the arse-licking Parisian slob had no idea what had happened. How could he, when he'd spent most of the drama cowering in the bedroom? He, on the other hand, had been out there the whole time and seen everything. And if he were so minded, well, there were stories he could tell…

Next thing he walks into his local for a glass and he's sitting there minding his business when a fat little bugger comes up to his table and says, 'mind if I join you?' And it's the arse-licking slob himself.

*

When they'd met on the boat taking them back to the shore after the explosion they hadn't exchanged a word. Now M. Troupelen's views on his article had come to the writer's ears. Not that the journalist minded – it must be jealousy, pure and simple. What interested him more were the old boy's impressions of Svetlana and her boss when he'd taken them out riding together.

'I said mind if I join you?'

M. Baudoin stood at the table, waiting. The *gardian* looked up, thought a few seconds, indicated indifference. The Parisian sat down and the waiter came.

'Another drink?' the journalist offered. 'Maybe I'll have the same.'

M. Troupelen's eyes were wary.

'Since you propose…'

M. Baudoin gave his order and a second bottle of white was brought, only this time it was a pricey Meursault.

'*Santé*, M. Troupelen.'

'And yours.'

They drank, and Baudoin began.

'My spies tell me you didn't approve of my piece on the Russian affair.'

Beneath his moustache, M. Troupelen's mouth tightened. The Parisian's directness had caught him off guard. Also he'd said it smilingly, without resentment.

'*Non, monsieur. C'est vrai que je n'ai pas apprécié.*'

Too right I didn't like it.

'*Voyons, mon cher* Troupelen, we're not enemies, *hein?* After all, we went through the attack together. And two people can witness the same event and come away with different impressions.'

Baudoin leant forward.

'I know you think my piece was a bit flattering, but between ourselves I'm not that great a fan of the President, not at all. Rather the reverse. But we journalists, we're creatures of our editors. The way they printed it, there were parts where it made me puke to read my own story! But I was thinking about a follow-up, so if I've got anything wrong, if new information were to come to light' – he beamed – 'I'll be more than happy to have another crack. For me the important thing is to get the truth on record.'

Playing for time – he had no idea where this was going – M. Troupelen put on his wiliest look. 'Well, there are things I could tell, I'm not denying…'

'Such as?'

'Can't say, not allowed to. I'm under oath. To the security services, the Quai d'Orsay…'

'But you tell things,' Baudoin waved an arm round the bar, 'to your friends, I've heard.'

'Not the *real* things.' The sly look again, as he held up his thumb and forefinger a centimetre apart. 'Only bits. And my friends are not the press.'

'And the security services? They must have talked to you. You've told them things, I imagine?'

'How can I tell them if they don't want to know?'

'Meaning?'

The *gardian* hunched forward, confidential.

'The authorities have their theories, and I have mine.'

'Which is?'

M. Troupelen gave a knowing laugh.

'You're smart, you Parisians, oh yes, very smart, but you wear big boots and I can hear you coming! Explain to me why I should tell you anything?'

'Because you're an honest man. You want the world to know the truth. You tell your friends things – they stay in this bar. You tell the authorities – they don't believe you. Because the things you know about him don't reflect well on him, perhaps?'

'Reflect well? You're joking! That *Président de merde,* that shyster!'

'I understand your feelings, the feelings of a man no one will believe. Whereas if you were to tell me…'

As he spoke, M. Baudoin raised his hands above the table, palms upward, tilting in M. Troupelen's direction. An ambiguous gesture. Did it signify *come on, why not open up, man to man?* Or could the cupped, tilted hands be presenting an invisible gift? M. Troupelen chose the latter interpretation.

'You're making me an offer?'

It was M. Baudoin's turn to look cunning.

'When I buy a melon,' his fingers made a probing movement, 'I feel it first.'

'Oh but it's ripe, I assure you. Ripe to bursting!'

'So allow me – '

' – *Un moment!*' Troupelen held up an alerting finger. 'What are we talking?'

When the journalist rocked his head, M. Troupelen looked hopeful.

'Hundreds, I take it?'

'*Ah, non!*'

M. Troupelen's moustache, raised in anticipation before, subsided like a tired dog.

The journalist smiled.

'No, not hundreds, *absolument pas*. But a thousand, more perhaps…'

'In that case…'

'You have more than a couple of phrases to offer me, I assume?'

M. Troupelen nodded eagerly, several times.

'And some impressions of the President's relations with his interpreter, I imagine?'

'Naturally. I took them riding, alone.'

'Excellent. In that case, I suggest we order dinner.'

'As you wish, *monsieur*.'

The waiter came, the food was ordered. When he'd gone the reporter felt in his pocket, took out a dictaphone – a small one, discreet – and laid it close to M. Troupelen's plate.

'*Vous permettez?*'
'*Pas de problème.*'
'*Alors, allez-y.*'

And the *gardian* told his story. Slowly at first, as though presenting evidence to the authorities, but as his feelings about the Russian President made his colour rise the words flowed freely, so freely he forgot to replenish his glass. Courteously and frequently, the reporter obliged.

'You have to imagine. Me, Pascau Troupelen, born in a slum of Marseille! And him, the President of all the Russias! But in France we believe in equality – a founding principle of the Republic! So when *ce Président de merde…*'

And off he went, recounting one by one the list of slights and indignities (some of them real, others clearly imagined) that he'd suffered at the Russian's hands.

M. Baudoin was sympathetic.

'I saw when she cut you off – we all did. And we thought, *ça alors!* This woman is more than an interpreter! So tell me, when they were alone together, how did they behave? When you went on the ride, did you notice anything?'

'*Ah, les femmes*, M. Baudoin… Don't get me started! I'll put it like this. It was evident from the beginning that there was something…something the wrong way round. That she had a certain mastery over him. No, I'm wrong! It was like two masters together. As if in some mysterious way the princess and the President were equals.'

M. Troupelen's eyes fell to his plate. What had he meant by that, exactly? He didn't know, he had puzzled himself. It was just an impression he'd had, at the time.

'The only subordinate in that set-up,' he went on bitterly, 'was me. They made that clear enough. And we southerners, we have our pride.'

'When you say she talked to him as though they were on equal terms, how did you know? They talked in Russian, didn't they? '

M. Troupelen grinned.

'*Ah, là!* My communist youth, monsieur! I have been to Russia you see, as a militant in the union of agricultural workers, and I picked up a bit of the language. *Durak,* that means idiot. *Ya lyublyou tebya,* I love you, and *peezdish* – that's fuck off. And when I got back I learned some more. *Ah oui! Les jeunesses communistes!* Young idiots more likely…'

'So what did they say to one another?'

'Couldn't hear. I told you, they rode ahead.'

'But on the blind, you heard him talking there. What did you hear when it happened? What did they do? I couldn't see clearly.'

'That's because you weren't there! The moment the trouble started, you shut the bedroom door.'

'I closed it a bit, I admit. All that noise! My ears – I've had a problem with my ears since infancy.'

'And your eyes, *monsieur,* your eyes! You have a problem there too? But I saw everything…'

'So tell me.'

'Well I was there, but I couldn't make head nor tail of what they were doing. When the ducks came over the guard lets loose with his Remington – boom boom! Couple of shots, and that was it. And when his boss opens up, he sort of pulls him back. *Ostorozhno!* he shouts at him – that means be careful! *Minuta!* he says, which means hold on a minute. And I'm thinking well while the pair of you are buggering about next to the windows the ducks are passing!

'And then?'

'Well then the helicopter and the explosion. It all happened together – you remember that all right, *monsieur, hein?* Even if you didn't see it, I did. Out there in the lagoon, that great geyser near the flamingo island. I see it and I'm afraid, I don't mind telling you. A helicopter, an explosion? I've been in a war and an attack is what I'm thinking, that's all it can be! A missile! Maybe there'll be another?

'You must have thought the same, wherever you were at the time. Under the bed, maybe? So anyway I make a dive for the floor but the President and his man – they don't move. Just crouch a bit, as if to get beneath the windows.

'Next thing it's over. No harm done, just that the blind's rocking a bit in the backwash and a window's blown in. At that stage we didn't know about poor Marc…'

'Marc?'

'Marc Dupleix, the young boatman who got killed. Anyway I look up from the floor and the President's still there, crouching. And the guard, Misha, what's he doing? Well you won't believe this, I could hardly credit it myself, but he's looking at his boss, sort of smiling. Then he sees me down there on the floor and he shouts:

'*Gospodin Prezident!* Are you all right?' And the President, he says, *ya nichevo*, meaning 'I'm fine.' Now if somebody fired a missile at me I'd be pissed off. I might even lose my cool. But them – it's like it's all in a day's work.

'Then you open your door, remember, you peer out and you don't look happy. 'What the fuck's going on?' you shout, and I say: 'Don't ask me!'

'Next thing the President's at the window that's blown in, as if to see what's happened, and the guard, he sort of lunges at him, tries to drag him away, and the President shrugs him off, cursing. *Durak* he's shouting at him – that means *con*, Monsieur, I told you. All very dramatic, but that's the Russkis for you. At which point you stop standing there gawking, your journalist's instinct kicks in so you whip out a camera and you take some shots.

'And when they stop the struggling and he turns round I see blood on his temple. Cut himself at the window, on the broken glass? Or maybe the guard's scratched him? Anyway they're standing there, grim-looking, the President with his clothes all messed up and this blood on his face, and there's you with your camera clicking away. And I'm thinking *merde*, he's in for it, they won't like this, taking pictures of the President in that state!

'But they didn't mind, did they? Stood there like a pair of squaddies back from the wars while you snapped away… All heroic he was, as if nothing's happened. And that's it. Next thing the gendarmes pile into the blind, a whole boatload. Dozy boatman's on the job now all right.'

M. Baudoin was leaning across, excited.

'One more thing. The guard. What was he wearing, under that leather blouson of his? Did you notice?'

'Strange you should ask, because when they're struggling – it was only a few seconds, like a judo clinch, he does that, the President, doesn't he? – anyway the guy's blouson gets pulled up and yes, I noticed. He had an arm holster under there – he would, wouldn't he? – and a kind of camouflaged vest, sort of flak-jacket. Didn't think nothing of it. Security man, isn't he? Probably wears them in his sleep.'

'But not the President.'

'Well that's the weirdest thing of all. When I first got out there and they're fiddling with the guns I heard the guard saying 'I brought you a vest, you're not wearing your vest! Put it on, *Gozpodin Prezident*, please put it on!' And he says *'Niet!, nye khochoo!'* That means no, I don't want to. And the guard, he tries again, tells him its for safety, that they're alone out there on the lagoon and there could be other hunters loosing off at the ducks, but the President's busy with the shotgun I brought him and he says 'Misha, you're beginning to annoy me, so fuck off with your bloody vest.' That's the way he talks, *monsieur*. So the guard gives up.'

The reporter frowned.

'A flak-vest, on a duck shoot? I still don't get it. There were rows of security men on shore, and no other hunters around. So who could harm him?'

'No one.' M. Troupelen swigged back his glass, and grinned. 'Unless...'

'Unless what?'

'Unless...' He glanced at the recording device. 'No, I'd better not say.'

The journalist reached across, picked up his recorder, extinguished the red light and buried it in his pocket.

'And so, unless what?'

In a parody of confidentiality M. Troupelen glanced around, leant across the table and said a low whisper:

'Unless they were expecting something all along.' He sat back, looking mysterious. 'That's my secret, *monsieur*. That's what I've never told anyone.'

'You mean – '

' – *Oui M. Baudoin*, that's what I mean. That the attack on the President was a fake, a comedy from start to finish!'

The journalist frowned.

'But the explosion, the waves hitting the blind, how can you deny – '

' – looking back, *monsieur*, and forgetting your rather extravagant description of events, tell me something. Would you say that you were ever in danger? You may have been afraid – so was I – but that was because we didn't know what the fuck was happening. No one had let us into the secret, had they? But whatever it was, a mortar or an exploding duck, look where the bloody thing landed! It wasn't even close!'

'The fact that they missed the blind – '

' – showed they never meant to hit it!' Troupelen glowed in triumph. 'With the guidance systems they have nowadays – those drone things, take off a man's balls if they want to and leave your cock standing – and they miss! Instead they land it right next to the island and smash up the boat of *le pauvre Marc*, God rest his soul. I knew him, fine young lad he was, saving up to go into the bull-fighting business.'

'But how would they have hit him, if it was all a charade?'

'Accident. Low in the water those boats, in the mist you don't see them. All they wanted was to make a big noise and a splash and avoid the blind.'

'When you say *they*…'

'*Les services, monsieur*. The Russian secret service, working with their old KGB boss. They must have been in it together. Come on, *monsieur*, it's you the journalist, you can work it out for yourself! He's got problems hasn't he, with his elections. Fucked up the country's economy with his Ukrainian adventures. So why not get himself blown up by terrorists? Give him no end of a boost, won't it? And it has, the TV says, he's a hero out there now. Must have all read your article! Yes, a phony attack. That's their mentality, how they do things.'

Baudoin pursed his lips.

'Don't believe me? Well then, answer me this. Why was it they didn't want me on the blind for the hunt? Said they did then afterwards not to bother. Didn't want no witnesses, *hein*?'

'But you were there.'

'Yes, but only to bring out the Remington. Then they couldn't get me off the blind fast enough. And you, they shut you in the bedroom, didn't they?'

M. Baudoin rocked his head and said nothing. Instead he took a mouthful of his first course: prosciutto. After giving him time to swallow M. Troupelen said:

'So what do you think?'

'About?'

'The melon.' He pointed to the journalist's plate. 'Nice and sweet, is it?'

'Oh yes. Very tasty.'

Mr Troupelen was a clown, was what Baudoin was thinking. A clown, a drunk and a provincial bore, though one who may have stumbled across something that could make him a fortune.

He went on eating.

'It's an interesting theory, I can't deny. Let me give it more thought. Meanwhile, another bottle perhaps?'

For the rest of the meal he listened as the *gardian* regaled him with bull-fighting tales, laced with accounts of what he'd do to any limp-wristed abolitionist bastard who tried to put a stop to a custom that had come down to them through the ages…

After a couple of brandies M. Baudoin called for the bill, glanced at it, took out his wallet, looked inside, and sighed.

'I seem to have only large denominations. In restaurants they don't like them. Perhaps you have a card? I'd be happy to make a contribution.'

M. Troupelen's brow furrowed.

'I thought maybe…'

A wink and a smile from his companion and his crestfallen expression lightened.

'*Une carte? Mais bien sûr!*'

He fished one from his wallet. The waiter arrived with his machine. He tapped in his pin number. The waiter processed it, left a receipt, and went.

'And this – this is my contribution.'

Taking two notes from his wallet M. Baudoin slipped them into the menu and slid it across the table. M. Troupelen glanced inside, saw the five hundred euro notes, grinned and said:

'I think that covers it.'

'Just one thing.'

M. Baudoin held up a hand.

'And what's that?'

'Your theory about the President. As I say, very interesting. But you can't sell the same melon twice. So if someone else gets onto you…'

In thirty years of introducing the pleasures of the Camargue to foreign hunters, some of them liable to complain about lonely nights in remote hotels, M. Troupelen had extended his services to arranging entertainments of a strictly private nature. To signify that confidentiality was guaranteed he had evolved a little trick: pulling down the corners of his moustache over his lips, as if his mouth was sewn up.

He did it now.

'Excellent. If I read nothing in the media about what you've told me, then there will be a similar sum.'

# 33

Tony lay contemplating the acanthus motif of the cornice twelve feet above his head. Like everywhere in the house the ceiling was high and the room spacious, giving it a cold, impersonal feeling. Though not at that moment. The room was Lisa's bedroom and they were lying side by side after making love.

It was not where he had expected to be at half past seven in the evening. To take his mind off the Camargue he'd called in for a drink, but after a couple of gins and tonics – normally Lisa's limit was one – they'd found themselves in bed and she'd fallen asleep beside him. The way her reserve could dissolve into tenderness without warning was one of the things he found endearing.

Cool and detached one moment, she could be warm and amorous the next. Maybe there was some echo here of his own nature, he told himself, a sensuality concealed beneath a diffident surface. A side of him Jean had shown few signs of welcoming in their years together.

Tonight their lovemaking had been less rapturous. There was too much on his mind, and she too seemed distracted. The first thing she'd asked after he'd poured their drinks was about the assassination attempt. The news had evidently taken her aback. His enquires about the man Sasha had hired who'd lived in France, then their trip to Marseille together – had he been afraid there was something in the offing? 'I'm just wondering. It seemed a rather large coincidence.'

He'd done his best to laugh it off. No use: Lisa wouldn't let go. Something in her had changed. Ever since Grekov had died she'd been worried about her future. Sasha had kept her on, she suspected, only because she knew her way round his father's papers and could help deal with the endless demands of probate. Now that that was done she was afraid he'd get rid of her. Ruth had been trying to persuade him to keep her on as a second personal secretary but Sasha was resisting: manic about his privacy, he preferred one person running his office to two.

Normally the most placid of women – something else he liked about Lisa – beneath her serenity there was a certain frailty, and something Ruth said had alarmed her: Sasha had disappeared from the house the morning of the Camargue attack, she'd told her, and hadn't been back since. Soothing her had not been easy; the news about Sasha had troubled him too. Hence their two double gins at five-thirty in the afternoon. Which was how they'd ended up in bed an hour later.

*

Lisa had woken up.

'I'm sorry. I've been so tired.'

'You're not sleeping?'

'Not well. Everything's been so unsettled. The assassination business was the last straw.'

He let a moment pass. He was thinking back to the message from Daudov that Ruth had taken giving his telephone number in the Thodys' house. It was what had prompted him to ask Tom Sandiman to have a go at hacking Sasha's mobile – he'd got the number from the intercepts at the flat – but no luck. For once Sasha had been efficient: the mobile turned out to be well secured.

'Lisa, you couldn't do something for me?'

She looked wary.

'What?'

'That phone message from Marseille you told me about. The one about Monsieur Thody. It would be handy to know if there've been any more.'

'You want me to ask Ruth to check his calls? On his personal mobile?' She looked at him, fearfully at first then with a hint of anger. 'I couldn't do that. Anyway he's not around, I told you. People are trying to contact him, get him to sign papers, give instructions, but he's never there.'

'Can't she just phone him?'

'She does, but she can't get any decisions out of him. He's not making sense. She thinks he's drinking, or on drugs. Have *you* seen him?'

'Not recently.'

'But you're still working for him, aren't you? And keeping an eye?'

'Well yes.'

He felt a sudden compulsion to tell her everything. Keeping his secrets to himself while she confided hers made him feel guilty, but that's how it was: a collision between his personal and professional obligations. His duty was to a dead man, yet somehow that made it all the more binding.

'And you?' he went on. 'Did Grekov – '

' – arrange for me to stay here? Not formally, he must have thought I would want to go. But he left me some money.'

'And if Ruth persuades Sasha to keep you on, you'll work for him?'

'I'm not keen – not for Sasha. But then I'm not keen to leave either. Twenty-two years I was with Grekov… I suppose you get spoiled. The security, this flat in the centre of London…'

His mobile rang.

'I'm sorry, I'd better – '

' – go ahead.'

He got up and answered. It was Jean.

'Can I ring you back?'

'No you can't. Where are you for God's sake? Penny's coming round tonight, remember? At half past eight.'

'Ah, yes. It's not looking as though I can make it.'

'You'll have to, even if you're late. She rang to say she's seen this place in Wimbledon. Two bedrooms, a nice road, walking distance from Heather's school. They're looking for a quick sale. Said she'd talk to you about it tonight, they want a quick decision, and she's going to need a bridging loan.'

'OK OK, I'll be there. I won't be long,' he said quietly into the phone.

He began dressing. Lisa watched him from the bed.

'Your family?'

He made a resigned gesture.

'So romantic. We make love, you ask me to steal some phone messages, your wife calls then off you go.'

He stopped doing up his tie, came to the bed, bent to kiss her.

'What can I say? I have to.'

'I know, you're such a dutiful person. Dutiful to Grekov, dutiful to your wife…'

'I'm sorry. It's just…' he shrugged, 'the way it is. I mean, we're mature people.'

'Perhaps that's the problem.'

Lisa gave him her most melancholy smile.

# 34

For the tenth time in as many days Tom Sandiman idled past the houses in the deserted square late in the evening. Since the Camargue drama Tony had asked for a take from the flat daily. The late October chill and endless drizzle was making downloading his device a chore, plus he was running out of disguises: there was a limit to the variety of hats, raincoats and umbrellas a man could possess.

When he'd done his stuff, in the Brompton Road he caught a cab to Chiswick. Tony answered the bell with a poor attempt at a smile. He hadn't been looking too good lately, Sandiman thought, his face lined and grey as if he had perpetual flu. Seeing him on his doorstep Tony was thinking the same about his friend. He stood there, a little hunched, his hat sodden, with a drip about to fall from the end of his nose.

After handing him his envelope in the hallway, he said:

'Tony, if it's all the same to you, d'you think we could, you know, vary the frequency? Like every other night?'

Tony looked out at the hangdog figure. Poor Tom was looking as old as he'd begun feeling himself.

'Just as you like. Couple more days, then we'll go back to three a week, OK?'

Sandiman said it was, and shuffled off.

It was past eleven. Pouring himself a whisky to help him sleep he took the envelope to his office, wearily. Why he went on doing this he didn't know; habit perhaps. For almost a week there'd been nothing: no phone conversations of interest, no visitors – and no Svetlana. He'd tried ringing her landline several times but she hadn't taken the calls. In the most recent recording she'd been sorting out her clothes. Was she off somewhere? In the circumstances it wouldn't surprise him.

The last news he'd had of her had been from Larry Merchant. Scrupulous as ever he'd gone on logging her movements in and out of the Residence all these months, sending him weekly clips. When he'd met him at a pub the previous day to drop off some money he'd passed him an envelope with a new photo.

'This one dates back couple of weeks. Looks like it could be the last. Don't see your lady with the Ambassador no more. Maybe his English has improved?'

The clip showed her sitting with him in the back seat, as usual, though with an unknown face in the front.

'And who's the new boy?'

'Andrei Kirilenko, new First Secretary for Cultural Affairs,' Larry explained. 'Replacement for Victor Bulagin.'

'The one with the spikey beard?'

'Yeah, that's him. Didn't last long, did he? Came in 'bout the same time as your lady friend six months ago and now he's disappeared. Uptight little bastard. Looked through you like you didn't exist, never so much as a good morning. Mind you, she was the same. Never saw 'em say a word to each other either. In fact never seen Bulagin talk to anyone, even on a phone. Can't have had too many cultural affairs to handle.'

He took out Tom's memory sticks, switched on his computer, plugged one in, settled back with his whisky.

The bedroom camera, morning. The curtains are half-open but the light is not bright – the big chestnut in the square is still in leaf and casts most of the room in shadow. Svetlana is up early – normally it's about eight but recently it's been around seven. After breakfast she comes back into the bedroom and resumes sifting through mountains of clothes, as though preparing to pack, when the telephone rings. She crosses the room, picks up the receiver.

'Hello?'

'Excuse me for disturbing you, *Mademoiselle*. My name is Baudoin. You remember me, *non*?'

Tony is listening indolently, from a reclining position. Now he sits up. Baudoin, the French journalist? The man whose article he'd read in the *Mail* and whose greasy, ingratiating features he'd seen in a Newsnight interview from Paris, extolling the Russian leader's courage in the Camargue?

It wasn't the first time. In the days after the attack wherever he'd looked on the media – French TV, CNN, the Moscow service *Russia Today* – Raymond Baudoin seemed to be there, enchanted to be the centre of attention.

And here he is calling Svetlana.

'Who?' she snaps into the phone.

'Raymond Baudoin. You were going to talk to me after the duck shoot, to give some impressions of the President, but we cancelled, remember?'

'I hardly think that's appropriate now.'

'Of course not, it's not about that.'

'Well what is it?'

'Something I was thinking of writing. Not for the magazine, but personally. A new element has come into play, you see, something I believe we should discuss.'

'I don't want to discuss anything.'

'Ah, but you will want to know about this before I write it. That I can guarantee.'

'I've told you, I'm not giving interviews.'

'I understand, it's natural, but I think we should talk. The problem is that things are not as they seem. About the assassination attempt I mean.'

Taking the phone from her ear she stares at the wall, uncertain.

'Where are you?'

'In Paris. Tomorrow I can be in London. My information, it is urgent.'

'Come to my flat at six tomorrow.'

She gives the address.

'Very well, I'll be there. And please, do not be alarmed. Providing we talk there will be nothing to fear.'

She puts down the phone, grabs her mobile, texts a message and stalks the room waiting for a reply. In a minute it comes. She reads it and, still agitated, dials a number.

'I need a taxi, quickly.' She gives the street address, listens a moment, says 'Dalston,' and switches off.

Now she is hurrying out of her skirt and jumper into a crushed T-shirt and tattered jeans that she retrieves from the bottom of a draw. Kicking off her shoes she replaces them with a pair of cheap-looking trainers, none-too clean. Tony has seen her do this before, dressing down after calling for a taxi to Dalston, presumably to go slumming in the studios and art galleries. Though why would she hurry off there now, in response to Baudoin's call?

And this time she goes the whole hog, putting on a pair of clear-lensed glasses (she doesn't wear glasses) to complete the transformation from Chelsea girl-about-town to art student slob. How come Baudoin has put her in such a state? The answer would come, he assumed, when Sandiman delivered tomorrow's instalment.

*

It was ten next evening when Tom dropped it off. At the ring of the doorbell Tony darted from his office. He was at the head of the stairs when his wife called up:

'That him again?'

Used to anonymous comings and goings over the years, normally Jean took no notice.

'Yes.'

'Comes every night now, doesn't he?'

'For the moment, he does.' He shrugged and made for the door. 'It's the job. No set hours. You know that, darling.'

Collecting the envelope after a *sotto voce* exchange with Tom he hurried back to his office, closed and locked the door.

The recording begins at seven. After her morning routine Svetlana gets back to sorting clothes, a seemingly endless process. He fast-forwards the film to six that evening. Now she is on the drawing room sofa, waiting. Dressed in a black silk number she is drinking something, nervily. At six precisely the doorbell rings. She jumps up, presses the intercom:

'*Oui, oui, c'est moi.* Third floor. Come straight up.'

She zaps the front door open, then unbolts it: since the Camargue affair she keeps the manual lock fastened.

'*Ah, bonsoir, Monsieur Baudoin. Entrez!*'

Her frostiness is gone. She is not charming, exactly, but correct. Baudoin enters.

'*Bonsoir, Mademoiselle.*'

'Can I get you anything?'

'If you insist.'

'A glass of champagne?'

'*Volontiers!*'

She goes to the kitchen. Baudoin's rotund figure is clothed in a light checked English suit, new by the look of it. While she's gone he takes a look from the window. The bedroom door is ajar, so he throws a glance in there too.

Svetlana returns with a bottle, and pours.

'*Merci. Santé!*'

They drink.

'You have a beautiful apartment, in a beautiful square.'

'Please have a seat.'

They sit opposite one another.

'M. Baudoin, I'm a little busy. I've come back from the embassy early to see you. I'd be grateful if you could tell me what it's about.'

'I am sorry, I shall be brief. You have read my article on what happened?'

'Of course. You were very complimentary about the President. A fine piece of reportage.'

'Well, that is kind, but now it appears that I am in a difficult position. I will be honest. What I saw – what I *thought* I saw – it may not have been the whole truth.'

'I don't understand what you're saying.'

'I am saying there is a different story. One that will explain why your leader was not injured, and why no one has been arrested. A story I have from an impeccable source.'

She gestures, curtly:

'Go on.'

'You are Russian, *Mademoiselle,* you follow what is happening in your country. With the President I mean.'

'Naturally.'

'He's done well out of the attempt to assassinate him, no? I mean the opposition, it is nowhere.'

'So it appears. The Russians are impressed by his courage, like you yourself. As I recall you wrote that he was a man in control of his emotions, of himself, of the destiny of his country.'

'And you, you shared my admiration. *So masculine, so noble! There's something so vital about him.'* Your words, *Mademoiselle.* As for me, I was writing on the evidence of the time. But the evidence has changed.'

'In what way?'

'A contact of mine has come up with something. Something that transforms the situation.'

'And who is that?'

M. Baudoin smiled.

'You're asking a journalist to reveal his sources?'

'If you could get to the point, M. Baudoin.'

'*Eh bien*' – the intake of breath is so loud that Tony hears – '*eh bien,* there was no assassination attempt. It was all a pretence. A show.'

Svetlana is sitting unnaturally upright. Tony too is rigid on his sofa.

'Bullshit! Absolute bullshit!'

'You sound angry. Why so angry?'

'And why are you telling me lies?'

From M. Baudoin, a sigh.

'I'm sorry, it's painful for you, with your loyalty to your President, your *patriotisme.*'

'Lies are always painful. You are going to write this?'

'I am a journalist. I write things for a living. Unless there is some reason why I shouldn't.'

'And if you don't, are you going to repeat your lies to the authorities?'

'My information, you mean? Naturally I will not. Why would I do that? They would not believe me – would not *want* to believe me. For the French it is a delicate situation. Diplomatic relations, you know about that. So the authorities would prefer not to examine things too closely. And you, *Mademoiselle,* you would not want me to involve the authorities, would you?'

Svetlana is silent.

'But the press…' He shrugged. 'The press could oblige them to take notice. Do not forget that a Frenchman died in this mock attack. It would not be the first time we have seen these comedies. I am not a specialist on Russian affairs but I have done researches. *Provokatsia,* you call them I believe? Provocations, pretending that something happened so as to provoke a certain situation. In this case to pin the blame on someone else and pretend the President was a hero.'

'That's absurd, grotesque. An invention.'

'That would be for the Russian people to decide, in their elections. They will hear about the mock assassination and they will make their decision. You see the importance of my new information?'

'And I'm telling you it's rubbish. Who would have done such a thing?'

'In Marseille, there are people willing to do anything. And remember the explosion. It frightened me, so loud, but it happened at a distance, with no risk. A blind, out there in the water, how could they miss? But they did. All they killed was an innocent Frenchman. Otherwise a broken window, that was all. And that photo, with blood on his face – '

' – the one you took. So you know it was real.'

'Certainly I took it, and certainly it was real. There had been an explosion. But a broken window, a nick on the skin?' He shrugged. 'It was nothing.'

He shoots her a sardonic smile. Svetlana glowers back at him.

'I still don't understand why you are telling me all this.'

'To warn you.'

'Against what?'

'If my article comes out, people will wonder about your own position. Whether you were involved.'

'If I was involved?' Svetlana is tense. 'That is outrageous. Why would I want to kill my President?'

'*Non, non,* I don't mean involved in an assassination. I mean in a *false* assassination.'

'I wasn't there. I was in the hotel. And I was unwell.'

'A good time to be unwell, if I may say so, with all that drama. One moment you were fine, I remember, the next minute unwell. To avoid going out to the blind, perhaps? And you know, people talk. Someone attached to the London Embassy – they will wonder if she knew something. You know, the beautiful spy…'

'Who else have you told about this calumny?'

'No one. It is you the first. And it is not a calumny.'

'And your source? He is spreading his lies to other people?'

'No one. Not the security people, not the police. I have arranged for that. So we are the only people in on the truth, and together we can fix things. We have the same interests, *non?* Why would you want such a thing to be said about your President? Not to speak about you yourself. And me – why would I want to write it? To make my first article look stupid? For people to laugh at what I wrote about the hero-President, say how naïve I must have been, so that I lose commissions in the future?'

'So you want money.'

'From you? *Absolument pas!* Why should I? You had nothing to do with it, it is not your fault, I am ready to swear it! It is just that your idol has let you down. So we must, you know, regularize the situation.'

'Explain.'

'I have come to you because I think your Ambassador might like to be aware of the position. Then he can consult the relevant authorities and take the necessary precautions. Of course, if he is happy to see the truth emerge, complete with pictures, new pictures –'

' – what pictures?'

'Of things I have not published yet. Of the flak-jacket, for example. I haven't told you about the flak-jacket in the bedroom. A hunter, in a flak-jacket? *Voyons, Mademoiselle!* It is the ducks who need the flak-jacket! Unless of course he was expecting an explosion, at a distance, and wanted to make sure nothing touched him, that nothing was left to chance. Yes, of that I have a picture, in his bedroom. Perhaps you saw.'

'How would I have seen? What are you saying?'

M. Baudoin spread his hands, smirking.

'I am saying nothing, nothing. I just thought that, if you had visited the blind earlier – '

'I was his interpreter, why would I do that?'

Svetlana stands up, her face pallid against the black dress.

'I think you should go.'

M. Baudoin finishes his champagne, and stands.

'Very well. I wanted to help you, you and your President, your manly President… But you don't want it. So I am at liberty to write my article.'

'I said I want you to leave.'

Tony stares at his screen, riveted by Svetlana, willing her on. *That's it, throw him out! Let him go ahead and publish! Show that the whole thing was a farce got up by the FSB and Sasha knew nothing about it – still less me! Go on, for Christ's sake, throw the bastard out!*

Svetlana makes an angry gesture, seems about to speak, then says nothing. Baudoin makes for the door.

'One moment.'

A squeak of heels on the parquet as Baudoin turns.

'*Mademoiselle?*'

'I'm sorry. The idea that people could say such things… What you told me was such a shock, for a moment I felt faint. I need some air. Maybe we'll take a walk in the square? Then perhaps a quiet dinner, if you would care to join me? So we can continue our conversation.'

'*Avec plaisir.*'

'I'll get my coat.'

She is in the bedroom. After putting on a coat and cap, she stops for a second in front of a mirror, fussing with her hairline beneath the woollen hat. Then they are gone.

Tony switched off his computer.

The whole thing a fantasy concocted by the FSB, with Daudov as their agent! Too good to believe... Though why shouldn't it be true? He'd seen the rumours Russian dissidents had put about the moment it had happened, read about the snickering blogs: '*Horrified to hear of the near self-elimination of our revered leader*', or '*Wishing you a botched recovery from your unfortunately botched suicide attempt.*' That was Russian humour, Russian cynicism, but here was proof – or at least evidence.

Had Sasha known that there would be an attack and believed it would be genuine? Surely not. Was Daudov under instructions to string him along, so as to implicate him? More likely. So the boy would be in the clear – along with himself.

By way of celebration he downed a second nightcap, then a third, and slept more soundly than he had for days.

# 35

Next morning, along with the hangover, the doubts set in. He felt sore about his failure to spot what had been going on before his eyes, and wary about getting things wrong again.

Something didn't fit. Baudoin's plan was clear – to use Svetlana as a channel to the Russian Embassy and the FSB, to get them to buy his silence. Yet she'd shared Sasha's view of the President. So why would she be unhappy at the idea of the pseudo-assassination being exposed? There could only be one reason: that if it came out that Sasha had been duped into bankrolling it he would be exposed to the world as the sucker he was. Not to mention the boatman, for whose death he would be held responsible.

It would have been good to talk to Dick Welby, but after serving out his notice he'd gone off for a diving holiday in the Seychelles. Better do what Dick had recommended: cut to the chase and confront Sasha.

To find out whether he was back at the house he rang Ruth's office – and got onto Lisa. An awkward moment. They hadn't spoken since their early evening tryst had turned sour. He ought to have rung, to soothe her, but somehow he hadn't.

'And how are you, Mr Underwood?' she said when she answered. 'It's some time since we've spoken.'

Sarcasm? Or discretion, because Ruth was in the room?

'A nasty virus,' he sighed. Lying to Jean, lying to Lisa, it was getting to be a habit. 'I'm better now and I need to know when I can see Sasha.'

'He's still not around,' she said curtly, 'I'll find out where he is and let you know.'

'It would be good to see you too,' he added.

'No hurry,' she said, detecting perhaps the lack of urgency in his voice, and rang off.

It was Ruth who phoned next day to say Sasha could see him at the castle that evening. The same morning a letter arrived from Mikhail containing a cheque for £50,000. 'From Sasha,' a covering note from Mikhail explained. 'He says is bonus.'

He stared at the cheque. Bonus? For what? His guilt lasted a full minute. If this was a gesture from Sasha to keep him sweet he felt sweeter already.

Over breakfast he told Jean they were in luck: he'd had a windfall that would help cover the cost of the bridging loan he'd arranged for Penny's new flat, which meant she could go ahead with the garden conservatory she'd been pining for ever since their fortunes had improved. The cost she'd worked out at £30,000.

'Don't do anything cheap-looking,' he said, a little grandiosely, getting up from the table. 'Even if it comes out at another ten grand.'

His reward was a kiss. It was a perfunctory affair, though unusual in recent months, when his absences and distractions had widened the subtle estrangement that had begun between them.

Telling her he had to go to the country to see his boss that evening and would probably stay the night at the local hotel, he drove down to Suffolk.

*

The castle rose up before him after a sharp bend in the road, though the sight gave him little pleasure. With its sandblasted stonework, neatly-pointed turrets and new ironwork it looked too fussily restored, giving it a phony antique air.

The security measures Sasha had insisted on didn't help. Arc lights and razor wire along the perimeter wall, aerials and surveillance cameras protruding busily from the gatehouse – he understood why poor old Grekov had been unhappy. The place was like a modern fortress. *Unsympathetic in an area of outstanding natural beauty'* had been the council's judgement on the plans, before a generous donation for a new playground in the village had eased them through.

The staff manning the entrance – selected, like all the security personnel, by Tony personally – must have mistaken his visit for an inspection, and penetrating his own defences wasn't easy. The car check, the identity-proving, the airport-type photographs and thumbprint recognition device – they seemed to take pleasure in obliging him to go through the hoops Sasha had obliged him to instal.

In the house he found him engaged in hanging pictures, an incongruous figure in the centuries-old drawing room. For a moment he stood watching him giving orders to the three workmen. The way the boy slobbed around in sweatshirt and grubby jeans, while he himself felt duty-bound to appear in suit and tie, like some butler or head waiter, had begun to annoy him.

When Tony entered he didn't look round. Absorbed in selecting from a row of canvases ranged along the walls he seemed dazed, maybe a little drunk. It was, after all, past six o'clock.

Eventually he turned.

'Hi Tony.' He flourished a hand round the walls. 'So, how do you like it?'

With its vast stone fireplace, cavernous hearth, reclaimed oak panelling and the antlers Lisa had found on one of their antique-seeking expeditions, the room had rapidly acquired a baronial look. To complete the sombre impression the pictures the workmen were hanging were Russian: vast winter landscapes and grandiose country houses with benign-looking landowners and idealized peasants. Even to the untrained eye they looked second-rate.

'Come on, Tony,' Sasha repeated, 'what do you think?'

What Tony thought was that the place looked dowdy and depressing.

'Very fine. But I don't remember the pictures.'

'Stuff dad kept in store. Didn't know he had them till Mikhail told me.' He turned to the workmen. 'OK, you can take a break.'

The three of them shuffled out. While Sasha went on contemplating his handiwork Tony stood by the mullioned windows, looking out. A maid relieved the silence.

'Anything to drink, Sir?'

A village girl got up in a Russian-style pinafore, she was lumpy, plain and freckle-faced. He remembered vetting her on the nod: she'd seemed agreeable and would be safer than someone prettier from her boss's proprietorial hands.

'Champagne, a bottle,' Sasha said after a moment.

'You want the opened one Sir,' the novice enquired, 'or a new one?'

'A new one.'

'And where would you like it, Sir?'

'In my office.'

He led him through a long, high corridor. Like the drawing room the office was panelled, overlarge and chilly. Boxes of books and papers lay around as if hurriedly packed and transported, together with still more pictures. He's imitating his father, Tony thought, looking round, constructing a personality in his image. And it wouldn't come off.

For a while they sat in their high-backed Jacobean chairs chatting about the castle's security, the garden, the moat, the village, and saying nothing. The girl brought the champagne bottle.

Sasha poured their drinks, then said:

'Hang on a second, I need a piss.'

Left to himself, in need of his drink but obliged to wait, Tony stared unseeing through a distant window. A sudden dejection overcame him. On the drive down he'd persuaded himself that the Camargue drama was over, and the threat to his job lifted. And after Sasha had got his fingers burned with Daudov, keeping tabs on his activities would be easier than before.

Now his upbeat feeling had gone. Sitting in these alien surroundings making conversation with a boss more than thirty years his junior, rich beyond measure and feckless beyond imagination, for the second time since Grekov had died he began asking himself: can I take another seven years of this? Of being a security adviser and in-house spy, a kind of double agent whose mission it was to save Sasha from himself?

From now on he'd be responsible for the security of this hideous mock-up of a castle, as well as the gruesome Belgravia house. And being down here reminded him of his affair with Lisa: a matter of circumstance, he saw now. Something about working alongside one another in the eerie, overblown mansion had driven them together like lost souls, the only ones in the place who were normal.

The truth was he wasn't suited to affairs with women. The money he'd been able to give his family had helped submerge his guilt about betraying his sick wife, but it was there. Deceit and double-dealing in his work was something he had lived with, a necessary part of his profession. Two-timing in his personal life was a different matter, something he couldn't rationalize away.

Back from the toilet, Sasha sat down and raised his glass.

'Well, cheers.'

'Cheers.'

'By the way,' Tony got out with a struggle, 'thanks for the bonus.'

'It's nothing.'

'I'm not sure I've earned it.'

''Course you have. You've done a great job down here. Pity dad didn't live to see it...'

The boy smiled, nervously. Tony was silent. He was waiting for him to say something about the Camargue attack being phony. Svetlana would have told him about Baudoin, and like Tony himself he must be mightily relieved. But Sasha stayed shtum, and given the source of his information he couldn't say anything before he gave him a lead. Instead he began chattering on about stuff he'd read on the Russian Internet, jokey as ever, though his voice was tense.

It was when they'd finished the bottle (it didn't take long) and he roared for another (the girl came quickly, she was learning) that finally an opening came.

Uncorking it Sasha said:

'So what are your MI5 friends saying about the Camargue thing?'

He was standing over him, filling his glass. Tony hesitated.

'Come on, Tony, they must have a view.'

'The message I'm getting,' he found himself saying, 'is that it was an inside job.'

Sasha's glass, halfway to his mouth, stayed poised in the air.

'Say again?'

'An FSB operation. To help him win the elections.'

He could almost hear the cogs in Sasha's drink-dulled mind grinding as he worked through the implications. Eventually he said:

'Impossible. It can't be.'

'Why not?'

'Because I know who did it, and it wasn't Moscow.'

Sasha slugged back his glass. Ignoring Tony he poured himself another. 'It was someone who did stuff for me – un-attributably. The whole thing was his idea. I didn't know what he was up to, I just gave him the money. And next thing I know there's been an assassination attempt.

'Must have been out of his mind. Stupid bastard didn't even make a proper job of it.' His laugh was brief and thin. 'And if the French pick him up, next thing they'll be onto me. Not to speak of the Russians. How deep in the shit can you get?'

Tony stared back at him. Either Svetlana hadn't told him about Baudoin, or the Frenchman was not just a blackmailer but a liar. This was his worst fear, the one he'd been doing his best to put to the back of his mind: that his story about the flak-vest and the rest was an invention, and that his own hope that Sasha and himself were in the clear was self-delusion.

'Come on Tony, say something for Christ's sake! How do I get out of this one? What do you advise? A chance to earn your bonus.'

Tony looked at the floor.

'How did your man do it?' he said. 'Is it true what some of the French press has been saying? An exploding bird? It seems a bit …exotic.'

'Don't ask me. All I knew was that he was thinking of creating publicity by buggering up the hunt using a bird to drop stuff round the blind. No one told me it would be a fucking bomb.'

'Nobody's going to buy that. He worked for you, you paid him, and if he's caught they'll find out. And don't forget, a man was killed.'

Sasha's glass went back to his mouth, urgently. By now he was drunk. Drunk and trembling, falling apart before him.

'So what do I do?'

'Come clean, before you have to.'

'Fucking hell Tony! That's the policeman in you coming out!' He hunched forward, frowning. 'You won't tell them, will you? I'll make sure you – '

' – just don't offer me money, OK?' Tony cut in like an irate father. 'I can't do anything for you unless you're honest with me. The first thing is, who else knows?'

'A girlfriend.'

'Is she reliable?'

'Absolutely.'

'No one else?'

'No-one.'

'So who's the girlfriend?'

'It's…private. I'd rather not say. I don't want to incriminate her.'

'Well there you go.'

Exasperated, with a gesture of renunciation Tony got to his feet.

'Where you going?'

'If you're not straight with me I can't help you.'

Sasha looked up at him, his glazed eyes pleading. Then lumbered to his feet and looked at his watch.

'Tony, can we talk about this tomorrow? I've got someone arriving for dinner.'

'OK, in the morning, I'm staying the night. But I repeat: if I'm going to help I need to know about everything, your girlfriend included. What time tomorrow? It had better be early.'

'Eleven? I'd ask you to stay in the house but – '

' – don't worry, I'm booked into the hotel.'

A car was arriving as he drove away. Inside he caught a glimpse of blond hair. Svetlana? Had she got more out of Baudoin, and come here to confer with Sasha? Maybe it was true, after all, and the whole thing was a Kremlin job. For Sasha's sake – and his own – it had better be.

# 36

Daudov did a line of coke, wiped his nose and stared into the mirror in the bathroom of his Pimlico hotel. He was happy with what he saw: a new man, minus the hippy hair and earring, in sober suit and tie. A man with a Ukrainian passport in his pocket with visas for London and Brazil, plus a bank account containing over four hundred thousand dollars, minus the couple of grand he'd spent on clothes at Jaeger's in Regent Street that morning.

Getting back into London had been a strain on his nerves: there'd been a query about the passport at immigration, though in the end they'd let him through. As the coke began doing its work he felt steadier. He sank into an armchair and looked round his £350-a-night suite.

Not bad for a lad from a Georgian mountain village. It was his determination to get away that had led him into the army. Joining up a year before the Russian invasion turned out to be a smart move: the war was short, he'd been out of the front line, he'd taken the first chance to get himself captured and spent a year in a prison camp. It was in the weeks before he was due for release that they'd taken him to see a Russian colonel in his office outside the camp.

'Have a seat,' the colonel said, 'I've brought you here so we can have a talk. It's part of the release procedure. You know, so there's no hard feelings. A drink, perhaps?'

It was the first of several meetings. At the last one the colonel had asked him what he'd be doing when he was released. 'Anything but stay in Georgia,' he'd said. 'I have a friend who's gone to live in Marseille, so I was hoping to join him, provided I can get some papers.' The colonel claimed to know someone in the Russian Consulate General, and had come up with a passport and a French visa, plus five thousand dollars 'to help him back into civilian life.' So there'd be no hard feelings.

Everything had worked out fine. The five grand had set him up in the dealing business, and on top of that there were the 300 euros they gave him when he met the colonel's Russian Consulate friend for a chat about the Chechen or Dagestani exiles he was in touch with, such as Kasym and his brother. It was enough to get by, though it was when he'd gone to London and they'd passed him on to Victor Bulagin, the First Secretary for Cultural Affairs, and he'd been instructed to get himself fixed up with Sasha, that the money got big.

After the Camargue operation it was going to be a lot bigger. In addition to his four hundred thousand – the remains of Sasha's million – in Rio another two million would be waiting, courtesy of Victor. No risk of anything going wrong there, because if it did the world would know about it. When he'd said that to Victor after they'd clinched the plan, it hadn't gone down well. The Russian had looked at him like he was shit.

'I don't care for your gangster talk. Of course you'll get your money, you're dealing with a professional.'

He'd never liked Victor, with his pointy beard and strutting manner. The man had a genius for making you feel bad about yourself, never ran out of ways of putting you down. He knew he was only half-Chechen, but that didn't spare him the jokes. You tell him your girlfriend's expecting and you're worried about the expense, hoping he'd up your retainer. Instead he says: 'Well congratulations, and what will you call your little Mohamed?' And roars his head off.

In London they'd rendezvous in art galleries in Dalston, him being cultural attaché, a different gallery every time, and even there he'd talk down at him. 'At least you could *try* to look interested,' he'd murmur as they stood in front of some pile of contemporary crap, 'even if you have the artistic sensibility of an orangutan.'

They'd got along well enough to put the Camargue operation together. Victor had come down to Marseille as soon as he'd got his message, and liked the idea of a mock assassination so much he'd taken it over, talked about it as if it was his own. Later he'd come down again, this time in a foul mood. After a hard night's drinking (the guy was a serious dipso), he'd let on that his Moscow bosses had turned it down. Though he was going ahead anyway, he'd told him, using 'unofficial channels'.

He hadn't pushed him about what he'd meant – Victor could turn stroppy in his drink – but it sounded like he'd got backing from outside the service. Not that it made any difference: all he'd needed was for someone to come up with the cash. When he'd told him about his idea of using a bird (it was Kasym's in fact, but what the hell) he'd loved that too.

Otherwise, nothing was ever good enough for Victor.

It would have been good to see the bearded little fucker now, ask him whether he was pleased with the operation, but then Victor would have found fault, and he knew what his gripe would have been: the dead boatman.

And it *was* his fault, no two ways. Fucking helicopter had put him off his stroke, he'd been so keen to steer the falcon well away from the blind that he'd brought it down too close to the flamingo island. Though think what Victor would have said if he'd erred on the other side.

It troubled him, the dead boatman, troubled him a lot. It was the first time he'd killed a man and he was sorry, sorry for the boatman and for the tearful young wife French TV had kept showing, though mainly for himself. A murderer! The French would keep after him now, wherever he was.

And there'd be no one else to take the rap. Kasym had nothing more to worry about, because he was dead. Some sort of fit while they'd been getting away, clawing at his head he was, going mental, and Batir had to hold him down. The last thing they needed at that moment, though it was soon over: a few minutes of threshing and shrieking and that was it.

They'd taken off his gendarme's outfit, wrapped him in the groundsheet and left him at the back door of a mosque Batir knew, so he'd get a proper burial. Amazing how Batir had kept his cool. *It was the will of Allah, peace be upon him,* was all he'd said, *and upon my doubting brother.* Scary, the way they talked. At least it would save him from paying Kasym his share, he'd thought, but Batir said he was to make sure it reached his wife and son, pronto, or else he'd talk. So he'd wired it off to Canada.

Brain seizure, he'd heard later, which was no surprise. He'd had these blinding headaches since childhood, apparently, and you could see there'd been something not right about him. Must have been half out of his mind all along, poor bastard, but then you'd have to be, to think you were going to assassinate the Russian President with a fucking bird. It was when they'd said on the car radio that except for a nick on his forehead he was in perfect health that Kasym had gone beserk.

Talk about tough luck: first the boatman, then Kasym. It was the boatman's death that had brought him to London. He'd have to stay out in Rio longer now, indefinitely perhaps, with Klara and the kid, and for that he'd need more cash. He wouldn't get it from Victor, so it would have to be Sasha.

And this time the one calling the shots would be him. He'd run over it in his mind a hundred times, knew word for word what Sasha would say and what he would reply:

'Mr Sasha, I need money.'

'Fuck off. I've paid you once, why should I pay again?'

'Because you did it the first time. How would you like the FSB to know that? And find yourself with a hole in the head, or some mysterious disease, like your dad?'

'I didn't ask you to kill him!'

'And I didn't. But you paid for the attempt, didn't you, which is all the Russians need to know. And Mr Sasha, please don't say 'this is blackmail!' because then I'll say, 'fine, it's blackmail. So go ahead and call the police.'

'How much?'

'Couple of million.'

And Sasha would say 'you must be joking!' and do his best to look tough, his eyes all hard but his face wobbly. So then he'd say:

'Come on Mr Sasha, I haven't got time to play around. A couple of million and you'll be rid of me, have your peace of mind. Worth it, wouldn't you say?'

'You're a greedy fucking bastard,' Sasha would shout at him, then pay up, same as he always did.

He got to his feet, ranged around the hotel room. The coke had fired him up, he felt good now, looking forward to the confrontation. Maybe he'd make it pounds, not dollars. But first he had to find out where Sasha was.

He tried his private mobile. No reply. He dialled his office. It was Ruth who answered.

'Mr Sasha, please.'

He spoke in a low voice with a reinforced accent.

'Sorry, he's not available.'

'Maybe I get him on country number?'

'You have it?'

'Somewhere I have it, not here…Maybe you give it me please?'

'Sorry Sir, we do not give numbers out.'

'OK, OK, never mind.'

'And your name, Sir?'

He put down the phone.

Sasha must be at the place in Suffolk. He knew where it was because he'd been there, at Bulagin's request. The idea had been to plant an informant amongst the security staff, but it hadn't come off. The guy Bulagin had in mind – a Latvian of Russian descent – had been weeded out by some security consultant the old man had employed to vet the applicants. Never mind, he'd picked up enough about the castle to know his way around.

He left the hotel and stood waiting for a cab to Liverpool Street station. Then changed his mind and walked towards Victoria Street. Sasha was weak but stubborn, the way weak men could be. He liked making him wait before coming up with the cash, but not today he wouldn't. There wasn't the time, he had a flight to make, needed to get out of the country. So he'd better take something along to persuade him to come across smartly.

The knives in the kitchen section of the department store in Victoria Street were confusing in their variety. A black and silver blur spread out before him. He lingered over the display. Carver? Too fierce-looking, and too long. It wasn't as if he was going to use it… A steak knife? Easier to hide, but they came in sets of six… A three-piece, for chopping? The small one looked good but the blades were too fat, wouldn't slip into a pocket… So maybe one of the steak knives. Short, serrated, scary…

'Can I help you, Sir?'

He looked up. A shop assistant, a young woman. Her tight blue frock, the store uniform, went with her light blond hair, caressed her rounded figure.

She smiled at him. Of course she smiled. His thousand-pound suit, his new haircut, his bank balance and his Georgian complexion, the blondes liked that. He grinned back, broadly, a power-smile. Give her a drink, take her back to his fancy hotel. For her he could make time.

'Yes you help me. You tell me name.'

The girl was wearing a name badge. He hadn't noticed, but now he did.

'Oh, so maybe here.'

He reached for the badge as if to check it, slipped it between his fingers. Her skin through the frock felt warm to his knuckles. He tweaked it towards him.

'*Katie*. Is nice…'

Removing his hand from her dress the assistant turned on her heel and stalked away.

Racist bitch… Like Victor and Sasha, racist bastards, all of them.

He turned back to the knives, which gleamed brighter. Yes, a steak knife it would be, with the black handle. He bought the half dozen set, left five on top of a toilet cistern in the store, hired a cab and caught a train on the East Suffolk service from Liverpool Street. On the journey he fell asleep and dreamt about what he would do if Sasha didn't play ball. Then woke in a sweat and took another line in the lavatory ten minutes before he arrived in Southwold.

# 37

When Sasha told Tony he had someone coming for dinner he wasn't lying, though it wasn't Svetlana. For days now she'd been out of touch. Desperate to contact her he'd spent half the afternoon before Tony arrived trying to track her down. Only she could tell him what his next move should be, without her he had no sense of what to do or where he was going.

He'd hesitated before wiring the ten million she'd asked for because he didn't believe the threat she'd appeared to make was serious, just her being dramatic. Then wired it anyway. The money had gone through – he'd checked with the bank – but there'd been nothing from her. He'd rung her landline at the flat, her official mobile, her pay-as-you-go mobile. No reply. Frantic, he'd got onto the embassy, something she'd told him never to do. Still nothing. 'She only here sometimes…Today she is away…' the Ambassador's secretary told him. 'No, we cannot take message.'

Svetlana had disappeared.

Another evening alone in his wintry castle (teething problems with the boiler) held few attractions. Before Tony turned up, for company he'd rung a girlfriend, Heidi Dutton-Rose, one of his swimming pool sports in London.

'Heidi, I'm down in the country… Yeah, the castle, it's finished. I've got a brand new pool down here, we need to baptize it.'

'Darling you're crazy! It's nearly five o'clock, you're miles away.'

'You'll be glad you came.'

'That's sweet of you, darling, I'm sure I would.' Heidi hesitated. Last time she'd come to the Belgravia pool she'd been glad to the tune of £3,000. 'But really I can't, I'm in London. Southwold must be three hours' drive. More.'

'Not if you're asleep. Hire a car, have a nap on the way, I'll leave the fare at the gate.'

To a girl who'd got to bed at five that morning, it wasn't such a mad suggestion. And so Heidi was awoken just after eight that evening by her driver informing the dead-eyed woman in the back of his Lexus that she was at Burntwood castle, and could she please settle the £375 fare? A sum the night porter supplied, doing his best to suppress his incredulity at the man's demand for a tip, not to speak of the length of leg that had preceded Heidi's exit from the car.

It wasn't the last surprise of the evening. Three hours later another taxi turned up at the gatehouse, this time local, from Southwold station. From it emerged a man of thirty in a smart suit, overcoat and broad-brimmed hat.

The visitor knocked on the gatehouse window. The porter opened it.

'I have come see Mr Sasha.'

'Who shall I say it is, Sir?'

'Tell him is Monsieur Henri.'

The porter hesitated. An automated lamp had come on outside the gatehouse, bathing the visitor in its rays. He didn't look like a Henry, he looked and spoke foreign.

'Hold on a moment Sir, I'll see if he's available.'

Closing the window the porter rang the security desk and explained. Security said they would ring back. M. Henri, meanwhile, had taken the liberty of coming into his office and was stumping up and down, frowning.

Except for the entrance in the castle, the lights were extinguished. Two floors up, in the master bedroom, Heidi lay drunk and asleep. Next to her was Sasha, drunk and spent, but awake with worry about what he would say to Tony next morning. The pair lay in a four-poster, a new and impetuous buy. It's attractions included its antique canopy and curtains, closed tonight against the chill of the vast, high room, its disadvantage its cramping size.

Beyond the curtain a pager bleeped softly. Sasha got up and went outside, into the hall. It was security, about Mr Henry:

'Sorry to trouble you, Sir, but the gentleman says he's a friend.'

Starkly awake now, Sasha stared from a window into the blackness.

'Tell him I can't see him. It's too late. Say I'll ring him tomorrow.'

The security man told the porter, then rang back.

'The gentleman says he has things to discuss tonight.'

'I told you, it's too fucking late!'

'I know, Sir, but he said to tell you 'better to discuss with you than other people.' Those were his words, Sir.'

Sasha stared on through the window. The night seemed blacker, the corridor colder.

'Oh all right. Let the bugger in for God's sake!'

In the gatehouse, Daudov unbuttoned his overcoat. It was hot in the small room, and beneath the hat he had pulled down at the sight of the CCTV camera in the corner, his head was sweating.

'He says you're to go in, Sir.'

The porter wrote down the taxi number. Mr Henry supplied his fingerprints but he was spared the airport-style scan: '*Let the bugger in!*' the boss had said, so he must know him.

The porter pressed his concealed button and the gates swung open. At the entrance to the castle a guard escorted Mr Henry inside.

'He'll be down in a minute, Sir.'

They waited. The cavernous hall, the silent guard, the feel of the knife in his overcoat pocket... Daudov's heart was audible to himself.

'You have toilet?'

'Yes, Sir.'

The guard pointed to a doorway. Daudov went inside then stopped, mesmerized. It was the lavatory that held his gaze, a lavatory that was nothing more than a wooden box. Nicely polished, but a box. An English castle with a latrine like the shithouse in his Georgian village, though without the stink.

Using the marble washstand he snorted another line – a line of courage – and went back to the hall.

A few minutes and Sasha came down, descending the broad flight of stairs wearing a white flannel dressing gown and loafers with no socks. Again Daudov found himself mesmerized, this time by the soft round whiteness of the Russian's ankles.

On the bottom step he stopped and glared at the figure in the hat and overcoat. In response to his questioning eyes, the hat came off and Sasha took in the face. Him, no question. Daudov dressed to the nines and without the excess hair.

'I look different, eh?'

'Mmm.'

'So sorry, Mr Sasha, I wake you up?'

'This way.'

Ignoring his commiserations he led him along the corridor to his office. Inside, Daudov stared around.

'A castle,' he said. 'A real castle. Is like from film.'

He had kept on his coat yet he felt himself shiver. He felt hot, but shivery.

'*Nu chto.*' Sasha mumbled, then switched to English. In English it was easier to put Daudov down. 'What the fuck are you doing here? I told you, no contact.'

'You must help, Mr Sasha. You know what has happen.'

'What happened had nothing to do with me. All I know is that I've given you money. Plenty.'

'For operation you gave it, but is gone. For the others, for travel, for expenses – is gone. For bird and for car and for visas – '

' – I'm not asking for an expense account. Though I see you got yourself some new clothes out of it.'

'Is gone, Mr Sasha, everything gone. So how I get away? How I live?'

'The deal was a million in dollars, and no questions.'

'Everything change now.'

'You're too right it has! Because of your stupidity! Nobody asked you to kill him!'

'But you ask, Mr Sasha, I remember.'

'What are you talking about? When?'

'In café, in London. I tell you I shoot Russians in Georgian war and you say now you have chance for a shot at President.'

'It was a joke, you lying bloody numbskull! A fucking joke!'

He fell onto a sofa, leaving him standing. Daudov stared down at him. Tonight he didn't feel small before him, he felt powerful, shivering a little with his feeling of power. 'No, no joke. It was you keep asking for something big. With President only big thing is – ' he drew a hand across his throat. 'So I think, he make joke, he not want say what he ask for. But I do what he no want say. You give me money and I do it. The President he escape but a French man die. It is for you he die, you who make me murderer! So now you help me.'

To the Georgian's coked-up mind all this wasn't a lie exactly, and his anger was sincere. When he said that Sasha had wanted him to kill the President he believed it, because beneath the lie he felt a kind of truth. It was Sasha and his obsession with the Russian leader that had given him his idea about the mock assassination, got him into this whole terrifying business, made a killer of him.

Sasha folded his dressing gown over his legs. He didn't like Daudov standing there, his forehead glistening, or Daudov talking back at him with that fixed bright light in his eye. Which was why he'd decided to buy him off. Another million would do it – though not until he'd knocked him about a little, made him feel some of the fear he felt himself.

'You're lying! I never asked you to do it, and anyway you botched it! You did what I never asked and you fucking botched it. And now you have the insolence to come whining to me for cash!'

Daudov had stopped shivering. Strangely serene, he smiled.

'Mr Sasha, I no like how you talk.'

'Well don't come blackmailing me.'

'Mr Sasha, you no ask me sit down. I come long way, I am thirsty, but you not offer me drink.'

'You can ask the fucking doorman on the way out.'

'Mr Sasha, you treat me like I am nothing, but maybe I more clever than you. You want me tell you things I know?'

'What is it you know?'

Sasha was frowning.

'You think is me do operation, but is not.'

'What are you talking about?'

'Is intelligence man control what you do. You no know that, eh?'

'You're raving.'

'You are angry, Mr Sasha. I like see you angry because you don't know about intelligence man. Is you who are stupid, Mr Sasha.'

He paused, staring down at him, enjoying his perplexed expression: his sagging mouth, his startled eyes.

'I don't believe you. What's his name?'

Daudov's lips came forward to form the B of Bulagin. At first the name wouldn't come, then he said it:

'Bulagin, Victor. He work for embassy. He know everything about you. The drug you take, what you do in Camargue, everything. Even he know – '

He stopped, his mind slipping in and out of focus, his forehead wrinkling in surprise at the echo of his words. *Bulagin, Victor.* He shouldn't have said that, should never have come out with the name. He'd dreamt of how one day he would tell him, for the hell of it, to make him sweat, but now wasn't the time. Not before he'd got the money, Bulagin's money, in Rio. He mustn't risk the money.

For a moment they stared at each other. Daudov thinking he mustn't say any more, Sasha's mind threshing.

'You're lying. And I want you out of my house.'

Daudov took a step towards him.

'I leave when I want. Is me give orders now. First you give me more.'

'Oh, come on, for fuck's sake, how much do you want? I'll give you your money – another million dollars.'

He stopped. Daudov had come a step closer, smiling now. Sasha was afraid and he liked that, the fear in his eyes drawing him on towards this fat pink slug of a Russian till he was standing over him.

At his approach Sasha pressed into the corner of the sofa, a hand gripping the arm.

'Pounds! Pounds I'll make it!'

Daudov glanced round the office.

'You have money here?'

'Of course not, not here for Chrissake! I'll give it you tomorrow – in cash. From Mikhail I'll get it. I'll ring him straight away. Tonight – now.'

In his reverie on the train Daudov had imagined how everything would happen. If Sasha didn't come across with the money he wouldn't just threaten him, he'd do it. Pull out the knife, close his eyes and do it.

But he *had* come across, promised him cash. Should he wait till he got it – take a later plane to Rio? But he'd told Sasha about Bulagin, couldn't hang around. If Sasha told the police…

He stared down at him. He had picked up the phone and was dialling. For Mikhail – for the money? Or for the guard in the hall – the police?

His left hand shot out to snatch the phone, his right into his overcoat pocket. As he leant over him with the knife the dressing gown parted over his chest, a plump fleshy chest that smelt of scent, like a woman's.

He had dreamt that he'd close his eyes when he did it but they stayed open, so when he lunged at him he saw Sasha draw his legs onto the sofa and thrust out his arms blindly. Then the easeful feel as the blade went in under the left breast, softly, soft as the hairless flesh.

*

'Kevin, good to see you. How're things?'

Kevin was the security guard on front door duty when Tony arrived next morning. A stolid-looking fellow with sideburns and a paunch, he was one of those he'd recruited from the village, in preference to the ex-army types and guys from the Baltic states, or wherever.

'Fine, Mr Underwood. Nice to have people down here, keeps me on my toes. Mr Grekov knows you're coming?'

'He does. Is he around?'

'Haven't seen him yet, I'm sure he'll be down shortly. Perhaps you'd like to wait in his office? You know where it is?'

'I do.'

Halfway along the corridor he heard high heels on the hall stairs.

'Good morning, Miss.'

Svetlana? Tony stopped to listen.

'Where's Sasha?' a woman's voice asked.

'Can't say, Miss. Maybe he's having a swim? They've got the heating working.'

'How do I get to the pool?'

'Here, I'll show you.'

It didn't sound like Svetlana. He walked back a few paces to check, in time to glimpse Kevin escorting a long-legged, long-haired blonde towards the back of the castle. No, definitely not Svetlana. A pity…

He went back along the corridor to the office and opened the heavy oak door.

# 38

Tony sat down with his pint and his French and English papers in the pub that had been his MI5 local. It had been a busy start to the day, and the first chance he'd had to look at them. The *Mail* and the *Telegraph* he dispatched quickly. It was days after Sasha's murder, there were a couple of follow-up stories, but for him there was nothing new.

Instead he began scanning *Le Figaro* and *Le Monde*. These days it had become a habit, good for his rusty French if not for his nervous system. *Le Monde* had found space for a brief report on Sasha, but today there was a longer, investigatory piece on the death of Raymond Baudoin.

*Fin Mystérieuse d'un Journaliste* was the headline.

'Baudoin could court controversy,' its chief crime correspondent wrote from London. 'But what no-one can work out is why anyone should hold a grudge so strong as to strangle the poor devil and dump his body in the Regent's Canal – in London a kind of collective grave for the least distinguished murder victims.

'One thing is certain: it can hardly have been the Russians. His description of their leader's heroic behaviour in the Camargue attack won him praise in Moscow's official media. The CIA? Conceivable, though that assumes they were behind the failed assassination in the first place, and that Baudoin had found out. All in all, a fanciful notion.

'Conspiracy theorists will be in their element,' the correspondent went on. 'Though as puzzled by this death as the French, the British are equally inclined to downplay rumours of international skulduggery. There are no indications that M. Baudoin was involved with intelligence services, his own or anyone else's. Suggestions of a link with the murder of Alexander (Sasha) Grekov, son of the recently deceased Russian oligarch, have been dismissed as speculative. There is no evidence they knew one another.

'M. Baudoin's sordid demise, French police are suggesting, bears the hallmarks of something more banal: sexual adventures, in a word. He was known to have a partiality for ladies of the night (he lived not far from the bars and clubs of the Gare du Nord), and he'd made a small fortune from his Camargue scoop. So the most likely explanation is that he fell victim to some sort of sexual scam. He would not be the first to discover that nowadays London nightlife can be more diverse and exotic than anything in his Paris locality.

'Other evidence points in this direction. His wallet and watch were missing and, according to British sources, there is speculation that the bruising around his neck could be consistent with some form of deadly erotic game.'

Finishing the article, Tony took a long draught of his beer. MI5, where he'd been that morning, were disinclined to spend much time on the Baudoin story. Like *Le Monde* they tended to accept the pre-liminary police conclusion of a sexual mishap. After his dinner with Svetlana, nothing more natural than a drunken sex addict in a foreign capital to get himself into dangerous company.

What interested MI5 more was the mock assassination, and on that it had been a gruelling session. The refrain he kept hearing from his former colleagues was why in hell's name hadn't he filled them in on what Sasha had been up to from the start?

Not enough evidence, a confidentiality agreement with Grekov, the risks of alarming a dying man – somehow he'd defended his corner. It was bullshit, but what alternative did he have? The truth – that he'd been worried about losing his job and had sworn he'd have nothing to do with MI5 after they'd hoofed him out – would not have gone down well.

*

The only good news these last few days had been about his payoff. The lawyer he'd consulted had assured him that although the agreement with Grekov had been for seven years, given that it was a condition of Sasha's inheritance, his executors would be obliged to pay up, 'his premature death notwithstanding'. Under Grekov's munificent contract a final year's salary would also be due.

So it wasn't all disaster. His daughter would get her Wimbledon flat, his granddaughter's fees would be secured, and she loved the new school. And Jean would go on getting her new treatment, to which she was responding.

Dick Welby was back from the Seychelles, and by way of celebration over his windfall he'd invited him to lunch. Bringing him up to date would mean a long session, something to which he was looking forward. Having someone he could talk to frankly would leave him feeling less lonely, worn down, mentally exhausted.

The restaurant was in Mayfair, a top drawer joint where he'd never eaten. *Convivial bar, a chic, upper-crust clientele, divine seafood at nose-bleed prices* the guide where he'd looked it up before coming had said.

Following the maître d' into the depths of the room, he glanced about. The review was spot on, the noise convivial and the clientele most certainly chic, to the point where even Tony could put a name to a couple of the celebrity faces. And the seafood looked superb. Passing the oyster bar he did his best to keep his eyes off a famous model, her splayed fingers picking apart a King prawn, her long bare legs pleasingly entangled in the chrome of her stool.

He sat at his table, resisted the urge to order a drink before Dick arrived, and waited.

'Tony.'

Dick was standing over him, horribly tanned and fit-looking, though it was a relief to see him. His trim little figure suggested an ability to navigate the most unpromising situation.

Dick sat down and studied his friend's drawn and pallid features.

'Jesus, you look awful.'

'In my situation so would you.'

'Tell me about it, I'm behind the game. The last thing you told

me was you were going to have it out with Sasha about his bungled
assassination, or whatever it was. The first English paper I got hold
of in the Seychelles told me he'd been bumped off. Next thing I saw
on French telly that some French journalist involved in the
President's visit was bobbing about in Regent's canal. You better fill
me in.'

Tony described the scene at Sasha's murder: how he'd gone to
see him at the castle that morning and found him sprawled on the
sofa in his office half-naked, blood all over him, like a stuck pig.
Then the scene got up by the girl he'd spent the night with, some
high-class tart howling like a banshee when the police told her she'd
be accompanying them to the station.

Not that she'd been long detained. The gatekeeper had pictures
of Mr Henri despite his broad-brimmed hat (there were low-level as
well as overhead cameras in his hut). In case of doubt, the fingerprints on the knife he'd left in the body matched the ones the porter
had taken, and to tie things up he'd managed to leave a blood-
smeared handkerchief in his taxi back to the station. Not a very professional operation, but then they'd found traces of his cocaine in
the hall toilet. He'd got out of the country smartly but been picked
up on arrival in Rio de Janeiro.

'So what's he saying?' Dick asked.

'Officially – nothing. The arrest hasn't been announced. They're
keeping it close for the moment.'

'And privately?'

'Brazilians let our man in the embassy talk to him. He did Sasha
all right. Went there to screw more money out of him, got drugged
up and knifed him.'

'And the Camargue?'

'It was an exploding bird – a mechanized falcon.'

'Jesus. And it was Sasha?'

'No.'

'So who?'

'No-one. There was no assassination attempt. The whole thing
was a charade and the President was never in the remotest danger.'

'So who the hell was behind it? The FSB?'

'No. Seems their hands were clean.'

'That would be a first. And the Kremlin? Was it some off piste operation, with the President in the know?'

'Not that either. Daudov was working for a mid-level FSB guy, Victor Bulagin. Cultural attaché so-called, and a serious drunk. Seems to have gone rogue when his bosses vetoed the Camargue operation. At which point he sold it to some oligarch pals. Rich crooks doing well out of the regime and scared to hell their man might lose the election.'

'Who else was in on it?'

'He was using these Chechen brothers. Poor dummies thought the assassination was for real. But they weren't jihadis. Turns out that the fellow with the bird – Kasym, the one I told you about – had this personal grudge over his dad being killed in the war. Bit off his head, apparently. Had a brain seizure when he heard Daudov had missed.'

'Anyone else?'

'The only other one involved was the personal protection officer on the blind. Bribed, I imagine, to make sure he didn't overreact to the explosion. That seems to have been the set-up.' He shrugged. 'Not that we'll ever know for sure.'

Dick gave a sigh.

'Nothing the Russians like better than a *provokatsia*, but pretending to bomb your own President is pushing it. So what happened to Bulagin?'

'Hopped it, after Sasha got his. Must have guessed it was his druggy friend. Either way, he'd gone. Just as well. Otherwise the Foreign Office would have had to decide whether or not to declare him *persona non grata*. If he'd been trying to assassinate anyone else, he'd have been out on his neck, but if it's your own President, the attack's phony and it's in someone else's country... Bit of a protocol problem.'

'And Sasha's girl?' Dick enquired. 'Svetlana, wasn't it? What's the deal with her?'

'Our man asked Daudov about her, in case she'd been in with

Bulagin, double-crossing her boyfriend. But Daudov hadn't heard of her, never met her. All they got from him were the bare bones, mind you. Ten minutes into the interview he blanked out. Some sort of blood poisoning, must have dosed himself up on the plane. Stuffed to the gills with coke and booze, and Christ knows what.

'He's been hospitalized, so it'll be a while before our man gets another go at him. Meanwhile they're keeping things quiet, for diplomatic reasons. Though eventually it'll all come out, when he stands trial for doing in Sasha and blowing up the French boatman.'

'And on Svetlana, what's your guess?'

'Last I heard she'd disappeared, though maybe she'll be back. See if her boyfriend's left her something.'

The truth was Svetlana was a bit of a blank. The recording of her meeting with Baudoin had been the last take he'd had from the flat. The day after he'd delivered it, poor Tom had gone down with pneumonia.

'And your good self?' Dick resumed, 'where does this leave you? In deep shit with the service, I imagine?'

'Will they cut my pension, you mean? No, thank God. The thing about Daudov's stuff is not just that it clears Sasha – lot of good that'll do the bugger now – but it exonerates me. Before he blanked out he confirmed that Sasha had never known it was going to be an assassination attempt, phony or otherwise. Which puts me in the clear as well. My nightmare was that it was genuine, that Sasha *had* been involved, and MI5 would come looking for me. Not to speak of the Russians and their polonium-packing killers.'

'So how do you stand now it's over?'

'I lose a job I should never have taken on and get my multi-million pay off.' With a dour smile, he spread a hand round the restaurant. 'Which accounts for this.'

Dick raised his glass.

'Well, good for you.'

'Can't say I've earned it. The job was to keep Sasha alive.'

'You did what you could.'

'Which was sod-all, it turned out.'

A moment's silence, before Dick gave a sigh.

'*Shit doesn't just stink, it sticks.* Looks like you were right.'

'I said that?'

'You did. About having anything to do with ex-intelligence people. That was before you went in with Grekov, though he was on the straight and narrow, God rest his soul. Anyway you're shot of it now, so why worry?'

'It's not the way I saw my career ending. And I'm out of a job.'

'Makes two of us. And to think I was looking for openings in the private security business.'

They had a cognac and cigar on the terrace, while Tony talked and talked. Finally he loosened up enough to tell his friend about Lisa.

'Oh Christ, Tony, that too? I'm sure the lady's a charmer, but if I were you I'd knock it off.'

'I have. Or to be honest, she has.'

Her letter, received that morning, was in his breast pocket.

Dear Tony,

I almost wrote 'Dearest' but I couldn't. People need to know what they mean to one another and I am not sure what I was for you: a lover, a diversion – or a source?

Obviously I've left the Belgravia flat. I thought it would be painful and it was, but I feel a kind of freedom.

Mr Grekov, now Sasha…Obviously there was a jinx on the house. On us too, it seems. We had a little happiness but the situation was false from the beginning, and we must not see each other again.

With affectionate memories, all the same,

Lisa

\*

The restaurant was a few streets away from the old MI5 headquarters in Leconfield House, Curzon Street, and on the way to Park

Lane for a taxi he stopped before the building. The name over the entrance hadn't changed, and except for a two-storey extension it looked much as it had when he'd come to sign on for the service all those years ago: anonymous, 1930s facade, blinds down, blank-faced as ever. In his time there'd been no sign on the door and there was none there now.

He stood for a moment, staring up. Flats, offices? He peered through the glass doors: a cavernous entrance hall, a peaked cap at a reception desk, a bronze sculpture representing nothing. About to walk on he noticed a grey limousine waiting, a chauffeur at the wheel, its engine whispering. Affecting an interest in a neighbouring window display he waited till two men emerged from the building, one a squat, jowly fellow with a briefcase, the other a spry young man in a striped suit.

At the sight of them the chauffeur leapt from the car to open the rear door: too late, the pin-stripe beat him to it. When the jowly one barked something at him from the back seat in what sounded like a Slav accent the young man thrust his head obsequiously inside the door.

'Certainly! Oh absolutely, Mr Palinsky!'

Closing it with a flourish he stood waiting and smiling till the limo – a Daimler Maybach Sedan – drove off.

Opposite was a private gambling club. Ambling across he made for the tail-coated doorman. Seeing him approach the fellow touched his hat, reached for the swing doors. Tony signalled not to bother.

'I just wanted to ask. That building, it used to be the MI5 HQ, right?'

'Leconfield? Yes, Sir. Been here thirty-nine years, used to watch 'em coming in and out, trying to look like they was nothing. Lucky I wasn't a commie, could have snapped the lot. Nice-looking secretaries they had though. Cut above the girls who used to work that corner.' He pointed along the road to the junction with Park Lane. 'My oh my, you should 'ave seen some of 'em in daylight.'

'And what goes on over there now?'

The doorman shrugged.

'Same as everywhere round 'ere. Money magicians, foreigners mostly.'

'So it'll be full of Russians.'

'I shouldn't wonder. Standard of the secretaries is holding up, mind you.'

Russians, Tony thought, lording it in the old MI5 HQ. It was as if his lot had taken over the Lubyanka.

He wandered further along the road. The Curzon street he remembered had a seedy air, but no longer. Today there were no ill-paid sleuths, no lamp-lit tarts, so far as he could see not too many Brits at all. Now it was Arab banks, a Lebanese restaurant, the Saudi Embassy with armed police at the gate, and up-market estate agents with their flats for foreign buyers at three grand a square foot and offices for hedge funders at similar rates.

For a moment the bitterness he'd felt at his dismissal from the service returned. It was people of his generation, he reflected, who'd done their bit to hold things together in the Cold War days. And for what? To make things what they were in the Mayfair of today: a sanctuary for financial spivs and high-rollers from the world over, the former adversary included.

Yes, a different country, you couldn't deny. Different in ways Tony didn't care for. And the worst of it was he'd become part of it, got himself mixed up in a crazy, alien milieu. Mikhail and his morning drinks, a safe full of millions, Grekov's nocturnal swims and make-believe castles. Meanwhile his son is convinced his dad's being poisoned, falls for a money-milking princess, gets himself involved in bogus Russian plots to assassinate their own president, and ends up dead.

Grekov had dreamt of modernizing his country. And how? By reinstating the Romanovs… But then what Mikhail had said at their first meeting was true. In the oligarch's house everything was out of time, a law to itself, a Russian reality with no connection to anyone else's. And the same was true of Russia herself.

# 39

The moment he came through the door Sun Fanying, a Chinese businessman of indeterminate age, liked the look of the Chelsea flat. The high ceilings, the generous proportions, the contemporary fittings, the view from the drawing room across the garden square – the place had everything he wanted. Only two bedrooms, but never mind: if his London investments worked out and his family joined him he'd buy something bigger. Meanwhile, for a man looking forward to some time out from his wife and children, and maybe some one-to-one entertaining, a stylish place to himself would not come amiss.

'Jus' one thing,' he said to the estate agent as they stood by the bedroom window. 'That tree – '

' – the chestnut?'

'Yes, chestnut tree. Chinese people, we like see long way from house, and that tree, it really big. From drawing room can see into square, from here no.'

'I'm not sure what we can do about that, Mr Sun.'

'Maybe you chop down, please?'

'To be honest, I doubt that's possible.'

'That is pity. Why not possible?'

'Well it's a conservation area, you see. That's one of the attractions of the flat.'

'But how I conserve view of square? For Chinese *feng shui* most important.'

'I understand, I love Chinese culture, I'm so sorry but there's nothing I can do.'

'Ah. If tree not cut down, how about you cut price?'

Mr Sun, an impish fellow, smiled as he said it. The estate agent was a well-shaped young lady, very nice, and he'd meant it as a joke.

Yet cut it they had, by two hundred thousand, to three million eight hundred, and he was happy with his bargain. A modern-minded IT entrepreneur, he'd never believed in that geomancy business, and the price reduction would help cover the renovations he planned.

Of particular concern was the bedroom. To counteract the darkening effect of the chestnut he wanted it redecorated in lighter colours, and it was when the decorators were working there that they found the camera. Next time the architect turned up the foreman showed it to him, grinning.

The architect examined the short round tube, less than the thickness of a cigarette lighter.

'What is it?'

'Miniaturized camera. Up in the bedroom chandelier, fitted into the piping, with a viewing aperture. Hate to think what they got up to with that. Whatever it was someone was keen to get it back. Fellow came to fetch it – that's how I got onto it, you'd never have known it was there. The boys were out the back having a bite of lunch, he sees the door open so he comes straight in. Seventy if he was a day, cheeky old bastard.

'Must have thought no one was here, but I was in the bathroom, having a leak. I come out and there he is up a ladder, tinkering with the chandelier. I ask what the hell he thinks he's doing, so he climbs down and says sorry. Come to collect it, he says, must have given him the wrong address.

'So when he's gone I have a close look in case he's done any damage – and there it was. See? Wired into the base of a specially adapted bulb. We had a search round, see if there was any more, and there's this hole in the drawing room cornice. Must have been another one in there. Got that one out sharpish, I suppose, while I was in the loo.'

Intrigued, Mr Sun got one of his technical people to check out the camera. The last recording was still in there, the man reported, hadn't been downloaded.

'So what was it?'

'I had a quick look,' the technician reported, 'and there was a woman. Looks like a spy camera, maybe not legal. Maybe better I throw away?'

'Not legal?' Mr Sun frowned. 'Yes, get rid of it.' He thought for a moment before adding. 'A woman, you say?'

'Yes, a young woman.'

'Well maybe make me a memory stick first.'

That night he went to bed early in his hotel. He was tired, he'd drunk one too many Rémy Martins – he loved French brandy, they didn't dilute it here. It was then that he remembered the camera. Before going to sleep he propped his laptop on his bed, slipped in the memory stick and settled back for his private viewing.

The start looks promising, like a film. 10.35 PM the timestamp says. The sound of the front door being unlocked, then closed. Voices – a man and a woman – speaking French. The woman is young. Black silk dress, low-cut, stylish shoes, haughty little nose. Expensive-looking lady, very nice. The man in a checked suit is middle-aged and paunchy – not the nice lady's husband, Mr Sun thinks, though she doesn't look like a whore.

They sit in the drawing room and have something from the drinks cabinet. The woman takes very little but the man drinks quickly. As they talk he sits close to her, very close, and puts a hand on her knee. Mr Sun thinks mmm, not too clever, she won't like that. But she leaves his hand where it is. And when he leans to kiss her she doesn't stop him.

In fact she seems impatient to move things on. Now she is getting up and they go together to the bedroom. When she goes into the bathroom the man noses around, stares up at the chandelier, straight into the camera. Then he lifts the curtain and peers from the window into the square, as if to check his surroundings. With that woman he should be a happy fellow, yet he looks nervous, and his face is red. Is he a bit drunk?

The woman comes back from the bathroom wearing nothing except high heels and pants. How casually she walks about, naked! Very good bearing, very good breasts. And so white! The man follows her movements with a smile. Yes he is drunk, his smile is dopey. He says something in French – a compliment perhaps. The lady does not answer. She is taking the covering off the bed and as she leans over her breasts waggle. Nice.

The man goes to the bathroom in his turn. The woman gets into bed, reaches for a switch, the lamp goes off. Mr Sun peers on at the screen. He hears the bathroom door open, sees the shape of the man fumbling around the room. The poor drunken fellow is lost in the dark – very funny, like a show!

'Ici!' the woman says, and he hears him stumbling towards the voice, climbing into bed.

A scuffling noise, then silence, then a sound like kissing? A pity he can hardly see. But now something is happening in the room. The bedroom door opens and a shadowy light from the drawing room shows someone coming in. The man in bed is surprised, breaks away from the woman as the figure enters.

A threesome? This could be interesting – but the man in bed shouts *merde!* and starts stripping away the sheets as if to get out of bed. And when the face of the figure turns his way, Mr Sun sees why. A beard! The third one has a beard, short and pointy! Two men and one woman, the Frenchman wouldn't like that, and nor would he.

So no threesome? Mr Sun will never know because at that moment the bedroom door closes. The light is gone, though he can hear. From the first man there is a stifled cry. Pain – or ecstasy? Maybe the three of them *are* up to something? More sounds of scuffling, then a sigh, then silence. Well, Mr Sun thinks, whatever it was, that was quick.

For a moment he listens on. The second man and the woman are talking in low voices, though it doesn't sound French, it sounds like Russian. He turns off the memory stick, disappointed. Such a pretty woman, with another girl it could have been good.

Finished with the laptop he tuned in to the CNN news on television, his nightly habit when he is abroad. Nothing about China, though an item from Moscow kept him watching. It was about the elections. He had business interests in Russia and had worried about the unrest on the streets. The election was over, it seemed, and it was a discussion about the aftermath, following the President's large majority. No surprise there, the CNN commentator explained:

'The allegation that he had set up the assassination attempt on himself in the South of France looked like finishing him off, but in the end it helped him.

'Viewers will recall his reaction when the truth came out during the sensational Daudov trial in Paris. The first thing he did was to fire a middle-ranking FSB officer, Victor Bulagin, along with a personal protection officer, Misha Yakovlev, who'd been with him in the Camargue, and whom Bulagin is thought to have bribed.

'At the time there was scepticism in the West. Had the President known about the phony attack all along? Was the FSB behind it, and Bulagin and Yakovlev merely scapegoats? On the other hand Western sources suggest that Bulagin was a drunk and a loner in league with a group of oligarchs with an interest in ensuring their man won the election.

'Following the amnesty the President declared to celebrate his victory, it is understood that Bulagin has returned home. Nor have Western governments made an issue of the bogus attack. The view is that the President would have won anyway, though by a reduced margin. In welcoming the newly installed Russian leader a White House spokesman said they will do business with whoever the people elect, and have no reason to doubt the Kremlin's version of events.

'Meanwhile, the Russian President has lost none of his old form. Here is his response when an interviewer, Svetlana Morensky, a former princess who has shot to prominence on state TV following her return to Moscow, questioned him about the attack:

'*Gospodin Prezident*. Western media appeared doubtful about the official explanation of the events in the Camargue, but to judge by your victory the Russian people believed you. They were also impressed by their President's conduct under what he believed at the time to be a genuine attack. Would you like to comment on that?'

'The West can think what it wants, it will not disturb my sleep. As for me, I did what any true Russian would have done in my place.'

JOSEPH CLYDE

'And what do you have to say about the intelligence personnel involved in the false attack? It is said that you were angry, personally affronted, by their unprofessional behaviour.'

'I was concerned for the reputation of a service to which I am proud to have belonged. I do not doubt their patriotism, and excess of zeal is not the worst failing. Yet such adventurist actions, even with the best intentions' – the President almost smiled – 'we cannot permit.'

'Now that an amnesty has been declared, the West is also saying that the intelligence people in question will be quietly rehabilitated. Is that true, *Gospodin Prezident?*'

'That will depend on the extent of their remorse. In the West too remorse plays a role in the judicial system, and it is right that it should. Don't you agree?'

Another hint of a smile.

'And finally, on that extraordinary day, what was your worst moment? Fear that this was a genuine assassination attempt?'

'Not at all. The worst of it was that it ruined a good day's hunting.'

'Thank you, *Gospodin Prezident.* And again, my personal congratulations.'

Mr Sun takes in the news report, drowsily. His Russian investments will be safe, there will be stability, it is all he needs. Yet he stares on at the screen, captivated by the interviewer as she introduces the second item. Her expression is a little stern, she is a bit too sure of herself, even with the President. But the legs and the breasts, very nice.

Finally he shuts down the TV, turns off the light, closes his eyes and begins sinking into sleep. Suddenly he starts awake. He has seen that woman. She was the girl in the threesome. A few minutes ago he was watching her, naked.

Impossible, he must have been dreaming – but no. That nose, that haughty face, he's sure of it, absolutely. He turns on the light, reaches for his laptop, slips in the memory stick, runs it again, but there is nothing. He has erased it.

# 40

Jean had made a fine job of the new conservatory, and Tony had adopted one of the luxurious armchairs for his TV viewing. With time on his hands, and in need of distraction, he was spending more hours there than he should, watching pretty much anything so long as it wasn't about Russia.

This evening he'd gone to fetch himself a nightcap and returned to find a BBC news item about an interview the President had given. Seeing the triumphant face filling the screen he zapped to another channel.

'I was watching that,' his wife frowned across at him, 'it's interesting.'

'Not for me,' Tony grunted.

'Well if you don't want to hear what he's got to say you can watch the interviewer.' Reaching for the remote she switched back to the programme. 'There, she's quite something, isn't she?'

A glance at her and Tony stared on, riveted. Svetlana, a TV presenter, interviewing the President? It was the moment she was asking him whether intelligence personnel involved in the bogus assassination would be rehabilitated following the post-election amnesty.

'That will depend on the extent of their remorse,' the President was saying. 'In the West too remorse plays a role in the judicial system, and it is right that it should.' After an infinitesimal pause he added: 'Don't you agree?'

Tony froze in his seat. There was something in the President's expression… A smile, was it? Or a smirk? *Don't you agree?* Maybe he was being fanciful, yet it was as if the question had been directed at Svetlana personally. If it was meant as a private joke his interviewer

**JOSEPH CLYDE**

wasn't amused. Her response – a curt nod of the head as she hurried on to the next question – betrayed a hint of irritation.

In recent months the suspicion that she'd been in with Bulagin from the start had lingered in his mind. Why did the two of them never speak to each other in the presence of the Ambassador, unless it was to disguise their association? Why had she hurried out in a panic after Raymond Baudoin had phoned her in her flat? And to Dalston, of all places – probably the art galleries where Daudov had confessed at his trial that he and Bulagin would meet. And why had she gone to Russia immediately after the Baudoin murder? Because even if something linked her to it, in Moscow she'd be safe from extradition.

All pure conjecture, of course. He'd bungled the whole thing before, he told himself, and he was probably getting it wrong again now.

'The purpose of the interview,' the BBC announcer signed off, 'was probably to draw a line under the whole extraordinary episode, and to put paid to any rumours that there was more to it than met the eye.'

'Look at you, gawking at her,' Jean said when the item ended. 'I told you you'd fall for her. A real Slav beauty isn't she?'

'Bit hard-faced,' Tony murmured.

'You think so? But then we see what we want to see in people, don't we, and you've always had it in for the Russians.'

'I'm just saying she seems to me a tough-looking cookie,' Tony replied wearily, in no mood to argue.

'Oh come on darling! You'll be telling me next that she's some sort of agent.' She sighed. 'Anyway you're out of all that now, and I can't say I'm sorry.'

'Neither am I,' Tony said, and took a deep swig of his whisky.